To my
Family

First published in Great Britain in 2002

Harry Gateaux copyright © 2002 Jeff Collard
The Witness Stones copyright © 2002 Jeff Collard
www.harrygateaux.com

ISBN 0-9542669-2-7
Published by
Channel Island Publishing
Unit 3B, Barette Commercial Centre
La Route Du Mont Mado
St John, Jersey, JE3 4DS
Tel (01534) 860806 Fax (01534) 860811
e-mail sales@channelislandpublishing.com

The Witness Stones

Jeff Collard

Channel Island Publishing

Inspiration, encouragement, support, fun, patience....All those qualities and more, from a very special person, have helped me write this book.

Thanks for being that person Janette.

CHAPTER ONE

Dominating the semi-darkened skyline of early morning, the Sphinx-shaped silhouette of Elizabeth Castle resonated gently to the dawn chorus of patrolling gulls. In their wake, the sleepy tranquillity of St Aubin's Bay stirred in sympathy with the 16th century fortification that it enveloped and stretched out its arms as it breathed the air of a new day.

As the aerobics continued, so attention was drawn towards the shadowed figure of a man who made his way cautiously along the castle's stone slab causeway which, like a meandering anchor line, seemed to tie the ancient monument back to its rock founded foreshore.

Having carefully negotiated the irregularities of medieval crazy paving underfoot, the man's progress checked occasionally as he paused to adjust the positioning of a large and cumbersome box-like object strapped across his shoulder.

Suddenly he stopped, crouched down and lowered the item delicately to the ground before standing and walking on a further few metres along the granite-weaved jigsaw.

From that moment on came the need for added vigilance as, with each advancing step, so increased the potential for infinite forward motion, a Newtonian consequence of the seemingly frictionless seaweed veneer that covered much of the pavement's age-wrinkled surface.

Instinctively, a more defensive gait developed before a succession of uncontrolled slides brought his advance to a halt. The man steadied himself, turned nervously and then walked in short purposeful steps back to the object and waited.

After half an hour or so the waiting ended as the sun finally showed its first signs of waking, peeping its head confidently over the horizon and throwing a soft golden glazed blanket across the wide expanse of the crescent-carved bay.

With the light now switched on, the silhouette of the man melted away, to reveal a person intent on preparing for a session of seascape photography. Tripod safely located, he stooped to retrieve a camera from the large equipment case which had been positioned with equal consideration for its safety on a flat granite slab, one of many making up the mosaic-like causeway. The kit of parts assembled, the man panned the camera slowly around.

His activity suddenly increased as he began tracking the flight of a pair of cormorants skimming their way effortlessly across the mirror flat Midas-touched sea which, with an almost undetectable momentum, continued to flood ever nearer and began its daily cleansing of the castle's circumferential foreshores once more.

The camera clicked.

For that instant, as the shutter opened, all appeared still. Indeed, for that small moment in time all seemed perfect, the apparent purity and colour of nature's offerings suggesting that a fine day awaited its participants.

An hour later, across the road at the Coburg Hotel, a dozen or so of those very participants were tucking into early breakfast in the ground floor dining hall.

Though the hall and indeed the entire hotel exuded a classical style of luxury throughout, it seemed, for a few at least at this still early hour, that appreciation of such luxuriant surroundings was in a distant, hitherto undiscovered corridor of their minds. For them, the advent of dawn away from the cosy wrappings of their beds appeared to be an alien experience as they struggled to come to terms with the reality that a new day had begun and they were a conscious, or in some cases perhaps a semi-conscious part of it. For the majority however, the transformation from bed to bacon and eggs appeared an easy one as they sat eagerly awaiting the day's bus tour, a journey to explore the Island's rich archaeological heritage.

6

As for the hotel itself, it dated from the early 1900s and was a true treasure of a building, its three storey external façades richly clad in traditional Jersey granite, with wonderfully ornate windows complimenting the well proportioned structure to stunning effect. In tribute to its Victorian designers, its orientation had been judged with pinpoint precision to offer the maximum number of rooms possible the luxury of a sea view.

At street level, a wide cobbled driveway curved its way past the sweeping granite steps that led up to the main entrance, a mainly glazed construction framed in highly polished stainless steel which, though of clearly modern vintage, blended sympathetically with the grandeur of the building it served.

Indeed, despite its age, the building had been admirably preserved and tastefully added to in more recent times, providing a subtle interaction of modern around the dominance of the old. That same care to preserve was equally reflected inside, with the large rooms, high ceilings and wonderful decor throughout in keeping with the regal splendour that the external image portrayed.

It had managed well over the years and more particularly in the recent ultra-competitive climate to maintain its standing as a premier Island hotel.

Year after year it continued to attract a diverse and often repeat clientele and, whether on business or holiday, many guests, where time permitted, seemed all too ready to participate in the numerous activities the hotel had to offer through its busy social itinerary.

One of those very activities was the ever popular day-long archaeological excursion, a once weekly event comprising a circular bus tour of the many Island sites which, though aimed primarily at those guests with a penchant for ancient history, appealed in equal measure to the small handful who simply sought an excuse for a day out.

As breakfast continued, the gentle buzz of early morning banter and clink of cutlery on plates was suddenly interrupted as, from a small raised platform at the top end of the dining hall, the public address system sprang to life with an announcement to confirm arrangements for the day ahead.

The eating and chat paused momentarily except for a solitary voice, that of an elderly chap named Bob who continued his mutterings oblivious of the silence that surrounded him. His wife Doris slid discreetly back in her chair and, extending her leg, gave her husband a firm tap on the ankle. All was finally still, save for a couple of tree-felling creaks as the agressor pulled herself slowly back to her seat.

En masse, the eyes and ears of those gathered were drawn towards the platform where an attractive young lady stood, microphone in hand.

'Good morning everybody,' she said in a bubbly, almost melodic manner.

The woman waited for a moment as a muffled chorus of returned greetings echoed pathetically around the room.

'My name is Melanie Winkley and I will be your tour guide for today. But please, to spare the formality, if you need to call me for anything, just plain simple Mel will do,' she continued, in a broad East London accent.

'You don't look simple to me,' called an anonymous voice from one of the tables.

While a light flutter of laughter danced around the room, Mel looked across in the vain hope of seeking out her comedian friend for future reference.

As the laughter evaporated she returned to her introduction.

'Can I welcome you all to today's archaeological tour. I trust everybody has now got a copy of the notes,' she continued as she waved her copy aloft before scanning the room again, this time for confirmatory nods and whispered variants of "yes thank you" from her audience.

'Good,' she said with a self-congratulatory smile, rewarding the fact that the first administrative task of the day appeared to have eluded any hitch.

'Our bus will depart from the front of the hotel at 9.00 am sharp. There's just one small change to the day's schedule to announce. If you can all turn to the map, shown on page four.'

She waited as this time the noise of frantically rustled papers filled the air. The wait continued, until the papyrus symphony had subsided.

'Due to a number of road diversions in force this week, we will still be following the route highlighted in red but, on this particular occasion, we will be completing the circuit in an anti-clockwise direction and not clockwise, as indicated. I only mention that fact because I see one or two familiar looking faces around me who have travelled with us on this tour before.'

'Yes and an excellent day out it is,' came another shout from the floor.

Mel smiled, a tiny hint of embarrassment in her cheeks from the impromptu cry of commendation.

'The revised route means therefore, that for today only, we will visit the site at Santille first and not last as is normally the case. From there we will travel around the coast, visiting a number of other sites, with a final stop at Cotte de l'Arbre before returning back to the hotel at around 4.30 pm,' she continued.

'Excuse me, dear,' interrupted Doris from her seat close to the platform. 'Can you please tell me what the lunch arrangements are. It's just I think that we've ordered picnic meals from the hotel and I'm not sure if I should collect them now or later?'

'Lunch of course, thank you for reminding me,' replied Mel as she looked down and nodded to acknowledge the questioner before raising her head to extend the response to her wider audience.

'I hope that you're all aware that we will be stopping en route for a pub lunch around one o'clock. For the few of you who have pre-ordered picnic meals, one of our kitchen staff will be along with them in just a short while.'

Doris nodded her head appreciatively in the direction of the platform, as around her stirred a cocktail of whispered lunch-related conversation.

As it did, Mel paused momentarily to draw breath, before summing up.

A hush suddenly returned.

'So please, may I remind you all just one more time. We depart at 9.00am prompt from the front of the hotel', she said, turning to look up quickly at the clock on the wall behind her.

'That's in around an hour and a quarter from now. So enjoy the rest of your breakfast and I look forward to seeing you all again soon. If you have any immediate questions, I will be here for a few moments longer.'

The eating resumed with the buzz of conversation noticeably raised a few decibels, the perky nature of the announcement, albeit brief, having clearly heightened anticipation of the days adventures ahead.

A young Scottish couple, the Milners, on holiday from Edinburgh, tried valiantly to keep up with the barrage of questions from their two young sons.

'Dad, Dad, what's arkology. Is it good?' enquired Andrew.

'Can't be as good as the beach. Why can't we go to the beach again today, Dad?' asked his younger brother, Munro.

'Yeah,' agreed Andrew.

'We want the beach, we want the beach,' he sang out, much to the increasing torment of his parents.

The conversation from surrounding tables softened momentarily as a ring of ears listened in covertly to the developing domestic.

'Quieten down and eat your breakfast,' said their father, Craig.

His wife, Alison, reinforced the parental stand.

'Yes, listen to your father. All that lovely food will make you both big and strong. We can go to the beach tomorrow.'

The two lads looked down at their plates, both of which were strewn with the rapidly chilling ravages of their part-finished breakfast. They whispered briefly to each other before raising their heads.

'Can we go boogie boarding as well tomorrow?' they enquired in unison. Their mother nodded and the boys sat back, their cheeky grins suggesting that they were content with the compromise package that they'd negotiated.

'Gee, such cute kids,' remarked a dark haired, gargantuan of a man as he rocked back in his chair towards Alison who was sitting at the table directly behind him.

'Yes, er, yes,' she replied in a slightly hesitant manner, the surprise of the interruption having caught her off guard. 'Yes, they do have their moments,' she continued.

The man's chair creaked as if to offer him early warning that it was not to be treated as a seesaw and that a repeat performance would most probably end in both tears and a reading on a seismograph.

He reacted immediately, returning the chair instantly to the ground with a dull thud. Safely back on earth, he then swivelled his body around, so that he was looking once more towards Alison. Again, the chair creaked unerringly.

'Hi, the name's Solomon but everybody just calls me Solly and this is my fiancée, Lauren. Everybody calls her Lauren,' he said smiling as he outstretched his 'T' shirt clad tree trunk of an arm across the table and offered his hand out to introduce a diminutive young lady with stunning blue eyes and shoulder length brunette hair, dressed in a bright green tracksuit jacket.

'Yeah, we're all the way from Denver, Colorado. Arrived yesterday, mighty long journey. All day on a plane, you know.'

He paused just long enough for Alison to get a word in.

'Pleased to meet you, I'm sure.'

Before Solomon, or Solly, could wind himself up for another oration, Craig interrupted.

'Yeah, we came down yesterday as well. Mighty long journey for us also. All day on a train down from Scotland and then on the boat.'

'Bonny Scotland where they have the tartans?' enquired Solly.

'Yep, the very same. Anyway I think it would have been quicker coming via the States with your good selves,' replied Craig.

'Oh Scotland, how beautiful. I've always wanted to visit your fine land,' said Lauren.

Craig let out a stifled laugh.

A momentary silence descended upon the two tables before Alison, after a gentle cough to clear her throat, began introducing her family. One by one, they exchanged smiles with their new transatlantic acquaintances. The final introduction reached Munro and, with his mother's tone of speech suggesting a polite acknowledgement to be due, he shyly lifted his face.

Suddenly, the young lad's face was transfixed, his eyes popping, while at the same time his mouth opened wide for tonsil inspection.

'Wow, look at the size of that man. He's like an elephant.'

Andrew started giggling uncontrollably as both parents fished frantically under the table with their legs to give the two youngsters a tap with their shoes on any piece of flesh they could find.

'I'm very sorry about that,' replied Alison, looking rather sheepishly across towards the American couple.

'Such cute kids,' Solly repeated as if dismissive of the elephant comment. He'd heard every jibe in the book about his size and his long developed immune system for such comment allowed them all to pass him by without pain.

'Do excuse us for now,' said Alison, keen to whisk her family off before any further humiliation could be attracted in their direction.

'Yeah, see you all on the bus,' said Solly.

The Milner's filed out quietly, Alison leading them carefully around the perimeter of the cluster of breakfast tables in the hope of minimising the amusing stare of those who had listened in on their son's breakfast time cabaret.

As they neared the exit, a minor misjudgement in the foot coordination department by Craig saw him brush the very last table at which sat the lone and diminutive figure of fellow guest, Andrew Price.

Craig stopped and looked across at the table's solitary occupant, the young man's head for that split second still bowed, his mind, it seemed, engaged in Tate Gallery mode and focused upon creating a carbuncle of modern art, comprising toast, the last scrapings of butter and a spoonful of raspberry jam.

As the table wobbled, the scoop of preserve flicked up in a short parabolic arc and splashed down onto the blue cloth napkin spread across the artist's lap.

'Whoops, so sorry about that, mate,' apologised the Scot.

His two sons looked at each other, giggled, and then glanced across the table at the jam-stained casualty. As they did so, Andy raised his head slowly, stared intently at each of the three for a few seconds and then returned impassively to his developing creation.

Craig turned towards his wife.

'Odd fellow,' he whispered, nodding his head discreetly toward the seated sculptor

'Come on you lot,' demanded Alison, 'before we wreak any more havoc.'

As they departed, Craig stared one more time at Andy, the young man's mind now re-focused and concentrated upon the execution of minor remedial works to his rapidly evolving art form with the napkin-collected conserve.

'Odd fellow,' Craig repeated.

A fairly regular visitor to the hotel, Andy had been affectionately nicknamed "Anorak" by a number of the hotel staff, a title attributed to his enthusiastic participation in the archaeological tour at least twice a year since its inauguration some six years previously.

The personal collection of archaeological literature which he had amassed in ever increasing volumes as each year passed had become almost legendary within the hotel's four walls and his knowledge of the subject was never in doubt, though his shy, introverted character often precluded the sharing of his talent amongst his fellow travellers.

Mel was always the first to note his presence on the trip, aware that her learned friend would correct any error in her presentation, however trivial, at some opportune time.

In the two and a half years since taking over as tour guide, she had slowly built up a friendly understanding of Andy's eccentricities although she knew little about him, except that his other passion, second to archaeology, was anything computer related. Indeed, she'd learnt from a previous visit during one of their rare conversations of any length that he had spent a short time, some years previously, working on Jersey, developing financial computer systems for one of the Island's specialist offshore banks. It seemed however that his stay then had been short, though it had allowed him sufficient free time to develop a keen interest in the ancient history of Jersey and surrounding islands.

As nine o'clock approached, Mel, her hair fluttering occasionally with each wisp of sea breeze, stood just outside the main entrance door, dressed smartly in a casual navy blue trouser suit and sturdy flat bottomed black shoes.

The dozen or so crowd, fresh from their bacon and eggs, slowly emerged, happy to gather on the granite steps as the warm glow of the morning sun began to sweep across, a radiance which served to further fuel the excited air of anticipation.

Very soon the hotel frontage was a cauldron of conversation, with some of the earlier arrivals striking up an introductory chat with Mel, their mentor.

'So how long have you been doing the tours, Mel?' asked one.

'Do you originate from the Island, Mel?' enquired another.

An avalanche of similar questions followed, many of those guests present keen to establish an early rapport with their host for the day ahead. She had heard the same questions so many times before on previous excursions, the only variation being that of the people who asked them.

Despite the predictability of each mini conversation, she maintained a characteristically professional composure, greeting each person with a warmly delivered response from her auto-bank of standard answers. On many an occasion the tedium of churning out the same information had her wishing she could develop a cassette recording of the standard questions and answers which could be played to the increasing throng of inquisitors while she sneaked off for a cup of tea.

Even for her, however, this particular morning's plethora of attention was becoming claustrophobic. Suddenly her prayers for a break in the interrogation were answered, as a shrill voice shouted out from behind her.

'MEL, MEL!'

Having turned, she adopted for a split second the persona of a goldfish at feeding time as an expression of stunned amazement washed across her face.

'Good God, Rachel Williams,' she cried with a schoolgirl thrill of excitement.

'Not quite,' replied Rachel. 'I'm now Rachel Astey. Went and got married, didn't I.'

'Well, whoever you are now, it's fantastic to see you again,' said Mel. The two girls locked arms momentarily in a celebratory hug to cement their impromptu reunion.

Rachel was an old college friend of Mel's with whom she had enjoyed many deeply mad escapades in times gone by. She had also been Mel's predecessor as tour guide at the Coburg Hotel and had played an influential part in securing the vacant position for Mel, following her return to the mainland those two and a half years previously.

'So where is the unlucky man?' enquired Mel with a cheeky giggle.

'Oh, the heathen has decided that a day of golf will be more rewarding than a day of cultural education. No matter, his loss is my gain. I'm quite looking forward to my day of freedom,' replied Rachel in a manner which suggested that, for the moment at least, she would prefer to be winding the clock back to her previous days of freedom at college with Mel, embarking on more mad escapades, with the inevitable chaos that followed in the duo's wake.

'Must be easily two years or so since we last saw each other? What a great surprise. I had no idea you were here. Didn't see you at breakfast,' said Mel.

'No. Sorry we both missed your chat but this morning's been all a little bit frenetic,' replied Rachel. 'Tony had a sudden desire to go for a jog along the Esplanade. I didn't want to be on my lonesome downstairs while he was out, so I had breakfast brought to our room. In fact he was that long, I ended up eating his breakie as well,' she continued. 'I've left him to it upstairs having a shower and...'

Suddenly the conversation was interrupted as the airwaves resounded to a less than orchestral sound of a chugging engine, a familiar sound to the two girls which signalled the arrival of their transport for the day.

'Still the same old racket then. Reminds me of some good times,' said Rachel warmly.

'Yep, good times indeed,' replied Mel.

'Anyway, great to see you again, Rach. We'll catch up with all our gossip later,' she added before spinning around and skipping quickly down the granite entrance steps to greet Cyril, the bus driver, who had just positioned the door of his vintage machine with great precision, adjacent to the kerb edge at the base of the hotel steps.

Mel looked up and waved through the open bus door. Cyril turned his head, looked down from his perched position at Mel and returned the welcoming gesture.

'Nice day for it, girl,' he said as he switched off the engine and then, with a quick stretch, arched his ageing back over the soft leather of the equally ageing seat.

Mel took a single stride up onto the lower step of the bus. Sweeping her hair back quickly, she then coughed gently once more to clear her throat before turning to face her expectant audience.

'Okay folks, all aboard,' she called, her authoritative cry tempered slightly by a cheery grin. Her initial attempts to rally the troops seemed lost amongst the now Richter scale volume of early morning gossip.

'COME ON folks, please, all aboard,' she repeated, this time more forcefully with an almost schoolmistress-like tone of command.

The noise of idle conversation diluted as the group began funnelling in a semi-orderly fashion down the steps towards the bus door. With the tiered formation in slow advance, Mel motioned those at the front forward a few accelerated paces to begin their climb on board. As they began to enter, each paused at the top of the steps to allow the exchange of simple one-line pleasantries with Cyril before continuing on to find a seat.

Soon Doris found herself at the front of the queue.

'It's not very big, is it, dear,' she said, taking a quick glance along the length of the pint-sized vehicle before looking across to her host.

'It's plenty big enough for our small group,' replied Mel, as she leaned down to offer an outstretched arm of assistance to her transport critic.

'Oh thank you, luv. Sorry to be a burden but I've not been the same since they did my hip. I'm sure it's going rusty, you know.'

Mel laughed. Having helped Doris to safely negotiate her entrance, she pivoted around in the expectation of attending to Bob, only to see him disappearing off in the opposite direction, back up the hotel's steps.

Doris, now seated, caught sight of her husband in retreat and swayed across to shout to him from the open window beside her at the front of the bus.

'Bob, Bob, this way, you silly old fool. We're going, not coming back,' she called, much to the amusement of those around.

He shuffled around, paused for a moment's cog-rattling computation of mind and then began a hesitant traverse back down the staircase to the waiting transport below.

Mel extended an arm and helped him carefully on board. Safely ensconced next to his wife, the procession of remaining passengers regained its earlier momentum, much to the relief of Mel who was conscious that a long and busy day awaited them and that time, as ever, was marching on remorselessly.

The remaining few seats of the small bus soon began to warm with occupants. Young Munro and brother Andrew, standing ahead of their mother at the top of the steps and linked by a firm parental grip, began scanning intently as best they could the length of the bus for available spaces.

As they did, Alison turned her shoulders to pan her eyes in the opposite direction across the road and pavement for any sign of her overdue husband who had disappeared together with Solly soon after breakfast to buy newspapers.

Andrew pulled at his mother's hand, tugging her arm. She turned for a moment and looked down at her son.

'Mum, Mum, there are no good seats left. I want a seat by the window.'

Immediately, Munro subjected his mother to a repeat dose of the agony by tugging her on the other side and reinforced his brothers concern that the prime viewing seats were disappearing fast.

'Excuse me,' said Alison, swivelling her body slightly and looking down to Mel who was still balanced on the bottom step of the vehicle. 'Do you think there's any chance of finding four seats close together up here so that myself and my husband, when he shows up that is, can look after the kids?'

'Maybe, let's see what I can do, if you can just let me by. Actually, it might be easier if you quickly jump off and then I can squeeze past?'

'Er, yes, of course. Sorry.'

Mel took one careful step backwards down onto the pavement, followed closely, but more awkwardly, by Alison, her hands still fused to those of her two sons.

Her already awkward progress backwards became even more contorted as the two youngsters, sensing disembarkation well before the expected time, began to offer resistance to their mother's retreat.

'Come on, kids,' said Alison firmly. 'The nice young lady is going to find us all some seats.'

With the welcome assurance that the retreat was apparently to their ultimate advantage, the lads' anxiety levels relaxed and they too were soon back on the pavement. Immediately they stared upwards and through the bus windows to follow Mel's progress along to the rear of the vehicle where she could then be seen chatting amicably with a number of passengers. Within seconds the bus started rocking as an indiscernible conglomerate of bodies and baggage began their relocation. Meanwhile back outside, the waiting Lauren had engaged in increasingly animated conversation with Alison.

'Any sign of the men yet?' questioned the American, referring to Solly and Craig's après-breakfast shopping expedition.

'Huh, God only knows where Craig's got to but he does like his daily newspaper. If they've not arrived on the Island yet, he's probably caught the boat back to the mainland to get one. I live in hope on that one,' said Alison.

'Gee, I hope Solly's okay,' said Lauren with an air of concern in her voice. 'He's not too familiar with this cute little town yet, you know.'

Suddenly Craig appeared on the driveway.

'Where the hell have you been? It's nearly time to go in

search of tomorrow's paper,' called Alison, her voice elevated slightly.

Lauren butted in immediately.

'Where's my Solly?'

'I'm afraid I lost him in town. Said he had to get some cookies and things for the journey,' replied Craig.

Lauren began to look around anxiously, unaware that the reality of the situation was that a man of such skyscraper proportions could not simply disappear on an Island that measured just nine miles by five.

Sure enough, within seconds of Craig's arrival, a white taxicab, its engine pointing skywards, pulled on to the drive and parked up behind the bus. The car door opened and a huge shadow cast itself across the steps as Solly made an ecliptic re-appearance, his arms filled to the rafters with bags of goodies for the day ahead.

'Sorry, sweetheart,' he called, looking across at Lauren who had broken ranks to meet him. 'Got lost again after I came out the shopping mall, didn't I. Ended up the other side of that damn tunnel again.'

'Gee hun, the shelves must be bare,' replied Lauren as she looked down at her husband's food hoard.

Before they could engage in any more conversation Mel was back at the bus door, beckoning with added fervour the final passengers on board.

'I've managed a re-shuffle inside,' said Mel as Alison and her family approached and prepared to enter. 'You've got the whole of the back row to yourselves. I should add that it's actually designed for three adults, so it might be a little bit of a squeeze I'm afraid.'

'The back row! Neat!' said the two young lads in unison.

As they made their way to the back their balance was interrupted as the bus suddenly dipped violently toward the kerbside front corner. The four stopped and turned as one to watch as Solly, complete with cookies, made his dramatic entrance, followed closely by Lauren.

Due to the musical chairs of people and possessions that had gone on moments earlier, only aisle seats now remained for the two Americans. Solly moved along the bus, eyeing up the remaining width and comfort potential of each vacant bench seat as he progressed, while each lone passenger, conscious of his imminent approach, tried to spread out as much as possible in an effort to reduce the attraction of the upholstered void beside them.

He stopped briefly and looked across at the solitary seated figure of Jamie Hart. Instantly the young man brushed a small jacket across from his lap to the cushioned leather space beside him.

'Er, I'm waiting for someone I'm afraid,' whispered Jamie unconvincingly.

Solly said nothing and moved on. Nearing the end of the bus he paused to exchange greetings with the Milners who by now were seated along the back row, their young sons' faces turned and pressed tightly against the rear window as they stared outwards to watch their small corner of the world go by.

Returning his attention to seat searching he looked across to the petite young figure of Kathy, who was sitting in the window seat immediately in front of the Scottish clan, her eyes squinting in a semi-sleep through the margins of her curly shoulder length dark hair.

Suddenly her eyes opened and popped like marbles as Solly unceremoniously planted his huge frame on the seat beside her, her yelps at the very real fears of being instantly puréed, muffled into obscurity amongst the mass of the American colossus and the mountain of cookie packets, which began falling like confetti around her. The seat creaked violently.

His wife, following closely behind, intervened immediately. 'Solly, look what you've done to that poor girl,' she said, looking across to the now desperate morsel, her whole body squeezed almost semi-cuboid into the corner formed by seat and window.

'I must apologise for my husband's lack of consideration,' continued Lauren as she leaned over to check on the continued breathing and general well being of the young woman.

The woman looked up and, chewing her face back into some approximate shape of normality, offered a pained smile.

'You might be safer somewhere else,' suggested Lauren.

As far as Kathy was concerned, there was only one answer to that simple proposal. Despite being rightly aggrieved at having claimed the seat first and now loosing her window position under such overwhelming circumstances, she had no desire to spend the whole day being squeezed like toothpaste through the gap between chair and window into the tartan row behind.

Solly, prompted by his wife, gathered together his cookies and stood up once again in the aisle, taking one step back to allow the girl to extricate herself with obvious relief.

Kathy paused to adjust her contorted dress which by now appeared to be almost back to front before moving to a vacant position near the front.

The big man returned to his hijacked seat and shuffled across to the window, so allowing Lauren to take the aisle seat, the relaxed expanse of Solly now forcing her to place her legs slightly askew into the passageway.

For a second time the seat creaked violently as Solly slid around to make himself comfortable.

Meanwhile, back at the door to the bus and last in the queue was Rachel who out of habit from her role years previously as a tour guide, brought up the rear, to ensure all were safely aboard. She met again with Mel at the foot of the steps, having completed her gallant contribution in ushering all the passengers on board.

'Thanks Rachel,' whispered Mel in quiet appreciation.

Rachel nodded.

Loading finally complete, Mel stepped aboard, fell back into her seat at the front of the bus and buried her head for a few seconds into her hands.

Stage two of what had already seemed like a day's work to her was complete and all present were aboard.

Cyril flicked the small switch on the dashboard to close the door.

Suddenly, a loud cry from outside rang out.

'WAIT, WAIT!'

Attention was instantly drawn back to the hotel's entrance as a youngish man, clad in black denim trousers and a red vest top, leapt from the hotel door, clearing the steps with a single athletic jump and who, with one further stride, mounted the steps of the bus, catching his small rucksack in the door as it snapped shut.

Cyril looked across.

'Sorry mate. Thought everyone was in.'

It was Tony, Rachel's husband.

Having extricated his bag from the heavy clam-tight grip of the door and wiped away a small smudge of door grease which had decorated one of the bag's straps, he continued up the steps.

Mel looked up from her front seat position, clearly startled by the man's dramatic arrival.

'Hi, I'm Tony Astey. Sorry about all that.'

Mel stared in silence at the man for a few seconds.

'Oh, right, Tony Astey,' she replied slightly hesitantly. 'I understood from Rachel that you were off to knock a few bits of plastic around the lawn.'

A ripple of laughter tee'd off and bounced itself around the bus.

'Yes, change of plan. Thought I'd indulge myself in some cultural enriching instead,' whispered Tony in response, under cover of the jovial exchanges around.

'Pleased to hear it. More the merrier I guess,' said Mel.

As she finished speaking and began scribbling the new name on the top of the guest list, Rachel leaned across from her seat into the aisle and lifting her arm waved towards her husband.

'Over here, Tone. So what happened to that game of golf?'

she said quizzically as her husband took to the vacant seat beside her.

Tony paused for a moment. 'Well. Umm. I changed my mind at the last minute didn't I. Decided that I'd prefer to share my day with you dear.'

'Oh, well, that's a first.'

As the couple continued their conversation, Mel made her way through the bus to take a head count.

She soon reached the Milner family at the rear of the vehicle '....9,10,11,12.'

She stopped. 'That's odd, should be 13 guests according to my list,' she muttered, her words just audible to those on board except Bob who was deep in sleep and seemingly immune to any disturbance short of a cataclysmic earthquake.

Mel turned and faced the front of the bus. 'Whoever's missing, please hold their hand up.'

Despite being a one liner as old as the archaeological sites they were about to visit, it was greeted by a further ripple of sympathetic laughter.

Returning to schoolmistress mode, she began ticking off the register of those expected. The first names on the list were those of the Alexanders, Doris and Bob.

'Bob Alexander?' she enquired in a firm tone.

There was a momentary silence.

'Yes, sorry luv, he is here but the silly old fool's still asleep,' replied Doris. The bus swayed to another ripple of laughter.

Mel continued on down the list, soon reaching the Milners.

'Craig Milner?'

Young Munro stood up just behind Mel.

'Yes, Daddy's here, Mummy's here, my brother's here but I'm not.'

Mel, startled by the shriek explosion of young words immediately behind her, turned and looked down.

The two exchanged a smile before Alison reached out and pulled the youngster back firmly into his seat. 'Behave yourself,' she said, as she switched back to authoritative mode.

Solly twisted his head around as far as the physical limits of his liana-vine neck muscles would permit.

'Such a cute kid.'

Mel smiled again and ticked the family from her list.

The name check continued.

'Andy Price?'

She waited expectantly for the characteristically muted acknowledgement from "Anorak".

There was hush.

She enquired again, this time slightly louder but again with no response. Scanning the rows of seats, it soon became very obvious to her that Andy was not aboard.

Mel paused in puzzled silence. She had definitely seen him at breakfast but it was clear that, for whatever reason, he'd not made the bus. On past tours he was invariably one of the first on board and always the most enthusiastic to get exploring.

Excusing herself and returning onto the pavement, she skipped quickly back up the steps to reception. Leaning across the desk, her feet for a moment left the lush carpet floor. 'Lucy, Lucy, are you there?'

Lucy, the manageress, appeared instantly from behind a dark burgundy coloured drape curtain at the side of the counter.

'Hi there, girl. What's up?'

'You haven't seen "Anorak" around at all, have you?'

Lucy's face paled momentarily.

'Oh yes, sorry Mel. Forgot to tell you but I found this folded scrap of paper here on the desk a little earlier. All it says is 'TOUR GUIDE, FROM ANDY,' she replied, passing the note across.

Mel took the creased note which had been folded approximately into quarters. Curiously, one corner fold was damp, which upon opening was found to have caused some of the ink to run slightly. The message was still just legible.

'Oh no, that's a great start,' she cried, spinning a quarter circle about her heels in animated frustration.

'What's the problem?' asked Lucy.

'Seems Andy's giving the bus a miss for some reason. He says here that he's meeting us at the Cotte de l'Arbre, though the message is a little smudged,' replied Mel as she fanned the note in the air just above her head.

'Isn't the Cotte the last site today. I thought you'd reversed the route because of the road diversions.'

'Quite,' replied Mel as she recoiled her quarter spin turn to face the reception once more.

'In a short while we'll be on the east of the Island and he'll be waiting on the west. I'm sure I couldn't have made the instructions clearer this morning, but then I wasn't expecting anyone to go under their own steam, I suppose,' she continued.

'He probably just switches off now when you're talking about the route, Mel, he's heard it so many times before.'

'Yeah, I guess you're right. Anyway, it's happened, so we need to sort it.'

'Do us a favour, Lucy. Can you phone Kay or Alan Le Badas at the Cotte boulangerie in St Ouen?'

'Is that the one at Plémont, just at the top of Puffin Bay?'

'Yes, that's it. It's just across the road from the site at Cotte de l'Arbre. Describe "Anorak'" to them and when they see him, perhaps you'd be kind enough to send someone over to pick him up and bring him to the bus. You can phone me then on the mobile to find out exactly where we are.'

'Yes of course, leave it with me, Mel.'

Lucy suddenly looked up and across to the large clock mounted on the wall across the staircase. Hey, you better get on your way, it's nearly 9.15.'

'Yes, better fly.'

'Okay if I can take this with me?' continued Mel, flashing Andy's scribbled note in the air once again.

'Yes, take it please. I'll only end up throwing it in the bin.'

'Cheers, Lucy, see you later then,' said Mel, smiling before picking up her notebook and mobile phone from the reception counter, turning and walking briskly towards the main entrance.

'All sorted, girl?' enquired Cyril as Mel skipped back quickly on board the bus.

'Yes, I hope so. Come on, let's get going. We've lost enough time.'

Mel took her seat at the front of the bus and then reached forward to drag down the vehicle's nearest sun visor as a laser shaft of sunlight arrowed in through the windscreen.

As she did, Cyril flicked the switch to turn on the engine. A small cheer filtered through from the back of the bus as the 1950's technology fired into excited action first time.

The vehicle shuddered gingerly across the cobbled driveway which curved down to the pillar-flanked exit that would lead on to the main Esplanade route.

A few metres before the that point the bus, without warning, lurched forward, as did its passengers, before coming to an uncompromising halt.

As all aboard settled down, their eyes became trained upon a cherry red, open topped sports car which had, without warning, entered through the "exit" route and was now nearly broadside with the front of the bus.

'You stupid idiot,' shouted Cyril as he leaned awkwardly through the open side window of his cab and looked down at the tweed-capped, young male driver below. 'You trying to get us all killed? You're meant to enter from the other side you know.'

The driver stretched across in his seat in a mirrored contortion of Cyril's current pose to get a full view of his lecturer.

'Yes, sorry about that old boy but I'm here for the tour. That is of course if this is the archaeological adventure?' enquired the man as he looked up to the cab for a response.

'Not so much of the "old boy". The name's Cyril,' came the indignant reply.

'Oh, sorry, no offence meant, sir.'

In her instantly self-imposed new role as diplomatic ambassador and arbitrator between the newly arrived tweed capped young toreador and the bull raged figure of Cyril, Mel jumped quickly to her feet and leaned across to flick the dashboard switch operating the door.

As the doors opened she hopped out onto the cobbles below and walked swiftly across to the car.

The driver looked over as she approached.

'Hi, the name's Luke, Luke Bass,' he said, flexing both hands from the car's mahogany steering wheel to offer a subtle wave of greeting.

Mel introduced herself before confirming that Luke was indeed intent on joining the tour for the day.

'I do apologise for the slightly unorthodox arrival but this morning's ferry was late and it's been a frightful rush ever since,' he added.

'Looks like you found time to wash the car, though,' said Mel as she looked down to see a heavy rim of water that had dripped from the body work and which had etched the vehicle's footprint temporarily on the tarmac below.

Luke paused before replying, turning his head to the side to stare out to sea through a small port-hole size gap in the granite wall.

'Yes, silly, really,' he said, as he turned his head back to face Mel once more.

'I simply wanted the car to look its best after the ferry crossing, so I took it around to the garage behind the hotel to hose it down before coming here.'

'And you couldn't have cleaned it later?' quizzed Mel as she puzzled over the apparent eccentricity that demanded the hosing down of an open top sports car following a sun drenched, flat calm ferry crossing.

'I had, I thought, accounted for all my passengers. To be honest, I wasn't expecting any more,' she added as she looked towards Luke with a slight vacancy of mind.

'No, no, of course. I do apologise,' said Luke. 'As I've said, it's been a frightful rush this morning. I only arrived an hour or so ago, quickly called in here at the hotel, saw details of the tour on the notice board but then had to dash out to drive my brother over to his girlfriend's cottage in St Martin, and then had to go to the car wash. As I raced back to the hotel, I saw the bus leaving, so rather rashly drove in the exit to stop you.'

'We don't race anywhere on this Island,' said Mel, 'Whether in a flashy sports car or in anything else' she continued.

'Hear, hear,' shouted Cyril, his head still strained into the fresh outside air through the small side window of his cab.

Luke sat impassively, an air of embarrassment at the apparent telling off showing in his face.

'If you still want to come with us,' said Mel, 'I suggest you drive your car SLOWLY around to the hotel's underground car-park and return here. As you're very well aware, we were on our way.'

'Yeah and don't scratch my bus while you're doing it,' shouted Cyril. Mel returned to the bus.

The passengers looked down, and swivelled their heads slowly to follow the car's path as it manoeuvred delicately around the bus and made its way towards the car park entrance.

As it passed by her window Rachel's head suddenly lurched forward as she searched out the face of the young driver in more detail. As he disappeared from her view, she completed the partial swivel in her seat to face her husband sitting directly behind.

Tony looked up.

'Don't I know that guy?' enquired Rachel.

'Who?'

29

'That guy down there in that car,' she continued, her voice raised excitedly. 'Isn't that the guy from back home driving that car, the one you used to call fishface or something?' she added.

'Er, Fish, oh ... Er, yes. Think it is,' replied Tony, a nervous hesitancy clear in his voice. 'Yes, come to think of it, he did mention last time we spoke that he was coming to the Island around this time.'

'Some coincidence he chose the same time to visit as us, isn't it? Remind me, what's his proper name again? asked Rachel.

'Er, Luke. Luke Bass,' whispered her husband as the apparent unease of interrogation continued. 'Surprised you still recognised him, Rach.'

'You know me, I've always had a good memory for faces. Not bad though, considering that it must be three or four years since I last saw him.'

At the front of the bus, Cyril, his head now free from the risk of decapitation from his fragile looking front sliding window, leaned back in his chair and began tapping the steering wheel as he waited frustratingly for the boy racer to re-appear.

Moments later, as the tapping intensified and began to threaten the onset of fatigue cracks opening up through every component of the bus, Luke climbed aboard.

Grabbing the uppermost brass bar, he pulled himself smartly up the last step to propel himself swiftly past Cyril before any further eye or vocal contact of hostility could be made.

He continued along the aisle in search of a seat.

The chilling stare of faces, a reward for his stunt-like entrance and consequential delay of departure, welcomed his every step forward, suggesting that sympathy, perhaps not surprisingly, was loaded heavily in favour of the driver.

As he approached Tony the new arrival paused for a split second, looked across and then without a word, walked on a further few paces before finally taking a vacant seat just in front of Solly and Lauren beside a large crate of mineral water bottles.

'What's up with you two then, Tone. Cat got your tongue or something?' whispered Rachel. 'I thought you two were mates?'

Before her husband could reply a cry came from the front of the bus.

'Any more young whippersnappers to come that I should know about?' shouted Cyril, looking across towards Mel.

'Hope not, let's get out of here before anyone else eh?' Instantly, Cyril turned to face the hotel exit and prepared for departure.

The door to the bus closed once again and the vehicle, this time without incident, rumbled its way cautiously across the cobbled driveway, to leave the confines of the Coburg.

CHAPTER TWO

With the granite pillars that guarded the hotel's exit now visible on parade in the vehicle's rear view mirrors, Cyril nursed the bus carefully across the short asphalt link and prepared to enter the gladiatorial mêlée of dual-lane, town bound traffic that now filled his forward panorama.

'Blimey, rush hour's running a bit late this morning, girl,' he said, turning his head smartly to look across at Mel. 'Hope it eases soon or we'll be eating lunch in this very same spot,' he added before spinning his head back to look somewhat helplessly through the windscreen at the impregnable fusion of slow moving traffic.

As the frustration of delay continued, he leaned forward and smothered his arms around the large steering wheel as he resigned himself, for the moment at least, to a patient vigil at the side of the road.

Suddenly, as if touched by the sympathetic hand of King Canute, the incoming tide of traffic stopped momentarily and invited the bus to join its throng. Immediately, Cyril pushed up smartly with his arms to propel his body back into his seat at the realisation that his silent prayer for a moment of freedom had now been answered.

'Hallelujah,' he shouted, raising his head skywards before easing on the accelerator and swinging the bus forward through its two lane arc to join the ranks of the combustion-engine procession.

As it began its slow crawl eastwards through town, Mel stood and reached for the microphone on the seat beside her. Turning to face the passengers, she found the need to grab a nearby brass rail with her free hand to correct her balance as the vehicle began its meander through the narrow labyrinth of St Helier streets.

Within seconds of her standing, the gentle hum of passenger conversation subsided as a wave of silence washed through to the back of the bus.

'Right folks, we're finally on our way, I'm pleased to report. Sorry about our delayed start,' she said, stretching her neck in a rather exaggerated fashion as she spoke to glance at each of the two co-conspirators responsible for that delay, first Tony and then Luke, who sat a few rows beyond.

Both men sat impassively and said nothing as the eyes of Mel and a few of her disciples silently radiated the two with guilt. The persecution at an end, she raised the microphone once again to her mouth.

Almost before the first few words of her continuing commentary had escaped, the microphone began to crackle wildly, painfully accompanied by an equally wild and high-pitched whistle.

Seated directly in the eye of the sudden audio-storm under one of the three ceiling mounted speakers, Doris quickly dived to her side and buried her head for some comfort deep into the pillowed chest of her husband.

Despite the double-edged attack upon him, from his wife's unannounced broadside in the midriff and the explosive rebellion of sound-waves from above, Bob remained unmoved, wrapped in the same deep sleep that he had enjoyed since soon after boarding.

Mel instinctively thrust the mutinous voice piece at arms length away from her, giving it several firm taps on the polished brass bar that crossed in front of her seat. As the force of the impacts began to increase exponentially, so increased the very real threat of reducing the offending item into its constituent atomic parts.

'Blimey, girl,' said Cyril. 'You'll snap my little truck in half in a minute,' he continued as Mel dropped the microphone to deliver its fourth and heaviest blow on the bar.

With that, the almost forgotten luxury of silence returned, to the obvious relief of tour host and assembled entourage, except that of the still comatose Bob, whose immunity to the harshest of any noise frequency or decibel level had now been proven to be un-paralleled.

Normal service restored, Mel stepped forward three small paces and leaned across to give a light tap on the shoulder of Doris who had one ear still buried firmly into her husband's chest while the other remained tightly cupped by her left hand. The hideaway opened one eye enquiringly and looked up.

'It's okay now, Mrs Alexander, it's sorted,' she said, waving the now innocuous though battle-scared microphone in front of her.

Immediately, Doris lifted herself from her protective cocoon and raising both hands brushed the ruffled up sides of her hair back into position. 'Oh thank goodness that infernal racket has stopped. I don't know what was worse, dear; listening to that squeal or listening to my husband's chest bits bubbling around in my ear.'

Mel giggled briefly and then stood tall to face the rest of the ear tingling passengers. 'Whoops, sorry about that folks. Just a temporary hitch, I hope,' she said before raising the sound piece again to return to her commentary.

'Today's trip will, I hope, prove to be a fascinating journey through time, tracking the evolution of early habitation on the Island. Our travels will take us from prehistory, through to the present day and should provide you all with an appreciation of the rich wealth of ancient sites and monuments that we have here on Jersey.'

A young voice suddenly interrupted from the back of the bus.

'Will they be as ancient as you, dad?' quizzed young Andrew as he looked up at his father with a mischievous grin. His brother, Munro, smiled broadly in unison, accompanied by a chorus of muffled laughs from nearby seats. Even Alison, not renowned for her ventures into outward demonstrations of jollity, afforded a quick snigger before deciding that order was to be restored.

'Andrew, don't be so rude. Apologise now, or you can forget the beach tomorrow.'

The youngster turned sheepishly towards his father. 'Sorry dad,' he said in muted repentance, his head bowed.

Apology delivered, he returned his attention to looking out of the rear window, while the others on board re-focused upon their host.

'Thank you,' said Mel. 'Right, well, incredible though it may seem to us now, many thousands of years ago when sea levels were much lower than those we see today, the Channel Islands as we know them now were part of the mainland coast of France. As the ice-caps of the glacial periods melted and receded, so sea levels gradually rose, flooding the low lying areas and in some cases enveloping high ground to form an island. Such an event happened right here in Jersey, around four thousand years or so before Christ. The period of geological time between approximately four and a half and two and a half thousand years BC is known more familiarly as the neolithic period and it is here that our adventure today will begin.'

Mel paused to take a gulp of air while some of her audience grappled with the seemingly incomprehensible notion that Jersey was, at one time in its past history, quite literally within walking distance of Europe.

'To fully understand the significance of the neolithic age, we need to take a further step back in time to the many thousands of years in prehistory during which a simple nomadic culture existed among the people who roamed the lands to seek food for their survival,' she continued.

'By contrast the neolithic period saw the advent of a race whose existence relied upon a settled culture of farming and hunting. In achieving this, they established their own sustainable communities and learned to live off the environment that surrounded them. The ideas and skills they learned were subsequently developed and improved as time and

36

technology progressed and were then handed down through subsequent generations. Our first stop today on this revised route will be to visit a dolmen on the eastern side of the Island. The monument would have been an integral part of one of these early settlements and dates from around three thousand BC. It also happens to be one of the best preserved of its kind in Jersey.'

As Mel paused again for a further short respite from her mobile lecture a young voice, this time Munro's, cried out from the back row.

'What's a "doll-man" missus?'

His mother stirred into action again, twisting around in her seat and fixing her eyes resolutely on her son. 'Munro, for the last time, behave. Wait until the young lady has finished talking, please. Any more trouble and you can forget the beach forever,' she said in a tone that suggested that her patience, for the moment at least, had been stretched to its elastic limit.

'But you promised,' replied Munro as Alison shuffled her body back into a forward facing position. The whispered mutterings of discontent continued beside her.

'Mum promised we could go to the beach. She promised. It's not fair, I hate this bus.' Protest delivered, Munro folded his arms tightly and slid down in the seat before drooping his head.

As Mel continued her commentary, his ears suddenly pricked up.

'Well young man, that as it happens is a very good question,' she said, straining her eyes to search out the diminutive figure of Munro at the back of the bus. 'Yes, a very good question indeed,' she repeated, hoping that her over-emphasised commendation would secure his interest for a little while longer.

Attention aroused, Munro immediately sat up straight and looked one way and then the next at each parent, grinning broadly with the self-satisfaction that even if his mum didn't want to hear him at least someone did.

Mel carried on, pleased in herself that the bait offered to the youngster had been taken in a single innocent gulp.

'The word dolmen is one used by archaeologists to describe a particular type of megalithic structure, the word megalith meaning large stone. Dolmens are thought by many to have been used in neolithic times as burial chambers for perhaps the more important members of a community. Excavations of a number of known sites have revealed human skeletal remains and artefacts, such as pieces of pottery and primitive tools. Typically, a dolmen comprises a chamber formed of four or more upright stones, with one or more large stones forming a roof, or capstone, over. Very often the chamber would have a passageway of stones leading to it and it is for this reason that a dolmen is also sometimes referred to as a passage grave. In some instances, the stone structure would have been covered with an earth mound. The one that we shall see shortly is a particularly fine example, although the earth mound has long since disappeared leaving just the exposed stones remaining.'

'Very interesting, dear,' whispered Doris as she leaned forward and patted Mel on the arm.

Mel looked across to acknowledge her plaudit before scanning her eyes around her still attentive flock.

'Well, I hope I've not lost you. I'll expand a little more on their history and function when we arrive at the site. There's also some more information on dolmens and the neolithic people in the notes provided - for the more studiously oriented ones in our group.'

'Well, that counts me out then,' shouted Solly. 'Only had time for baseball at High School,' he continued.

Mel forced a sympathetic smile before concluding her presentation. 'That's it from me for the moment, so sit back, enjoy the journey and above all, enjoy the day.'

This time a very genuine expression of relief decorated Mel's face as she nodded appreciatively to acknowledge a spontaneous round of applause from her guests.

Curtain call complete, she switched off the microphone and sinking back into her chair placed it, in the same movement, onto the seat beside her.

Hibernating into a moment of welcome solitude, the amphitheatre of conversation behind her picked up again.

Meanwhile, towards the rear of the bus, Solly leaned forward and placed his huge shovel-like hand for support around the top of the bench seat in front, upon which sat Luke.

As the laws of mechanics swept into action the seat, complete with occupant, lurched backwards and creaked wildly to the extent that imminent and catastrophic structural failure of the framed piece of furniture appeared to be the next inevitable consequence.

Instinctively, Luke turned his head to search out an answer to the unexpected and dramatic movement, a movement that risked launching him, ejector-seat fashion, into the back row. As his upper body swivelled, he found himself almost eyeball to eyeball with the planetary figure of the huge American.

'Hi, the names Solly.'

Luke's head retreated like a tortoise, until the sharpened image of his chair-wrecking assailant came into focus.

'Sorry about that, sir. Pleased to make your acquaintance,' said the big man.

'Yes and pleased to make yours too, I'm súre,' replied Luke as he reached forward awkwardly with his arm and shook his new friend by the hand.

'Do tell me, sir,' continued the American. 'Was that you in that mighty fine looking convertible back at the hotel just a few moments ago. MGA isn't it?'

'Yes it was me, and yes it is an MGA. Actually, it's a 1600cc, 1961 roadster, to be precise,' replied Luke. 'You've an interest in classic cars, have you?' he continued as he sought to extract some common ground for conversation with his newly acquired travel companion.

'Yeah, you might say that,' interrupted Lauren in a manner

39

that suggested an air of sarcasm. 'Our parking lot back home looks like a freeway,' she added.

'So how long have you had her?' continued Solly.

Luke paused for a moment, to think.

'Er, must be close on two years now, I suppose.'

'Gee, can't be many places better than your lovely Island to enjoy the little beauty.'

'Yes, I'm sure you're right. But I don't actually live here, you know, well not any more. I brought her over on the ferry this morning with my brother. We're from the mainland. Only here for a few days jolly and the chance hopefully to catch up with a few old friends.'

As the two immersed themselves ever deeper into an enthusiastic abyss of Anglo-American classic car talk, so they became increasingly oblivious to the lush picture-postcard views that continued to fill the windows of the bus as it progressed sedately towards Santille.

Leaving the frenetic buzz of the small metropolis, the bus crossed the metamorphic parish boundary between the townscape of St Helier and the countryscape of St Saviour.

A short distance on the vehicle slowed to a crawl as it rounded a heavily shaded tree lined bend in the road and tucked in closely to allow the small procession of cars that had been following patiently in its wake to pass.

Mel reached for the microphone.

'If you all would like to look across to your left, you will see a large grass covered earth mound. This mound covers a very famous passage grave, an internationally renowned site called La Hougue Bie.'

Instantly, a ripple of passengers leaned across to the left side of the bus for a better view of their first site of the day. The vehicle mirrored the same movement as the windows filled with a montage of expectant faces and cameras.

'We will in fact be visiting this particular site later. You should have some excellent photo opportunities then.'

At the announcement the cameras retreated as the tide of over enthusiasm shuffled back to their respective seats.

With everyone including Mel seated the bus moved off, soon beginning a sedately paced descent down through the Parish of Grouville. It slowed momentarily as it passed the reservoir, the flat motionless waters reflecting the cloudless blue skies above as they warmed rapidly to the infusion of uninhibited sunshine.

From the small glistening pond at the roadside end of the reservoir, several excited young children abandoned their frantic duck feeding session to turn and wave feverishly to the chugging bright red bus as it crawled by.

A few on board, including Mel, returned the gesture before joining in a chorus of laughter as one of the children, forgetting she still had a fist full of bread morsels, waved them into the air like confetti much to the noisy delight of the resident ducks who, as one, made a vocal dash for the irresistible feast of generosity that lay scattered on the grass around them.

The vehicle continued on its way for a few kilometres more before turning from the main road into a narrow lane, the eerily shaded entrance a result of a heavy shroud of tree canopy that arched across it from both sides. Several hundred metres further on, it emerged from the tunnel of foliage and back into bright daylight.

As the lane began to widen slightly, Cyril eased on the brakes and guided the vehicle onto a short dusty strip of verge. Bumping across several small ruts, it threw a few wisps of dust past the line of windows on each side before finally coming to a halt.

Mel stood up and turned. 'Right, folks, we're now here at the first site, Dolmen de Santille. If you look over again to your left through the small copse of trees in the distance, you should be able to make out a few large stones. They form part of the dolmen.'

As had happened just moments earlier, the bus rocked immediately to one side as the eager entourage jostled for position to find the best view.

41

The rocking motion suddenly took on a new and dramatic dimension as Solly, fresh from his exchange of car related trivia with Luke, then joined with the mass flow of other bodies towards the viewing side of the bus.

As it rolled violently, the air became a spaghetti-like tangle of arms as the passengers, fearing the aged vehicle was about to capsize like a boat in a storm, reached out to seek extra support from any piece of fixture they could find.

With the migration of occupants, for the moment at least, now temporarily at an end the oscillations settled down allowing the minds of those present to refocus upon the task of searching out the site in the distance.

'Yes, yes, I see the stones. Look there, I see them,' shouted Munro from the back.

'I want ...'

He suddenly stopped, sensing the ominous first signs of his mother in swivel mode on her seat.

Before further parental control could be exercised the airwaves filled again with the now familiar tone of Mel's voice.

'As we can't park any closer, I'm afraid that we're going to have to walk it from here. Should take us about ten minutes maximum. I'm sure a little stretch of the legs on this fine day will do us all good,' she gibed.

'Can I ask the younger ones amongst us not to play on the stones when we arrive at the site. I'm certain you would all like to do your bit to help preserve them for another five thousand years.'

As a unilateral murmur of approval echoed around, Alison turned to face her two sons. She stared at Andrew and Munro each in turn and without a word, though her silent, intense stare said it all; 'NO playing on the stones.'

The bus door squeaked open.

'Please be careful when you get off as this is quite a narrow road,' warned Mel to the group as they all began to stand and gather together their possessions.

'If we can all meet up outside, I'll then lead you around to the site.'

She placed the microphone back on her seat, picked her notepad up and then skipped her way quickly down the steps and onto the ground below before dragging her sunglasses down across her eyes from their perch on top of her head.

With the preparation for disembarkation intensifying back in the bus, Doris turned her head, leaned across and whispered into her husband's ear from close range.

'Bob, Bob, wake up dear. It's time for a walk.'

With no discernable reaction, short of a brief involuntary grunt, she repeated the invitation, her increasing anxiety at the possibility of missing the group exit now paralleled by an increase in her tone.

'Bob, Bob, come on, dear, wakey, wakey. It's time for a walk.'

With the decibels raised, Bob's head twitched slightly, his eyes still closed.

'I don't want to talk. I want to sleep,' he mumbled, subconsciously.

'No, not a talk, a walk, you silly old fool. Come on. Everyone else is going.'

As her demands continued, she began nudging her husband's arm firmly in the hope of stirring a heightened level of activity that at present still registered perilously close to zero, as indeed it had done since soon after departure.

Pulses of life temporarily restored, the two raised themselves gingerly from their seats and shuffled into the aisle, to join the orderly evacuation.

As the couple began their nervous negotiation of the steps, Mel stepped quickly back on board and extended her arm to assist their descent.

With their safe landing back on terra firma, the exodus behind them continued. As it did, Solly still seated, prepared for his exit. With a cry of effort fuelled anguish, he rolled forward in his chair into a semi-standing position, before the penalty of consuming four packets of biscuits in half an hour sent him crashing unceremoniously backwards from where he came.

Lauren, having witnessed the abortive take-off, quietly congratulated herself for escaping to the aisle just seconds earlier before leaning over to her husband and relieving him of the remaining packets of goodies which lay scattered across his lap and the adjacent seat. Food debris removed, he prepared himself for his second attempt at lift-off.

As the countdown began and the booster rockets began to fire up once more, Lauren silently prepared herself for the line; "Houston, we have a problem." As the rehearsal continued, she turned to face the Milner family who were waiting patiently for a clear passage.

'I'm so sorry for the delay, guys.'

The Milner quartet looked up.

'Would the rest of you care to go first?' added Lauren, mindful that if the family waited for Solly to successfully disembark it might well be the middle of next year before they themselves got off. She crossed the aisle to take up a holding position in the adjacent row of seats as the clan filed out.

'Okay, sweetheart. It's now or never,' said Lauren, looking across and smiling at her husband. As the adrenalin of his imminent levitation, or so he hoped, began to pump, Solly ruffled up the lower portion of his 'T' shirt and mopped a film of sweat from his brow. He took a deep breath and then in one flowing movement, rocked back a few degrees before springing from the seatback to convert the propulsion into a forward motion.

With the considerable momentum of his mass acting in his favour, the energy projected him to his feet and into a standing, though slightly crouched posture, an enforced consequence of the buses restrictive headroom.

Mission accomplished, Solly wiped his forehead with a repeat brush of his " T" shirt as the sweats of perspiration from his recent efforts made their continued runs for freedom.

'Come on, let's catch up with the others,' said Lauren.

The two dropped down from the bus and joined the tightly massed group which had assembled along the narrow crescent of dusty verge between the vehicle and a high semi-grassed mud bank that stood as a man-made weather break barrier protecting the seasonal potato fields beyond.

For now though, this year's treasured harvest of the famous Jersey Royals was well in the past and the field now stood as a neatly ploughed square in the patchwork quilt that encapsulated the ancient site within.

As the group waited, Cyril, the only person now left on board, opened his flask of coffee, produced two foil wrapped digestive biscuits from his jacket pocket and spread his newspaper out across the steering wheel as he prepared to take full advantage of his short break.

Mel suddenly reappeared at the foot of the steps.

'Only be the usual twenty minutes or so,' she said, as the driver rolled his eyes down from his paper and looked across.

'Take as long as you like, girl. Want to check how the horses did at the weekend.'

'Well don't buy a luxury yacht and sail off into the sunset with your winnings until we return,' joked Mel.

'Huh, chance would be a fine thing. I had a "dead-cert" fiver on the favourite last week. Called himself "luckycharma". Would you believe it, he fell at the first fence. I'll tell you what, Mel. If my fortune does change one day and I do sail somewhere with my winnings, it'll probably be on a lilo.'

Mel laughed, then turned and brushing her way courteously through the scrum of waiting bodies that greeted her, stepped cautiously onto the partially grassed mud-bank to gain a welcome height advantage on the group around her.

The heads swivelled as one to follow Mel's arm which pointed along the road.

'If we walk straight up the road here first and then follow it around to the left for about five hundred metres or so, we'll eventually find the sign for the dolmen and three granite steps leading up to the short track which takes us to the site itself. Please do try and stick together, for everyone's safety. We'll stop at the granite steps for a quick breather before the final short hike to the dolmen.'

Mel dropped down off the bank and walked on briskly ahead, in an effort to catch up with an advance party of three eager adventurers who, despite Mel's earlier plea to stick together, were now dolmen bound, having left the group quietly under cover of her concluding few words to the others.

Before long, the trio, comprising Tony, Luke and Jamie, had converted their initial speed walk into a trot and then a sprint.

Andrew and Munro snatched at the tight handgrip placed on them by their parents. 'We want to race with them as well, mum,' they pleaded.

'You're going nowhere,' said Craig and Alison in a stereophonic cry of parental accord.

The two lads huffed, shrugged their shoulders and looked ahead with the others to see the three men eventually disappear from sight.

Mel turned to wait the few seconds for her main group to join her.

'Shouldn't waste your time on them, Mel,' shouted Rachel. 'They're just a sad bunch of idiots. My pet hamster's got more sense than those three Olympiads put together,' she continued.

A ripple of laughter jogged its way through the party.

Now back in touch with the main group, Mel, like the pied piper, led her merry gang forward, this time at a more comfortable, weather respecting pace. Immediately behind her followed the Milner family, their sons' hyper-activity now impeded following their failed race request by the even firmer hand clenches from their parents.

Dominating the middle ground in the people convoy walked Solly, his massive frame dwarfing all those around him to Lilliputian proportions.

In his shadow a short distance back followed Doris and Bob, their ever diminishing progress carefully monitored by last in the line Rachel who had recognised the couple's struggle against the energy sapping effects of the warming sun.

Mel stopped as she approached the sharp left hand corner in the road to allow the lengthening procession to regroup.

Compact again, she turned and walked on to the second junction and the meeting point steps where the three sprinters had gathered, all looking on this fine bright morning as if they had just endured a long session in the sauna.

'Hope it was all worth it?' said Mel as she glanced at the three pathetic morsels, their heads drowned in sweat.

'Must remember not to sit next to you lot today,' she continued.

'Yes, hope the hotel's given us a supply of pegs for our noses later,' added Rachel.

Though not wishing to promote the three's rebellious achievement too much in front of the now fully assembled group, Mel nonetheless felt obliged, as their host, to politely enquire upon the result.

'Okay, so who won the Santille sprint?'

'Oh, he won by a mile, went off like a train,' said a semi-breathless Luke, pointing over towards Tony who, like himself, was crouched over at the waist with hands extended onto knees to prop his race exhausted body.

Suddenly Mel's attention was drawn to Jamie.

Adopting what appeared to be an alternative and contorted recovery posture, the third residue of apparent athleticism sat a few metres away from the other two on the roadside, his body flopped backwards across a grass swallowed boundary stone.

'Been in the wars, have we?' enquired Mel as she focused upon a series of bloody abrasions on his hands and arms.

Jamie slowly raised his head, a hint of anger glazing his eyes.

'Yes, no thanks to those guys,' he replied, looking across uncompromisingly at first towards Tony and then Luke. The two accused glanced over towards their battle-scarred competitor. 'They seemed intent on wiping me out from the moment we got going,' he continued. 'I don't think they wanted me to join their stupid race. You'd have thought the finishing line was their personal domain.'

'Yes, sorry about that, mate. No harm done I hope,' said Tony as he stood and took a few steps forward towards the injured man's resting place.

Jamie pushed his arms against the granite wall and sat up.

'Only if you call a hole in my knee-cap no harm. What are you, some sort of human bumper car or something,' he said, a conspicuous tinge of anger now pulsating in his voice. 'First you try and shoulder barge me into the hedgerow and then you blatantly trip me up.'

'Well I can only apologise,' replied Tony.

'Yes, me too. It was only a bit of fun,' interrupted Luke.

Tony quickly wiped his sweaty palms on his tracksuit trousers and offered his hand across to Jamie for a handshake gesture of apology.

Jamie remained impassive.

Suddenly, a large shadow threw its chill blanket across Jamie's sitting position as Solly stepped forward into the sporting arena.

The men looked skywards, into the stratospheric abyss that contained the American's all-consuming figure.

'Come on guys, make up. You're acting like a bunch of high-school college jerks.'

Solly's summing up completed, Jamie began weighing the options of dismissing the peace-plan or maintaining his war of silence with the considerably less formidable frames of Tony and Luke.

The calculation was instantaneous. Though clearly pained, Jamie rolled forward and pushed himself to return to a standing position, before he too dried his hands crudely on his trousers and then offered the right one across to his two English counterparts in turn to seal an enforced handshake of truce.

'All yours again, young lady,' said Solly.

Mel nodded in appreciation of the American's diplomatic success at achieving the entente cordiale between the warring factions.

Confrontation diffused, Mel walked forward a few metres to the start of the narrow track that would take them on the final leg of their short hike along to the dolmen.

'If we can all stay close together this time please, I'll lead the way. And that means all of us, please,' she said, her request for some degree of order directed primarily towards the athletic trio who had all collapsed in a sweaty recovery mode just beside her.

Before proceeding she raised her arm to point out a moss-covered sign above her head. Though slightly weather-beaten and concealed behind the thickly leaved branches of a mature sycamore tree, the sign was still just legible.

PUBLIC FOOTPATH
DOLMEN DE SANTILLE - 3000BC.
50 YARDS AHEAD

Mel stepped aside as young Munro, who had managed to finally break the hand-clamp grip of his mother, suddenly ran forward and stared up at the sign before raising the camera that hung around his neck and immediately snapping a photograph of the semi-obscured, algae veneered sign.

'What on earth do you want a picture of that mucky thing for?' enquired Alison who had instantly leapt forward to interrupt her son's enthusiastic photographic shoot.

'Oh, please mum, just this one please, please.'

'No, Munro, come on, son. You've not stopped clicking that thing since we set off.'

The youngster stood for a moment, looked up at his mother

and then again at the metal post before quietly returning his simple camera, rather reluctantly, into its scruffy leather case.

With the camera secure, Alison grabbed her young son's hand and looked across at Mel.

'These kids seem to forget that us parents have to pay for these photos, don't they? We went to Menorca last year and he somehow managed to take sixteen shots of a cloudless blue sky. He reckoned one was a photo of the moon, would you believe?'

Mel laughed discretely to herself before stepping onto the granite steps and turning to quickly check on the well-being of her eager explorers.

'You okay at the back there?' she enquired, her voice slightly raised. 'What about you and Bob?' she added.

'Oh, we're not too bad, thank you, dear,' replied Doris wearily, her clear exhaustion, not to mention her husband's, suggesting that her typically British response had been one out of politeness for her host and immunity from embarrassment, rather than one which truly reflected the energy sapping toll that the short walk had taken out on the two of them.

Bob, who had finally succumbed to the heat and had taken up temporary residence seated in the shade of a small privet bush, raised his head slowly to acknowledge some degree, if only minor, of well being.

Rachel bent down to where he had come to rest.

'Fancy a drink of water?' she said, placing a small clear bottle into his open left hand which lay palm up at his side. As the cool object came into contact with his drying skin, Bob's fingers slowly coiled to clamp the bottle.

'Oh thank you, young lady,' said Doris. 'You're a real treasure. Can we adopt you at all?'

'You better ask my husband,' replied Rachel with a warm friendship-filled smile.

Re-hydrated, Bob, assisted on each side by his wife and Rachel, slowly returned to the vertical.

'Okay folks, let's go,' said Mel. 'Just a few more yards and then we can have a longer rest.'

In single file, the group made its way carefully up the granite steps and along the short, dusty and heavily tree lined track.

Within a few metres some of the monument's perimeter stones came into view.

'Wow, look at those,' said young Andrew.

'Oh, Double Wow,' agreed his brother. 'Look mum, look, it's "Stoneyhedge",' he yelped excitedly.

'Think you mean Stonehenge, son,' said his father, smiling as he followed, ever watchful, behind.

Suddenly Andrew shouted again.

'Look, look, I've found some "knee liffic" pottery.'

Those close by stooped over to view the young amateur archaeologist at work as he squatted down at the edge of the track, his mother having now released him from her handhold in the vain hope that he was now on safe nuisance-free ground.

Alison stepped forward.

'Oh Andrew, put that down immediately,' she demanded. 'It's just a dirty piece of brick. Put it carefully in the hedge now and wipe your hands with this,' she added, pulling a fresh white tissue from her trouser pocket and waving it in front of his eyes.

With Andrew cleansed of brick dust and back in line, Mel beckoned the group on.

They soon emerged from the track into a small oval shaped grass covered clearing, its outer perimeter a seemingly impregnable mesh of trees, bushes and thistles.

Dominating the central area, though slightly elevated from their present vantage point, stood the magnificent geometric array of ancient stones.

Greyish in colour and displaying the weather-beaten pits and scars of the past five thousand years, each stone had its own fingerprint of identity that extended from its unique shape to the pastel patchwork of green, black and brown lichens that speckled its surface.

Before closing in on the monument for a more detailed look, Mel paused to continue her much versed commentary on the history of the dolmen that lay before them.

'The Dolmen you can begin to see ahead dates from about three thousand years BC. It was first excavated in nineteen thirty two, during which five human skeletons were found, together with numerous stone axe heads and items of pottery.'

'But no bricks,' whispered Craig to his wife.

'Many of the artefacts recovered from that particular excavation and indeed findings from a number of other excavations around the Island, are on display at the museum in St Helier. If you get time, I strongly recommend a visit. It's a fascinating collection,' said Mel.

'Okay, if we move on now, I'll just lead you around to the front of the passage, at which point I'll leave you to spend a short while exploring the site for yourselves. I will of course be about if you have any questions.'

As she began leading the party around to the left, so the interior of the dolmen began to open up with each advancing stride.

Suddenly she stopped without warning, so abruptly in fact that the four members of the Milner family following closely behind collided with her.

Both Andrew and Munro, in an effort to over-dramatize their comic appreciation of the collision, fell to the floor and rolled around in the grass giggling hysterically to themselves.

'Get up from there now, you silly boys,' said Alison uncompromisingly.

Instantly the two lads jumped to their feet and, assisted by their mother, brushed a sticky deposit of grass from their trousers.

'What's up Mel?' enquired Craig.

'I'm not sure, but over there, under the capstone,' she said, her arm extended and pointing into the heart of the stone ringed site. 'Looks like someone sleeping?' she continued.

Silence descended on the group as the collective eyes of the people assembled homed in on the mysterious resident.

Craig stepped forward.

'Stay here, I'll go and have a look,' he said, as he looked across at Mel and then his wife.

'Munro, Andrew, stay with your Mum until I come back,' he said authoritatively.

'But I want to come with you, dad,' said Munro.

'Yes and me, dad, please,' pleaded Andrew.

'Munro, Andrew, here, NOW,' ordered Alison.

The lads reacted instantly to the call to order and stood one either side of their mother, each holding one of Alison's outstretched and expectant hands.

The group stepped back as Craig made his first strides towards the entrance passageway of stones.

'Solly, go with him,' said Lauren as she offered a pathetic nudge to her husband in the impossible hope of assisting his propulsion forwards.

Silence descended again as Mel and the others watched the two men, looking more like David and Goliath, walking over to the capstone. Solly propped himself against the massive granite slab which covered the chamber, leaving the ever more agile Craig to squat down and examine the bundle nervously. Seconds later he suddenly backed away, still crouching, until he sensed he was clear of the stonework overhead.

The two men engaged in a short conversation before turning and walking slowly back. Their body language suggested that something was seriously wrong.

As they returned to where the group stood, Mel broke away and stepped forward a few paces to meet them.

'Craig, what on earth is it?' she whispered.

'It's a body, a young m-m-man,' replied Craig, the shocked realization of his discovery triggering a slight stutter in his speech.

'I think he's dead …' he continued '… And I'm certain he's that young lad from the hotel.'

Munro, stretching inquisitively from his mother's clasp to listen in on the attempt at a private conversation between

Mel, Craig and Solly, ensured that the efforts made by his father to avoid distress to those around failed almost instantly.

The young lad rocked back towards his mother.

'MUM, MUM. They've found a dead person in the cave.'

'Oh, wow, a real dead person. Is it a real caveman?' interrupted Andrew.

Alison tugged painfully at the two lads' arms as their announcement conspired to send a shock wave of terror, rumbling through the group that began to shuffle around nervously.

Mel reacted instantly and turned to face her entourage, a few of them clearly traumatised by the situation that now presented itself.

'Okay everybody. I'm afraid that for the moment I'm going to have to ask you all to return to the bus,' she said, her last words beginning to falter as she fought with the emotional turmoil caused by Craig's discovery.

She turned to search out Rachel.

'Rachel, can you see everyone back, please, and explain the situation to Cyril. Tell him to keep everyone on board and wait for my return. I'll wait here with Craig and Solly, if that's all right?'

Rachael nodded her acknowledgement of her ex-colleagues request before turning and leading the party away in a silence of disbelief, the excitement and humour since the start of the day having evaporated in an instant.

As they retreated, Mel reached for her bag and pulled out her mobile phone. She fumbled for an instant with the buttons before pressing *Memory # 10*, a direct line through to the police station in St Helier. It was a number she had programmed some years previously but which she had not had cause to use until now.

Flanked by her Scottish-American guardians, she waited anxiously as the dialling tone began.

CHAPTER THREE

The silent vigil of Mel, Craig and Solly as they waited for an acknowledgement to the telephoned emergency call was, to their collective relief, short-lived.

'St. Helier Police, can we help you?'

'Yes, Yes … Hello police ... police,' said Mel, a breathless hesitancy choking her response as she strained every muscle to maintain her composure.

'Yes, this is St. Helier police. Can we help you, madam?'

She paused and drew in a deep breath before speaking again.

'My name's Melanie ... Melanie Winkley. I'm the tour guide for the Coburg Hotel. We're on a group tour at the ...'

The final words failed her.

'Please, just take your time, Miss Winkley,' said the calming voice of the female controller.

'My name's Sue,' continued the woman hoping that the more personable approach would help to dilute the increasing rushes of nervous energy that appeared to be flooding Mel's body.

The line went quiet for a moment as Mel paused and drew a deep breath.

'Hi, Sue, are you still there?' she enquired eagerly, the tone of her voice rising anxiously as she spoke.

'Yes, I'm still with you. Just take your time. Now you were about to tell me where you were.'

'We're at the Dolmen de Santille in Grouville with a visitor party. We've found a body ... a dead body … of a young man. He may be from our hotel?'

Mel drew another breath, this time deeper, as the enormity of that last disjointed statement began to register in her mind.

'And you are sure that the person is dead?'

'As sure as I can be, Sue, without actually seeing the body myself. Two of the hotel guests in my excursion group found it, you see.'

'Right. Understood, Mel. I'm arranging for immediate assistance as we speak. If I can just ask you for some information while that back up is en route.'

'Yes…yes, of course, how can I help?'

'The incident area itself, is it as you discovered it?'

'Er, yes, as far as I know.'

'And how many guests do you have with you all together?'

Mel paused for thought. Though fully mindful at the start of the day as to every necessary detail about her party, including the total number, that same mind was now clouded into mild obscurity by the unfolding drama of more recent events.

She pressed the phone against her shoulder, allowing her two free hands to quickly search her bag for the pink sheet of paper that contained the corrected register of names.

'Hi again, Sue ... Sorry about the delay. The total is fifteen. That's one five, which includes myself and our bus driver, Cyril, who is waiting in the vehicle about ten minutes walk away.'

'And the group are still there with you?'

'No, I've sent them all back to wait in the bus. It seemed the best thing to do in the circumstances. There are just the two men who discovered the body left with me at the site here now.'

'Okay, that's good Mel. As I said earlier, assistance is on its way. If I could ask you to stay exactly where you are, that help shouldn't be too far away ... Just one final thing for the moment though.'

'Yes?' enquired Mel tentatively.

'Can I quickly take a note of your telephone number? It's only routine, in case we need to call you back.'

Mel hesitated.

As before, a simple request for information that under normal circumstances she would have expected to regurgitate routinely proved elusive, as the trauma of the morning's discovery continued to blockade every automatic door to her cerebral database.

Seeking a manual over-ride, she reached into her bag again

56

and, pulling out a small red diary, thumbed frantically through its pages.

'Yes, yes, here it is,' she said quickly, her panicked response fusing the words, it seemed, into one.

As she began relaying the digits of the number to Sue, the numbing silence that had shrouded the dolmen site since the gruesome discovery of the body suddenly became displaced by the distant, though clearly approaching, sound of an emergency siren.

Attention returned to the dusty footpath leading to the site along which approached two smartly suited young men.

Mel walked across to meet the duo.

'Good morning, madam. Would you be Miss Melanie Winkley?' enquired one as he glanced into his small notebook.

Mel nodded.

'I'm Sergeant Shaun Carak and this is my colleague Sergeant Kevin Ledouche,' he continued as the two waved their identity cards in the still air.

Mel said nothing.

'I understand you have just been speaking with my colleague back at the station, is that correct?'

'Er ...Yes, that's right, sergeant ... I believe her name was Sue?'

This time it was Shaun's turn to offer the confirmatory nod.

'Okay, and where exactly is the body you've found?'

'Just over there in that stone chamber ... Can you see, it just looks like a bundle of rags from here,' replied Mel as she stretched out her left arm to point.

A blanket of silence descended and wrapped itself around the site as Shaun and Kevin turned and walked briskly across to the granite enclosure to make their initial study of the scene.

Mel, Solly and Craig looked on impassively.

The "pin drop" observance continued as the two men retreated.

As they did, the figure of Shaun could be seen speaking into his mobile phone.

Within seconds the vacuum of noise which had bubble-wrapped the monument, albeit briefly, began to erode once more. That same noise gradually intensified until very soon the narrow, arid, dust-covered lane was flooded by an incoming tide of pulsating blue lights and sirens.

As Shaun and Kevin moved in to continue their conversation with Mel, so continued also the blue invasion of uniformed officers, their numbers, it seemed, multiplying with each passing minute as further posses made their arrival.

With Mel engaged in detailed discussion, Craig and Solly watched in a bewildered stupor as the whole theatre of operation unfolded before them.

As the plain clothed minority began to take stock of the scene so the uniformed majority, under the direction of their complementary uniformed sergeant, fragmented and began setting about their delegated tasks with the feverish and purposeful industry of ants on a nest.

Their co-ordinated efforts initially seemed focused upon the establishment of an improvised incident room. With the sophistication of a race not far removed from that of the neolithic people themselves, the temporary shelter comprised a heavy and battle-weary pale blue tarpaulin slung crudely across an obliging tree branch of a nearby oak, with the two grass skimming perimeters of the sheet tied tent fashion to the ground.

The open ended pseudo-wigwam complete, the orchestrated activity continued as the blue army relayed a seemingly house-move volume of boxes and crates to the shelter's focal point.

Soon the full complement of site investigative props was in place, with the minor exception of a tape to link the ring of steel stakes that now marked the boundary to the incident area.

This time it was the turn of the re-grouped ensemble of officers to observe as their sergeant, a diminutive figure of stocky build, walked the site perimeter and linked each metal stake with blue and white striped plastic tape, tying off at each one rather bizarrely with an elaborate looking twist and knot.

'Knew he'd be useful for something,' whispered one of the men to his colleagues.

'Yes, didn't you know he is the station's crochet champion,' added another.

The others laughed.

The wisecracks ceased as the sergeant completed his circumferential journey.

As he made the final few steps back to his troop, the forensic team comprising two men arrived, each laden with heavy looking shiny steel boxes.

The sergeant paused and, after a swift exchange of pleasantries, turned to watch the duo walk around the taped perimeter to the front entrance of the recently completed control room. Shaun and Kevin, their initial discussions with Mel now at an end, followed closely behind.

The four stopped for a few minutes and stared intently at the pale blue tunnel structure that confronted them.

The group of officers responsible for its construction tried to listen from a distance, hoping to learn from the developing discussion whether the men's conversation was in quiet admiration for the improvised dwelling or one of consideration as to its structural integrity.

Appearing to side in favour of the latter, the forensic duo disappeared through the front entrance before re-emerging moments later via the rear and onto the dolmen site, dressed head to toe in snow white coloured overalls.

The scene now adopted two focal points, the inner zone dominated by the chamber where the forensic investigation took on a more analytical bias, and the outer zone beyond the cordoned ring where the transient migration of uniformed personnel continued to and from the site.

Mel, Craig and Solly, now flanked by two such uniformed officers, continued their patient watch and wait in anticipation of further instruction.

Some thirty minutes or so later the ever changing focus of attention was redirected once more as all eyes present, except those at the chamber, were suddenly drawn back to the track which accessed the site from the lane.

Approaching at speed, appeared a youngish looking man riding a red mountain bike and wearing a bright red crash hat. As he advanced ever nearer, he found himself ducking his head and contorting his upper body several times, to avoid the peril of a painful swipe from the gnarled limbs of some awkwardly overhanging tree branches.

The drama of the spectacle then increased with the two-dimensional flexing suddenly becoming three as the rider found himself at the same time juggling with the control of the bike which was sliding continuously on the earthy marbles of the dry dusty track.

For Mel's two guests, the perpetually moving body made the determination of any readily discernable facial features difficult if not impossible.

It soon became apparent however, courtesy of mutterings from the many officers present, that any knowledge of even the faintest of facial features was, in this case, not necessarily a pre-requisite for determining the man's identity.

Whispers began to circulate among their ranks suggesting that there was only one person this side of Mars who could make an entrance of such eccentric pantomime, their very own Inspector Harry Gateaux.

'Stand back lads and lassies, here comes Cyco,' announced one.

The "Cyco" tag had been one long attributed to the Inspector and seemed particularly apt in view of his fanatical addiction to, it seemed, all things sport related. He was the ultimate competitor, with an inbuilt though controlled determination and aggression to win at whatever he participated in, whether it be a heart stopping bike event along a precipitous rocky north coast headland or an opportunity to buy a hotel in Mayfair during a simple game of monopoly.

That will to win had very clear parallels with his work. Every avenue and every occasional cul-de-sac of each case he led was pursued with a keen and unrelenting vigour and intensity until he and he alone was satisfied that the time had come for the files to be successfully closed. In everything, except the dress code department, he was accepted as the consummate, if slightly unorthodox, professional.

The suspicions, if indeed any had existed as to the rider's identity, were soon erased as the Inspector, clad in his trademark tracksuit, closed in on the waiting congregation.

Soon the whites of his eyes were in full view and, with those same eyes soon filling with the battalion of police officers just several yards ahead of him, he slammed on his brakes and brought the bike to a skidding, though apparently controlled halt.

He balanced athletically for a moment. Seconds later and with equal athleticism, he jumped from the machine and lifting its lightweight frame with one hand, swung it swiftly across his body to prop it against a nearby tree.

In the same flowing movement of seamless energy he swivelled around, nodded to the throng of nearby officers and then without a word stooped down under the blue and white striped tape ringing the incident area.

The perpetuallism of the motions continued to the dizzy gaze of those close by as, having cleared the tape and sprung instantly to a standing position, he jogged briskly, still clad in his red crash hat, over towards the capstoned cist.

'Hi lads,' he called, as he swapped greetings with his two station colleagues, Shaun and Kevin, who had themselves now returned to within metres of the chamber entrance.

The two men nodded, before Harry's attention was drawn towards the stone tomb itself where the forensic duo, kitted out in full-length white and looking paradoxically like two snowmen lost in a summer wilderness, were busily occupied with their initial photographic survey of the scene.

'So what have we found so far?' enquired Gateaux, as he looked back at Shaun for an instant briefing.

Before his sergeant could utter the first syllable of a response, Jeff, the senior forensic scientist, aware that the Inspector was now close by, broke away from the camera for a moment and turned, snapping the white latex gloves from his hands as he did so.

'Good to see you again, Harry. How you doing?' he said, offering his arm at the same time to shake the Inspector by the hand.

Gateaux turned a few degrees to his side.

'Yes, very well thanks Jeff.'

'I was just about to quiz Shaun but you've got in first.'

'So what exactly have we got?'

'Well, we've one body, white, male, probably about thirty years old.'

'Has the Doc been on site yet?'

'Yes, you've just missed "H". She left about ten minutes ago,' replied Jeff, referring to their mutual friend, Doctor Heather Short, a local GP.

'That'll teach me to be a little earlier in future,' said Harry.

'I do like my chats with "H",' he continued, the latter abbreviation being a colloquialism by which the young doctor was affectionately known by her friends.

'No worries, I'll catch her later then.'

'Anyway, she confirmed the guy's dead,' said Jeff, jumping the conversation back onto its investigative track. 'But he's apparently not been gone long, perhaps sometime within the past couple of hours. Certainly this side of day-break,' he added as he relayed the doctor's preliminary findings to the Inspector.

'Any ideas yet upon cause of death?'

'Nothing concrete at the moment but some interesting finds.'

'Such as?' enquired Harry, his voice lusting for more information.

'Well, if you just come over to the chamber for a second, I'll show you.'

As the two men walked the final few steps to the megalithic stone enclosure, Harry raised his hand skywards flicking the buckle to his crash hat and removing the headwear before tucking it smartly under his arm.

Jeff crouched to prepare himself for a forward shuffle into the chamber. He turned smartly and offered a small blue plastic torch across.

'Can you look after this, please, mate?'

The Inspector reached out with his free hand to accept the baton.

'Cheers Gats, it's just that we'll need it inside until the lads have rigged up a spotlight.'

Soon the two found themselves squatting claustrophobically under the imposing fifteen tonne roof slab of pink weather stained granite which skimmed their heads and threatened a self-inflicted scalping from any ill-considered movement. The intimidation of the ancient canopy seemed compounded by its precarious support along three sides upon four knife-edge wafers of similar granite stone uprights.

'Can see why you needed the torch,' said Harry as his eyes adjusted to its miserly illumination.

Jeff side stepped along, crab-like, and placed his hands delicately under the victim's head.

'You see here? A fresh cut just above the eye,' he said as he carefully rolled the body's head a fraction to one side.

'What is not so obvious, but perhaps which is more significant, is that the poor chap has a broken neck. Either injury could, I suppose, have been caused by the guy somehow hitting his head against that stone,' he continued, pointing to a small triangular shaped granite stone close to where the victim's head rested.

'What do you mean somehow hitting?' enquired Gateaux.

'Well, the lad's about the same height as us, I would say and we're stooped fairly uncomfortably in here. I think it would have been very difficult, if not impossible, for him to have fallen with any great force on to that stone and to then have ended up in this position with the injuries I've just described.'

'Yes, now you mention it, I guess he couldn't have crunched himself much tighter in here if he'd tried, could he?' replied Harry as he leaned his own body forward and scanned the victim's contorted shape from head to toe. 'And the ground around him looks quite disturbed,' he added.

'Yes, indeed.'

'So how do you think he came to arrive like this. Do you think it's conceivable that he might have dragged himself in here?'

Jeff paused for a moment's silent consideration.

'Well, though a dragging scenario might explain why there are very well defined blood stains on each side of this small stone, it doesn't seem plausible with the severity of the neck injury. It's still early days, but I think it's fairly safe to say that if he had sustained this outside the chamber, which is my guess, then he wouldn't have been able to drag himself a millimetre in any direction ... And certainly not under here.'

'Not an accident then?'

For a second time Jeff paused.

'Maybe not. I know what I said a short while ago might suggest that as a conclusion but to be honest, I must keep an open mind for a little longer. Perhaps another couple of hours or so on site and I'll be able to give you a better picture. As soon as we've finished here I'll get the body back to the labs for a post-mortem. That's when I can give you some real answers. Hopefully, some preliminary findings for tomorrow morning.'

'Okay, fine, I'll catch up with you later then, Jeff, but anything you find out, I want to know straight away.'

Still squatting, Harry shook hands with his scientist colleague before initiating his escape.

As he tried carefully to reverse blindly out of the chamber his head suddenly cracked against a rogue and immovable projection of the igneous rock above.

'Urgh ... Who put that damn thing there,' he joked bravely as he crouched lower and began rubbing the injured top of his head furiously, though rather awkwardly in the cramped confines of the chamber.

'Whoops, sorry, mate. I did mean to warn you about that,' said Jeff. 'Perhaps you should have kept that cycle hat on after all,' he continued as a small laugh echoed around the chamber walls.

'Oh, it's not your fault, mate, but you can still buy me a pint for that later ... to numb the pain,' replied Harry as he began his second attempt at a retreat, his head this time ducked lower to the extent that it now brushed his knees.

His exit safely negotiated, he stood, rubbed his head one final time and then turned, to walk the several paces back towards the spot where the main group patiently waited.

Stooping under the blue and white tape, he found himself face to face with Mel who had walked forward to meet his return.

'Hi there girl!'

'Hi, Gats,' replied Mel, her head slightly bowed, the normal jovial tone of her voice now suppressed by the air of melancholy that infused within her.

'Didn't think you'd ever give me business?' continued the Inspector as he tried to re-light the fun loving smile that was the trademark feature of his good friend.

Mel raised her head slowly, her pale ashen face and piecing stare suggesting she wasn't in the mood for Harry's ill-timed attempt at his infamous humour.

Though well intended, his lack of tact under the present circumstances was instantly understood.

'Sorry, Mel,' he said, patting her consolingly on the side of the shoulder.

'Yes, me too,' she replied. 'You just caught me at a bad moment, I'm afraid. I'll be okay in a minute,' she continued, as she lifted her hand to wipe a lone tear from her eye.

Respecting her hint of a plea for a moment's space, Gateaux

turned and exchanged small talk with one of the officers. Conversation complete, he turned to face Mel who, to his relief, responded with a brave characteristic smile.

'Okay, Gats. I'm all right now, thank you. What do you want to know?'

'Well, I understand from my sergeant that it was your good self who alerted us earlier. Is that correct?'

Mel nodded in agreement.

'And I also understand that the victim may have been a guest from your hotel?'

'Yes, we believe it to be a young man called Andrew ... Er Andrew Price,' confirmed Mel, a chilling hesitancy returning for a moment to her voice. 'Though I should add that I've not seen the body at close quarters myself.'

'So who discovered the body then?'

'Oh, Mr Milner found it ... And Mr Neilson,' replied Mel, standing back a pace as she spoke and offering out her hand to introduce the Inspector to the Scotsman who stood a few metres further along to her left.

The Inspector stepped past and turned his attentions to Craig.

Before he could continue any further word of inquiry his eyes were drawn hypnotically to the voluminous figure of Solly who had just returned from the shaded canopy of a nearby tree, where he had spent the previous ten minutes protecting himself from the very real possibility of meltdown.

As Harry's eyes rolled slowly from bottom eyelid to top, his trance-like state was broken as a shout rang out from the direction of the dolmen.

'Inspector, over here.'

Gateaux looked across his shoulder to see Jeff beckoning him back to the capstone chamber.

Excusing himself, he spun around and headed for the epicentre of forensic activity, this time scissor jumping over the perimeter tape.

'What is it?' he asked, squatting down once again in the stone enclosure.

'I've just found this,' said Jeff, lifting the left hand of the body and carefully rolling back the unbuttoned sleeve of the man's shirt to reveal a black fabric watch strap with the partial remains of a broken timepiece attached.

'Unfortunately, no sign of the watch hands or cover though. With any luck we'll find the missing parts later when we get this place fully lit.'

Harry braced himself on the large stone roof slab and leaned across the body for a closer look before arching back and beginning another now rehearsed reversal from the chamber.

'Don't go yet, Harry.'

The Inspector halted his crab-like escape and pressed his arms to the ground to brace his body.

'So what else is it, Jeff?'

'Well, apart from the watch, we found this small diary in the top outer pocket of his jacket.'

'Yes, and ...?' enquired Harry, his response slightly pained by the inner screams from his knee joints that insisted on some instant relief from their compressed discomfort.

'It's not exactly the busiest diary I've ever read,' replied Jeff as he flicked quickly through the proliferation of blank pages. 'But interestingly, if you turn to today's date, it has an entry written in thick black pen. Do you see here?' he continued as he offered the small blue covered book across to the Inspector.

Harry turned slightly, to allow a small shaft of sunlight from outside to illuminate the page.

3456BC/8.00am/Coburg.

'And that's all?' asked Harry.

'Yes. That message, together with his arrival and departure times to and from Jersey are the only entries for this month.'

The two looked at each other in bewilderment, hoping the

other could offer a plausible explanation for both the message and the apparent disappearance of the watch components.

With no such explanation immediately forthcoming and the arrival of irreversible knee damage imminent, Gateaux handed back the book and then backed slowly out of the chamber.

'Once bitten, twice shy, eh, Gats?' called Jeff as he watched the Inspector's shrivelled departure.

Back in the welcome infinity of bright daylight, Harry stood and angled himself for a moment against the capstone before starting a series of squat repetitions to rejuvenate his semi-contorted joints.

'You need to get fit,' joked Jeff as he leaned his head out.

The Inspector laughed.

As the exercises and joviality continued, Mel shouted across. 'Gats, do you need us for the time being. I'm keen to get back to the others?'

Muscles and bones suitably realigned, Gateaux pushed himself to the vertical and jogged lightly back to where Mel and the others stood, flicking his legs high behind him as he did so.

'You okay?' enquired Mel concerningly.

'Yes, just a bit of cramp, I think. Can't swing a cat in that place, you know,' he replied. 'Anyway, sorry we've kept you for a little while. I'll arrange for someone to see you all back.'

The Inspector beckoned one of the police officers standing guard over the cordoned off perimeter to the back of the monument.

'Can you find a couple of your colleagues to see this young lady and the two gentlemen safely back to their bus and then accompany the group back to town?'

The officer nodded.

'Oh, and can you ask Sergeant Carak to follow you back to the hotel also. He's just over there,' added Gateaux, pointing to his left.

'Yes, no problem, sir,' replied the officer, nodding his head firmly.

Harry turned to face Mel.

'Before you go, do you think your guests would voice any objection if we asked them to stay together as a group in the hotel until I return? They might have some useful information, bearing in mind the victim was possibly staying at the Coburg. I really need to quiz them all before they get back into their holiday routines again.'

'Okay, I'll see what I can do but I can't make any promises. Many of them have only got a day or two left at most. Can't imagine they'd want to spend the last throws of their holiday cooped up in a hotel with your mob crawling all over them, particularly when it's sub-tropical out here just now.'

'Yes, guess you're right but see what you can do anyway, it would be a great help.'

'Well, I'll do my best, Gats.'

As Mel, Craig and Solly disappeared back down the lane with their police officer escort, Harry returned to the chamber to speak with Jeff once more.

Their discussion was suddenly interrupted by the distant sound of the bus firing up into action.

Immediately, activity on the site temporarily halted, as those remaining looked up and watched the bright red bus, flanked front and back by two police cars, move off lethargically on its way back to St Helier.

Their heads swivelled as one, tracking the vehicle's slow chugging departure from view until it was swallowed whole by the dense avenue of trees that fringed the end of the lane. That disappearance marked the cue for those on site to return to their duties.

Before Harry and Jeff could resume their conversation they were both called over by Nick, the second forensic scientist, who was busying himself with a tape measure at the inner edge of a low grass covered earth mound which surrounded the site, broken only by the stone lined passageway leading up to the chamber itself.

'Harry, this is Nick Warren, a new member of my team. He's

just joined us from the mainland,' said Jeff by way of introduction.

The two nodded to each other before Nick squatted down and rested his arm on the steep side of the low bank.

'See this here?'

Harry and Jeff's eyes followed Nicks arm as he pointed with his free hand across the rough and rambling grass cover to a strip which appeared flatter than the surrounding area.

In unison they then propped their bodies against the low bank to allow them to stoop over, press-up fashion, to its outer face. In position, they continued to watch as Nick slowly traced the outline of the flattened area with the edge of his hand, over the crest of the mound and down the outer slope to the edge of a privet hedge which formed part of the densely vegetated perimeter of the site.

Hand geometry complete, Nick looked across towards his two spectators.

'This grass has been flattened fairly recently by either a weight having been laid on it or dragged along its surface. Too early to say which at present.'

'Our victim perhaps?' quizzed Harry.

'Perhaps. I'll be processing some of the measurement data I've collected later. Should give us some idea of weight and size of the person or object placed here,' explained Nick.

'I've also got to look at that privet, just at the edge of the mound. It has some fresh damage to it which may be related.'

'Fine. Okay, Nick,' said Jeff. 'If you can concentrate on this area for a while, we'll compare notes later.'

As Jeff was speaking, Harry walked carefully around the flattened grass zone and in two strides stepped smartly onto the mound before jogging quickly the few steps down the outer edge, breaking his accelerating descent by reaching out to grab the lichen stained and roughened bark of a large tree trunk in front of him. He quickly rubbed his hands together to remove the chlorophyll-gloved veneer of nature's offerings.

'Just want a quick look at this damaged hedge,' he said, glancing back to Jeff and Nick.

Jeff joined him on the outer side of the bank. The two squatted down and looked closely at the base of the dishevelled bush.

'I reckon something's been dragged through here. There's very definitely a gap and the ground is full of freshly snapped twigs and leaves. What do you think?' enquired the Inspector.

'Yes, that's actually something we're looking in to,' replied Jeff. 'No pun intended of course.'

'So do you know what's on the other side of here?'

'Well, there's a wire tied timber stake fence and then open fields to a country lane and a few farm cottages beyond. I've already looked,' interrupted Nick.

As the Inspector began to stand, he noticed a flicker of red through the broken foliage.

'What's that Nick?' he enquired, pointing gingerly though the hedge so as not to spike his fragile cycle wear on the random minefield of occasional thistles.

'Oh, that's a marker flag, sir.'

'Marking what exactly?'

'It locates the position where we found what we believe to be the victim's small red and blue rucksack,' replied Nick. 'It has the initials "**AP**" marked in thick black marker pen on the inside and a pocket of it contained a Coburg room key. We've checked with the hotel. They did a bit of investigation of their own and confirm they did have a guest called Andrew Price,' he added.

'Well that would tally with the suspicions of the tour group as to the lad's identity,' replied Harry. 'Anything else?' he continued.

'Yes indeed. Strewn close by the rucksack we found two empty beer cans, a plastic lunch-box, some partially eaten chicken sandwiches and a partly eaten apple. Rather bizarrely, we also found a few traces of what would appear to be the same picnic food caught in the top of that sapling just there.'

Harry looked across to his left. 'Bit early for a spot of lunch, isn't it?' he enquired, lifting his arm to glance at his watch.

'We'll fathom that one out later I'm sure?' replied Nick.

'Come on Jeff, let's leave your man to it. He's obviously on top of things here,' continued Gateaux as he hopped back quickly across the mound and back into the inner sanctum of the dolmen site, followed closely by Jeff.

The two walked back towards the tented tree house.

'Um, this is beginning to get very interesting,' said Harry, a buzz of excitement electrifying his voice. As they entered the already exhausted looking wigwam, the Inspector turned to Jeff.

'Right, mate, I'm finished here for the moment unless you need me to stay, of course?'

'No, we're okay for now, thanks. Plenty to keep us occupied. Think we can excuse you for now.'

'Okay, I'll get back to the hotel to catch up with Mel and any guests that she might have press ganged into hanging around. Contact me there as soon as you have more news.'

Leaving the tent, Gateaux chatted briefly with a couple of the police officers before jumping on his bike, donning his crash hat and pedalling back down the dusty track to the junction with the lane.

Once there, he balanced motionless and checked each way was clear of moving traffic before bouncing the bike like a pogo stick down the few granite steps and then through ninety degrees to land on the tarmac lane. He had advanced a few metres, when he heard the faint cry of a female voice.

Gateaux stood acrobatically on his bike and looked up and across the narrow lane to his left. There, at the front white painted gate and entrance to an immaculately landscaped garden beyond stood a short middle-aged elegant looking lady, clad in gardening gloves and holding a couple of potted geraniums.

'Excuse me, young man. Can you tell me what all this frightful commotion is about?'

Harry slid from his saddle and with one leg each side of the cross bar, walked the bike over to where the woman stood, stopping with the front wheel resting on a narrow grass verge which trimmed the spotlessly white painted low panel fence.

He introduced himself before establishing that the retired woman, Eva Morlaix and her husband, Pierre, owned the bungalow which nestled cosily in the centre of the flower-blanketed garden.

Introductions complete, the Inspector relayed the grim discovery of the body on the site opposite.

'Oh my, how horrible,' said Eva, her face paling instantly. 'I heard all the noise but didn't want to interfere, you know how it is?'

With the plants still in her hand, she turned and walked briskly across the snooker table lawn to the open front window and looked through into the lounge to where her husband was sitting, listening to the radio and dabbling with his daily newspaper crossword.

'Pierre, Pierre, come quickly, something dreadful has happened.' The alarm in Eva's voice brought her husband running around to the front of the house, the paper still in his hand.

'What is it, dear?' he enquired, placing his arm warmly around her shoulder. 'And who's this gentleman?' continued Pierre, looking across to the tracksuited figure of Harry.

'Oh, this is a police Inspector. They've found a body at the dolmen.'

Soon Pierre found himself in conversation with Gateaux.

'We had no idea. We heard the coach party go by earlier and then your people showed up sometime shortly afterwards. Just assumed there had been some trouble within the tour group and to be quite honest we didn't want to get involved. We're too old for that sort of thing.'

'Yes, prefer to keep ourselves to ourselves, you know,' added Eva, in support of her husband's previous comment.

'So what exactly have you found?' continued Pierre.

'Well, as your wife has said, we've found the body of a young man in the dolmen.'

'What, actually in the chamber itself?' enquired Pierre further, his curiosity now intensified at the news that a major drama was unfolding under their very noses.

'Yes, but that's all I can tell you for sure right now. It's still very early stages in our investigations.'

'Yes of course, we understand,' said Eva, as she swayed her head to one side to see past Harry, allowing her to view a group of police officers who were beginning to load some white plastic bags into the back of a small van. She looked back at Gateaux as he began to speak.

'I'm just off back to town now, but perhaps if the two of you are available this afternoon I could pop back and ask you a few questions, if you don't mind?'

'As long as the questions are about gardening I should be all right,' said Eva.

'I don't think I'll catch you out on that subject.'

'I must say, this is one stunning garden,' he continued as his head made a wide sweep of the lush lawn and profusion of colour that flooded his view.

'Oh, you are so kind.'

'What time can we expect you later?' interrupted Pierre.

'Shall we say around three o'clock?' suggested Harry.

'Yes, I don't think we have anything on this afternoon,' confirmed Pierre, looking at his wife to seek her approval.

'That's okay with me, dear.'

Appointment confirmed, Gateaux jumped back into the saddle and lifted the bike wheelie fashion on its back tyre, ready to spin it from the narrow grass verge back onto the lane and in the direction of town.

'Fine, bye for now,' he said as he waved the couple goodbye and raced quickly off down the gradual decline of the lane. Ten minutes or so into his journey, his mobile phone suddenly sprang to life with a crudely digital rendition of Beethoven's Fifth. Immediately, he slammed on his brakes and slid the bike to a halt at the side of the road before hopping off, lifting the cycle onto the pavement and laying it against a stubby granite garden wall.

Un-zipping his jacket halfway, he reached inside to retrieve his phone from the inner pocket.

'Hello, Gateaux speaking.'

'Hi Harry, it's Jeff again. We've been scratching our heads here over part of that mysterious entry in the diary. I was chatting with one of the officers here who claims that he's a bit of an archaeology buff. He just wonders if that apparently cryptic message '3456BC' may in some way simply relate to the age of the dolmen?'

There was a brief pause.

'We've checked the date on the information board at the entrance to the site and it does suggest that the dolmen dates from around three thousand BC, so 3456BC might be plausible. What do you think?' he continued, the words of his message occasionally indecipherable, courtesy of an ill-disciplined phone signal.

'Think I understood most of that,' replied the Inspector.

'And there's another thing ... ' added Jeff before another weak signal suddenly curtailed the message.

'Jeff, Jeff, you still there mate?'

'Hi, Harry, yep still here. Think we nearly got cut off for a moment.'

'Right, so what was the other thing you were about to tell me?'

'Well, you'll remember how the body lay when you saw it a little while ago. I think you described it as crunched.'

'Yes, and?' said Gateaux demandingly as a sense of urgency crept into his response.

'Well, my same amateur archaeologist friend here thinks it could be significant. I don't know much about ancient history but it seems that these dolmens may have been burial sites in their time. Apparently the classical burial position, if you can call it a burial, was for the dead body to be placed simply on the ground of the covered chamber in a quasi-foetal position like the one we have here?'

'Very interesting. You might have something?' said Gateaux.

'With every respect to your man on site though, I think we might need some professional help on this one,' he added.

'Anyone in mind?'

'Yes. I'll phone Janette Mariner. She's the head archaeologist at the museum. What she doesn't know about this site and its past is probably not worth knowing. I'll see if she can make a visit straight away, while the body's still in situ. Jan should be able to tell us if there's any substance to your hypothesis. Might be useful to expand our fragile knowledge of these ancient structures at the same time. It could be relevant later. Anyway thanks again, Jeff. I'll be in touch.'

Before there was any chance for a reply, Harry had cut the line and was already dialling the museum.

'Good morning, Jersey Museum. Can I help you?'

Within seconds the Inspector was through to the Archaeology Department.

'Hi, Janette, it's Harry. Listen, I need a big favour from you,' he said before expanding on the morning's events and the mysterious entry in the victim's diary.

'Any possibility of meeting me at the dolmen de Santille in say fifteen minutes ... PLEASE. I'll buy you a huge drink sometime as a reward?' he said, an element of grovelling edging his request.

'Okay, smoothy, as long as that huge drink is a bit stronger than a mug of tea. I'll just clean up here and I'll be straight over but I can't spare you too long. I've an important meeting here in town soon.'

'Any time will be appreciated, shouldn't keep you too long.'

'Right, I'm on my way.'

Harry signed off and, with lightning fingers, dialled the site.

'Jeff, it's Harry again. I've phoned Janette at the museum and she's coming over now, so I'm heading back.'

'Okay, see you soon, and don't overtake too many cars on your bike.'

Gateaux laughed before placing the phone back in his pocket, zipping up his tracksuit and jumping back on the cycle.

Approaching the track leading to the dolmen, he pulled up sharply outside the cottage bungalow opposite. Eva, who was still gardening looked across. 'Is it three o'clock already, Inspector?'

'Huh, certainly seems like it,' said Harry, smiling before pressing on the pedals again and powering himself up the granite steps and back onto the track. He parked his bike as before and walked over for another discussion with Jeff.

Several minutes later, there was a shout from the perimeter cordon at the front of the site.

'Excuse me, sir. There's a Miss Mariner to see you.'

'Excellent, can you send her over, please?'

Harry refocused on the tent through which emerged the young archaeologist, wearing a fluorescent yellow safety jacket, black jeans and light brown suede boots.

'Hi, Jan, you are an absolute star,' he said in praise of her prompt arrival.

'Couldn't refuse a huge drink, could I,' she replied with a warm grin before lifting her hand and brushing a wisp of blonde hair away from her eyes.

'Jeff, have you got a moment?' shouted Gateaux as he beckoned his colleague across to where Janette and he stood.

Introductions over, the two men's quest for some cultural enrichment and the search for information to advance their enquiries began.

'We've had a suggestion, Janette, that the "3456BC" entry in the victim's diary, which I mentioned to you on the phone earlier, might be related in some way to the age of the dolmen,' said Gateaux. 'Could that be possible?' he continued, looking up enquiringly at his learned adviser for an answer.

Janette's response was instant. 'Well, the structure is certainly old. I've done a fair bit of study on it over the past couple of years and what I can tell you, is that it's definitely more recent than 3456BC. Probably nearer 3000BC as the sign suggests.'

The two men listened intently.

'And even if it was close to this 3456 figure that you're suggesting, there's simply no technique available at present that would allow even the most informed archaeologist to age a structure such as this that accurately, certainly not to within a particular year. I just wish there was.'

'Oh well, looks like that theory's heading for a crash and burn,' said Harry as he looked across towards Jeff.

'Fair enough. It was worth a punt,' replied Jeff.

'Have you talked about the victim's position yet,' he continued, this time returning the enquiring glance back towards Gateaux.

Harry shook his head firmly and then turned through one angle of the discussion triangle to look at Janette.

'Would you have any problem in having a quick look at the body in the chamber?'

'Is it important that I do?' she enquired, a nervous anxiety clouding her reply.

'Well, it could be. It's only that the body appears to be tightly crunched up in what resembles a foetal shape. It might be nothing, just coincidence perhaps, but was this not a method by which bodies were frequently placed in these stone tombs in more ancient times?'

'Oh, we have been doing our homework, haven't we?' she replied, her expression still riddled with nervous energy.

'So, can you look in the chamber with us?' enquired the Inspector as he repeated his earlier invitation.

'Well, I suppose so … If it's going to help you out …'

'Great, thanks, it's much appreciated,' replied Gateaux

immediately, before escorting the young archaeologist forward and into the semi-darkened gloom of the chambered monolith.

Their studies complete they returned to the refreshing taste of open space. Janette, her face wan, paused for a moment and drew a deep breath.

'You okay?' enquired Jeff.

'Yes, fine now, thank you. Just a bit of a shock, that's all.'

'Yes, sorry we had to put you through that little ordeal. So what did you make of the victim's position?'

'Well, you were right earlier when you said these chambers were most probably ancient burial sites and that the foetal orientation for the rested body was characteristic. But it's a little bizarre to think that this particular situation five thousand years on is in some way related, isn't it?'

'And we still haven't firmly concluded yet whether our victim was alive or dead when he arrived here, don't forget,' interrupted Jeff.

'We do know though that he was well acquainted with the historical background to these particular monuments and their customs. If he did die at this site alone, perhaps he felt the adoption of such a position to die to be symbolic,' added Harry.

'And what if he was dead when he arrived?' enquired Jeff.

'Well, that's a bit more worrying. Might suggest some sort of ritual burial perhaps,' replied Gateaux.

'Oh, how ghastly,' said Janette as the temporary restoration of colour to her cheeks evaporated once again.

'Of course, the resting position of the body may be purely and simply a historical coincidence,' said Harry as he sought to dilute the hypothesis of horror under discussion.

'Well, I hope that is the case, for the poor chap's sake,' added Janette, as she began to take a few small steps backwards.

'Time to go?' enquired Jeff.

'Yes, sorry gents but I need to make a bit of a dash. I've a meeting back in town in ten minutes and I did say that I couldn't be too long,' she replied.

Harry nodded.

'Our apologies for keeping you, Jan. Appreciate your time and input. Will you be around in the next few days if we need to pick your brains again? I'd like to quiz you a little more on these dolmens, for starters?'

'Might be, if it means a huge meal to go with that huge drink you promised me for coming here this morning?'

'Education comes at a high price, doesn't it?'

'In your case, yes. Seriously though, I'm out and about this week, supervising some restoration work over at Gorey but the museum should be able to track me down if you need me.'

'Excellent,' said Harry.

He turned to speak to Jeff.

'Okay, I'm off to the hotel. Try not to phone me again 'til I'm back this time. My pedals are beginning to wear out,' he said, laughing.

'I'll do my best, mate.'

Janette and Harry paced slowly across the site, leaving Jeff to return to the chamber.

'You're not still on that thing are you, Gats. Doesn't your salary extend to something with four wheels?' said Janette as the Inspector grabbed his bike and placed his red crash hat back on his head.

'Better than a car any day, girl. You'll have to try it sometime.'

'Well, actually, as it happens, I've just bought a bike, a lovely marine blue colour with yellow flashes. But you did say you wanted me here early so it had to be the car. I'm not as quick a cyclist as you yet.'

The jovial exchange of banter continued as Gateaux, complete with bike, led Janette back down the track to the lane.

As the Inspector set off en route for St Helier, Jan lifted the rear hatch of her small burgundy coloured car and having placed her fluorescent jacket neatly in the corner, slammed the boot lid tightly shut before walking around and jumping into the driving seat. Completing a tricky three-point turn in the lane, she looked up to see the red-capped head of Harry disappearing into the distance.

Within minutes of her journey back to town beginning, she soon found herself in the wake of the pedal-mad Inspector. She slowed momentarily in the two-wheeled slipstream as both bike and car negotiated a shallow, though blind, bend in the road.

As the road opened up she moved out and accelerated away smoothly. Running parallel, Janette shouted loudly through the open passenger side window.

'Pedal faster, Gats, you're slacking,' she shrieked, offering a farewell wave from the car as it filled to her laughter. The smiling and giggles intensified as she looked in her rear view mirror to see Harry's reciprocated gesture, his two hands raised high off the handlebars.

Ten or so minutes later, Gateaux entered the outskirts of St. Helier. Stopping for a short break, he dragged the bike on to the pavement and stood to take in the panoramic view of the sea wrapped town ahead, before taking two large gulps from his bike-mounted water bottle.

Suitably refreshed, he jumped back on the bike and began his accelerating advance down the hill towards the sun-drenched metropolis below, his head and body tucked in as tight as he dare in an effort to optimise his aerodynamic shape.

The land speed record having just eluded him, the Inspector slowed as he completed the rapid navigation of the hill and soon found himself on the crimson paved boulevard which ran alongside the marina. In the distance, the grand façade of the Coburg was now in his sights.

CHAPTER FOUR

Removed from the hazards of road traffic that had taunted the latter part of the Inspector's journey from Santille, the course ahead along the marina-fringed boulevard now demanded an immediate transition in concentration.

In contrast to the avoidance of painful liaisons with town bound traffic successfully performed moments earlier, the new challenge became one of avoiding similarly painful liaisons, though of a less metallic kind, between cycle and ice-cream licking, randomly directional, pedestrians who shared the same path.

Harry's pace slackened off as a pushchair-laden armada closed in. Safely through the sea of bodies and machinery, he stepped upon his pedals and began accelerating away, his view impaired occasionally from the reflective glare of glistening waters that now tracked his progress.

Suddenly his attention was drawn towards a green and white liveried racing yacht, steering delicately towards a berth adjacent to the chain-fringed pavement just ahead of him.

Instantly, he recognised the craft to be the *Silly Billy,* a yacht upon which he had helped crew some years previously, a pastime that he now, albeit with some regret, had sacrificed to the past in pursuit of his numerous other interests.

As he passed, he slowed momentarily and glanced down towards the stern where a group of wine drowning thirty-somethings were amassed.

Just as his head began to arc slowly back to the route beyond, a hand suddenly shot up from the party gaggle and waved frantically in the Inspector's direction.

'Harry, old boy, how the devil are you?' shouted a lone male voice from the craft, the greeting just audible above the crescendo of jocular banter that filled the back of the boat and echoed around the granite stoned walls of the marina basin. The vocal chords belonged to Phil Thomas, a wealthy local property developer and owner of the floating wine bar.

Phil's head swivelled as he watched Harry fly past, the Inspector raising a hand from one handlebar to acknowledge his good friend's greeting with a single wave.

'Sorry, can't stop Phil. Man on a mission and all that. Catch you later for a pint maybe,' he shouted, the last words of his sentence lost in the salt-water air as he disappeared rapidly out of earshot.

Within minutes of leaving the confines of the marina complex, Gateaux found himself back on the Esplanade roadway and closing rapidly on the two towering granite pillars that graced the entrance to the Coburg.

Several metres short of the entrance he snatched heavily on both brakes. The bike twitched momentarily with the sudden deceleration, allowing the semi-blurred view from his speedy approach to return into focus.

At that same moment the Inspector slipped into auto-pilot, twisting his body slightly to correct the bike's split second instability which for many a less experienced and agile rider would surely have ended in tears for both machine and operative.

With the control restored, he continued his advance, this time at a more conciliatory pace and without pedal power, as the momentum of his arrival continued to act in his favour. As the frictional forces of nature began to erode away at his progress, so he picked up the pedalling once again, though this time less aggressively, dropping down through the gears as he did so to allow a more cautious navigation between the twin pillars.

His life-sized game of croquet successfully completed, he immediately adopted a semi-standing position in an effort to suppress the impending discomfort as he began to negotiate first a pink granite-set speed hump and then the irregular cobbled surface of the crescent driveway that would lead up to the curved expanse of the hotel's entrance steps.

At the base of the steps, Harry stopped and with both feet still on the pedals, performed his party piece bike-balancing act as he looked around to search out a suitable resting place for his machine.

'Just leave it propped against that wall, Inspector,' shouted an imposing male voice from the top of the steps.

Gateaux, his balance momentarily broken by the surprise call, dropped both feet from the cycle onto the granite-cobbled roadway.

Stability of man and machine fully restored and the risk of both toppling as one like a felled tree now being of no further concern, Harry rocked his head back as he scanned the airwaves to the top of the steps from where the cry had originated.

Vision elevated, he found himself squinting heavily in an effort to seek out some clarity of image through the laser-like reflection of sunlight that bounced from the glazed entrance porch.

There, positioned just to one side of the main revolving entrance door, his scorched sight began to focus slowly upon the immaculately costumed figure of a doorman.

A solidly built looking gentleman, his face heavily tanned, the figure stood with hands clasped tightly behind his back exaggerating his upright, almost sergeant major stature. Perhaps in his early fifties, he wore an eye-catching bright red and gold braided tunic, so bright in fact that the Inspector found himself squinting his squint to control the compounding of pain from both sun and the seemingly equal radiance of the man's uniform.

As the scrutiny continued he saw the tunic to be complimented with equally bold matching trousers, both items of which were sandwiched between a wide brimmed matt black top hat and a pair of mirror-polished black shoes.

'I presume you are the Inspector?' enquired the man in a very precise manner, a suggestion of Scottish ancestry in his accent.

'Yes, indeed I am. How incredibly perceptive of you,' replied

Harry, his voice raised slightly to project it adequately to the topmost step.

Before inquiring further as to the man's apparently clairvoyant talent, Gateaux sought first to find safe refuge for his two-wheeled transport, upon which he was still propped.

'Any chance of leaving my bike around here somewhere?' he asked, raising his voice for a second time to allow it to reach the elevated heights of the main entrance.

'Just tuck it around the side there, sir,' replied the doorman, extending out his red and gold clad arm to point to the start of a low granite wall that bounded the steps to one side.

'I'll keep a safe eye on it for you. I'm never too far away from here.'

With that, the Inspector stood tall on his toes and pulled the bike smartly forwards from under him before lifting the frame with one hand and walking it to its temporary resting place as directed.

The doorman who by now had made his way down the few steps to pavement level watched in silence as Harry parked his treasured machine, exercising great care as he did so to use the saddle and handle-bars as cushioning props to protect the custom painted metallic frame from the merciless perils of the sandpaper-rough stonework.

With the bike safely located, Gateaux turned and walked around to the base of the stair where the doorman was now standing.

'Wouldn't have been able to lift it like that in my day, sir. Needed three strong men to lift a bicycle when I was a lad.'

Though rarely short of some whimsical repartee, Harry resisted the temptation on this occasion of suggesting to the man that he was already aware from his school history lessons that penny farthings had been particularly cumbersome creations.

'Yeah, wonders of modern science, eh?' he replied, choosing to adopt the more diplomatic route.

Pleasantries seemingly complete, the doorman returned to his more formal ushering mode. 'If you would like to follow me, sir, we have been awaiting your arrival,' he continued as he began making his way back up the steps.

Harry followed closely behind. 'Tell me, do I look so obviously like an Inspector?' enquired Gateaux as he reached the uppermost step, his curiosity still aroused by the man's apparent talent for sleuth-like deduction.

The doorman laughed. 'Suppose if I said yes, you'd offer me a job in the CID, wouldn't you? If you want the truth, the whole truth and nothing but the truth, then the answer is that one of your colleagues phoned ahead to inform us that you were on your way. I have to say their description was pinpoint accurate.'

'Obviously ... So who was this smart Alec then?'

'Ah, now that would be telling, wouldn't it,' replied the doorman, lightly tapping his nose twice as he spoke to indicate that that particular person's identity was remaining firmly under his top hat.

Before Gateaux had a further opportunity to interrogate his pillar box coloured usher, that same person had extended out one arm, this time to push open the ornately etched glazed door located immediately adjacent to the revolving entranceway while the other arm motioned Harry into the building.

'If you'd care to walk just over to the main reception, Inspector, and ask for Lucy, our manageress,' he said, his arm still extended to point across to the desk just beyond.

Having thanked the man for his assistance, Gateaux entered the resplendent opulence of the foyer area, the centre piece of which was a large spotlessly clean and shimmering crystal chandelier suspended from an equally spotless and glistening gold chain that extended high into the intricately vaulted ceiling above.

Lucy, right on cue, appeared from her small office adjoining the reception zone.

'Can I help you, sir?' she asked in a quietly calming southern Ireland accent.

'Yes, I'm Inspector Gateaux from St. Helier police. I believe you are expecting me?'

'Yes, of course, the famous cycling detective. Pleased to meet you, sir.'

Harry smiled uneasily at his apparent and perhaps dubious notoriety as some kind of circus act. 'Please, just plain Harry will do. I'm not that keen on all that sir stuff.'

'No problem. That's fine by me ... Harry,' replied Lucy, with a warm smile.

A momentary hiatus in conversation then followed as the two looked impassively at each other and waited for the other to utter the next line. The minor interlude was suddenly broken as almost inevitably the two began their next lines simultaneously, filling the air around the desk with a garbled spaghetti of words that would have sounded alien to an alien and had any self-respecting de-cipher machine running for the main door.

That cryptic garble ceased as the two stopped speaking, stared at each other for a second and then laughed in a sharing of mild and mutual embarrassment.

'Sorry Lucy, after you please.'

'Thank you. Bit of a shock to us all, this morning's events,' she said.

'Yes, I'm sure. I presume the group returned safely enough in the coach?'

'Yes, no hiccup's there. Everyone arrived about an hour and a half or so ago accompanied by two police officers. Oh, and one of your detective colleagues arrived just a few moments before you also. Think his name was Shaun. Would that be right?'

'Yes, that will be my sergeant, Shaun Carak.'

Harry leaned against the desk and propped his chin on his forked hand. As he did, a large ball of sweat rolled from his forehead and splashed across one corner of the visitor's book over which he was resting.

Lucy spun around quickly and snatched a tissue from a box perched on the table behind her.

'Oh, I do apologise,' said Gateaux as Lucy swivelled back to the main desk and began dabbing delicately the offending moisture from the treasured document before the ink from any of the literary contributions had a chance to smudge.

'Most inconsiderate of me.'

'No harm done. Perhaps you'd like to quickly freshen up in the cloakroom over there?' she suggested hurriedly as another bead of sweat begin its journey ominously across the Inspector's brow.

'Yes, probably not a bad idea,' replied Gateaux as he turned and made his way to the cloakroom located just to the side of the main entrance doors.

With the Inspector having disappeared in search of blotting paper, Lucy reached down below the counter, to emerge seconds later, with a small box of cleaning miscellany. Lifting the visitor book, she treated a new white coloured cloth to a quick inaugural waltz across the mahogany desk-top to rid it of any residual constabulary moisture before bringing the dance to a conclusion with a rejuvenating glide from polish and duster. As she replaced the book and returned the cleaning items below decks the Inspector re-emerged from the cloakroom.

'Now that's a lot better. Perhaps I should have done that as soon as I arrived. I do apologise again.'

Lucy resisted the temptation to offer any word of hygienic agreement.

'Now, where were we?' enquired Harry, this time adopting a bolt upright standing position a few steps back from the desk-top which now reflected the sparkle of the chandelier above in celebration of its recent waxing.

'I was just saying, Inspector, that the tour group had returned to the hotel safely.'

'Yes of course.'

'Fortunately, Mel who is our tour guide …'

'Yes, I know Mel,' interrupted Gateaux.

'Right, well she thankfully had the presence of mind to ring us from the Santille site as soon as the tragic event began to unfold, so we had a chance to get ready for their return. She subsequently passed on your request for us to keep as many of them as were willing together here to await your arrival.'

'And exactly how many were willing?'

'Well, believe it or not, we seem to have the full compliment.'

'Fantastic.'

'But they seem keen not to be kept too long, particularly with the weather as it is outside just now.'

'Yes of course, Lucy, that's understandable.'

'We've set up the "Beauport Room" as a makeshift holding area. Everyone should find it comfortable enough. It has all the necessary facilities and we're about to lay on plenty of food and refreshment, so fingers crossed, everyone should be happy for a while ... Well, as happy as you can be, given the circumstances.'

'Yes, quite,' replied Harry, nodding.

As he finished speaking, the automatic door to the long ground floor corridor beyond rolled open and a dapper dressed gentleman in his early thirties appeared, his swept back dark hair and pin stripe suit suggesting the attire of a whiz-kid financier.

Harry, his arms still folded, swivelled about his waist and watched as the man approached.

'Hi there, Shaun.'

'Morning, sir.'

Harry spun back to face Lucy.

'I think you said you had been introduced to my sergeant?'

'Yes ... Yes, we met earlier.'

The two exchanged a synchronized nod of silent acknowledgement.

'Don't call him the city slicker for nothing do they?' laughed Harry, glancing as he spoke towards Lucy. 'You wouldn't believe he's spent much of the morning over at Santille would you. He's not got a speck of dust on him.'

Gateaux turned to Shaun whose expressionless posture suggested that he had been un-phased by the Inspector's cheap jibes.

'So have you had a chance to assess the situation here at the moment, sergeant? Lucy tells me that everybody is in the Beauport Room.'

'Yes, that's correct, guv. There've been a few restless moans and groans as you might expect. I think everyone would rather be outside enjoying the warm sunshine but generally they seem to be okay. All understand the delicacy of the situation and seem keen to assist where they can, so long as their inconvenience is short-lived. I've left PC's Simon le Pain and Gavin Daniels down there with them at present.'

'Good, okay. I think it's probably time I went and joined them.'

'Of course, sir.'

Harry turned again to face the desk.

'Thanks for everything, Lucy. I'll catch up with you again later maybe.'

With that he stepped back and then followed Shaun through the sliding doors and along the burgundy and blue patterned thick pile carpet that lined the corridor beyond.

The two men soon found themselves at the entrance to the *Beauport Room,* its name grandly etched in a polished mahogany panel over the door.

They nodded in acknowledgement to the two police officers flanking each side before entering.

Passing through into the cavernous grandeur of the room, the echoed din of conversation slowly damped down, as those present turned their curiosity towards the sergeant and the new face of the Inspector, casually dressed in black tracksuit and dust covered training shoes.

Mel who was sitting closest to the door talking with Rachel

immediately excused herself and walked over to welcome the two new arrivals.

'Hi, Gats.'

'Hi, Mel. How are we all doing?'

'Not too bad. I took a quick register as soon as we got here. Everyone was present and correct then and we've had no one leave the room since our arrival.'

Harry, Mel and Shaun gathered tightly around in whispered discussion.

Suddenly the concentration of that conversation was broken as a large paper dart plane whizzed between the three, its wing brushing against Harry's nose as it did so before hitting the oak panelled wall close behind and falling to the floor. Almost before the origami glider had come to rest, young Andrew and Munro appeared at speed and, diving one each side of the triangular discussion group, slapped one hand each simultaneously on the homemade toy.

'It's my turn to fly it,' shouted Andrew.

'No it's not. It's mine. Let it go,' insisted his brother with an equally childish aggression in his voice.

As the lads tugged and twisted at the fragile craft, its form changed without the slightest resistance from the sleek aerodynamic speed machine of moments earlier to a crumpled mass with the aerodynamic efficiency of an avocado.

With both youngsters' concentration focused intensely upon wrestling the last sinew of rigidity from their paper creation, their mother appeared.

While Harry busily stroked his nose to determine if the mid-air collision between aircraft and proboscis had drawn blood, Mel and Shaun looked across at Alison.

'I do apologise,' said Alison as she brushed delicately behind the three and then stepped over the two young arms that were still snaking wildly across the floor below her.

Her sons, each holding one end of the now ragged paper dart, raised their heads, the remainder of their bodies still prostrate upon the floor.

'Right, you two. Up now, this minute,' she demanded in what had become on this day a well-rehearsed instruction of discipline.

The two lads stood at once and looked on in silence along with the gathered masses as their mother, for the moment, became the focus of attention herself. 'Over there to your seats right now and no more planes. If you misbehave again there will be no ice-creams later,' she said, her facial expression close to an explosive state.

'But dad made the plane for us,' replied Andrew.

'Well, your silly dad should know better, shouldn't he? I'll stop his ice-cream as well.'

Mel sniggered in unison with more general laughter around the room before forcing her clenched hand to her mouth in an effort to prevent the development one stage further to all-out hysterics.

With the boys now standing, Alison grabbed both lad's arms and marched her captives speedily back to their seats, this time adjusting her still eye-bulging stare in the direction of her husband who by now had rushed for cover and buried his head deep into the table-cloth sized newspaper in a desperate search for safe refuge.

'Don't think you can hide behind that,' she said, slapping her hand against the top of the newsprint with sufficient force to cause the top to fall flat, exposing the full expression of Craig's guilt-ridden face.

Craig raised his eyes momentarily and glanced at his wife as those around looked on keenly for the next development in the family conflict.

'You're as bad as your sons, you know.'

Craig huffed and snapped the paper taut in a further attempt to hide behind the printed screen from the continuing taunts. A muffled sound of laughter echoed a second time around the room. As the jollity began to subside, the Inspector broke ranks from Mel and Shaun and advanced towards the centre of the room.

'If I can have your attention just for a short while please.'

A pin drop silence descended.

Craig, sensing that the ordeal of his public humiliation was now past, lowered the paper slowly on to his lap. The hushed atmosphere was broken almost instantly as the door to the men's cloakroom at the end of the hall opened with the eerie creak of a haunted house movie. A few seconds passed by before through it appeared the tired looking figure of Bob.

Slowly he walked across towards his seat beside Doris while the Inspector and his audience watched patiently.

'Take your time, sir, there's no rush,' reassured Harry as he sought to calm the old man's anxious though failed attempts to accelerate his breathless body across the room.

'Yes there is. I want out of here,' whispered Jamie as he scanned sideways along the seated crescent of bodies in search of some group consensus to his plea.

'Sorry about that, folks,' mumbled Bob as he finally flopped unceremoniously into his seat.

'It's that coffee you know. It goes straight through me, I'm afraid,' he continued, referring to the drink that had been provided for him some ten or so minutes earlier.

Doris nudged her elbow into her husband's side. 'You silly old fool. They don't want to hear about the problems in your basement.' Laughter bounced around the room before being replaced by a vacuous quiet as attention gradually turned towards the tracksuit clad figure standing in its centre.

'Thank you. My name is Inspector Harry Gateaux.'

'Did someone mention cake?' interrupted Bob. 'I'm famished.'

'Shush,' whispered Doris as she leaned to one side and gave him another light nudge on the arm.

'You will all, I'm sure, be aware by now of the tragic incident earlier this morning at the Dolmen de Santille during the tour,' continued Harry. 'I hope you can understand our request that you remained as a group here at the hotel and I'm very grateful

94

to you all for giving up your valuable time. To assist us with our initial enquiries, we will be looking to take a statement from each of you. That done, we can then leave you to continue with your holiday break without any further distraction from us.'

Muffled words of conversation relayed along the seated group of detainees. Suddenly a pause in the fog of indiscernible dialogue allowed the soft voice of Doris to be heard.

'Is there any chance of a window or two being opened. It's getting rather warm in here, don't you think?'

Immediately Tony, Luke and Solly who, like many around them, were desperate for air but had been too embarrassed to cause a break in proceedings, jumped to their feet simultaneously and reached for the window catches nearest to them. Within seconds, a refreshingly light sea breeze began to be drawn into the room.

As the audience began gulping like goldfish to take deep breaths from the injection of new salt rich air, so Gateaux continued his introductory statement. Before he could utter his first word, there was a shout from the back of the room.

'Who are you, Mister?'

It was Andrew.

'Shush,' said his mother, jabbing him with her elbow.

'Ouch, that hurt,' squealed the young lad.

'I'm sure you'll survive. Now behave,' said Alison, her patience now worn micrometer thin.

The Inspector smiled at the innocence of the young man's question.

Craig leaned out and turned his body to talk across his wife to his son Andrew who was sitting on the other side.

'The man is a police inspector and he locks young people up if they keep on talking.' Andrew's face paled.

'Don't scare the poor kid,' said Alison, turning to her husband and giving him one of her infamous laser stares.

'Thought you wanted them to shut up, luv?'

Alison said nothing.

'If he's a policeman, dad, why's he wearing those silly clothes?' enquired Munro, pointing. 'I thought policemen wore those pointy hat things and had whistles.'

'Not these days they don't, son,' replied Craig quietly as a further carnival of laughter lit up the room.

'Look, quiet you lot, NOW,' said Alison firmly as she leaned forward in her chair and fired another jab-like stare at Munro, Andrew and then her husband. The three sat upright and looked forward as the Inspector coughed lightly and prepared to continue with his instruction.

'Thank you,' said Gateaux. 'The statement process I've just mentioned should not, I hope, take too long, and is just a simple matter of routine so I would ask you not to get unduly concerned. Your tour guide, Mel, will, in the next few moments, compile an order list from the tour register. We will then circulate it amongst you, so that you are all aware in which order these interviews will be taken. Sergeant Carac and I will be conducting them in there,' he continued, pointing at the far corner to a door marked *Games Room*. As if tied together by a common chord of string, the seated ring of faces turned in unison and glanced at the door.

'Perhaps I should add that during the interview we will be asking you for a contact telephone number and address, just in case there should be a need to speak with you again at a later date. Right, that's all I have to say for the moment, so I'll hand you back to Mel,' he concluded.

The Inspector retreated several steps and leant against the oak panelled wall close to Shaun who was propped up in a similar manner.

'Thank you, Inspector,' said Mel as she replaced Gateaux in the centre of the room. 'Can I firstly thank each and every one of you for your continued co-operation in this difficult matter. I know the Inspector has extended his gratitude already, but I just wanted to reinforce that appreciation on behalf of the Coburg Hotel. Now I'm very aware that you're all bursting to get back outside and brush up on those tans,' she added.

'Yeah, you don't have to remind us,' whispered a voice.

Mel paused. 'Yes, well anyway, we will be doing our very best not to keep you for a moment longer than we have to. To make your wait a little more comfortable you will I'm sure be relieved to hear that complimentary food and refreshments will be arriving very soon to keep you going.'

'Now you're talking,' whispered the same anonymous voice.

'If you have any special dietary requests or need any other assistance then please do come and find me and let me know.'

'What about those of us who have picnic meals with us?' enquired Kathy.

'I've eaten mine already,' interrupted Solly.

'Yes, for those of you who do have picnic meals and haven't eaten them yet, you can either have them now of course or keep them for a snack later. If you wish to leave them in the hotel's fridge for later, please pass them on to one of our kitchen staff when they arrive shortly.'

Her few words of thanks and domestic instruction completed, she spun on her heel through a semi-circle and looked back towards Gateaux who was still propped up against the wall.

'Is that okay for now, Inspector?' she enquired.

'Yes ... Yes, fine, thanks very much, Mel.'

Gateaux looked across to his sergeant. 'Can you, Simon and Gavin, keep an eye on this lot for us while Mel and myself quickly disappear back to reception and sort out this interview list?' he said, nodding across to Mel who was now standing a few metres in front of him.

'Yes of course, no problem, sir.'

Mel and the Inspector turned and together walked back to the main function room door. A few strides from the exit, Gateaux suddenly stopped, jumped around and looked back in the direction of his sergeant.

'Yes, sir?' enquired Shaun who had been following the couple's departure.

'Just one other thing. Can you buzz the station and see if they can lend us, say, three more guys to help us here for a few hours?'

'Not a problem, guv. I'll do it straight away.'

Harry nodded and then rotated as he completed his walk towards the doorway where Mel now waited. No sooner had he reached it than he found himself in retreat, standing aside to allow a six trolley convoy of food and drink to pass through. As the train-like procession, it's cargo still covered from view, made its way across the floor of the hall a waft of fresh pastries began to fill the air.

The six white and blue uniformed waiting staff, three male, three female, parked their respective trollies in an orderly line along the far side of the room adjacent to the line of windows opened minutes earlier.

As soon as they were in position, the sextet, with chorus line synchronicity, leaned forward and peeled back the blue and white chequered linen to reveal a Himalayan-high assortment of savouries, desserts and refreshment.

If the bakery-like aroma had not provided the catalyst for a mass movement of bodies towards the food, then the sight of it in the flesh certainly did. Within seconds the stampede had begun as Tony, then Rachel, followed by Luke and an all too eager Solly initiated the rush for the queue. Soon the chain reaction of movement involved all present like bees to the proverbial honey pot.

As the line of hotel guests waited in keen anticipation, their concentration was divided between muted group conversation and monitoring progress as the finishing touches were made to the presentation of refreshments before them.

'They better hurry up. I'm starving,' whispered Luke. 'And they better hurry up with all this detective stuff as well,' he continued, this time his voice raised just slightly in an effort to attract some mutinous support from his parading comrades.

One of the attendant officers, Gavin, looked across towards the dissenting voice and stared.

'It's all right for you mate,' said Luke. 'You're not on holiday are you?' he added as he returned the intimidating glance.

'Yeah, I don't really know why they feel the need to keep us all here,' interrupted Jamie.

'Well, I guess they're just looking for any pointers we may be able to offer them on the guy while we are all still on the Island. Perhaps they suspect some sort of foul play or something,' said Craig as he contributed to the growing debate from his position at the back of the queue.

'Is foul play what footballers do, dad?' enquired Munro.

The two lads looked up at their father inquisitively for an answer.

'Yeah, sometimes,' replied their father.

'Well, if they do think the guy was done in and it happened this morning, then they need to look elsewhere for the baddie, don't they?' said Jamie.

'I guess you're right. I remember seeing the lad at breakfast,' added Craig.

'Well, there you are then,' interrupted Luke as his eyes panned the tightly formed queue which by now was slowly developing a concave profile as the ensemble moved in closer to share their views.

'What do you mean?' enquired Lauren.

'Well, we were all on the bus straight after breakfast and we stayed as a group up until the moment the body was discovered. Am I right?'

Luke paused and scrutinized his attentive audience, to be rewarded by a spontaneous cocktail of agreeable nods and shouts of 'Yes'.

'Well, I may not be Inspector Clouseau but in my book that unanimous support equates to a fairly watertight alibi for us all.'

The chorus of agreement repeated.

Suddenly the air of huddled conversation was suffocated by the sound of jangling crockery racing towards the hall along the corridor close by.

The food line turned and observed a young lad arriving with a seventh trolley at the door. With the trolley equivalent of a handbrake turn, he then spun it through ninety degrees and continued its progress to a position just in front of the expectant guests.

'Won't get far without these,' announced the lad as he looked up and laughed.

Like a magician in trick mode he pulled back the linen cover cloth to reveal a confused array of plates, napkins, crockery and cutlery, its randomness an inevitable consequence of the stunt trolley arrival seconds earlier.

Everyone watched as the waiter hurriedly began to re-gather the items and arrange them in a more presentable manner. As he did so, the Milner youngsters broke away from their position towards the back of the enthusiastic procession of food magnets and moved in on the tabled feast for a closer inspection. Andrew pointed his finger across to a large plate on the end table.

'Wow! Look at that chocolate cake,' he said excitedly, the joy in his cry brought on by the lad's now close up and hypnotic appreciation of the cake and the myriad of assorted sticky goodies that surrounded it.

Before his brother could add his paralleled seal of approval their mother broke ranks and marched across. 'How many more times must I tell you? This is your very, very last warning,' she said, grabbing the two by the arm before dragging them hurriedly back towards the end of the queue. As the two scuffed their way across the room their heads remained turned towards the tables with eyes firmly transfixed upon the dark creamy cake.

'Now stay here and wait your turn like everybody else,' demanded Alison as they returned to take up position.

Doris and Bob suddenly appeared, having just completed their stroll from the end of the room. Rachel, who had watched the elderly couple's laboured last few strides stepped to one side.

'Doris,' she shouted.

Doris looked up.

'Would you like to return to your seats and I'll bring some food and drink over to you?'

'Oh, how very kind. Are you sure we can't adopt you, dear ... Er, could we have just a few sandwiches and two cups of tea. Oh, and perhaps a couple of pieces of that delicious looking fruit cake?'

Her instructions communicated, she tugged on Bob's arm through which she was linked.

'Come on. Let's get back to our seats.'

'But I've only just got here.'

'Yes, I know. But that nice young lady who helped us this morning is going to bring some food over to us.'

With that, the couple turned and shuffled slowly back to their chairs while Rachel set about collecting together their lunch request.

Food safely gathered and delivered, Rachel returned to her place next to Tony at the front of the queue.

The line began to advance steadily, watched keenly from long range by the deeply scrutinising eyes of the young Scots.

It was soon Solly's turn to find himself in front of the dessert trolley, his tray already well laden with, it seemed, a body-weight equivalent of savouries. The towering sight of the food consuming machine of Solly closing in on the chocolate cake now brought Andrew to a state of heightened anxiety, so much so that he felt the need to press the palms of his hands together in silent prayer.

It seemed all too obvious to the two lads that if the big man continued with the same passion for cake as he quite clearly had for sandwiches, then they were going to be lucky if they had the cherry on top to fight over.

As the American pondered his next move, the two youngsters ears locked in to the titan's vocal selection process.

'That chocolate cake looks mighty fine, sir,' said Solly pointing.

'Please no, no,' whispered Andrew as his muted pleas to the heavens continued, this time more intensely.

His brother, hearing Andrew's cries, joined in muttered discussion of events before them. 'I bet he scoffs it all and we end up with some yucky boring apple pie or something.'

Solly stood for a few seconds, his head moving almost robot fashion to view four quadrants of the trolley containing strawberry flan, apple pie, raspberry meringue and the much admired chocolate cake.

'Think it'll have to be the apple pie for now, sir.'

'Yes. Yes. Yes,' cried the young Milner duet from the back of the queue.

Cyril, who was standing just in front of the lads, turned and looked down at the two whose faces were now each decorated with grins of anticipation.

'Looks like your luck's in, boys.'

The two youngsters looked up gleefully and nodded.

With most guests seated, Andrew and Munro, flanked each side by their parents, approached the line of trollies.

Alison looked to her husband as he picked up a tray.

'What do you want, Andrew?' quizzed Craig as he placed four sandwiches, a handful of cherry tomatoes and a large scoop of coleslaw on his plate.

'Don't want none of that. That's just for rabbits and adults.'

'That may be the case,' interrupted Alison. 'But you're not getting any cake if you don't have some salad beforehand. It will make you fit and healthy.'

'So will chocolate cake,' protested Andrew quietly, his head drooped as he stared at the floor.

'Sorry, what was that?' enquired his mother who had missed the content of the garbled retort from her son.

'Oh nothing, mum.'

Munro, who had caught his brother's comments, began to giggle.

Craig and Alison said no more, filling the plates for their sons with a token supply of savouries and salad. Suddenly the hiatus in the conversation was broken as the family arrived in front of the colourful array of sweets.

'Would it be a silly question to ask you what you would like, Andrew?' enquired Craig, looking down as he spoke to his son whose body was now pressed tight against the trolley, his eyes fixated on the chocolate cake of which half now remained.

'I'll have some raspberry meringue and my son will have a slice of that cake, please.'

'Can I have a big bit, please, Mister?' interrupted Andrew.

'Yeah, and me, even bigger than my brother's bit,' said Munro as he added his vocal weight to the serving process.

'You will have what you're given,' insisted Alison.

The Milners, finally laden with food and drink, returned to their cluster of chairs.

Suddenly the unmistakable stars and stripes voice of Solly called out.

'Craig!'

The Scotsman looked up.

'My good friend here, Luke, was just asking if we had any idea how that lad had died, from what you saw at the site,' enquired the American.

'Well, I didn't get a good look, to be honest, but I did notice that he had what looked like a big bruise on his head.'

'Well it's simple, then,' interrupted Tony. 'The kid must have hit his head when he was sniffing around that stupid monument.'

'I believe his father is preparing to come over to identify the body,' added Jamie.

'Is that right?' enquired Lauren.

'Yes, I overheard Mel talking to that sergeant chappie earlier. I believe they're expecting him here sometime tomorrow?'

'Tomorrow? As in Thursday?' quizzed Luke.

'Yes. Thursday, if it's that important to you,' replied Jamie, his voice slightly raised to emphasise the reply to his questioner.

'Oh, poor man, flying over to this beautiful Island to identify his son's body,' said Doris.

'Yes, very tragic,' said Rachel.

'Wonder if they'll bother carrying out a post-mortem,' enquired Tony.

Alison leaned forward and looked across at the questioner.

'Do we really have to talk about this? I'm trying to eat my food here.'

The group session of small talk paused as each person searched for a new subject with which to divert the increasingly morbid topic of mealtime conversation.

'So, when you off back home then, Solly?' enquired Rachel.

'Oh, this Saturday, sadly. Think it's the one thirty afternoon flight to London and then an evening flight back to the States. And yourself?'

'Yes, Saturday as well. Same flight I believe.'

'But missing out the bit to the States, of course,' interrupted Craig.

Solly turned to Luke.

'I presume you're back on the ferry sometime, are you, buddy? Guess that MGA of yours is just a bit too big to squeeze in the overhead lockers?'

The others laughed.

'Yes, back on the ferry ...'

Before Luke could complete his sentence, Mel and the Inspector reappeared.

'Sorry to interrupt your lunch,' said Mel as she walked around in front of the crescent of chairs. 'But if we could just have your attention for a few moments more, please.'

A buzz of conversation from those seated extinguished itself.

'The Inspector and myself have now drawn up an order list for the taking of statements which we will circulate very soon. We have decided to see Bob and Doris first, followed by the Milner family and then the remainder of you will follow soon after. Please may I repeat the hotel's thanks for your continued patience and co-operation.'

Mel walked over to Doris and Bob. 'Have the two of you finished your snack?'

'Yes, thank you dear. Very nice indeed, though I do prefer brown bread for sandwiches actually.'

'I'll try and remember that for next time,' said Mel smiling. 'Well, if you're sure you are ready, perhaps you'd like to follow me?'

'Have we far to go?' asked Doris.

'Come on Bob,' she continued, linking with one of his arms and, with the added assistance of Mel, lifting his weary body to its feet.

'Where are we off to now?' he enquired.

'They want to ask us some questions.'

'What, about the sandwiches?'

'No, about this morning.'

'Why, what happened this morning?'

'Never mind,' said Doris as she led her husband off in the direction of the Games Room where the Inspector waited, his arm propping open the door until the two were safely inside.

'Shaun, are you ready?' called Gateaux, looking across the room towards his sergeant who was involved in quiet conversation with one of the waitresses.

'Yes, sorry, on my way guv,' replied "Romeo", turning smartly and walking briskly through into the makeshift interview room.

The door closed behind them.

CHAPTER FIVE

The antique train station clock, its imposing arctic white face staring proudly from high upon the oak panelled wall at the far end of the Beauport Room, chimed resoundingly to announce the arrival of a quarter past two,

A recovered relic of a bygone locomotive era on the Island, its clockwork monotone still crisp and seemingly devoid of any ageing weariness, was suddenly interrupted as the door to the Games Room, and improvised interview area, opened on to a now vacated Beauport suite, vacant that is except for the lone and imposing figure of Solly.

The big man, who had been pacing the length of the function area with the increasingly strained and lethargic mobility of an ocean going super tanker, turned in a wide arc to face the door and looked on in eager anticipation of the re-emergence of his wife, Lauren, who now possessed the dubious honour of being the final tour party interviewee.

'Thank you very much Miss Nielsen,' said the Inspector as he held the door wide open and offered his hand to usher the elegant American politely forward. Her cheeks popped into a rosy smile as she saw her waiting husband.

'Hi there, hun, all finished?' he enquired as he dropped the huge shadow of his left arm and wrapped it carefully around her slender shoulders.

'Yes, I think so, cherry pie,' she replied, glancing across at Harry in an appeal for confirmation of her freedom.

The Inspector gulped uncomfortably in an effort to swallow the embryonic development of a laugh, unavoidably triggered by his "funny" muscles as they tickled wildly with the obtuse notion that Solly, a megalithic being of the homosapien race, could in any way, shape or form, be likened to a fruit dessert.

From where Harry stood, the only possible justification for

107

the use of such a metaphor was in visualising the giant American as a wholesale consumer of such pastries.

As the fuse that he feared might lead to an explosion of laughter continued to fizz away at his vocal chords, Gateaux turned his head away from the couple and putting his clenched hand to his mouth, fired a single deep grunting cough into the tightly rolled fingers. Composure momentarily restored, he turned back to face the couple again.

'Do excuse me please,' he said, in apology for the cacophonous treat from his larynx seconds earlier.

'Sorry, Inspector, but are we free to go now?' enquired Lauren.

'Er, yes, yes, we're finished with you now, thank you,' replied Harry, a slight hesitancy apparent in his voice as the threat of spontaneous laughter continued to tease uncomfortably within him.

Unleashed from the shackles of the interview, Lauren smiled broadly.

Gateaux reciprocated, unsure as to whether the American's gesture was one of relief on account of her imminent exit or a reaction to her curiosity regarding the Inspector's facial contortions of the previous few seconds.

'Thanks very much to you both for your time. I hope you enjoy the last few days of your holiday. Let's trust they won't be as dramatic as the last few hours.'

'Well, thank you kindly for that, sir. Gee, we've a lot to tell the folks when we get back home, haven't we, hun?'

'Certainly have,' replied Lauren, her words slightly stifled from the effects of the restricting stranglehold that her husband affectionately held her in.

The big man took a step forward towards the Inspector, sliding as he did so his huge arm from Lauren's shoulders where it had perched since her return from the interview room.

With the anchor removed, Lauren let out a quiet sigh of relief as her weight halved in an instant and her fragile looking frame concertinered back into something resembling its natural form.

'Well, I guess we'll see you around,' said Solly as he shook Harry firmly by the hand.

'Yes, see you around,' replied the Inspector.

Farewell pleasantries complete the couple turned as one before walking the dozen or so steps across the room to the exit and into the corridor beyond.

'Bye, cherry pie,' whispered Shaun as he paused for a short escape from post-interview tidying duties.

As the covert repartee floated past Gateaux's ears, the fuse inside his funny zone ignited, sending a powder keg of explosive laughter resonating around the now empty floor.

No sooner had the Americans departed, so Mel walked in.

'Hi again, Gats ... Oh, and hi, Shaun,' she said, as the young sergeant popped his grinning face out from around the corner of the games room door.

'Okay, so what's the big joke?' she continued as the infection of jollity spread to her own cheeks.

Harry raised both his hands and began waving them innocently towards her.

'No, nothing to do with you Mel, I promise. I'll tell you later when I've recovered.'

Suddenly, the ear-to-ear grin which had filled Harry's face since Solly's "cherry pie" departure evaporated as his eyes began to wander involuntarily around the Beauport Room's empty shell.

'Where the hell's all that gorgeous food gone. I'm starving?' he cried. 'Has that Yank polished it all off? I thought he looked slightly more voluminous on the way out?'

'Don't worry Harry,' interrupted Mel. 'I've put by some sandwiches and a huge portion of fruit trifle for you. If you just give Lucy a call back at reception when you're ready, she'll show you to the dining room.'

The Inspector's cheeks puffed as an expression of relief decorated his face.

'Mel, you are an absolute treasure. My stomach is forever in your debt.'

'Is that a line you learned at charm school, Gats? You can say such the nicest things when you put your mind to it,' she said, her response wrapped generously with a cheery tone of sarcasm.

'I try my hardest,' replied Harry.

'Anyway, if we can just leave food aside for the moment, how did the interviewing go, if I may be so bold to ask?'

'You can ask, Mel, but there's not a lot to say,' said Shaun. 'They were all very similar, the same account a dozen or so times over, it seemed. To be honest, it was beginning to get all a bit tiresome,' he continued.

Two short coughs popped from Harry's cheeks.

Shaun looked across to where the chesty eruption of noise had originated.

'Tiresome it may be sergeant but you'll soon learn in this game that every grain of information is potentially a field of useful study material and a possible rich harvest thereafter.'

'Very philosophical, Gats. Did you come up with that yourself?' enquired Mel.

Harry nodded.

'Can see I'll have to start calling you Plato soon then,' she added. 'Incidentally, you mentioned during my interview earlier something about wanting another chat sometime. You haven't forgotten, have you?'

'No, definitely not, Mel. I know we've had a fairly detailed statement from you on the day's events already but I just wanted to pick your brains a little more, if that's okay? You've known the victim from a few of the tours in the past and I just thought that another chat, after you've had some time to unwind, might bring new details to light. Allow us to build up a better picture of our Mr Price.'

'Yes, sure, that's not a problem at all, Harry. I'm around all afternoon.'

The Inspector hesitated, raised his head and stroked his lightly bristled chin as, close by, his brain engaged in thought mode.

'Could be a little tricky this afternoon unfortunately,' he said, dropping his head to look at Mel. 'I'm shortly returning to Santille and afterwards I've a few other potential witnesses to speak to. So today is probably out,' he continued.

'Well there's always this evening, Gats. That's of course, if you're not too busy?'

As the fingers returned to the bristled chin, the Inspector's thought mode re-engaged momentarily.

'Tonight, er yes, fine by me, as long as the prospect of spending an evening talking shop doesn't phase you?'

'No, not at all, anything to help.'

'Great, okay, you're on, Mel. How about meeting up at 'Popeye's at, say, eight o'clock then? I'll book a table ... Oh, and don't even think about bringing your purse. The evening's on me.'

'Thanks, fantastic, ' replied Mel excitedly, with a glowing smile that translated into the self same words. 'I'll take it all back. Perhaps you were a graduate of Charm School. I'll see you later then,' she added before spinning smartly on the rapidly diminishing heel of her left shoe and then, like the Americans moments earlier, disappearing from the function room and into the corridor beyond.

The Inspector turned to face his sergeant. 'Right, Shaun. I'm going to head back to Santille now, that is of course after an urgent appointment between my stomach and some food back in the lounge. Going to join me?'

'No thank you. I had a good stuff before we started.'

'Oh great. Look after number one season is it?'

Shaun said nothing.

'Well, as you're fully fuelled, perhaps you can start busying yourself around the hotel. Burn off a few of those calories.'

'Busy myself?'

'Yes, have a chat with the staff and some of the other guests we've not yet spoken to. See if anyone knew anything of Andrew Price. Don't forget what I said earlier though. Any information might be useful information,' replied the Inspector. 'I'll have my mobile if you need me. Should be back from Santille around five I hope,' he continued as he began edging his way along to the exit. 'Oh, and before you do begin quizzing anyone, find out from Lucy which room Price was staying in and give it the once over.'

'No problem, guv.'

'If I don't see you later, sergeant, we'll get our heads together first thing in the morning back at the station and see what we've got from today's efforts. I'm hoping also that we should have some indicative post mortem results from Jeff by then.'

Instructions relayed, Gateaux turned and, spurred on by his ever-screaming appetite for sustenance, made a brisk departure. Within milliseconds of his exit and with the smell of food in his imaginary sub-conscious, the brisk walk had developed into a light jog in the direction of the main entrance. In no time the Inspector found himself at a deserted reception, or so it seemed. Propping both hands firmly on the solid dark mahogany desktop, he lifted himself up, his feet tip-toeing on the floor to periscope his vision over and below the desk from where he could hear a curious rustle.

His eyes locked in upon the diminutive figure of Lucy, seated at a small side table, with her head buried deep among a spiralling mountain range of invoices and staff rotas. Aware that her attention was being sought, Lucy looked up.

'Hi, sorry to interrupt you, but ...'

'Sandwiches?' she replied enquiringly.

The Inspector's head twitched.

'Is clairvoyancy a pre-requisite for working in this hotel?' he enquired, a reference to his encounter with the doorman a couple of hours earlier.

'I'm sorry,' said a bemused looking Lucy who with good reason had missed the relevance of the Inspector's remark.

'No nothing really. Just something that happened earlier,' replied Harry, by way of vague explanation. 'But yes, you are quite right. I have come about the sandwiches. I'd like to interview them next if I may, followed by the trifle.'

Lucy returned a molecule of a giggle, a more than generous reward, she considered, for the Inspector's borderline attempt at spontaneous humour. As the molecule vaporised, she stood, pushed her chair away from behind her and walked around to the front of the desk.

'If you'd just like to follow me I'll show you the way.'

Soon the two found themselves in the opulently decorated lounge, occupied only by an elderly couple seated in the far corner who, between petite mouthfuls of their afternoon cream teas, were quietly sharing the panoramic view of the bay through the large window beside them.

'If you just sit here, Inspector, I'll get Liane to organise lunch for you,' said Lucy softly, pointing to a wrap around black leather clad sofa chair.

The leather crunched softly as Harry sank into its luxuriant jaws. As he did so Lucy disappeared through a door opposite marked *staff only*.

No sooner, it seemed, had the door swung closed than it arched back in the other direction as in walked a young waitress clad in the hotel's blue and white striped uniform and carrying a large tray of food and a pot of tea.

'Thank you very much,' said Harry as Liane leaned across and placed the tray delicately on the low, glass-topped table at his side.

She stood in silence momentarily as the Inspector scanned the feast before him. Scanning complete, Harry looked up. 'Fantastic, thanks very much again.'

The waitress returned a nervous giggle, before turning and disappearing with a quick shuffle back through the door. Her exit provided the trigger for Gateaux to begin his re-energising process. Reaching across, he picked up a dark blue napkin from the tray and opened it out neatly across the lap of his cycling trousers.

The tidy placing of the cotton cloth marked the end of civilised ceremony as the Inspector's etiquette then transcended to a feverish relay, moving food rapidly between plate and mouth. As the gastronomic demolition continued the elderly couple, sitting innocuously in the far corner, switched their attentions for an instant from the tranquil beauty of the sun-drenched bay to the unorthodox spectacle of primeval animal behaviour provided by the Inspector in the middle of the room.

They muttered quietly to each other before twisting their chairs in unison further towards the window and refocusing their eyes upon the infinitely more pleasing sight of the bay.

Lunch complete, Gateaux lifted the napkin from his lap and quickly wiped his mouth before folding the cloth tightly and placing the small cotton cushion beside the neatly placed stack of three empty white sandwich plates and glass trifle bowl.

Re-fuelled, the Inspector raised himself from the clutches of the body-swallowing chair before turning and following the etched dark brown timber panelled signs along the maze like route back to reception.

Lucy, who seemed barely to have re-acquainted herself with her desk and the stack of invoices and rota preparations, looked up again as Harry reappeared and propped himself again across the counter.

'Surely you've not finished already?' she enquired, an expression of bewildered consternation written across her face.

'Yes, absolutely gorgeous food, thank you. But it's one of those too much to do and not enough time days unfortunately,' he said as he raised his hand to his face to wipe a single rebellious crumb from the side of his mouth.

'I should be careful with all that fast eating. You'll give yourself indigestion later, if you're not careful.'

'There's probably not even enough time for that today.'

'Maybe not, but I'm sure it will find time for you later.' warned Lucy, patting her stomach lightly.

Harry returned an appreciative nod in recognition of Lucy's apparent concern for his well-being.

'I must be away now. Things to do, people to see and all that. Thanks for all your help, Lucy ... Oh, and can you thank Mel for the food. Just sorry it was such a rush.'

As Gateaux spoke, his clear state of increasing hyper-activity moved him into taking a few quick strides backwards towards the main door. He raised the palm of his right hand to wave his farewells for now at least towards Lucy who returned the gesture instantly. With that, he turned and stepped outside. He stood still for a short while to allow time for his eyes to adjust from the relatively low intensity of the hotel's interior to the now laser brightness of the still, sun-kissed blue skies.

His optic regions suitably recovered, he squinted as he arched his body back to look skywards, opening his chest as he did so to take a deep breath of long overdue fresh air.

'Are you okay, Inspector?' enquired the doorman who was on his way back up the steps, having just seen a couple of guests safely to their waiting taxi below.

'Er, yes, thank you. Just appreciating some well deserved sea air. I've been cooped up inside there for the last two hours or so,' he continued, nodding once towards the entrance door.

'Think I'll grab some of that with you ... Not quite as fit as I used to be,' said the doorman as he reached the top step, his reply somewhat fragmented as he paused occasionally to catch his breath.

'Well, I'll leave you to it then. But don't grab it all,' said Gateaux.

'No time to waste,' continued the freshly oxygenated Inspector as he leapt athletically three steps at a time down the granite staircase to the pavement below. Back at street level, he turned and looked up. 'Thanks for keeping an eye on the bike for me.'

'No problem at all, sir. Seems a well behaved bike ... Just wish they were all like that.'

Gateaux laughed before disappearing from view as he walked round the side path to where his cycle was parked.

The disappearance however proved to be short lived as, within seconds the Inspector, complete with red crash hat, cruised past the entrance steps on a slow freewheeling descent down the cobbled driveway towards the exit. He raised his head and, tapping the brakes for an instant, glanced up for a final time towards where the doorman stood.

'Cheers for now. Perhaps see you later, if not, tomorrow,' he shouted, the extra decibels injected into his voice to propel his words adequately to the top of the steps.

Farewell delivered, his eyes returned to the route ahead. As he closed in rapidly upon the two imposing granite pillars that marked the end of the driveway and the boundary to the hotel complex, his mind refocused towards the imminent entry into the lions den of mid-afternoon traffic.

From the relatively quiet confines of the hotel's inner sanctum the noise levels suddenly took a quantum leap as Harry crossed the Coburg's outer threshold and joined the bubbling casserole of vehicles beyond.

Safely negotiating a series of intricate traffic weaves, he soon found himself back in the hassle-free green oasis of the Jersey countryside, bound for Santille.

The pleasing return to peaceful solitude allowed his mindset to re-adjust, this time collating and organising mentally the various sinews of investigative information that had come to light during the day. His mental computation became so intense and absolute that the ride to the site became a journey reliant almost wholly upon the abilities of the Inspector's sub-conscious autopilot. Indeed, such was the occupation of mind that the three miles between town and Santille passed by as an irreverent blur. As the Inspector neared the start of the track that led to the site a voice rang out from the picture postcard garden just across the road.

Harry pulled hard on his brakes and came to a rapid, though

slightly bike-twitching halt. Steadying himself with both feet dropped firmly to the road surface he turned to see Eva, a small trowel still clasped firmly in her left hand, looking towards him over the short lush green privet hedge that picture-framed the garden.

'Lovely day for it,' said Harry.

'Oh yes, can't waste glorious weather like this,' replied Eva as she waved her trowel skywards.

'Is it three o'clock already?' she continued.

'No, not just yet,' said Gateaux, raising his arm and quickly viewing his blue fabric-strapped watch. 'I've just got to check how my colleagues are progressing over at the site. Should be back with you in around fifteen minutes if that's okay?'

As he finished his sentence Pierre appeared, crunching his way along the gravel path that lined the side of the house.

'Did you call, dear?' he called out, oblivious of the Inspectors presence.

'No, it's okay,' cried Eva. 'It's just that lovely Inspector Cake,' she continued, turning to greet her husband who had now arrived beside her.

Pierre looked across the hedge and grinned whimsically towards Harry.

'The Inspector's popping back to see us in about fifteen minutes, dear.'

'Oh, if you're coming back that soon we'll go and put the kettle on for you,' added her husband.

'No, please don't go to any trouble on my part.'

'It's no trouble at all young man, no trouble at all. We'll be pleased to have the company,' replied Eva. 'I've made you some sandwiches and some trifle as well. Just a little something to fill your fragile frame and keep you going,' she added.

The Inspectors face paled. Having consumed an army's worth of similar goodies moments earlier at the hotel and aware that a further intake of food so soon after might only be possible with the assistance of a crowbar, Gateaux began to rapidly scour his

117

mind's vocabulary in search of some diplomatic words of polite refusal.

Before his response had fully gelled, Pierre spoke.

'Oh yes, my good wife's made you a lovely spread and the trifle is full of gorgeous fresh fruit from the garden. Only picked this morning as well. I'm sure you'll love it.'

The couple looked on in quiet anticipation of an appreciative response from the Inspector. Harry said nothing, his face, it seemed, in a state of suspended animation.

'Is everything okay?' questioned Pierre as Gateaux's apparently dreamy reticence continued.

The Inspector shook his head a couple of times as if to wake himself from his food-drunken stupor.

'Sorry, miles away I'm afraid,' he replied. 'Yes ... The food is a very kind thought. Thank you very much,' he continued, a slightly forced smile decorating his face as he resigned himself to an acceptance of the well intended and friendship-filled invitation to afternoon tea.

'Good, we will see you very shortly then, Inspector,' said Eva with a quick farewell wave.

As the couple turned to move back to the house, so the Inspector mirrored their movement and spun round with his bike to face the track that led up to the dolmen site.

Lifting his leg to jump back onto the machine he winced suddenly as he experienced a painful tightening of his stomach muscles.

Instinctively he lowered the trigger-limb to the ground, propped his arms at full stretch against the handlebars and set about seeking instant entry to the de-stress department. Maintaining the semi-crouched position he stared blankly down at the ground and took in a few controlled deep breaths, until the creases of anguish written across his face began to erase. As they did, he pondered as to whether the discomfort just moments previously had signalled the onset of indigestion as warned of earlier by Lucy or constituted a mutinous reaction by his body towards the imminent prospect of a second meal in an hour.

Whatever the cause, it was clear to him that the short journey back to the dolmen was one that would not be travelled comfortably by bike. The residues of discontent continued to burn uncomfortably as he pushed the cycle the few metres across the lane and then carried it up the three granite steps. At the top he paused to take further deep intakes of air before continuing the pedal-push along the narrow dusty track.

As he entered the tree ringed clearing that enveloped the pre-historic stone structure, Jeff walked across to meet him, having witnessed from some distance the Inspector's uncharacteristically lacklustre progress along the track.

'Tell you what, mate, those things go a whole lot better if you sit on them,' he said, pointing to the red mountain bike which had been placed carefully against its now accustomed tree.

'Is that right?' replied Harry. 'D'you know what, I'm always being criticised for not reading the instructions first,' he continued with a grin, still riddled with the pained expression which emanated from ongoing events lower down his body.

'You all right, Harry?'

'I will be in a minute. Just a bit of cramp, I think?'

'You'll burn yourself out soon if you're not careful. You need to slow down a bit.'

'Can't see me doing that until er ... I'm six foot under,' replied Gateaux, a semi-disguised wince interrupting his reply. 'And even then the box will be hopping around. Anyway, on to more serious things. What have you got for us?' he continued.

With Jeff leading, the two men began walking back towards the dolmen.

'Well, in addition to the broken neck and facial cuts which I mentioned to you last time, we've also found a very heavy bruise on the left side of his face possibly consistent with a fall,' said Jeff, as the two neared the megalithic chamber. 'That may have resulted in the neck injury, of course. That or a blow on

119

the head from some form of blunt implement perhaps. Difficult to say exactly which at the moment,' he added.

'So what's your gut reaction?'

'Keep trying to put me on the spot, don't you, Harry?'

'All part of the job, mate, I'm afraid.'

'Well, my personal view, off the record of course, is that whatever the cause, the guy was almost certainly dead before he arrived at his final resting place here.'

'Right, well that's a start.'

'An unofficial start, remember.'

With that, Jeff turned his head and glanced across the stones towards the grassed mound beyond. Gateaux's head moved in parallel as if connected by a puppeteer's string.

'Nick's been working overtime on that flattened area of grass and the local zone of ravaged shrubbery we looked at earlier,' said Jeff, pointing. 'Might as well see how he's getting on now you're here,' he continued before weaving his way carefully through the outer ring of smaller granite stones and then turning sharply to his right and walking slowly towards the perimeter mound. The Inspector followed closely behind.

Nick, oblivious of their imminent arrival, remained crouched at one edge of the perimeter grass covered mound, his head bowed in total stillness to allow his eyes to focus at very close range upon seemingly each and every fibre of greenery in front of him.

Five or so metres short of the study area the two stopped and observed in silence as Jeff's assistant engaged in an apparent session of micro-gardening, very delicately scraped away at a small patch of moss infused grass in front of him with a small trowel.

The operation, of almost brain surgeon intricacy, concluded with the careful lifting of a small soil covered sample and its placement with equal care into a clear plastic bag which he held by his fingertips in his other hand.

Jeff's and the Inspector's silent vigil continued, as they

searched out an opportune moment to interrupt Nick's hypnotic fixation upon the grassed bank.

His mind still wrapped around the task in hand, Nick carefully squeezed some unwelcome air from the sample-filled bag and then tied it with a simple single looped knot. Recovering a white tag from his overall pocket, he inscribed in large digits the number 24 on both sides, using a thick black marker pen retrieved from the same pocket.

With the tag then secured around the knotted top of the polythene pouch he placed it finally into a black plastic tray at his side, a tray brimming with a family of similarly sealed and labelled bags. As he reached for his clipboard, Jeff advanced a few paces and leaned his body slowly forward. His colleague looked up as the shadow of Jeff's outline crept across the sample filled tray.

'Sorry to interrupt you, mate, but is there any chance you can spare us just a few moments?'

Still in the crouching position, Nick placed the clipboard on its edge against the side of the bank to act as a prop and, swivelling his upper body, turned and looked up at his superiors standing a few metres beyond.

'Sorry, sir, I didn't quite catch you then. Miles away, as always.'

'I was just wondering if you could spare the Inspector and myself a few moments?'

'Sure, no problem at all, sir. As it happens, that's the last sample for now anyway. Just give me a second while I log it on my sheet.'

Administration concluded, he leaned across to place the notes on top of a small polythene sheet that lay on the crest of the grass bank before standing and arching his back.

As his spine contorted, he stretched his arms behind him and pressed deep into his lower back with the outstretched fingers of each hand. The impromptu exercise routine continued, as the articulation of body parts moved to the legs with first a couple of short squats, followed finally by a brisk rubbing of his overall clad calves and knees with cupped hands.

As he stood and took a deep inhalation to mark the end of the flexing, the silence that had accompanied the theatrics was broken by stereophonic laughter from the other two.

'What's this, Nick. You getting ready for a marathon later or something?'

'I wish! No it's just that I've been crouching down in the same squatting position so much this afternoon I think evolution was very close to concluding that I wanted to be a frog.'

At the realisation that the exercise, thought moments earlier to be the eccentric display of one overdosed on sun rays, was in fact a genuine display of battle fatigue therapy following a long day in the field, Jeff's laughter gave way to more sympathetic words.

After exchanging a few pleasantries of concern and well being for the recovering Nick, the conversation returned to the case in hand.

'So what have you found there?' enquired Gateaux, pointing down towards the tray of bags that were now beginning to sweat profusely from their continuing exposure to the still intense heat of the sun.

'Well, sir, we're working on the theory just now that the victim's body was brought through to the site at this point from the field over there,' said Nick, pointing to a patch of dusty oat-coloured earth beyond which was just visible through the local area of disturbed shrubbery.

'As far as these soil samples are concerned, we're sending them off to the forensic laboratory in Southampton tonight. What we're hoping for is a positive trace of any fibres that may be contained within the scrapings from the flattened grass and shrubs. That would clearly add some weight to our theory.'

As Nick finished his sentence, Jeff stretched across to the tray and laid a white sheet over it in an effort to preserve the contents from further solar cooking.

'Thanks, sir,' said Nick. 'Was just about to do that myself.'

'And if there's nothing unusual reported in the samples, Nick, then presumably it's back to the drawing board, eh?' quizzed the Inspector.

'Quite.'

'So what about the victim's bag and the food and drink items that you found scattered over there?' enquired Harry, pointing towards the red flag in the adjacent field. 'Any more on that?'

'Yes, a bit of a development on that, sir. We've recorded and collected the scattered food and drink items found in that field and all have been sent to the same Southampton laboratory. What adds to the mystery, though, is that we found a few smaller crumbs of what appears to be food from the same lunch box on that hedge, as we said earlier, and just on top of the bank over to your left,' he added as he took a few strides forward and indicated to a patch of grass ringed at ground level with yellow tape.

'Interesting,' said Gateaux.

'There's a slightly more bizarre twist to this little tale, though, Inspector,' continued Nick.

'Oh yes, and what is that?' asked Harry as his investigative pulse began racing at a familiar pace.

'Well, this same patch of earth is absolutely sodden. Smells like beer,'

'And if anyone knows what beer smells like it's this man,' interrupted Jeff, patting his colleague firmly on the shoulder.

Gateaux laughed as he knelt and then moved in on the suspect patch of ground for himself.

'Phew,' he cried as he rocked back and returned to a standing position.

'I now know what they mean by getting high on grass. You'd fail the breath test with one whiff of that,' he continued.

'I assume soil samples from here are off to the laboratory as well?' asked the Inspector.

'Indeed, sir,' confirmed Nick. 'Hopefully we can link the beer and indeed the food scraps here to the picnic bits we found in that field.'

'And what conclusions could we draw if that were to be the case?'

'Well, thinking aloud, perhaps the guy, for whatever reason, chose to have an early lunch and then lobbed the leftovers across the hedge in to the field.'

'Together with his rucksack?' enquired Gateaux.

'Yes, maybe. It all sounds a bit odd, I know. As I said, I was only thinking aloud, but I guess it deserves a little more thinking time?'

'Okay, thanks for the moment, Nick,' said the Inspector before returning his attention towards Jeff.

'When we first looked at the body in the chamber you showed me a blood stain which you assumed was from the victim and which was on the other side of that rock to where the head now rests. If the guy was dead before he arrived here as you are suggesting, unofficially of course, have you come up with any ideas on how that stain got on the other side?'

'Yes, I've been doing a little head scratching on that one, Harry.'

'And?'

'The obvious conclusion, I guess, is that the person, or persons, responsible dumped the body and then rolled it into the final position. A few scuff marks on the ground suggest it has been moved at least once. But I agree it remains a question to be answered. Unfortunately, we're no closer really to solving a lot of mysteries in this case.'

'So when can I expect some concrete facts to go on with?' enquired Gateaux, an eagerness for the possession of some incontestable findings clear in his tone.

'Well, my plan is still to carry out the post-mortem later today if I can find the time. We've arranged for the body to be removed in the next half hour or so. As I said earlier, I'm hopeful that some preliminary conclusions should be with you sometime in the morning, I hope.'

'And I'll be chasing Southampton for some urgent results tomorrow on the food and soil samples, though the tests might take a couple of days,' interrupted Nick.

'Fine. Anything else?' enquired Harry as he panned his eyes across the faces of both men. The two shook their heads.

'No, I'll be off in a short while, just as soon as the body has been removed,' continued Jeff. 'I'm going to keep Nick here with a few officers to carry out one final detailed search of the whole area. I suggest we keep the site cordoned and secure for the foreseeable future, just in case we need to revisit for any reason.'

'Yes, I agree, Jeff,' replied Harry. 'I'll make contact with the Constable at the Parish Hall shortly, just to keep him in the picture.'

As the Inspector finished his sentence the back pocket of his cycle top rang out to a symphonic encore.

'Excuse me, gentlemen. It's that good old "jelly-bone" again.'

Jeff and Nick took a few steps sideways and engaged in quiet conversation.

Harry, meanwhile, arched his back forwards and twisted his left arm behind him to extricate the plastic coated orchestra from his shirt. With the mobile glued firmly to his ear he began a slow meander away from the others and headed for one of the few vacant spaces at the edge of the site.

'Hello, Gateaux.'

'Sir, it's Shaun at the hotel.'

'Hi, how're you getting on? Have you looked in Andrew Price's room yet?'

'Yes, we're actually in the room now,' replied Shaun excitely. 'But we didn't need the key. The door was already unlocked. Added to that, the window to the outside was wide open as well. I think someone beat us to the search, guv. It's a complete mess.'

'Can we be sure, sergeant, that it wasn't Andrew who left the room as ...'

125

The Inspector's inquiry was suddenly curtailed as the phone began to hiss wildly in its search for a stronger signal.

'Shaun, Shaun, you still there?'

'Yes, sir, sorry, I missed the last piece of your message.'

'Damn phone. Don't know why I didn't stick with my cocoa tin and a bit of string,' said Harry. 'Anyway, I was asking if you could be sure that it wasn't our victim who left the room in the state you've found it?'

'We've checked that possibility out, sir. Lucy tells me that the maid doesn't begin her cleaning round until after eleven o'clock and, as we know, the body was found well before then at Santille.'

'Is it possible that the maid, for whatever reason, forgot to do his room today?'

'We're ahead of you on that one as well, guv. We've spoken to the chambermaid who assures us that she cleaned the room this morning. We've checked her list to be doubly sure and that clearly indicates the room as having been cleaned at eleven twenty five. If we needed any further confirmation, it turns out that a new visitor's information pack was being introduced to each of the rooms today as they were cleaned. I'm looking at the pack for this room, right in front of me on the table. Lucy's with me and she's insistent that the pack must have been delivered this morning and could not have arrived any day earlier.'

'Is it too early to say if anything is missing from the room?'

'Yeah, I was coming onto that, guv. Lucy has checked the room inventory and all hotel items seem to be present and intact. However, when we quizzed the maid, Rozella, again, she said that the guest ...'

The Inspector interrupted.

'By guest, you mean Andrew Price?'

'Yes, that's right. Rozella remembers always having to clean around Mr Price's lap-top computer. He was, as we have learned, a bit of a computer nut. Well, all we have left here is a tangled mess of cables and some computer books and discs scattered on the floor. No sign of the computer anywhere.'

'And the computer was there when Rozella cleaned the room?'

'She thinks so. But one day apparently is much like the next, so she wouldn't put her hand on her heart.'

'Okay, so we're left with two possibilities. Either Andrew took the computer with him or someone else took it for him. Any idea which might be the more likely, Shaun?'

'Difficult to say right at this instant, but whoever took it was in a mighty hurry. The evidence here suggests it's been just crudely ripped from the sockets. I can't imagine a computer enthusiast such as our victim wishing to cause serious damage to his own equipment.'

'Unless of course he had to leave the room quickly and had something of value saved on it perhaps?'

'Well, yes, it's a possibility, guv.'

'One other thing, Shaun. You mentioned the room window to the outside being open. Is that significant,' said Gateaux as the tide of questions continued to flow.

'Could well be, sir. Transpires that there's a major new annex wing under construction to the rear of the hotel, which this room overlooks ...'

The phone hissed loudly again.

'Sir, can you hear me?'

'Yes, carry on sergeant,' replied Harry, his voice enthusiastically fuelled with adrenalin as developments continued to be relayed from the hotel.

'The site has a ring of scaffold slung around it for the full two storey height, with a timber plank deck at first floor level close to where we are standing. Looking at it, I reckon there's probably only about a metre gap or so between the temporary walkway and the sill to the open window of this room.'

'So do you think it's conceivable that either our victim or another person could have gained access, or made their escape, via the scaffold?'

Shaun paused as he pondered over the Inspector's hypothesis.

'Well, yes, I suppose so,' he replied with a slight hesitancy in his voice as his brain tried to compute the visualisation of somebody traversing the bridge of fresh air between external platform and stone sill.

A further pause followed as the sergeant strained every calculative sinew in the hope of a moment's gift in the art of parabolic analysis that would allow him to provide the Inspector with a more scientific and meaningful response.

'I shouldn't imagine you'd need to be a stuntman to do it, guv. A few ounces of athleticism and a bit of bottle should be enough. Unfortunately, I'm a wee bit lacking in both those departments or I would have tried it myself.'

'You seem okay in the bottle department when I've seen you in the bars,' quipped Harry. 'And you can sort the athleticism out with a few hard games of squash. That would cure it.'

'Think I'd prefer to be un-athletic if that's the only solution,' replied Shaun, his retort meeting with a resounding shout of 'wimp' down the phone line.

'Anyway, anything else to tell me sergeant?'

'No, that's it for the moment, guv.'

'Right. Can you arrange for an officer to stand watch outside the bedroom door and a second to patrol the scaffold area until I return? You'll probably have to search out the building site foreman to sort that one out. And while you're there, have a word with the guy. He might have something useful to tell us.'

'Okay, sir. So how long before you expect to be back?'

'I'd think at least another hour. I'll have a word with Jeff here on site to see if he can lend one of his people to join us back at the hotel. I'll rely on you to keep the room secure until then, all right?'

'No problem, guv. Consider it done.'

As the Inspector pulled the phone away from his ear, his social sub-conscious clicked into gear.

'Shaun, Shaun, hang on a moment.'

'Still here,' came the immediate shout of reassurance.

'Shaun, can you do me a big big favour. I've promised Mel a meal tonight and I've not got the number for the restaurant on me. Could you phone "Popeye's" and book a table for two in my name, for eight o'clock?'

'Yeah, I'll do it straight away, guv.'

'Thanks. Catch you later then, Shaun. I'll save you a doggy bag from the meal.'

Pressing the button to end the call, Harry walked the few paces back towards the two white clad figures of Jeff and Nick, placing the phone back into his pocket as he did so.

'I'll tell you what, mate. I'm glad I don't pay your phone bill,' said Jeff.

'Yes, thankfully, it's not me paying either,' replied Gateaux with a broad grin.

'Interesting call?' enquired Jeff.

'Yes, very interesting, actually,' replied the Inspector before continuing on to relay the unfolding hotel dramas to the attentive duo.

'Gets more intriguing by the minute, doesn't it?' said Jeff.

'Certainly that. I'd really like to give the hotel room a detailed look over before the day's out. Do you think you could spare us one of your "S.O.C.O." guys back at the Coburg in, say, an hour or so?'

'I would think so. Nick should be free sometime later. He's probably fed up by now looking at grass, anyway, and getting his hands plastered in chlorophyll. It'll be a nice change for him.'

'Yes, you can stare at green thick pile carpets instead,' said Harry, as he looked across to Jeff's assistant.

'Um, I better not start digging holes in that.'

Harry laughed.

'Right, time to make a move. I've just got to have a chat with the couple living across the road and then I should be able to meet Nick at the hotel. If, for any reason, I don't make it, then

Shaun should be around somewhere,' he continued before exchanging handshakes with the two men and then turning and making his way briskly back towards the start of the lane. Suddenly he stopped and spun around.

'Oh yes, just one more thing.'

Jeff looked across.

'Any sign of those missing watch bits yet?'

'No, sorry, still a blank on that one, Harry.'

'Okay, no worries. I'll speak to you later. I'll leave my bike here for a short while, if that's okay?' said Gateaux, patting the saddle twice as he spoke.

Jeff nodded.

A short jog later, Harry found himself at the front gate of the cottage. He stretched his upper body across for a periscope view of the garden beyond.

Eva, still at one with the flower bulging earth around her, looked up from her kneeling position on a small blue cushion that was tucked closely under the shadow of a large rhododendron bush.

'Pierre, Pierre, it's the Inspector,' she announced excitedly, turning her head as she spoke and maintaining the elevation in decibels, to fire her message through the open side window of the ivy walled cottage.

'Okay, dear, kettle's on,' came the instant retort from the cottage as Eva pushed her trowel into the grass beside her and prepared for her return to the vertical.

Having witnessed her first failing at a re-adoption of the standing position, Harry quickly flicked the wrought iron catch to the gate to open it and, having carefully guided its spring powered return behind him, crunched quickly the few paces along the pea-shingled pathway towards Eva's side.

'Let me help you,' he said as he extended his arm down towards her.

Eva looked up appreciatively towards her knight in shining armour.

'Oh, how very kind of you.'

Safely back on her feet, she locked her arm inside Harry's as they slowly made their way back to the cottage.

Pierre met the two at the door.

'Hello again, Inspector. Good to see you again,' he said, with the same childlike exuberance as had been displayed by his wife just moments earlier.

Pierre took a step back to allow Eva and her escort to pass through the hallway and then beyond into the lounge.

'Thank you young man,' she said as she unhooked her arm from the Inspector's clutches and rolled herself back into a soft pale blue linen covered armchair located to the side of the open fireplace.

'Great to get the weight off your feet, isn't it, Inspector?' she said with a sigh of relief.

'Indeed,' replied Gateaux as he dropped into the middle of a wide, cushion-overdosed sofa that faced a large granite inglenook.

'What a glorious room,' he continued as his eyes began to wander around the wall-to-wall display of museum-worthy artefacts. His gaze was drawn towards a light brown stained wooden box, perched precariously on a narrow shelf just above the fireplace. Suddenly two large hands wrapped themselves around the waist of the object and lifted it carefully down.

'Lovely piece, isn't it?' said Pierre. He motioned the Inspector to take the box from him.

Harry pressed his feet into the floor, rocked forward from his soft sunken resting place on the sofa and cupped his hands solidly around the handcrafted curiosity as if his very life depended on it.

'It's a Victorian veloscope. Only a handful left in the world, as far as we know.'

As Pierre spoke he lifted a small maple leaf patterned wooden table across to the Inspector's side.

'Here, place it on this.'

Harry stretched his back and leaned across to give the antique a delicate and silent landing on the table.

'Look through the eyepiece and turn that handle,' said Pierre as his historical commentary continued.

Gateaux contorted his body once again and clamped his right eye limpet-fashion to the timber-moulded eyepiece.

Turning the handle, as instructed, he stared hypnotically as the seemingly animated, sepia-brushed image of a Victorian family group walking along a pier rotated before him.

'That's fantastic,' he said. He removed his eye away momentarily and exercised his eyelid with a quick rubbing motion from the back of his finger.

'Let me show you a few more of our little treasures.'

The Inspector sat back in the chair for a few moments and allowed his host to parade a number of equally intriguing *objets d'art* that decorated the shelves of the four walls around him. As the items moved in and out of his possession, Eva shared the detailed commentary on each with her equally knowledgeable husband.

The three suddenly looked up as the small brass-cased carriage clock on the mantle piece chimed to signal three fifteen accompanied, coincidentally, by a whistling noise from the kitchen.

'That'll be the kettle,' announced Pierre.

Immediately, he turned and replaced a small oil painting of a seascape that he had been about to offer for closer viewing back onto the wall before retreating from the room.

Just a few minutes elapsed before his return, carrying a large tray containing three white coloured bone china cups and saucers and a large floral painted white china teapot.

Eva and Harry looked on as he placed it carefully on a mosaic-tiled coffee table beside the vacant armchair, opposite his wife. Without a word, he vanished before reappearing seconds later with a larger tray filled to overflowing with an assortment of sandwiches and the trifle.

'Tea, Inspector?' he enquired.

'Lovely, thank you. Milk, no sugar, if you would be so kind?'

Pierre poured the tea and passed one cup to Gateaux, followed closely in the other hand by the first wave of food offerings.

'Please help yourself,' he insisted, thrusting a silver plate stacked with crust-less triangular cut white bread sandwiches under Harry's nose.

As the fresh sight and smell of savouries wafted up and teased the two triggered senses, the militancy of uprising within his whole body that he hoped had been overcome, began to repeat its menacing drumbeat.

Gateaux gulped, and then again.

'You sure you're okay, young man?' enquired Eva.

'Er, yes, I'm fine, thank you. It's just been a very busy day,' he replied, his unconvincing response a distant dream from any Oscar nomination.

'Yes, I can imagine you've had to pack a lot in, you poor soul,' continued Eva as she yielded to the Inspector's pathetic appeal for clemency.

'And it seems that there's a lot more to pack in before the day's out,' said Gateaux, his response a reference both to investigations that would continue after this visit, but more immediately towards the plate of savouries which continued their intimidating hover in front of him.

He picked up two of the sandwiches and put them on his plate before placing the plate in the same motion on to the wooden table beside him.

Before Eva and Pierre had time to launch into their next enthusiastic session of antique showings or food related conversation, Gateaux produced a small notebook and pen from a sleeve pocket stitched on his cycle shirt and began his overdue question time with the couple.

Like a tennis match, the conversation ebbed and flowed from left to right as Eva and Pierre alternated in their responses.

133

Flicking over the fourth completed page of healthily scribbled notes, the activity stopped briefly as the clock chimed away.

'Four o'clock already,' said Harry, raising his head. 'Where does the time go?' he enquired, looking across at Eva and then swivelling his head to look at her husband seated in the armchair on the other side.

'Believe me, it moves a lot quicker as you get older as well, young man,' said Eva, sharing the gathered wisdom of her past years.

Harry quickly rustled back a page of his notes and looked to his right at Pierre.

'You said a few moments ago that you got up at seven thirty this morning and after some house chores were both in the garden by eight thirty.'

'No,' said Pierre instantly. 'Only my wife was in the garden at that time. I stayed in here reading the paper. That is of course until Eva told me of the commotion outside when your people arrived.'

'And did you notice anything out of the ordinary earlier, before all that activity?'

His question delivered, Harry's eyes pendulumed between the two interviewees. He waited patiently, occasionally repeating his eyeball gyration, as the two sat in silence, oiling the cogs, to cast their minds back to early morning.

'Can't think of anything in particular,' announced Pierre.

'What about you, dear?' he continued, looking across the thick oval shaped lilac patterned rug towards his wife.

'No, nothing really unusual. I do remember André calling by to deliver the eggs. That must have been around nine, I suppose, and the next thing I remember was the tour group arriving some time after.'

'Can you remember how long after?'

Eva turned her head slightly to one side, away from both the Inspector and her husband and dipped into an apparent trance.

Suddenly she looked up.

134

'I'm not very good with times Inspector. But I suppose the group turned up about half an hour after André left ... Oh, and another thing.'

'Yes?' said the Inspector, his ears pricking up expectantly.

'I remember hearing Woody on his tractor in the field opposite, but I couldn't tell you whether that was before or after the tour group arrived.'

'Woody's on holiday,' interrupted Pierre. Went to St Malo with the family last week. I'm sure they're still away.'

'Oh, silly me, Inspector. I do apologise. It must have been another day I'm thinking of. I did say I'm not very good with times.'

Despite the seemingly erroneous comment, Harry noted the tractor incident quickly in his book, writing <u>WOODY/HOLIDAY?</u> in large letters and underlining the entry as if he felt it merited some hitherto undisclosed importance.

'And that's all you can recall?'

Silence wrapped around Eva's chair as she dipped her head again and stared on this occasion deeply into her lap.

As her journey to the twilight zone and beyond clicked over to the first minute and then the second, the Inspector interrupted the woman's apparent meditation in an effort to spark as yet un-travelled avenues of thought in her mind.

'Did you see any other people in the lane, or perhaps some other vehicles?'

'Well, let me see,' she replied, looking up momentarily before dropping her head for a further time.

'Come on, dear. I'm sure the Inspector wants to get home sometime tonight,' said her husband.

'No it's okay,' replied Harry instantly.

He looked across at Pierre and offered a discreet smile.

'Take your time. There's no rush,' he continued, turning his head back to look at Eva, her head still bowed.

'Just as well,' muttered Pierre.

Eva glanced at her husband and then turned to face Harry.

'I can only remember André and the group from the hotel but then, they come by every Wednesday this time of the year ... Though it's normally in the afternoon,'

'What about traffic?' asked Harry, as one final prompt towards extracting additional vital grains of information.

'Er ... Well, André's van of course ... Oh yes, and a funny old car.'

'Funny old car ... What funny old car, dear?' enquired Pierre.

'Oh, it was a sweet little thing. Reminded me of our younger years,' replied Eva.

The Inspector sat up straight, slid himself to the front edge of the chair and, digging his elbow into the top of his leg, propped his chin on his raised hand. 'Do you know what type of car it was?' he enquired, an added bite of the growing optimism exciting his voice as he began to smell the imminent arrival of a further thread of information to accompany the "André" and "possible tractor" items already committed to ink written scribble in his book.

'Think it was a red one, maybe blue, can't really remember. Anyway, it was one of those conversionals.'

'Think she means convertibles, Inspector,' said Pierre.

Harry nodded and then turned again to Eva as she continued her conversation. 'André would know ...'

There was a short pause.

The two men's eyes looked intently across the room in eager anticipation of the conclusion to Eva's apparently unfinished sentence.

'Yes, André would know, I'm sure of it. I remember they pressed their car horn to ask him to move his van. I think they were in a hurry, you see.'

'They? Was there more than one in the car?'

'Oh yes, there were two men, one driving and a passenger.'

'Your friend André. Do you have his address to hand at all?'

'He's over at Le Castel farm, just down the lane on the left hand side,' interrupted Pierre. 'In fact, you'll probably pass it on your way back,' he continued.

'Thanks,' said Harry as he quickly scribbled the details into his rapidly ink swelling notebook.

Suddenly Eva rocked forward in her chair and pressed her arms to elevate her body slightly.

'Inspector, you've not touched your sandwiches yet and your poor tea's going cold,' she announced, looking across at the still orphaned plate on the table beside him.

Harry looked down at the food which he had hoped, in the time he had been speaking, had perhaps been abducted by aliens.

The aliens were clearly elsewhere.

His eyes then moved a fraction sideways where they focused on the now less than inviting veneer of tannic enriched scum that was rapidly completing its spiralling journey to seal the top of the cup of tea. He reached across for the plate of disowned savouries. As he raised the first and began taking a series of pea sized bites from it, the clock chimed four thirty.

'I am very sorry, but I really must be going. Still lots to do, you know.'

'Oh, can't you stay just a little while longer,' asked Eva invitingly. 'Pierre will make you a fresh cuppa, won't you, dear,' she said, looking across to her husband.

Pierre instantly launched himself forward in his chair and prepared to return to active mode in answer to his wife's request.

'No really, I really must be off,' repeated Harry, an injection of some urgency creeping into his reply, the urgency spurred on by the fear that should he stay he might succumb to either stomach failure or tea poisoning.

As he spoke, he leaned across very slowly to return the plate containing three remaining sandwiches and one randomly pecked sample to the small table.

'Sorry I can't stay longer,' he said as he closed the cover sheet of his notebook and began taking to his feet.

'Oh, and you've not finished your tea nor had any trifle yet,' said Eva, a mild hint of disappointment fringing her response.

'Yes, I do apologise. Perhaps next time? Could I perhaps pop back in the morning if you're free. I'll take the opportunity to visit André at Le Castel and look around that farm opposite at the same time?'

'Yes, please do, Inspector. You'd be welcome to call in any time, any time at all,' replied Eva.

'Thanks,' said Gateaux before pushing up on the arms of the chair and rolling himself forward on the balls of his feet to effect his release from the body swallowing fabric of the seat.

With the Inspector back in a standing position, Eva began similar rocking motions to extricate herself from her wrap around chair.

'Please, please, don't get up. I'll see myself out,' said Gateaux.

Pierre looked up. 'Okay, Inspector, what time can we expect you tomorrow?'

'Well, I'm in the office first thing but how about say eleven or eleven thirty?'

'Yes, that sounds okay. I'll just check the diary.'

Pierre reached over to his side and retrieved a large calendar from the floor, a large print of Monet's waterlillies decorating the page.

'Yes, that's okay, Inspector. Eva has church cleaning in the afternoon but we're free all morning.'

'Fine, see you then,' replied Gateaux, raising his arm to wave the two chair-sunken onlookers farewell.

Back in the sandwich-free air of outside he looked quickly at his watch, which read four forty-two. As he walked back up the lane to retrieve his bike he reached around to grab his mobile phone and began dialling. The connection was instantaneous.

'Hi, Shaun, it's Harry.'

'Hi, guv.'

'I'm running a bit late. Don't think I'll make it back to the hotel tonight. Have Jeff's people turned up there yet?'

'Yes, Nick's been here a while now, guv. He's carrying out a microscopic search of the victim's room as we speak.'

'Great. Can we meet back at the station first thing tomorrow then as arranged? See if Nick can join us as well. That's of course if he's finished everything at the hotel?'

'Yes, sure, sir.'

'Oh and Shaun, before you go, did you remember to book a table for me at 'Popeye's' tonight?'

'Yes, all done, guv. One table booked for eight o'clock.'

'Good, thanks again. I owe you a pint. Anyway, must dash.'

'Okay, sir ... And bon appetite for tonight.'

The Inspector packed away his phone and turned off the lane to begin his way back along the dusty trail towards the dolmen.

'Evening, Inspector,' said a patrolling police officer at the end of the track as he slowly paced the entrance to the now eerily deserted site.

'Yes, good evening, Barry,' replied Harry as he wandered past and then reached across to pull his bike away from its sycamore tree resting place.

'I was beginning to get worried about that thing. I thought you'd forgotten it.'

'No chance of that. Inseparable, us two,' replied Gateaux before grabbing the frame of the bike with two tightly locked fingers, spinning it around and jumping back into the saddle.

'See you soon Baz,' he said, as he prepared for departure.

'Yes, goodnight, sir.'

With early evening closing rapidly, Gateaux pressed down hard on the pedals and accelerated away from the site. As he began distancing himself from the megalithic focal point of the day's events, his mind slowly began to uncoil and close in rapidly upon the infinitely more appealing prospect of a restaurant night out.

CHAPTER SIX

'Good morning, sir,' greeted Shaun brightly, tapping twice against the frosted glass pane of the open door as he entered the Inspector's office.

The compact office located on the first floor and adjoining the main central corridor nestled in the heart of a labyrinth of other similar rooms that in turn were served by a series of arterial sub-corridors. The investigative maze that resulted was well matched, it seemed, to its collective title as the CID.

In dramatic contrast to the rest of the department, Gateaux's office always presented itself to be, without equal, the quintessential model of organisation. Between two wall-mounted pin boards located behind his desk, stood a stack of four white enamelled shelves along which paraded, soldier-like, rows of red and black plastic box files. From their elevated position each row looked down upon a rank of similar files that neatly fringed on three sides the Inspector's large desk and in so doing enveloped an ageing computer, monitor and keyboard.

As Shaun conducted a quick inspection of the guard, his mind entered a momentary black hole of confusion as he considered the surely inconceivable notion that the Inspector's reputation as that very model of organisation might be one born out of myth. Unlike other days and for some hitherto undiscovered reason it now appeared that the Inspector's territorial space had entered the previously uncharted waters of chaos.

'That looks interesting,' said the sergeant, the only words he could find in his current state to describe the large open clam-like creation of tin foil that sprawled like an over-used table cloth across the keyboard and document files on Gateaux's table.

He leaned over and looked into them martian looking craft to find it contained a weighty pile of neatly cut sandwiches.

'Must say I'm a "two croissants and juice man" for breakfast myself.'

The Inspector looked up.

'It's a Red Cross gift from Eva and Pierre Morlaix,' quipped Harry before returning his eyes to the tabletop and the savoury mountain that provided the uncharacteristic blanket of disorder across the middle of his table.

'Thought I'd escaped their food party yesterday but these were waiting for me when I arrived this morning,' he continued, rocking backwards on his chair.

'Gee, there's a lot there, guv,' said Shaun as he moved in for a closer scrutiny. 'Looks about two loaves in this lot,' he added.

Harry rolled forward in his seat back to the table and carefully lifted with both hands the duvet-sized bowl of foil. 'Don't feel like helping me out with a few do you?'

The sergeant looked down at the top layer of granary bread sandwiches that had begun oozing a less than desirable mix of tuna, sweet corn and mayonnaise.

'Um, perhaps not just now, sir but I shouldn't worry about any waste. We've our resident gang of vultures across the corridor,' he said, laughing, a reference to his dustbin-lined colleagues close by. 'Just leave what you can't finish in there. They'll be reduced to crumbs in seconds, I promise you,' he continued as he lifted his hand across his shoulder and pointed behind him towards the offices beyond.

'Yes. Good idea. I'd hate to see them all go to waste,' replied Harry as he gathered the foiled flaps of the food parcel and twisted them together before placing the package precariously on an adjacent table. Package deposited, he quickly rubbed his hands over a nearby bin to eject a few rogue crumbs from his fingers.

'So it took longer than you thought at Santille yesterday, did it guv?'

'Yeah, sorry I couldn't make it back to the hotel later on, but I just couldn't force myself away from the Morlaix's, what with

142

their little antiques cabaret and sandwich banquet, and then of course I was out in town afterwards.'

'Oh yes, I nearly forgot to ask, guv. How did the meal go last night with Mel?' enquired Shaun, a glow of expectation glazed across his face as he awaited a response with which he could fill the gossip corridors of the neighbouring offices.

The Inspector paused. 'Yes, it was a very pleasant evening.'

'Is that all?'

'That's all you're getting.'

A silent plea for more information appeared on the sergeant's face.

'If you think there's anymore to know, you'll have to use your detective skills and find out for yourself, mate.'

'Well, that's doomed to failure if I've got to use my own detective skills, sir.'

'You said it,' replied Gateaux.

'So did the Morlaix couple come up with anything useful over afternoon tea?' enquired Shaun, a slight tease of sarcasm in his voice.

'As it happens they did and there's a lot to follow up on. Can you round up Kevin, Bazza and Nicki? We'll all meet in room four in ten minutes. You can tempt them with those sandwiches if there's any resistance.'

'You won't tempt Bazza with gold bars today, guv. He's on leave, taking his family to the air show.'

'Gee, that guy's about as useful as a raincoat in the Sahara. When you want him he's not there and when you don't he's around you like a leech.'

Shaun laughed. 'In fact there are a few off today, with the Battle of Britain display later this afternoon.'

'To be quite honest, Sergeant, I'd completely forgotten about that this morning until you just mentioned it. Well, we'll just have to find someone to make up the numbers then.'

'There is young Ami Jeune, sir, who joined us at the start of the week?'

'Fine by me. Should be useful experience for her. In at the deep end and all that. Let's face it, she's got to start somewhere.'

'I'll include her then?'

'Yes, sure. Let's see how we get on with Kevin, Nicki and Ami. Oh, and can you grab a cup of tea for me while you're out and bring it along to the meeting. I need something quickly to wash down my breakfast.'

'Okay, one tea coming right up and I'll see you in room four with the others in a few moments,' said Shaun as he leaned across to gather the pack of sandwiches and then began his retreat towards the door.

The Inspector nodded. 'I'm just going to phone forensics, see what they've got for us. Then I'll be right with you. Do you know if Nick is joining us at all?'

'No, he phoned in a short while ago, guv, with an apology. Seems he's had to pop over at short notice to Santille again.'

With that the sergeant disappeared, leaving Harry to an intensive five-minute session of phone conversation with his scientist colleagues.

The salient details of the discussion committed to ink, Gateaux gathered together his paper jammed clipboard and notebook and left his office for the twenty pace journey along the dimly lit corridor to room four at the end of the passage.

'Morning everybody,' he announced, as he walked purposefully in through the door of the meeting room and made his way to the front.

'Morning, sir,' echoed the quadraphonic response, mimicking the cry of an eager group of spotty faced students awaiting classes.

There was a short silence as the Inspector took stock of the few pieces of furniture at his immediate disposal.

'Someone's been busy at the boot fair?' he said, a hint of desperation in his voice as he dropped his notes onto a small oak effect table decorated copiously with cup stained blemishes and then sank himself uncomfortably into a crudely distorted orange coloured plastic chair.

He shuffled around in the seat for a few seconds to force all four legs to engage positively with the floor.

'Trust you to get the best one, guv,' called Shaun.

Gateaux looked up and smiled.

'Is that mine, sergeant?' he said, pointing to a white mug of tea on the table with the graphics I'M A MUG FROM SOUTHAMPTON UNIVERSITY embossed on its side.

'Yes, it is, sir. The machine tea came out like village pond water so I thought I'd make a proper brew.'

'Very commendable.'

Before beginning his briefing, Harry reached out and lifted the mug slowly towards his eyes for a close inspection that confirmed an apparent veneer of chilling tea on the surface accompanied by a floating intrusion of unidentifiable flotsam.

'You sure this isn't pond water?'

The others laughed.

'It was okay when I made it,' replied Shaun, his face painted with a mild expression of anxiety.

Harry gave the mug a swirl and then braved a quick gulp. 'Actually, it doesn't taste anywhere near as bad as it looks,' he concluded.

Instantly, Shaun's face filled with relief, the suspicion that he might be clinically incapable of cooking up a decent cuppa having now been demonstrated to be without foundation.

Gateaux placed the mug back on the table and looked up to the seated row of four attendees in front of him. 'Thanks for your promptness.'

Commendation delivered, his attention moved to the young, fresh faced recruit with a short bob of dark brown hair and complementary tan who sat at one end of the row.

'And I presume that you are Ami?'

'Yes, sir,' she replied, a hint of nerves sprinkled within her short response.

'Enjoy the holiday?' enquired the Inspector as his detective instincts were drawn for a moment to his new colleague's solar painted glow.

Ami conjured a short giggle.

'Yes, very good, thank you, sir. I went to Tenerife for two weeks with my boyfriend. Incredibly hot and sunny.'

'As we can see.'

'Did you bring us back some sticks of rock as a present each then?' interrupted Kevin.

"Order … Order," called Gateaux in true parliamentary style. 'Holidays aside, sadly. Let's get back to more mundane tasks,' he added as he sought a halt to the increasingly tangential threads of discussion.

'For those of you not familiar with the events of yesterday … and for those of you who are …' he added, looking across at Shaun whose eyes had appeared to wander momentarily.

'… I'll give you a résumé of the case so far.'

The four looked on intently as Harry stood and turned to face a large glossy white board mounted across the end wall of the room. The observing continued as he gathered up an assortment of coloured thick felt-tip pens that littered the tray under the board and then proceeded to describe the findings thus far, with a multi-coloured presentation comprising words, flow-charts and dubiously scribbled art work.

A little under two hours had passed during which time the board had been transformed from its snow white origins to a creation more resembling the superimposed images of London, Paris and New York metro maps, each line of the rainbow spaghetti important in its own right, indicating, where eyesight permitted, a name, a place, a time, or an event.

'I think that's enough for the moment. Shall we take five?' suggested Gateaux as he looked along the line of his apparently hypnotised audience who had been entranced by the firework frenzy of coloured pen before them.

'I need a break. My throat feels like sandpaper with all that talking,' he continued, a slight hoarseness in his voice reinforcing his plight. The others stood as one and waited their turn while the Inspector led the exodus from the room, returning soon afterwards with yet another mug of steaming tea in one hand and a bottle of mineral water and a clear plastic beaker stacked together in the other. His quartet of troops followed a short distance behind.

'At least there's no icebergs and sand dunes in this mug,' said Harry, looking first at his brew, still steaming like a power station chimney, and then across at Shaun.

'Incidentally, sergeant, I left the remnants of that last drink you made for me with forensics. It was starting to set the last time I saw it,' he continued.

A short breeze of laughter stirred around the room.

The laughter diluted to another silence as the Inspector placed the drink on the table and then stood tall to face his audience.

'Right, time's moving on and I've got to be off in an hour or so to visit a few places and a few people back at Santille. So if I can quickly finish off the introduction and bring everyone up to date we can all be on our way.'

Reaching down to his desk and retrieving a lime green felt marker, he turned back to face the wall-mounted board.

'Right, where did we get to?'

The attentive eyes of his studious ensemble returned to the proliferation of information in front of them and watched as Harry quickly traced the route of his last commentary prior to the refreshment break.

A further half an hour or so of Inspector-led presentation continued before he finally placed his pens on the table in front of him and looked up at his team, seated in a concave formation before him. "That's it in a rather big nut-shell. Now's the time for us to fill in the gaps,' he said, as he turned to his side and glancing back at the board, described a wide circle of air with his hand around the carnival explosion of colour.

'No gaps to fill in, sir, unless you get busy with that duster,' interrupted Nicki.

Her colleagues laughed. 'Yes, they'd pay a fortune for that at the Tate,' added Shaun.

The outburst of humorous accord increased a decibel or two as Harry spun round again to study his unconscious creation of modern art, though his closeness to the piece prevented the full appreciation of its *Pollock*-like appearance.

'Any questions at this stage?' he asked, spinning back to face his gaggle of art critics and looking invitingly along the seated line at Ami, Kevin, Nicki and Shaun, for any contribution.

'Do we know much more about the victim, guv? ... His background, for example?' enquired Nicki.

'Yes, we've covered a lot but not really touched too much on that side of things yet. Suppose now's as good a time as any,' replied Gateaux. 'We know he originates from the Winchester area. Seems his mother died when he was a teenager and he's lived with his father, on and off, ever since. The local constabulary over in Hampshire are digging around to find out more information for us. I am right in saying that, aren't I, Shaun?'

The sergeant sat up smartly in his seat.

'Er ... Yes, that is correct, sir. I've been in contact with Inspector Scally at Winchester CID both yesterday afternoon and this morning. In fact, we sent an e-mail photograph of the victim across to them last night. Apparently the lad's father has since confirmed it was indeed his son, not that there has been much doubt locally as to the victim's identity.'

'And he's flying out today to make the formal identification?'

'Yes, guv. We've a car on stand-by to pick him up from the airport. He'll be on the mid-day flight from Southampton and is due to return to the mainland sometime on Saturday morning.'

'And you've booked Mr Price senior in at the Hotel Amadeus, as agreed, have you?'

Shaun nodded.

'The Amadeus is on the other side of town, isn't it, sir?' enquired Nicki.

'Yes. We thought it would be better to try and maintain the father's anonymity by keeping him away from the Coburg Hotel. It also avoids him being pestered by too many sympathisers, however good their intentions might be,' continued Gateaux, explaining the logic behind the decision to the others.

'If you have any questions for him, please direct them through myself. I don't want him feeling too pressured by an endless stream of inquisitive visitors, official or otherwise, okay?'

The four seated in front of him nodded in unison.

'You mentioned, guv, during the discussion earlier that the victim had a passion for archaeology and computers?' remarked Nicki.

'Yes, I've spoken at length to the tour guide, Mel, who knew Andy Price as a familiar face at the hotel. Seems he was a bit of an egghead when it came to archaeology, a particular fascination of his. Appears also that he had an equal fascination, if not more so, for computers. A "techno nerd of the first degree" was how Mel put it. Seems to have been well suited to his title,"Anorak Andy", bearing in mind his apparently obsessive nature with the two subjects. As I said earlier, as a person everything at present suggests that he was a bit of a loner.'

The Inspector paused and took a quick sip from his mug of tea.

'What isn't in doubt is that he has been an annual visitor to the hotel for a number of years and, incredibly, has attended at least one of their archaeological tours each year over the course of the last six. The hotel's records confirm that.'

'Now, that's what I call enthusiasm,' said Kevin.

'Indeed,' replied Harry. 'Archaeology aside though, we also understand, as I've already touched on, that he had worked for a short period in the Islands at some point in the past. Some type of specialist computer related work for one of the offshore trust banks,' he continued.

'Do we know which bank exactly?' enquired Ami.

'No, not at this stage. That's something we'll need to follow up on very soon.'

Harry paused as his colleagues before him scribbled feverishly in their notebooks.

'Any other questions?'

'Yes, I have another,' said Ami keenly, raising her hand as she spoke to accept the Inspector's invitation for contributions.

'You've talked about some possible connection between the current building works at the hotel and the ransacking of the victim's room that is believed to have occurred sometime early afternoon yesterday.'

'Yes, that's correct. Glad to hear somebody else was listening. It's just one of many leads we're pursuing. Shaun, perhaps you can fill us in on that as well?'

'Yes, guv. The room that was occupied by our victim backs on to the site of a large new two-storey annex which is currently being built as an additional accommodation wing at the back of the Coburg. We noted during our look around his room yesterday that the access scaffolding to the site runs straight past its rear elevation window.'

'So that was a possible route of entry for any intruder?' enquired Ami further.

'Yes, or exit if indeed there was an intruder,' said Gateaux.

'How do you mean, guv, no intruder?' enquired Nicki, a slightly bemused expression bathed across her face.

'Well it has to be considered that the ransacking may have been self-inflicted, for whatever reason. We have to remember that the main door to the room was open when we arrived, as was the window at the back. Forensics have since told us that there appears to have been no forced entry at either,' replied the Inspector.

Nicki nodded.

'Still on the building theme, sir,' said Nicki. 'You mentioned this morning that during one of the victim's previous visits a couple of years back, he became embroiled in some form of complaint with the same firm of building contractors who are working on the hotel right now … A complaint that may have cost one of the labourers his job.'

'Yes, that's quite right. We believe the incident happened a couple of years or so ago during a contract to clean the external façade of the hotel. Seems that particular contract was a totally unrelated one to the building construction that is on going at present. We've already asked the hotel to search out as much detail on that particular incident as they can find.'

'Okay, guv,' said Nicki as she continued to jot the essential details in her book.

'Did you have any luck in speaking to the foreman at the current site, Shaun?' enquired Harry, looking across in expectation towards his sergeant.

There was a short hiatus as the sergeant completed the final compilation of notes in his own book.

'Not exactly, sir, but I've got a name. They call him Sumo, apparently, on account of his size. Not only is he the foreman though, it seems he owns the company as well. I've arranged to see him later. He wasn't on site yesterday afternoon when I called.'

'Well if our man Sumo's as big as his name suggests, mind you don't upset him when you find him.'

The others laughed as they began to visualise for themselves the forthcoming David and Goliath tête-à-tête.

'Right, folks. If we're all finished, I think it's time for some action?' said Harry.

The room fell silent for a brief moment.

'Nicki and Kevin,' called Gateaux, looking directly at the couple.

The two looked up.

'We know the victim had a broken neck and a bruise to the side of his face. Forensics have now told us that they found several small flakes of blue painted rusty steel in his hair close

151

to the impact point on his face and several flakes down the back of his shirt. They also found a fair amount of sand on his clothes.'

'So a blow with something metallic or a fall onto something metallic?' suggested Nicki.

'Yes, forensics are putting their early money on a fall. They've already carried out a test on the sand type and have pinpointed its probable origin to a location somewhere along our south coast area. So the first thing I want from you two is to organise a detailed survey of anything you might think relevent on the beaches along the south coast bays. Probably best if we start close to the hotel and then move out around St Aubin's Bay. I've already arranged with downstairs for you to borrow some of their bods to help. Anything that can stick to a magnet, I want to know about, whether it's a drawing pin or a boat. All right?'

'Is it worth reminding everyone about the air display today, guv,' interrupted Kevin.

'Yes, good point,' said Harry nodding feverishly.

'Now, in about three or so hours time, the Bay is going to start filling with spectators, so that's all the more reason to begin with St Aubin's Bay first.'

'Anyone know what time high tide is?' enquired Kevin.

'I believe it's around mid-afternoon?' suggested Shaun.

The Inspector paused and raised his arm to look at his watch. 'In that case, it looks like it's your lucky day then, the two of you,' he said. 'Seems that you've a few hours before you get your feet wet,' he continued, looking first at Nicki and then Kevin.

The walls of the room again splashed with laughter.

'Actually, the tide issue raises an interesting point,' added Harry. 'I suppose we've probably had at least one high water already since the incident yesterday so it's highly likely that the area we are looking for has been disturbed or washed completely. You had better speak with Harbours sometime and get from them as much data as you can on the pattern of tides of recent days. It might be useful?'

'Yes, sir,' replied Kevin.

'The main focus initially though is to find that blue painted metal object. And if it is in the Bay we must try and locate it before the Biggles gang arrive,' said the Inspector, in reference to the impending aeronautical extravaganza. 'Otherwise you'll not see the sand for sky-watchers or rising water.'

'Yes, understood, guv,' said Nicki nodding.

'Anyway, after you've both finished down at the beach come back here and, if you've any time left, begin compiling a dossier on Andrew Price. We should be able to add to anything you find, or tidy any loose ends, when I speak with his father either later today or tomorrow. Might be useful if you liase with Shaun sometime and get the contact details for our Inspector Scally over at Winchester. Also, speak with Social Security and try and find out some employment history. Is that okay?'

'Yes, no problem,' replied Kevin.

'Who're going to be busy bees then?' whispered Shaun as he looked across the seated arc to his right.

'Sorry, what was that?' enquired Harry.

'Nothing,' replied the sergeant as the cheeky grin that had accompanied the comment suddenly disappeared with a quick sweep of his hand across the face.

'Glad to hear it. While I've got your attention though, Shaun.'

'Yes, guv?'

'Can you continue speaking with people back at the Coburg and while there try and catch up with this Sumo character over at the building site. Also, track down Lucy and see how she and the hotel are progressing with that search for those records on the cleaning contract of a couple of years ago. They promised they'd call with some details but I've heard nothing yet.'

'That should keep me out of trouble.'

'Another "busy bee" around the hive I trust?' said Gateaux as he homed in upon the whispered taunts he had caught earlier between his colleagues. 'Okay, that just leaves Miss Jeune to sort out.'

Ami looked up nervously.

'If you'd like to tag along with me for the afternoon we'll pop over to Santille. I'll quickly show you the scene of crime and then I've a chat to finish off with a couple of local residents there that I began yesterday. Following that, there are a couple of farms close by to visit. Should be a lot easier with the two of us.'

'Okay, sir.'

'If it's all right with you we'll grab a bite of lunch while we're out.'

'Yes, that's not a problem with me.'

Gateaux raised his arm and looked at his watch. 'Time to move out, guys. We've spent enough time cooped up in here,' he said, as he reached down and grabbed a tightly rolled plastic carrier bag on the floor just to his side. 'I suggest we all meet up here again later today at around, say, four thirty. If any of you find anything remotely useful in the meantime let me know straight away. I'll have my mobile with me. You all know the number.'

As he stood he looked across at Ami. 'I'm just off to jump into my cycle gear.'

As he spoke, he waved the carrier bag in the air. 'Should only be a few moments. I'll meet you outside in the compound in a short while,' he added, as he began to make his way towards the door.

'Hope you've brought your cycle clips, girl,' interrupted Kevin.

Unfamiliar with the cycling eccentricities of her new boss, Ami's face paled instantly. As a light chorus of laughter filled the room the teasing banter of repartee continued in its shadow.

'Didn't anyone warn you that if you go out with the Inspector on a visit you have to sit on the handle bars,' said Shaun.

'Yeah, just keep your legs free of the spokes and you'll be all right,' added Kevin.

As the laughter intensified from the vocals of Shaun and Kevin, so in direct proportion did the continued retreating of colour from the new recruit's face, together with the paralleled body language of unease.

With the paled expression turning to one of increasing lifelessness Nicki stepped across in front of Shaun and gave Ami a gentle pat on her back.

Ami flinched, as if startled, before swivelling her head to face her colleague.

'Don't listen to that bunch of wasters. They're only messing about. Just ignore them. They shouldn't have been let out of nursery at such a young mental age.'

At the sudden realization that her employment conditions did not require her to engage in a bicycle circus act, an expression of relief returned instantly to Ami's face, boomeranging the temporarily mislaid colour rapidly back into her cheeks.

With normal service of apparent harmony suitably resumed the five, led by Harry, left the room to begin each of their allotted duties. Once through the meeting room door they funnelled their way along the corridor, eventually reaching the open foyer area.

Like the Red Arrows that would light up the sky later in the day the quintet fanned off in four diametrically opposite directions, Gateaux to the locker room, Ami to the compound and Kevin and Nicki for a session of beach combing, leaving the lone figure of Shaun to make the short walk back to the Coburg to continue his investigations.

Within minutes of leaving the foyer area the Inspector reappeared in the asphalted compound at the rear of the building, his chameleon-like change having been completed from casual blue shirt and tie to the more sporty attire of his trademark black tracksuit and red cycle helmet.

Ami, her head propped by her arm against the roof edge of a small white patrol car, looked up and watched as Gateaux vaulted monkey fashion over a yellow painted handrail that fringed the rear door, so by-passing the three steps down to road level.

He landed feet together beside the waiting Ami. 'Hi, won't be a second,' he said as he completed his theatrics by trotting past the bewildered looking young recruit and across the heavily patched up surface of the compound to a flimsy tin clad lean-to opposite in which his treasured bike was stored.

In a party piece display, well-rehearsed on many a previous occasion, he quickly lifted the bike up by its frame, spun it around with one finger and then pushed it forward in the same flowing motion.

'Pay a lot at Covent Garden to see that, Harry,' shouted a voice from the far end of the yard.

The Inspector turned to search out the mysterious heckler.

'Oh, hi, Danny,' he replied, waving across to his station colleague.

'You'll need to do more than that to impress the girls,' added the man before disappearing quickly from sight round to the front of the station.

Gateaux turned back towards Ami.

Instantly she ducked her head a notch and rubbed her hand across her face in an effort to massage an imminent fit of giggles back into a facial form that resembled anything closer to stoic normality.

Normality in limbo, she looked up.

'Do you know the Santille site at all, Ami?'

'Well sort of, sir. Used to play there as a kid.'

'Good. How about if I meet you at the end of the lane that leads up to it, just before the road narrows in, say, about twenty minutes. Do you know where I mean?'

Ami nodded.

'Right. See you soon then,' said Gateaux as he leapt onto his bike and sped out of the ring-fenced compound.

His exit coincided with the arrival of Nicki at the threshold to the rear door. Having descended the steps she skipped across to her colleague's patrol car and leaned forward to look in through the open window.

'Good luck, girl.'

Ami, busily engaged in adjusting the seat, looked across.

'Yes, thanks. So what's with the Inspector and all this cycle stuff?'

'Oh, don't worry about "Cyco",' replied Nicki. 'He's okay, just a bit of a fitness freak, that's all. You'll probably pass him along the road. Just look out for a mountain bike rider, pedalling like a maniac, with a flashing blue light strapped on his head.'

Ami laughed.

Good wishes delivered, Nicki stood back and lifted her hand to wave as her new associate manoeuvred the vehicle carefully from its space and departed the compound gates in pursuit of the Inspector.

Meanwhile, back at the hotel, Shaun had just completed his speedy return.

'Hi again, Lucy,' he announced as he was ushered through the main entrance door by the doorman into the quiet reception area beyond.

'Oh, hi Shaun. Back for the second half are you?'

'Yes, something like that. Tell you what though, if the Inspector has his way, I'll soon have to re-direct my mail here.'

Lucy chuckled.

'Anyway, glad I caught you,' continued the sergeant.

'Oh, I shouldn't worry about not finding me here. I'm turning into part of the furniture as well.'

Shaun grinned.

'I understand that Inspector Gateaux spoke to you yesterday about searching out some hotel records? They related to an incident involving the dismissal of a builder's labourer a few years ago while our victim was a guest here. Any chance you've tracked anything down yet?'

Immediately, Lucy disappeared behind her desk. She reappeared seconds later with a buff coloured file marked *Coburg Facade Cleaning 1998 - Internal file*. 'I had a quick look through this as soon as I found it,' she said, handing the file across the desk into the expectant hands of the sergeant. 'There's a note in there registering the complaint from a guest, one Andrew Price, back in 1998.'

'Fantastic. I'll read it for myself in a while but what seems to have been the nature of the complaint exactly?'

'I've not read much of it but it appears that Mr Price had a little altercation with one of the builders involved at the time in the external façade cleaning. Seems he complained that they were creating too much dust that he felt was a risk to his computer. The problem seemed to just escalate from there really.'

'Do we know why he had the computer with him?'

Lucy paused before replying.

'I think the answer to that one is eccentricity. Seems he was never without his box of tricks when he visited this place. I don't know what he used it for and as far as I know no one ever asked him.'

She hesitated again.

'Some follow up notes I've read seem to suggest that the argument about the dust became a bit personal. Of course the hotel, in the interests of our guest's comfort, had no option but to intervene and sent a letter to the building contractors, Messrs Colcroft Construction,' she continued. 'Basically the letter insisted that their man, a Mr Alec Walsh, be removed from the site. There's a copy of that letter in the file,' she added, pointing as she spoke towards the folder that was now held in a vice-like grip in the sergeant's left hand.

'And that communication was the trigger for the man to be dismissed from the site?' enquired Shaun.

'Yes, we have a letter to that effect from the builder. But more than that, they continued in the same correspondence to say that Colcroft Construction considered Alec Walsh's future with them to be totally untenable so they had dismissed the guy altogether. The hotel subsequently praised the contractor for their prompt and professional response to a difficult situation for both parties and the issue, it seems, was then forgotten. As far as I know the Hotel Group has always had a good working relationship with Colcrofts and I guess they didn't want to spoil that in the interests of present and future work with us.'

'You've more expansion plans then, have you?'

'Oh yes, never ending. The hotel's part of a very large development consortium, you see. There are some fairly ambitious proposals in the pipeline, particularly for the Waterfront area and further afield, over at Gorey.'

'Sounds exciting?'

'Oh, it's all very exciting. But the detail's all a bit hush-hush at present. So it's a case of watch this space, I'm afraid, sir.'

'Okay, I won't pry any longer. Guess it's just instinct with me. And please, just call me Shaun.'

Lucy smiled.

'Is there any problem if I borrow this for the rest of the day?' continued the sergeant, raising the document folder and placing it back on to the reception desk. 'I'll photocopy any relevant extracts and return it in the morning, if that's all right?'

'Have it as long as you need, Shaun.'

"Cheers."

'Anything else at all?' she enquired, a sense of urgency creeping in to her invitation. 'It's just that I've got a few important chores to get sorted.'

'Of course. Sorry to keep you ... I'll let you get along. It's not as if I've not got a lot to get on with myself. Just one thing. I was hoping to do a walk of the hotel later and see if anyone had any useful information to add to our inquiry. Would that be in order, Lucy?'

'Yes, that's fine by me, Shaun. As you might expect, the hotel has now informed all staff and guests of the current situation. The feedback has been very encouraging. Seems everyone's keen to co-operate in any way they can.'

'Great. Thanks for doing that, Lucy. Should make our task a little easier. I'll see you later then?'

'Look forward to it.'

Suddenly, the reception phone rang out.

'Hotel Coburg. Lucy speaking, can I help you?'

As she listened attentively to the caller's inquiry she looked up towards the tall figure of Shaun and silently mouthed the words "could be a long time".'

Lip reading translated, the sergeant exchanged a silent wave of farewell and then retreated in the direction of the main lounge for a quick résumé of the file's contents prior to his next engagement on the adjacent building site.

Ensconced within the mid-morning solitude of the empty lounge, Shaun sat himself comfortably and began thumbing his way slowly through the folder's randomly assembled contents, pausing just occasionally to highlight a page or point of relevance with a fluorescent orange sticker. Exercise complete, he laid the file carefully on top of a number of other documents in his case before closing the cover, snapping the locking catches securely shut and then standing to make his way back along the wide and lavishly decorated corridor towards the main entrance foyer.

'Morning again, sir,' said the doorman.

'And a very good morning to you as well. Perhaps an introduction is a bit overdue,' replied Shaun. 'Sergeant Carac, St Helier police,' he continued as he extended his arm and shook the man by the hand.

'Joseph Masters is the name but most people just call me Joe. Pleased to make your acquaintance. You're not looking for a bike minder as well, are you sergeant?'

'Oh, so you've met my boss, I take it?'

'Yes, nice chap. He popped by yesterday. Not for me to say, perhaps, but he seems a sandwich short of a picnic on that bike of his.'

'He's not short of any sandwiches right now,' said Shaun as

he conjured a mental picture of the Inspector bursting at every seam, courtesy of Eva and Pierre's foil wrapped hamper. 'Tell me Joe, what's the quickest way round to the site office from here?'

'For the annex extension?'

The sergeant nodded. 'It's just that I used the back entrance yesterday, you see, but it was a bit of a trek.'

'Oh, there's a much easier route,' said Masters as he beckoned the sergeant through the main door and began descending the granite steps. 'See that white hoarding there?' he added as he stopped half way down the staircase and pointed towards the left hand side of the building.

Shaun took a few careful paces across in front of the doorman to improve his view from their elevated position.

'Oh yes.'

'Well, if you just follow along there you'll soon come across a green gate flanked by a couple of skips, one white, one blue. One is normally full of site junk and the other is full of sand. The site hut is just inside the gate.'

'Great, thanks for your help,' replied Shaun before twisting his body slightly and continuing the final few steps down to pavement level.

The short orienteering course safely negotiated, the sergeant paused for a moment to read the heavily soiled and concrete splattered sign on the front of the green gate.

COLCROFT CONSTRUCTION LTD.
ALL VISITORS MUST REPORT TO SITE OFFICE

With a gram of effort and a kilo of trepidation, he leaned upon the ill fitting and dilapidated swing gate and entered the site. As he did so, a man dressed in a day-glow yellow jacket, white coloured plastic hat and mud encrusted black boots emerged from the nearest of a terrace of three rather shabby looking prefabricated site huts.

The man looked across to the arriving suit clad figure.

'Excuse me,' said Shaun. 'Is Sumo anywhere around today?'

'Yeah, he's in that office, mate,' said the labourer in a hard monotone, turning as he spoke to point to the adjacent hut.

'Cheers,' replied the sergeant as he walked forward, climbed the four creaking timber planked steps and knocked on the door.

'Entré,' shouted a deep gruff voice from inside.

The same nervous twinge that had accompanied his entrance to the site returned for a moment as he wrapped his hand around the gnarled aluminium door handle and turned it.

Inside the room he found himself at the head of a long table, covered completely in a thick tablecloth of drawings around which sat three men.

The trio looked up and stared as one at the pinstriped entrant in the doorway.

'Any of you called Sumo by any chance?' enquired Shaun with a calculated dose of diplomacy as his eyes looked around the table at two of the men with the combined fat excesses of a beanpole and the third who looked as though any safe exit from the hut would require the building's wholesale demolition.

The two beanpoles looked across to the top end of the table where sat the third man, of planetary proportions, sporting a wrap around black beard, thick wiry hair, and the general demeanour of one who had just swung in from a pirate ship.

'Guess it must be me?' said the giant as he looked sideways at each of his two seated colleagues.

His two sidekicks laughed.

'If you're flogging double glazing, I've already got some,' he continued as he raised a cigarette from an ashtray on the table and took a quick puff.

Shaun looked on impassively. 'Sergeant Carac from St Helier CID,' he announced, reaching across and flashing his identity card in a rhombic circuit to each of the men in turn through a light haze of cigarette smoke before returning it to his top pocket. 'Any chance of a word in private?'

'And which word would that be?' enquired Sumo, to a further accompaniment of the increasingly irritating vocal display of amusement from his slender compatriots.

Shaun weathered the storm of comedy for a few seconds before speaking.

'Some time … Please … Today,' he continued, as his patience began nudging rapidly towards the "wearing thin" zone.

'Right, you two out,' said Sumo as he looked uncompromisingly towards the two plaster covered stick insects.

The men jumped instantly to their feet and made their way from the room, each looking at the snappily dressed intruder intently from close range as they brushed past him. The door slammed shut.

'So what's the problem then, pal?' enquired Sumo.

Shaun pulled up a seat, brushed the veneer of dust quickly from its top with the palm of his hand and sat down.

'I understand you're the owner of Colcroft Construction?'

'Yeah, that's right. So what's the interest? You want to buy some shares in the company or something?'

'Not quite. I presume that you are aware one of the hotel's guests was found dead yesterday?'

'Yeah, news travels faster than light around here. So what's it got to do with me?'

'Well, nothing, I hope, but we're just trying to gather together any information that we can that might assist with our inquiries.'

'Okay, so what do you want to know, but you'll have to make it snappy. I've a big concrete pour to supervise in five minutes or so,' said the big man, a slight agitation knotted within his response.

Shaun explained the sequence of events leading to the discovery of the body the day before and then reached inside his jacket pocket to produce a small photograph.

'This is our victim, a guy called Andrew Price,' he said, reaching forward and holding the photo in front of Sumo's rotund and bristle filled face.

'Ugly young geezer ain't he?'

Shaun remained unmoved.

'Never seen him before in my life. What did you say his name was again?'

'Andrew Price.'

'Nope, still doesn't mean anything to me.'

'Do you mind if I ask your men around the site if they know of him?'

'Ask em what you like but I'd change out of that suit first into something a bit more dirt-proof. And you'll need some boots and a hat as well. You can have any of those bits if they fit,' replied Sumo, pointing to a jumbled assembly of mud-ravaged clothing under a nearby desk. 'Don't worry, they're all designer labels. I picked them up from a recent Paris show,' he sneered.

Ignoring the cheap jibes, Shaun rolled forward in his chair for a closer inspection of the mismatch of rags. As he did, the door to the hut suddenly flew open and a young lad popped his head inside the room.

'Concrete's here, boss,' he shouted before retracting his head back like a turtle and slamming the door shut behind him.

'Right, that's me gone,' said Sumo. He pushed himself away from the table and stood up.

Shaun immediately sat upright and reached out to brace the table and its cargo of drawings as it took an unerring leap to one side of the room.

'Got to go, mate. Nice speaking with you and all that,' announced the foreman as he donned his blue coloured site hat and made his way to the door.

'Before you go,' said Shaun. 'Do you recall a contract here in 1998 to clean the façade walls?' he continued as he, too, rose to his feet and took a step backwards to stand at one side of the door.

'Should I?'

'Well, I only ask because the hotel records say that it was your company who carried out the contract.'

'Well, why ask me then?' replied Sumo, an air of defiance in his hurried response.

'I ask because there appears to have been an argument at the time between a hotel guest and one of your men, a Mr Alec Walsh. Can you remember the incident?'

'Who the hell do you think I am, Brain of Britain? 1998 is a long time ago, you know, kid,' replied the foreman as he turned to look out of the site hut window.

'Look, I've got to go otherwise I'll be charging the police force a few grand for some knackered concrete,' he continued, a heavy hint of foreboding salivating in his voice.

Shaun took a further step to his side as the imposing figure of Long John Silver's brother, minus the parrot, bulldozed past and reached for the door handle before making his way outside.

The sergeant followed. 'I'll call by again later then. Maybe have another chat and perhaps speak with some of your lads,' he cried as his words chased the disappearing figure of Goliath.

'Look forward to it,' said Sumo dismissively as he vanished into the dust-shrouded jungle of the building site.

Shaun turned and made his way back to the hotel.

'Did you find the boss man on the site then, sir?' enquired Joe as the sergeant re-entered the reception area.

'Yeah, could hardly miss him really. Was he the reason for the eclipse over here in '99?'

'Yes, he's a bit on the large side, isn't he?'

'A bit abrasive with it as well.'

'You're not wrong there, sergeant. I should have given you some advance warning but I just assumed that you might have bumped into him yesterday when you visited the site in the afternoon?'

Shaun paused for a moment, as he considered the likely source of Joe's apparent knowledge of his previous day's movements.

'Yes, I did visit the building site yesterday but the foreman wasn't there,' he said. 'Though I've met him now, for my sins.

That aside, you seem very well informed on my whereabouts, Joe?'

'Err … Yes … Quite an efficient grapevine around these parts,' replied Masters, an apparent air of hesitancy clear in his response.

'Obviously,'

The doorman smiled nervously.

'Right, Joe. Time to move on, I guess. Lots still to do. While I am here though, is there any chance you've got a few moments to run through your account of events yesterday or indeed anything from the past that you think may be relevant perhaps?'

'Er … I'd like to help you, but I'm waiting for a coach load of new guests from the airport just now,' replied Masters, the same nervous hesitancy still echoing in his voice. 'They are overdue already. Maybe later sometime, sergeant?'

'Okay, so how about if I pop back when I've finished walking the corridors upstairs then,' suggested Shaun.

Joe nodded but said nothing.

One hour and two circuits of the hotel's five star corridors later, the sergeant found himself back in the reception area.

'You'll wear your shoes out if you are not careful,' said Joe.

'Yes, think you're right. I'll have to get one of those golf buggy things.'

As Shaun completed his response the mobile phone in his jacket pocket sang out. 'Excuse me,' he said.

He turned and began walking slowly towards the corridor.

'Hello, Carak speaking.'

'Shaun, its Gateaux. How are you getting on?'

'Hello, guv. Not too bad. Lucy dug out the file on the '98 contract. Contains some interesting notes on the incident with our victim. I've spoken briefly with the construction company next door but I'll need to pay them another visit later. Just caught them at the wrong time, that's all.'

'So what are you up to at the moment, sergeant?'

'Well, I'm in the middle of a hotel walkabout, sir, quizzing a few staff and guests. Nothing much to report yet. Having said that, there are still plenty of people left to speak to. I'm just having a little breather and speaking in reception with Joe.'

'Joe, who's Joe?'

'The doorman, sir. He seems to know you … And your bike.'

'Yes of course,' replied Harry. 'So, is the hotel busy at the moment?'

'To be quite honest, guv, it's a little on the quiet side in here. I think there's been a mass exodus for the air display.'

'Okay, well, just keep plugging away. Ami and myself have finished over here at Santille and we'll soon be on our way back to town. I'll send her across to give you some assistance if you need it.'

'Sure. More the merrier. And it'll save my calves from exploding. Are you returning to the hotel with Ami as well?' said Shaun.

'No I'm off down to the beach,' replied Harry, a splinter of excitement edging into his response. 'Nicki has just phoned. It seems they may have found our mystery object.'

'Fantastic … What is it?' enquired the sergeant keenly as he shared in the thrill of the discovery.

'Apparently it's a steel box containing deckchairs. It was found just below the sea wall about five hundred metres along the beach from the front of the Coburg. I understand that Jeff and Nick are on their way down there now to have a closer look.'

'I presume it's busy down in the bay, sir?'

'Yes, apparently so. Kevin's just phoned me, in fact. Seems they've got half the public looking in the air at the aircraft whizzing over and the other half staring at the steel box which our people are gathered around.'

'Sounds infinitely more productive than walking around here, guv?'

'Maybe but we don't know for sure that the box is the object we're searching for yet, sergeant, do we? Carry on with what you're doing for the moment. Ami will be with you shortly and don't forget, we're all meeting up again at four so you've only an hour or so to go.'

'Okay, see you later,' replied Shaun, a detectable sign of despondency clouding his response. Having returned to the entrance door, he was just about to speak to Joe when the hotel shook to the violent roar of jet engines overhead.

'What the hell was that?' he cried, a panicked glaze filling his eyes as he crouched in an effort to get an upward view through the entrance windows.

'Think it may be the Sukhoi Flanker, that Russian Jet,' replied Masters calmly. 'Quite an impressive piece of kit, isn't it? You'll have to get one for that mad boss of yours. It's nearly as quick as his bike,' he added, laughing.

'Must say, I'm impressed with your aircraft knowledge, Joe.'

'A requirement of the job on days like this, Shaun. The guests are asking for information all the time. Yesterday Lucy gave me the show's programme to memorise, so I'm in trouble if I don't know the answer myself to any question. As it happens though, I'm a bit of an aeroplane enthusiast anyway, which helps.'

'Yes, I'm sure it does. Incidentally, are you still waiting for that coach?' enquired Shaun.

Masters nodded. "Still no sign of it. I've now been told that the plane's delayed for two hours. Nothing to do with the show. Technical problems at Birmingham apparently, whatever that means.'

'So could you spare me a few minutes now, then, for our little chat?'

The doorman paused for a moment's thought.

'Er … Yes, I suppose I can just now. But I'll have to interrupt you if any guests need me.'

'Of course,' replied the sergeant. 'Might as well go outside in the sun and catch a bit of the display while we're talking,' he added.

'Fine by me,' said Masters enthusiastically, as he ushered the sergeant out through the main door and onto the small granite terrace at the top of the staircase.

'I take it you're aware of yesterday morning's events at Santille?' enquired Shaun.

'Yes, absolutely tragic for everyone involved.'

The sergeant pulled out the photograph of the victim from his jacket pocket and flashed it in front of Joe's face.

'So it was that lad, was it? The poor blighter.'

'Yes. His name is Andrew Price. You remember him as a guest, do you?'

'Yes, sergeant but I don't know much about him. I do recall seeing him around the hotel though. He's been quite a frequent visitor over the course of the few years I've worked here but he wasn't exactly what you would call talkative.'

'Did you see him about yesterday morning at all?'

As Joe paused to consider his movements of the previous day his face visibly began to pale as an apparent expression of anxiousness began to erode further his earlier air of confidence.

'Are you okay?' asked Shaun.

'Er, yes, I'm fine,' he replied, as he tried, rather unconvincingly, to regain a composure which it seemed had once again eluded him momentarily.

'I was just asking if you recollected seeing Andrew Price around the hotel early yesterday morning,' repeated the sergeant.

'Yesterday … Er, yes, of course. No, sorry, I mean no. I didn't see him because I took part of the morning off … Didn't arrive here until just after 10 am,' replied Masters as he fumbled his way through the response. He hesitated again and took a short and conspicuous deep inhalation of air.

Shaun waited until the aerobic exercises had ceased. 'Get up to anything interesting during your time off then?' he enquired probing the reason for the doorman's absence from duty.

'Er … Er, yes, I spent the first half of the morning up at the airport … Watching some of the early arrivals for today's display. You get quite a few of them coming over a day early, you see.'

'And after that you came straight back here to work?'

'Yes, that's right, sergeant. Straight back to work.'

'I guess the world of aviation offers an interesting hobby if you enjoy that sort of thing,' said Shaun. 'I must confess that the only plane I know is the Spitfire,' he continued, as he conceded his limited knowledge of aircraft recognition, which started and ended with the historic World War Two fighter plane.

'Oh, they're all fascinating machines. Coincidentally, my favourite happens to be the Spitfire,' replied Masters, a child-like enthusiasm propelling through his voice.

'Actually, now I think about it, Joe I'm sure I saw a Spitfire parked on the grass at the airport yesterday when I drove past? I assume you saw it there too? You must have got a real buzz, particularly with it being your favourite plane.'

Masters paused again, this time longer, before responding.

'Er … Yes … It was good to see it again yesterday morning,' he replied, the account oddly seeming to lack the fervour of one claiming to be an ardent follower of one of aviation's masterpieces.

'So why aren't you out there today joining in the fun?'

'What, with a grandstand position up here?' replied Joe as he raised his head skywards and swept his arms across the kerosene scarred sky in a wide arc. 'And they're paying me at the same time. Best of both worlds really.'

'Yes, I suppose you've got a point there,' said Shaun, smiling. 'If we can just return to the events of yesterday.'

'Yes of course.'

'While you were up at the airport do you know who covered for you here at the hotel?'

'Er … No one in particular as far as I'm aware. I think Mel and Lucy simply shared the duties as best they could though

Mel of course would have been busy also with the tour group from early morning onwards. Think they call that sort of thing, these days, "multi-tasking", don't they?'

'Oh, don't start me off with all that ridiculous management jargon,' said Shaun. 'The people who make up those phrases need to get out a bit more,' he continued.

The doorman, his face still pained with an apparent taint of unease, nodded in agreement.

'Any more to tell us then, Joe?'

'Not really. As I said, the lad was a fairly frequent visitor and he just seemed happy in his own little world.'

Suddenly Shaun flinched for a second time as another unannounced explosion of noise filled the air and bounced around the natural amphitheatre of the bay.

'It's all right, sir. It's one of ours, a Tornado F3.'

The two looked skywards once more as the new arrival performed its aerial ballet.

As quickly as the grey blur had appeared so it was gone, together with the last pulsating echoes of its all-shattering power.

As the skies recovered from their trauma, Shaun relaxed his head from its elevated perch to find the figure of his colleague, Ami, standing beside him.

'Where on earth did you come from?' he enquired with the surprise of one who had just witnessed a rabbit being plucked from a magician's hat.

'Oh, I crept up the steps while you were looking across at that plane. The Inspector said you might need some help.'

'Yes, he said he was sending you over here. Quick, let's get inside before our ear drums get beaten up again.'

He turned to Masters whose eyes remained locked on the heavens.

'We're off now, Joe. Thanks for your time.'

'Whenever,' replied the doorman, his head still raised in mouth watering anticipation of the next morsel from the feast of flying around the bay.

171

Shaun and Ami made their way quickly back inside the hotel just as the momentary peace became disturbed by the distant sound of another approaching aircraft.

'How's your hotel walkabout going then?' enquired Ami.

'Well, I've covered ground and first floor, just third and fourth floors to go. All I've been doing is simply knocking on room doors and presenting a photograph of our victim in the hope that someone might have known him or seen him around the hotel. That said, it's not exactly been Piccadilly Circus around here this afternoon. I'm convinced I would have had more success searching for people to interview on the Mary Celeste.'

'It's been that bad, has it, Shaun. Sounds like one of those days when you'd rather watch paint dry?'

The sergeant hesitated, scratched his head vigorously and then began to take a few paces around the foyer.

'You okay? I can hear your brain ticking from here. What's on your mind?' enquired Ami as she watched a few contorted spasms begin to twitch across the sergeant's face accompanied by a frenetic few seconds of chin scratching.

'Something you just mentioned, actually Ami. Paint … Skip. Yes, paint, skip,' shouted Shaun excitedly.

'Sorry?' enquired a bemused Ami.

'You'll find out in a few moments,' said the sergeant.

He stepped smartly past his colleague and leapt quickly across to the reception desk.

'Lucy, can I quickly borrow the phone please, it's extremely urgent?'

'Yes of course you can. Use the one in my room. It's a bit more private,' she replied, motioning the two around behind the reception counter and pointing towards her office door.

Shaun dashed forward, dived for the phone and began dialling.

'Hi, guv. It's Shaun at the hotel.'

'Hi. What's up?'

'That blue metallic box and the sand.'

'Yes, what about it?'

'What's the latest thinking on it, sir?'

'Well, forensics have taken numerous bagged samples of paint and sand away for testing. I'm actually standing beside the box at this moment, and it does appear to bear all the hallmarks of our mystery object. Why do you ask?'

'Well, something Ami said has just reminded me that there's a blue painted skip on the building site next door which I've just visited, and guess what? It's filled with sand,' replied Shaun, his tone of voice rising with each word as the fever of anticipation continued to flow through his veins.

'Has the skip got any dents on it?' enquired Harry.

'Dents,' replied the sergeant. 'I think it's had a herd of elephants fall on it at some point in its life?'

'Okay, wait there, Shaun and I'll phone Jeff. He's only just this minute left. Can we meet you in the hotel? I reckon we'll be there around four thirty.'

'Fine by me, guv. We're not going anywhere.'

'Ironic, really, isn't it?'

'Ironic, sir?'

'Yes, our infamous metallic objects. It's a bit like that old saying: you wait for one bus to turn up and then two arrive at the same time.'

'What buses, guv?'

'For buses, read box and skip, sergeant,' came a shout down the phone.

'Oh yes, sir, very good … So what do you want to do about our group meeting later?'

A silence filled the line for a few seconds.

'Um … Yes, it's getting a bit tight on time, isn't it?' replied Gateaux, as the verbal interlude was suddenly broken. I've still got to visit the victim's father at the Hotel Amadeus. There're a few things I'd like to ask him.'

'Has Mr Price made the formal identification of his son's body yet, guv?'

173

'Yes, he did that as soon as he arrived earlier this afternoon. I'll see how he's bearing up after I've visited the building site. But as far as our internal meeting is concerned, I suggest we cancel it for now. Can you let everyone know? Rearrange another gathering for 9am prompt back in room four tomorrow morning.'

'Understood, sir.'

'I'll catch you later then, sergeant.'

'Thanks for the use of the phone, Lucy,' called out Shaun as he placed the receiver down.

'Okay,' came a cry from the reception desk.

'So, do you think Andrew Price may have fallen on to the builders skip?' whispered Ami.

'Well, it's a possibility and certainly worth a look. We'll have to wait and see what forensics find when they call by later. The guv'nor said he would be here with them around four thirty.'

'Okay, so shall we make a start knocking on the rest of the doors then?'

Shaun nodded. 'If we take a level each?'

'Fine by me,' replied Ami. 'I'll take three if that's okay. Less stairs to climb,' she added with a cheeky giggle.

'Think I can live with that. Let's say we meet back here at around four and then dive into the lounge for a coffee. We can use the time before the boss arrives to compare notes.'

'Sounds great,' agreed Ami.

'Yes, I reckon a coffee's the least we deserve after our efforts today. Especially as the others are now down on the beach sunning themselves,' continued Shaun.

Ami laughed.

'Okay, I'll catch up with you soon then,' she said as she began her advance towards the staircase.

Suddenly Shaun called out.

'Oh and just one other thing before I forget.'

His colleague stopped and turned, allowing the sergeant to make up the few strides to meet her.

'You probably caught the gist of the conversation a second ago, but basically the guv's just said that as it's all getting a bit frantic this afternoon he's putting off our late afternoon get together until nine in the morning.'

Ami responded instantly with a smile that suggested relief.

'That works out quite well actually with me. I was hoping for a quick get away tonight as it happens.'

'Looks like your prayers have been answered,' said Shaun. 'Come on then. Let's get to work and earn that coffee,' he added as the two picked up the pace and headed for the main stair.

CHAPTER SEVEN

$\mathbb{W}$ith the industry of Thursday's investigations now events of the day before, the crime team assembled in room four and prepared for the imminent arrival of the Inspector and the start of his re-arranged briefing.

'Morning again, everybody,' announced Harry as he walked in through the open door allowing it, with a subtle nudge of his elbow, to swing back and close behind him.

'Morning, sir,' came the instant response from the assembled choir as they joggled in their seats towards a more attentive posture.

The quartet watched as Gateaux made his way quickly to the front, placed a large box file and a bundle of papers held together by a thick rubber band on the table and then turned away from them to face the presentation board.

With the room bathed in a monastic silence, Harry panned across the snakes and ladders image of coloured lines and scribbled text, now serving as an aide memoir to the previous day's discussions as he endeavoured to decipher the endless branches and sub-branches of information.

It seemed at first, from the apparent unease of his body language, that the multi-layered, multi-dimensional and very much multi-coloured product, despite being barely twenty four hours old and produced in the Inspector's own fair hand, had perhaps sub-consciously resulted in a mind puzzle that would have had Einstein or Pythagoras reaching for a stiff drink.

'Kind of like "groundhog day" isn't it, sir?' said Kevin.

'Yes, there's more than a slight hint of déjà vu, or at least there would be if we were all here,' replied the Inspector as he swivelled back to the front and focused in upon the one vacant chair of four beside Nicki.

'Anyone know where Shaun is?' he continued, his tone

suggesting that he was not overly impressed by his sergeant's apparent rebellion on promptness.

'I trust he's not got lost in all that fog out there?'

A muted laughter from the others wisped its way around the room.

'I could hardly see my handle bars when I cycled in this morning.'

'Shaun did mention something about calling in first thing on the building site next door to speak with that foreman again,' announced Ami.

Harry looked across. 'Did he say what time he expected to be here?'

'He said if he did go he'd make sure that he was here for the meeting, sir.'

'Perhaps Sumo's run out of toast and eaten him for breakfast,' jested Kevin.

As the laughter returned there was a tap on the opaque glass panelled door.

'Come in, sergeant,' shouted Harry.

The door opened.

'Morning, guv. Morning everyone,' said Shaun as he took a long exaggerated stride into the room and closed the door behind him. 'Sorry I'm a bit late.'

'Well, you're here now so take a seat. You can tell us all about Sumo later,' said Gateaux.

'Actually, sir, that wasn't the reason why I was delayed.'

'So it was the fog then,' said Kevin as he leaned back in his chair and looked sideways towards the recent arrival.

'No, it wasn't that either. I've just had a call from Winchester. There's been a major development.'

'Which is?'

'Well, guv, it appears that there was quite a substantial fire at the Price family residence in Winchester overnight.'

'Do we know how serious?'

'Inspector Scally reports quite extensive damage.'

'I presume that Mr Price, the victim's father, is so far unaware of the incident?'

'That's correct, sir. Our agreement was for all communications to him to go via you. Incidentally, how was your meeting with Mr Price senior last night?'

'A little depressing really, as you might expect,' replied Harry, his tone reflecting that same sense of despair. 'As you know, the formal identification was made by him yesterday when he arrived. The poor man is totally devastated.'

'And today's news is not going to help the cause,' interrupted Nicki.

'Indeed not. Looks like another visit soon to break it to him.'

'So did you learn anything when you spoke with him last night, guv?' enquired Shaun.

The Inspector shook his head.

'Nothing we didn't already know, unfortunately. Back to the fire … Do we have any idea of the cause, sergeant?'

'Too early to say yet, sir. I asked the very same question to Inspector Scally. He did say he would call us back later this morning with a further update.'

'Any word on whether the computer equipment suffered much damage?' enquired Kevin. 'It's just that forensics were in the early stages of sifting through endless computer files at the house when I spoke with them yesterday,' he added.

'Again, too early to say, mate,' replied Shaun, turning his head as he spoke to acknowledge his colleague's question.

'Okay, let's leave the fire for the moment until we are more fully aware of the facts. From what Shaun has just told us it seems we won't be at that stage until later this morning when Inspector Scally up-dates us,' said Gateaux. 'Right now we'll focus on our joint efforts from yesterday. I'm sure there's a lot to talk about?'

His seated colleagues nodded and murmured in agreement.

The Inspector's strategy finalised, he turned back to the board and cast his eyes analytically across its contents. 'Time to sort the wheat from the chaff I think,' he said loudly, as if wishing to bounce the message off the wall to his audience behind.

'The metallic object first. Now, you are probably all aware that yesterday's beach combing exercise by Nicki and Kevin yielded a large blue painted steel box on the beach side of the sea-wall about five hundred metres along from the hotel.'

The four nodded.

'Forensics found what they considered to be a fresh dent in one corner of its lid, around which some paint had flaked away, exposing a very small area of bare metal. The fact that there is very little rusting on this suggested the damage to have been caused within approximately twenty four hours of its discovery.'

'It did look a very exciting find initially …' interrupted Kevin as he looked up towards Gateaux. '… And what appeared to seal it, of course, was when forensics found those fibres of clothing snagged in the frame. Whether or not they belonged to our victim remains to be seen, of course.'

'Yes, I must admit that at first sight there seemed little doubt that the deck chair box was our mystery object,' confirmed Harry.

'A sort of "open and shut case" at that stage, was it, sir?' called out Shaun.

'Very clever,' said the Inspector, offering a token smile of appreciation for the early morning one liner.

'Anyway, it might well have been the classic "open and shut case" had Ami and Shaun not thrown into the ring the blue painted and sand filled skip located in the building contractors compound next door.'

'You can always rely on someone to spoil the party can't you?' said Kevin, as he looked one way and then the next at his colleagues. 'Did it have all the hallmarks of our box?' he continued.

'Well it had more bashes on it than a blacksmith's anvil, if that's what you mean?' replied Shaun. 'And like your beach box, it turned out to have some fibres snagged in it,' he added.

'Okay, okay,' said the Inspector as he stepped into the ring. 'It's not a competition, you know.'

The early noises that had suggested the start of a jovial point scoring discussion between the two sparring partners came to an abrupt halt.

'Unfortunately, nothing is ever simply black and white in this business,' said Harry.

'Going back to the beach box, guv. What size was it exactly?' enquired Ami.

'Well it's probably the size of a large wardrobe. We traced the owners to a local cafe. Seems they use the thing for storing deckchairs. The box itself is mounted upon a small extremely rusty steel frame which is semi-buried in the sand.'

'And forensics, I presume, are looking at the two objects in detail, are they?' enquired Kevin, as he looked across to the Inspector.

'Indeed.'

'Have they come back to us yet with any conclusions?' asked Ami.

'Yes, they have. I phoned Jeff just a few minutes prior to this meeting. It seems that their metallurgical expert, a Dr Maurice, is looking at paint samples from both items as we speak.'

'Great. That's some progress in the right direction then,' said Shaun. 'Did they have news on the testing of any of the fibre samples?'

'I did enquire but the answer at the moment is "no",' replied Harry.

'So how far away from coming up with something are they, sir?' enquired Nicki, her question edged with a hint of urgency.

'Yes, well, I know it's all a bit frustrating but the sort of answers we're looking for are unfortunately never instantaneous. Jeff tells me that the Santille results are very close and he's pushing the laboratory at Southampton for a swift response also. He's promised to call me later, by which time he should have the much awaited post-mortem report.'

'Just have to wait patiently then, I guess?' added Nicki.

'I'm afraid so,' confirmed Harry with a firm nod.

'You did say, guv, that the box or crate, or whatever, containing the deckchairs was positioned directly below the sea-wall?' enquired Shaun.

'Yes, that's right.'

'And its lid is, what, perhaps two metres or so beneath the level of the footpath that runs along the top of the wall?'

'Yes, about that.'

'So let's just assume for the moment that this box is our object,' suggested the sergeant. 'Then a possible scenario is that the victim fell, for whatever reason, from the wall, hit the crate and then from there toppled down onto the beach below?'

'Yes, that's one possible theory we're working on at present.'

'So was anything found on the beach around the box?' enquired Ami.

'Unfortunately not. If there was anything to find, it was either disturbed by a person or persons or perhaps by the sea. We've checked with the harbour-master and it turns out we had one particularly high tide between the time the body was found and the time the box was discovered. It would have given the area around it a thorough washing.'

The Inspector paused for a moment.

'Of course we mustn't forget that it's conceivable, as an alternative train of thought, that the victim fell onto the skip at the builder's site from the walkway scaffold that winds its way past the window to his room.'

'And I suppose it's also just possible that neither the beach box nor the skip have any relevance to this inquiry at all?' said Nicki.

'Yes, that must remain at the back of our minds,' replied Gateaux.

'If there was a fall involved, sir, will forensics be able to tell us if it was an accident or as a result of an assault?' enquired Ami.

'I would hope so.'

'And I presume that they would be able to tell us if he died instantly as a result of any fall?' enquired Ami further.

'Yes, they should be able to tell us that also.'

'If he did die close by the hotel, then someone or somebody has clearly moved him to his final resting place at Santille,' suggested Shaun. 'And if he didn't die instantly then there's always an outside chance, I suppose, that he made his own way to Santille.'

'But why would he choose to do that?' said Kevin.

'Why indeed?' interrupted Harry.

'There's an endless array of permutations and scenarios in the pot just now. Before we start clouding our minds too heavily with them I suggest again that, as with the fire incident, we wait for some more information before we spend valuable time speculating,' he added.

Discussion over, the Inspector turned, picked up a ball of blue cloth from the tray under the board and began rubbing away carefully at selected pieces of coloured text, scribble and diagrams before annotating the remaining notes and hieroglyphs with the fresh details which had recently come to light.

'What's happened to the modern art then, guv?' called Kevin, a passing reference to the previous day's rainbow coloured pictogram, approximately half of which now survived as a more condensed and comprehensible record, or so Gateaux hoped, of investigative data gathered thus far.

'*Mondrian* now, is it?' he continued.

'Oh, we are cultured, aren't we?' interrupted Nicki.

'Since when have you been a follower of abstract art?' she added.

'Tell you what. I would have paid good money for the original,' said Shaun.

'Okay, lets move on,' said the Inspector as he called his troops to order. 'Victim's background?' he said boldly, turning

183

to tap the same phrase twice with his pen on the board beside him.

'Nicki, did you and Kevin yesterday have a chance to uncover any more background on our victim, after you finished down at the beach?'

Nicki lifted her head and coughed gently.

'Certainly did, sir. Proved quite an interesting last hour or so to end of the day. Kevin spoke to Inspector Scally at Winchester CID while I phoned around to get some local information on Andrew Price.'

'Did Winchester have anything useful to tell us?' enquired Harry as he switched conversation and looked across towards Kevin.

'Yes, quite a bit actually, guv.'

The conversation ceased momentarily.

'Well?' enquired Gateaux, his voice infused with a large question mark of anticipation as he attempted to prompt his younger colleague into sharing his discoveries with the others.

'Sorry, sir. Well, it seems that apart from his dad whom we know he lived with, on and off, there was no other immediate family.'

'What about friends?'

'None. Seems he was a bit of a recluse by all accounts. All a little sad really, I guess. That aside, the local CID did find lots of evidence at his house, well, his father's house that is, confirming his passion for archaeology and computers.'

'Such as?' enquired Harry, as his probing continued.

'It appears, sir, that Andy's bedroom was a wall-to-wall library of history books and artefacts. He also had an adjoining room that had been converted a few years back to a computer study. "State of the art" is how Inspector Scally described it.'

'Um … Interesting,' said Gateaux.

'Yes, but what we don't know yet, guv, is how much of that survived the fire.'

'Anything else, Kev?'

'Yes, not quite finished. It seems from their investigations that our victim wasn't short of a few bob. Inspector Scally, having quizzed a couple of authorities on the subject, reckons that the book and memorabilia collection alone, which included apparently both recent publications and some rarities, is probably worth in excess of ten thousand pounds.'

Harry's eyes illuminated.

'What makes it even more interesting is that the lad's father said that the collection had only really grown significantly over the last couple of years or so. And, in that same time, according to Mr Price senior, his son also paid off in full the outstanding mortgage on the father's house as a Christmas present ... That was a gift of around thirty grand, would you believe?'

'Now that's what I call a Christmas present,' said Harry as the computation of the victim's apparent affluence began to click away in his mind.

'Don't you ever tell my dad that last bit, Kev,' interrupted Shaun. 'I only bought him socks last year.'

'Is there more?' enquired the Inspector.

'Most definitely is, guv. The Winchester team did some similar studies on the computer equipment in the victim's room at his home. Seems like that gear, again which the father says had been accumulated over the last two or three years, is probably worth ... wait for it ... in the region of about ninety thousand pounds.'

'Wow,' cried Shaun.

'Any chance I can have the kid's old job?'

'If indeed he had an old job. When I spoke with the father yesterday he gave me the impression that his son had not worked since returning from his contract in Jersey,' added Gateaux. 'On that note, did you find anything at all that might help us into establishing exactly when Andrew Price finished his work over here?'

'I think Nicki has some details on that, sir?' replied Kevin. 'You tracked down an employment record, didn't you?' he continued, giving his colleague seated beside him a feather-gentle nudge with his elbow.

The Inspector's eyes tracked a notch sideways and looked directly at Nicki.

'Yes, I phoned the Social Security office, guv. They had no record of a Mr Andrew Price.'

'Did they consider that unusual at all?'

'They're looking into it as we speak. The anomaly may have something to do, guv, with the short period that his employment lasted.'

'Or so we are led to believe at the moment,' added Harry.

Nicki paused for a moment.

'As I drew a blank there, sir, I then followed up the lead that Mel gave us during her interview when she recalled Mr Price junior talking to her about a bank that he had worked at on the Island.'

'And where did that take you?'

'A long way as it happens, guv. I didn't realise you could squeeze so many finance houses on to such a small lump of granite.'

'And you hit the jackpot eventually, did you?' enquired Gateaux as he sought to prise the name of the bank from Nicki's lips.

'Certainly did, sir. After numerous phone calls to the personnel departments of a succession of the banks, I had a return call first thing this morning from the AMC bank in town. They confirmed that a Mr Andrew Price had worked for them for six months during the latter part of 1999.'

'Fantastic,' replied Harry with relieved excitement. 'That seems to tie in nicely with the time-scale his father was talking about.'

Nicki nodded in agreement.

'Did they tell you anything else, Nicki?'

'Not at the time but they do still have his file on record along with his CV, pay details, that sort of thing. In fact, I've arranged for Kevin and myself to meet up with the AMC's manager, a Mr Dwight Henderson, later today.'

'Good work,' said the Inspector, with a firm nod of appreciation to his colleague.

'Teachers pet,' whispered Shaun.

As Nicki cupped her hand over her mouth to muffle an escaping giggle, Gateaux swivelled his head, and his attention, back towards Kevin.

'Returning to the victim's apparent affluent lifestyle, do we know, Kev, if the father ever expressed any curiosity as to the source of his son's acquired wealth, particularly when it seems he's had no recent work or source of income?'

'I understand, sir, that Winchester did quiz the father about that and he confirmed the question had been put to his son. The answer he received was that all the money had been made here in Jersey. Mr Price senior appears to have accepted that as an explanation and the issue was never raised again.'

'If that is the case then he must have been on some fairly serious money over here for six months?' suggested Shaun.

'Quite,' said the Inspector.

'When you visit err ...,' he continued.

The name he searched for having eluded him for a split second, Harry turned for a glance at his board where he had been continually updating the previous day's carnival coloured aide memoir.

He spun back instantly.

'Kevin, when you and Nicki visit Mr Dwight Henderson later at AMC, ensure that you pick up on the salary side of things. See if Andrew Price's earnings could have justified the levels of spending we've seen and his existence out of work for nearly three years,' he said.

Kevin nodded.

'As for the research that Winchester has been carrying out, do we know if the victim made any money from his computer work? Ninety thousand pounds worth of kit must have been useful for something.'

'Interesting point that, guv. The mainland office tells us that they've traced a bank account in his name but the monies deposited there have never amounted to anything more than a few pennies.'

'Presumably they're continuing with that as a line of inquiry?'

'Yes, sir. When I last spoke to them yesterday they were trying to find traces of any other financial accounts and such-like. I guess, though, that the fire which we've recently learned of is tying up their resources right at this moment?'

'Yes, that's probably the case?'

'Money issues to one side though, guv, the apparent sophistication of his computer set-up remains a bit of a mystery. Inspector Scally said they found his room littered with computer games, internet literature and that sort of thing.'

'And you were suggesting a little earlier that forensics in Winchester had only just begun to sift through the data?'

'Yes, that's what we are led to believe, sir. It seems there was file upon file of computer data in his room and each piece was going to be downloaded to see if it was of any relevance. It will be a mammoth undertaking by all accounts.'

'Made all the more difficult, perhaps, by this morning's news?'

'Yes, possibly, guv. Inspector Scally was telling me that such was the complexity of the set-up that they've had to call in specialist 'I.T' assistance. That team of experts were due to arrive and begin their analysis on site this morning.'

'Let's just hope they've something to analyse,' interrupted Nicki.

'Let's hope so,' said Gateaux.

'Returning to the internet interest again, Kevin, I assume Winchester will be speaking with the telecoms people as well?'

'Yes, sir. That line of enquiry is already being followed up and a local telecoms group over there are compiling a list of all calls made to and from the victim's address. But, as with the computer files, it's going to take a little while. Seems again that there's absolutely reams of such calls to sift through.'

'Anything more?' enquired Harry, looking first at Nicki and then to her neighbour.

'No, nothing really,' replied Kevin as he looked to his colleague for consensus.

Nicki nodded. 'We will of course be in regular contact with Hampshire and we have a few more lines of inquiry on the Island, including the meeting with AMC later. We'll update you as soon as new information becomes available, sir.'

'Thanks, both of you.'

Commendations awarded, Gateaux returned to the board and annotated his felt scribbled notes before placing the pens down in the tray under the board and spinning around to face the front.

'I keep telling you, you're going to wear those heels out soon, sir,' said Shaun.

'Yes, you'll need those shoe mending people before long,' added Kevin.

'Cobblers,' retorted Shaun.

A wave of laughter trotted around the room.

'You two are wasted here,' said the Inspector.

'We could have told you that ages ago,' said Nicki as she rocked forward in her chair and smiled across at Ami.

'They should be on the stage ... The next great double act,' continued Harry.

'Take over from Bill and Ben, perhaps ...' suggested Nicki.

'... Assuming they can pass the entrance exams, that is.'

The Inspector laughed as the tennis match of banter continued before a short manufactured cough from Gateaux brought his small army of investigative soldiers back to attention.

'Okay. I think that's enough for the moment. Let's have a quick break for tea. We'll continue in, say, five minutes.'

Almost before he'd finished his invitation, that same small

army had dismissed themselves and were heading towards the door.

Having been dubiously refreshed, courtesy of the kitchen chemistry set that amusingly called itself the "de luxe" drinks machine, the group retook to their seats and awaited the Inspector's resumption.

'Right, Shaun,' said Gateaux.

'Yes, sir?'

'Can you tell us all how you got on with our friend Sumo at the building site next door? I understand your meeting with him yesterday was curtailed somewhat?'

'Didn't upset him did you?' said Nicki.

'Certainly hope not, he looks a bit of a nutter if you ask me ...' replied the sergeant. '... Anyway, it turned out that he couldn't spare me much time yesterday. He had to dash off to see to a delivery of concrete, or so he told me. I'd hardly had time to sit down in his site hut before he was kicking me out again.'

'And that's why you went back this morning, Shaun?'

'That's right, sir. Thought I'd catch him while I was still a familiar face. It also gave me the opportunity afterwards to chat with a few of the guys on site.'

'So how did your brief audience with him go?'

The sergeant paused before replying.

'I'll tell you what, guv. If anyone ever tells you that the cave man is extinct, don't believe him. Just tell that person to visit next door and ask for Sumo. I'm sure one of his ancestors must have been Fred Flintstone.'

A chorus of laughter filled the room.

'So, did we learn much from our woolly mammoth hunter then?' enquired Harry, his voice raised slightly above the ever-diminishing noise of jollity from the others.

'Well, not an awful lot yesterday, sir. He was aware that one of the hotel guests had been found dead. I showed him a photo of the victim but he said he didn't recognise the face and that the name Andrew Price meant nothing to him. I'd just touched on the subject of the contract that his company carried out at the hotel a few years previously and the incident during that involving Mr Price and one of Colcroft's men.'

'Yes and ...?'

'Well, no sooner had I mentioned the subject when, as I said, I was being shown to the door.'

'Weren't you telling me earlier, Shaun, that you'd managed to find out from the hotel management some more detail on that previous building contract?'

'Yes, quite a bit more actually, thanks to Lucy who, it turns out, is herself a main board director of the Coburg Hotels Group. She managed to track down the hotel's file on the project which was carried out back in 1998 - and a comprehensive record it was too. It mentioned the very incident between Mr Price and Colcroft's operative, Alec Walsh. The paperwork even had a copy of the letter from the hotel group demanding the removal of the Colcroft man from the site and a copy of the subsequent response from Colcroft's. That letter was signed by a Mr Adrian Gills who, in real life, turns out to be none other than our friend Sumo.'

'Did you find out any specific details of the case at all?'

'Well, apparently, guv, the contract itself basically involved cleaning the external façade of the hotel from a scaffold access platform that, like the one at the moment, wrapped around the building. It seems that our victim, Mr Price, stepped on to the scaffold from his room to complain to the first labourer he found about the dust being generated. Coincidentally, his room then was the very same room that he had on this occasion.'

'Interesting,' said Gateaux. 'Is that significant, do you think?'

'I did quiz Lucy about it but she couldn't trace any record of any particular room requests from Andrew Price which might have suggested that he favoured one room over another.'

'Okay,' said Harry. 'Sorry, I took you off the scent then. You were just about to tell us about the incident in '98,' he continued.

'Yes, guv. The basis of his complaint appeared to be that Andrew Price claimed that the excesses of dust were a risk to his computer equipment that he had with him in his room at the time. The first labourer he met turned out to be this Alec Walsh character who, it seems, didn't take too kindly to Mr Price's accusations and allegedly gave him a bit of verbal overload for his trouble.'

'And that led to Mr Walsh being removed from site?'

'Yes, sir, that and more. The letter contained in the hotel's files received from Adrian Gills confirmed that the man had been dismissed from Colcrofts altogether ...'

Shaun hesitated for a moment and looked down at his notebook before completing his sentence.

'... And, I quote, 'for gross misconduct',' he continued, looking back up towards Gateaux.

'So what did Sumo have to say about the incident?'

'Well, as I said, he gave the impression yesterday during our curtailed chat of being just a tad evasive and a bit twitchy about the whole episode.'

'And this morning?'

'Well, again that twitchiness was still there. I mentioned the letter to him which appeared to jog a few of his memory cells. He suddenly remembered the incident, confirmed the guy had been sacked and then assured me that he'd not seen Alec Walsh since giving him the boot.'

'Did you believe him, sergeant?'

'Well, initially I had no particular reason not to.'

The Inspector's face contorted slightly to an expression of puzzlement.

'Sorry, I don't quite follow. What do you mean 'initially'?'

'Well, during my second chat with him this morning I spotted a few job sheets pinned to a notice board in the office. First names only mind, but one of them just happened to be a chap by the name of Alec. I asked Sumo for the surnames of all those listed on the sheet and next thing he throws a bit of a mental and kicks me out again. Some pathetic excuse this time, about a meeting to go to. He did seem particularly agitated at my request though.'

'So what happened next?'

'Well, having been evicted from the site hut, sir, I then took the opportunity to quiz a few of the guys around the site. All of them denied any knowledge of the victim but, significantly, some knew of Alec Walsh. Turns out he's spent quite a bit of time on the site just recently. Seems the man now has quite an elevated position in the Colcroft hierarchy?'

'Um ... Sounds like our friend Sumo's got a very selective memory, doesn't it?' suggested Harry.

'Yeah, you might say that, guv. Definite candidate for Amnesiacs Anonymous.'

'Sorry, what was that you said, Shaun, I've forgotten?' interrupted Kevin.

'Sad man,' whispered Nicki.

'Right, Shaun,' he said, refocusing his line of thought, which had temporarily derailed following Kevin's short offering of humour.

'I suggest we offer Mr Sumo and the invisible Mr Alec Walsh the opportunity later to volunteer their services at the station for a few more focused questions. Can you organise that when we're finished here?'

'And if they are not keen, sir?'

'We'll cross that bridge when we come to it, sergeant. Just emphasise to them that a visit of their own volition would be in their own interests.'

As Harry finished talking there was a knock on the door.

'Come in,' he called.

The door opened.

'Sorry to trouble you, guv, but there's a Jeff Monet on the phone from forensics,' informed the female messenger. 'He says it's extremely urgent.'

'Thanks, Sally,' said Gateaux.

Immediately he stood and began walking towards the door.

'Excuse me, all, for just a few moments,' he said.

'I've put the call through to your office, sir,' continued Sally, as the Inspector made his exit quickly out through the door.

Ten minutes later the Inspector reappeared. His colleagues turned and watched in silence as he made his way bullishly towards the front table.

Pausing for a moment, he stood and stared, an expression of accomplishment written across his face.

'Post-mortem results?' enquired Shaun optimistically.

'Not quite, but some interesting developments nonetheless. Good news and bad news as always. The bad news is that the Southampton laboratory is still working on the paint, sand and fibre samples recovered from both the beach box and the skip. So nothing conclusive yet.'

'And the good news, sir?' asked Nicki eagerly.

'Well, the good news is that one of the tractors appears to hold some vital clues.'

'Tractors, what tractors?' enquired Kevin as he looked to each side for some moral support to his claim for a lack of communicated information.

His plea failed.

'Think you might be a candidate for Amnesiacs Anonymous after all,' said Nicki, whispering again.

'Okay, a little reminder for those of you who haven't been listening or reading my board notes one hundred per cent,' replied the Inspector, looking across intently at his seated colleague.

The others laughed.

'On Wednesday, the day of course that the body of Andrew Price was discovered, I spent some time speaking with Eva and Pierre Morlaix, a retired couple who live in the picture postcard cottage at the end of the track leading up to the site.'

'The Sandwich King and Queen of Jersey,' interrupted Shaun.

'The what?' asked Nicki.

'Oh, ignore him. It's a private joke,' Harry replied, with a dismissive stare towards his sergeant.

'Now where was I?'

'Your chat with the Morlaix couple,' said Ami.

'Thank you. See someone's listening. Well, during my interview with Eva Morlaix, you others will remember that she thought she recalled hearing a tractor working in the field around the dolmen site on the morning the body was discovered.'

'Yes, it's coming back to me now,' interrupted Kevin as he endeavoured to recover his minor loss of credibility.

'Anyway, Eva guessed at the time that the tractor was being driven by a guy who goes by the slightly curious name of Woody,' said Gateaux as he resisted the temptation to offer any sarcastic commendation towards his colleague's apparent return to alert consciousness.

'Woody owns the Cobnut Farm close to her cottage, has done for years and runs it with his family. Eva's guess seemed plausible at first - that was until her husband, Pierre, threw a spanner in the works by informing his wife and me that the farm was closed and the family were away on holiday.' he continued.

'And that fact was confirmed by Woody's brother,' interrupted Ami.

'I thought the family were all on holiday?' enquired Nicki.

'Well, they are, except for the brother. He's the only member of the clan not involved in the farm. Seems he runs some computer consultancy in town. Ami and myself happened to bump into him yesterday,' said the Inspector. 'He was at the "Cobnut" when we visited. He's taken a weeks leave and is staying there to look after the place while the rest of the family are away,' he added.

'When we spoke to him initially he confirmed that no tractors had been operating on that day or on any day this week,' interrupted Ami, looking up first at the Inspector and then to her colleagues seated at her side.

'So are we saying that Eva's confused the days or is simply a sandwich short of a picnic?' enquired Kevin.

'She's certainly not short of any sandwiches,' interrupted Shaun.

The Inspector's stoic expression suggested that the subject matter of his sergeant's quip was now well past its sell-by date.

'No, I didn't get the impression of any confusion on her part,' continued Harry. 'She seemed fairly adamant that she had heard a tractor in the field on the Wednesday morning. Of course, if she was right, then it was being driven by someone who, as we understand, plainly should not have been there.'

'But Ami's just said that Woody's brother told you that no tractors were running,' said Shaun.

'Yes, he did at first but when we questioned him again a little later it turned out he had to go into the office early on the Wednesday and didn't make it back to the farm until mid-afternoon. As a result, he was clearly in no position to be able to say categorically that machinery had not been interfered with on that particular morning. Anyway, Eva's little tractor mystery nagged away at me all night, so I had all the vehicles on the farm checked over at first light this morning.'

'Anything found Sir?'

'Well, it seems that a small blood stain was found in one of the machine's front loading buckets and has been positively matched with that of our victim. A fingertip search of the same bucket and analysis of some dusty debris also found the missing parts to the victim's watch. If you remember, the watch we found on Mr Price's wrist at the site had clearly been broken and both the hands and the glass cover could not be traced …Until now.'

'So the body had at some point been in the tractor bucket?' said Kevin.

'Certainly seems that way,' said Harry as he turned back to

his board and, in a small area of uncluttered space, began drawing in thick black pen a rough sketch of the site, the farm building and the lanes that circumnavigated it.

He reached for a red marker before continuing.

'All the evidence at present suggests that the body was brought to Santille from town and was then transferred to the tractor and driven to the site across the field at the back of the dolmen monument. Forensics have now had a closer look at the tyre marks in the field and confirm a return trip to the dolmen site was made by the tractor in question. On arrival at the site, the body appears to have then been dragged through the hedge, over the mound and along the grass to its final resting place. We found heavy staining from the grass, which matches that at the site, over his clothes.'

'But why go to the trouble of nicking a tractor when all the person, or persons, had to do was simply carry the body up the lane?' enquired Kevin.

'Most probably because they didn't want to risk being seen by Eva or the local grocer, André, both of whom we suspect would have been outside at the time the body was dumped.'

'Were there any prints on the tractor?' asked Nicki.

The Inspector looked over.

'Well, yes there were quite a few, but of course they may all be from members of Woody's family, whom we've now traced to a holiday hideaway in France. They've been informed of events and are providing a full collection of prints so at least we can compare theirs to those found on the tractor and see what's left.'

'Was there anything else found in the tractor, sir?' asked Ami.

'Yes indeed,' replied Gateaux with a grin. 'Thought I would save the best bit until last.'

He paused as if to inflict some teasing pain of suspense upon his colleagues.

'Well, guv?' said Nicki, her eyes seeming to pop with anticipation.

'Well, in addition to the watch pieces, forensics also found a wristband of coloured beads with a small brass surfboard looped into it. From the profile we've built up about Andrew Price, it would seem very unlikely that it was his.'

'So it belonged to the person that put the body in the tractor bucket then?' suggested Shaun.

'Or maybe one of Woody's family left it there?' added Ami.

'Yes, maybe. Hopefully the former,' replied Harry.

'As I have said, we've managed to track down the family. In addition to their fingerprints, we'll be asking if the bangle belongs to them.'

Once again the Inspector hesitated.

'Any other questions on what we have covered so far?' he enquired, casting an inviting radar sweep of his eyes across the seated arc of colleagues.

'Yes, sir,' said Kevin. 'You mentioned yesterday something about a car being seen in the area.'

'That's correct. So you were listening after all?'

Kevin smiled, the black mark awarded to him earlier in the day now hopefully erased.

'Eva remembered what she described as a funny old car driving past her cottage early on the Wednesday morning. We tracked down André, the grocer, yesterday who also recalled seeing the old car and two people inside, one driver, one passenger,' continued Gateaux.

'Regular Miss Marple your friend Eva,' said Kevin.

Laughter filled the small room once more.

As it began to dilute, Shaun raised a finger quickly just to the side of his head.

'Yes Shaun?'

'Any 'ID' on the vehicle guv?'

'Unfortunately not. The only common ground we obtained from Eva and André is that it was coloured red and looked old.'

'That sounds suspiciously like my motor,' said the sergeant.

'No, when I say old, I mean old.'

'Still sounds like Shaun's car,' interrupted Nicki. 'Something falls off it every time he turns a corner.'

'Well, Shaun's wreck aside, it seems that we're probably looking at a vintage machine, a classic car. I've asked a couple of the lads downstairs, Simon and Gavin, to get a sack full of relevant books from the library and pop over to see Eva and André again. See if we can get a positive fix on the *funny old red car*.'

'So you think the car's related to the crime then, sir?' asked Nicki.

'Well, it appears to have been the only vehicle on the road in the area that morning apart from the grocer's van and the tour coach which arrived later. We must trace it if only to eliminate it from our inquiry.'

'What about an 'ID' on the two people in the car, guv?' asked Ami.

'Not much to go on there, really. The witnesses concurred on the number in the car but that's where the agreement starts and ends unfortunately. Eva reckoned it was two young lads, one of Mediterranean appearance, and André thinks it was a middle aged couple.'

'Those descriptions must cover about fifty per cent of the Island's population?' said Kevin. 'Should be easy to trace them,' he continued, a thick strand of sarcasm woven in his response.

'Right, it's nearly mid-day,' said Harry, looking at his watch. 'Is there anything else from yesterday's inquiries that we've not touched on yet?'

Shaun raised his hand.

'Well, sir, I had a chat with the doorman, Joe, at the hotel.'

'Yes, and ...?'

'I asked him if he knew of the victim, Andrew Price, or indeed remembered having seen him on the Wednesday morning, prior to the tour bus leaving.'

'And what did he say, sergeant?'

'He said he had seen Mr Price on quite a few occasions on account of the lad's frequent stays at the Coburg. As for Wednesday, it transpired that he wasn't on duty at the time in question. He took the early part of the morning off. According to him, Lucy and Mel took over his responsibilities as best they could.'

'He was there when we arrived mid to late morning, I remember talking with him,' said Gateaux.

'Yes, I spoke to him then as well, guv.'

'So where did he get to before then?'

'He didn't seem too sure himself at first, sir. Then he said that he been up at the airport.'

'Doing what exactly?'

'Seems that some of the vintage aircraft for Thursday's display came in a day early and performed a small display around the airfield. I checked with Lucy this morning and she confirmed that Masters had made a point of citing his plane-spotting pursuits as the reason for requesting part of the morning as leave.'

'Did you doubt his account then?'

Shaun paused for a moment, before replying.

'Well, I didn't at first I suppose. It was very clear from speaking to him that as far as aircraft were concerned he knew his stuff and it was perfectly understandable that he'd want to be at the airport to see the early arrivals at close quarters on that Wednesday morning.'

'So, what's changed your mind since then?'

'Last night's newspaper actually, guv. It carried a lead story about yesterdays air show - in particular the disappointment that the Spitfire had been grounded on the mainland due to engine problems. Consequently, it couldn't make it over to the Island for either the Guernsey or Jersey shows.'

'So how does that cast suspicion upon the doorman's story then?' enquired Gateaux.

'Well, when I was chatting with Joe yesterday morning I

suggested to him that I'd seen a Spitfire parked up at the airport on Wednesday when I drove past. When I prompted him he claimed to have seen it there also. We now know it never got here.'

'I didn't know you were a closet plane spotter, Shaun?' interrupted Nicki as she curled her fingers on each hand and then put them across her eyes in a playful imitation of flying goggles.

'That's just it, I'm not. I only thought I saw a Spitfire. But now it turns out it wasn't that aircraft at all,' continued the sergeant.

'So what did you see then, mate, an overweight pigeon?' suggested Kevin irreverently as more jovial airwaves rippled around the room.

Shaun waited patiently for his verbal humiliation to cease.

'I checked with the airport staff who, when I pointed out where it had been parked, said it must have been the Hurricane,' said Shaun as the banter silenced. 'I've looked through a few books since and the two aircraft are fairly similar.'

'So, could Joe have not made the same mistake?' enquired Ami.

'A very slim chance of that I would guess. The planes are similar as I said, but there're some very identifiable differences for the trained eye to spot. I admit I'm not well up on aircraft but I think Masters most certainly is. Lucy said as much. I simply find it very hard to believe that he could have confused a Hurricane for a Spitfire.'

'So are you saying he's trying to hide something?' enquired Nicki.

'No, not necessarily. But what I am saying though, is that his alibi for Wednesday morning doesn't seem too convincing.'

'So, if he wasn't at the airfield, where was he?' enquired Nicki further.

'That's clearly something we need to establish,' said Harry, rubbing his chin with the palm of his hand.

A veil of silence dropped on the room for a brief moment.

'Right, if there are no more questions I suggest we break for an early lunch,' said Harry as he seized the opportunity to call for a mid-day break.

'And later we'll speak to Sumo ... And our Mr Walsh, if we can find him that is?' said Shaun.

'Yes,' confirmed Harry.

'I'll go to the front desk on my way to the canteen,' said the sergeant. 'See if they can spare anyone to go and pick the two of them up. What time shall we aim to speak with them, guv?'

'Well, I've planned a quick meeting with Gavin and Simon straight after lunch. Then I'm going to visit Mr Price at the Hotel Amadeus. So we could aim to be ready for a chat with the pair around three o'clock maybe,' replied Gateaux, looking quickly at his watch.

'What shall we do about the doorman, Joe,' enquired Shaun.

'Yes, I was just about to mention him myself,' replied Harry as he looked across at Nicki and Kevin.

'You're off to visit the AMC bank later, aren't you both?'

The two nodded.

'Get us some money while you're there if there's any going spare,' interrupted Shaun.

'Oh, and a job application form,' he added.

'I'll organise the leaving card then,' said Harry before refocusing upon Nicki and Kevin.

'If you find yourself with any time after your bank visit, perhaps you could do a little scratching around behind the scenes on our doorman friend, Joe Masters. But keep it discreet if you can and try not to get Lucy involved. I'd like to keep our suspicions out of earshot of the hotel for the time being.'

'Understood, sir,' said Nicki.

'And what do you want me to do, guv?' enquired Ami.

'How did you get on with Shaun quizzing the guests at the Coburg yesterday afternoon?'

'Wasn't overly productive actually, sir. I think everyone was outside watching the planes. I knocked on all forty-four doors on the fourth floor and had three replies. Nothing useful to report unfortunately.'

'Okay,' said Harry.

'Can you go back to the hotel this afternoon and walk the floors again. We need to speak with as many guests as possible that were in the hotel on or around Wednesday.'

'Right Sir, I'll do my best.'

'Can't ask for anything more than that.'

'And don't forget to put a new pair of shoe soles on your expenses form,' added Kevin as he moved his left foot to one side and tapped the outside of Ami's boot.

'Right,' continued Harry, slamming shut the large box file on his table. 'Think it's high time we all went to find some well deserved food. If we hang around here any longer there'll be nothing left,' he continued as he stacked the files neatly on his desk and stood.

'I'll second that. Don't want that bunch of Neanderthals from downstairs scoffing it all,' said Shaun.

With that, he and the others began to get up from their seats.

'Keep in touch everyone and back here for five prompt,' said Harry as the group began shuffling subtlety towards the door.

As the attempt at a covert exit continued, a misty chorus of disapproval began to whisper through the air at the prospect of an end of week extension of time into their early evening.

'I won't keep you long I promise,' said the Inspector as he opened diplomatic channels in a pre-emptive move to quash the suggestion of an imminent uprising among his front line. 'I need to be away myself fairly pronto later, anyway, so I hope we'll only be ten or fifteen minutes maximum.'

A murmured recovery of morale rippled along the parade line as the pendulum of grievance swung from rebellion to relief.

'Excellent. So five o'clock it is. Shaun, after you've been to the front desk can you quickly phone Winchester. They said they would have an update on the fire about now. We can talk about it over lunch. Be useful to have a bit more detail in my mind so that I'm better prepared when I break the news to the victim's father this afternoon.'

'Understood, sir,' said Shaun.

'I'll see you all in a moment then,' he added as he brushed quickly past his colleagues and disappeared out of the room.

'Right, come on then the rest of you, din dins,' cried Gateaux before walking ahead of the remaining three and ushering them out of the room and onward towards the canteen.

The door closed solidly with a clunk behind him.

CHAPTER EIGHT

The library-like tranquillity of the station's canteen that had surrounded the Inspector's lunchtime discussion with his colleagues was suddenly shattered as the room echoed to the sound of a rapidly invading army of fellow lunch-seeking occupants.

Fired by the food fuelled enthusiasm of its new arrivals, the small dining area located on the ground floor soon found itself increasingly consumed by the sound of clinking cutlery and lively conversation.

'Looks like it's time for a swift exit,' suggested Harry as he began to shuffle uncomfortably in his seat.

'Yes, it's getting just a tad claustrophobic, isn't it?' agreed Shaun as he looked up to see their seated area coiled by the python-like strangle of the food bound queue.

Without further word and in mirrored synchronicity the two men stood, lifted their crockery-laden trays and meandered their way through the obstacle course of bodies towards the kitchen's serving hatch.

'Fantastic meal again, Joyce,' said Harry warmly as he stooped forward and extended his arms to pass his tray across the small sill to the diminutive blue apron dressed figure of the canteen's supervisor beyond.

'Yes, superb,' said Shaun, standing a short distance behind.

'Oh, you're too kind, gentlemen,' replied Joyce, a glow of mild embarrassment resonating in her cheeks.

She looked down at the Inspector's returned white china. 'Cor, wish everyone enjoyed their meal to the last morsel like you, sir. Wouldn't have any washing up to do at all if they were all this clean, and I've cleaned some plates in my time, I can tell you. Thirty-five years this November,' she announced proudly.

'Thirty-five,' cried Harry, an air of consternation filling his reply. 'That anniversary will have to call for some celebration, perhaps I'll cook you a meal?'

'Oh, that'll be nice,' she replied as Harry took a step to one side to allow the waiting Shaun to offload his tray.

'I shouldn't agree to one of the guv'nors meals, Joyce. We can't afford to have you away with food poisoning, can we?'

'Oh, I'm sure Mister Gateaux is a lovely cook,' she replied, her voice sautéed in sympathy for the Inspector at the suggestion that he might be the Doctor Crippin of the gourmet world.

'Only joking.'

'That's okay then, Sergeant Carac.'

Trays and compliments successfully delivered, Gateaux turned and followed his sergeant towards the exit.

Propping the swing door open, Shaun motioned the Inspector through.

'So what happened to Ami, Nicki and Kevin?' enquired Harry, as their paths crossed.

'Oh, they all left about fifteen minutes or so ago, guv.'

'Really? I didn't see them leave.'

'I think you were still in the shadow of your trifle dessert when they disappeared,' added Shaun with a cheeky grin.

'Yes, I guess it was a greedy portion. Perhaps a visit to the gym might be on the cards very soon ... To repent.'

Shaun laughed.

With the smell of canteen food now behind them, the two picked up the walking pace and began their return to the mazy cluster of drably decorated offices on the first floor. As their advance continued, the Inspector rolled his sleeve back to snatch a glance at his watch.

'Gee, it's nearly one thirty,' he said, a hint of surprise pulsating in his voice.

'Well, I suppose we did have a lot to discuss over lunch after another busy morning, sir.'

'Yes, and I suspect we're in for an even busier afternoon,'

replied Harry, the adrenalin-dosed response prompting his pace to accelerate a further notch.

Shaun's rate increased in parallel, a necessary reaction to maintain an audible and coherent discussion in the voluminous and word swallowing tunnel of the corridor.

'I'm quickly off back to my office,' said Gateaux as he approached the staircase at the end of the passage. 'Simon and Gavin from downstairs said they're popping along around two o'clock. I bumped into them on my way to lunch and it seems that the little soirée at Santille for some vintage car chat with Eva and André activated a few of the desired memory muscles,' he added.

'And what have you planned after that?' enquired the sergeant, a suggestion of breathlessness apparent in his reply.

'Out of condition are we?' enquired Gateaux as he looked across his shoulder to his lightly perspiring colleague. 'That game of squash is always on offer, don't forget. Anyway, in answer to your question, sergeant, as soon as I've seen Simon and Gav, I'm cycling over to see Jeff again to see if those post-mortem results have been finalised yet. He did promise them to me this afternoon sometime. On my way back, I'm going to call in to the Hotel Amadeus to break the news about the fire to our Mr Price.'

'I don't envy you with that job, guv.'

'No, I'm not exactly relishing the prospect myself. To be honest, I really should have visited him this morning but we had a lot to get through and it's only since your recent chat with Winchester that we've fully established the facts.'

Shaun nodded.

'When I get back we'll sit down with Sumo and Walsh,' continued Gateaux. 'Any news of our two builders at all?'

'Not sure, sir. I'll pop along to the front desk in a moment and see if they've tracked down the dynamic duo yet. As soon as I've spoken with them I'll give you a call on your phone. So what else do you want me to do while you're away?'

'Where do we start?' replied Harry as he tilted his head carefully backwards.

With his gaze focused momentarily on the corridor ceiling, so his mind focused on the myriad of unfinished tasks. 'Can you squirrel yourself away in room four? Go through that pile of Wednesday's witness statements again from the tour group. See if there's anything we've overlooked. Also, have a think about the information we've collected to date. We still need to make some sense, don't forget, of that note the victim left at reception prior to his disappearance. You might have a chat with Mel again to see if she's remembered yet where she put the slip of paper after reading it. It could well be a vital clue, if only we can find it?'

'Anything else, guv?'

'I must say you're showing a very commendable, dare I say uncharacteristic, display of keenness today, Shaun. You after a pay rise or something?' said Gateaux, smiling broadly. 'If you do have any spare time you could think again about that curious entry in the victim's diary, "3456BC",' he added, his mind appearing to switch to calculative mode from the moment he mentioned the brain-teasing number and letter combination.

'Okay, sir, I'm on the case right now. So when can we expect your return?

'Well, I'm still looking to be back around three. Our chat with Sumo and Walsh should then lead us on nicely to our get-together with the others planned for five.'

'You did say our meeting later wouldn't carry on for too long, didn't you, guv? It's just that Bev is out tonight and I've agreed to look after the kids.'

'Well, sergeant, I suppose its duration depends on how busy we've all been.'

'Oh,' said Shaun, as a wash of concern splashed unerringly across his face.

The Inspector hesitated before replying as if to tease the pains of a possible late finish a little longer. 'I shouldn't worry yourself too much. As I said earlier, I need to be away fairly smartish tonight as well. Mel's invited me as a guest to the Coburg's evening beach barbeque over at St Ouen and I'm still hoping to get to the hotel before then to have another chat with Lucy about a few things.'

Shaun's anxious expression vaporised immediately.

'Catch you in a little while then,' added Gateaux as he pushed open one of the two swing doors and broke instantly into a semi-jog back to his room, leaving Shaun to return, via the front desk, to room four, armed with his assortment of delegated tasks. He seemed barely to have skimmed the first few pages of his notebook when there was a tap on the door. As he swivelled in his chair and reached across, it opened.

To his clear surprise it was the Inspector, clothed head to toe in a blue streamlined nylon cycling tracksuit, his red crash hat tucked tightly under one arm and a book under the other.

'That was quick guv.'

'Yes, Simon and Gavin were waiting for me and thankfully the chat with them was brief and then Jeff didn't take as long as I had been expecting.

'Did you get to the Amadeus as well, sir?'

'Yes, though that was quite a brief visit as well.'

'Evidently,' replied Shaun, his face still struck with amazement at the Inspector's lightning quick circuit.

'The father was in quite a state when I arrived and you can imagine what reaction the news of the fire had on him,' said Gateaux.

'Um, not good, I guess?'

'Mr Price is keen to get back to the mainland today rather than tomorrow as originally arranged, so we've booked him on a mid-afternoon flight back to Southampton, fog permitting of course. If we need anything else from him then we'll do it via the Winchester office.'

'I don't think he will be flying anywhere in the near future, guv. The airport's still effectively closed due to this weather. Has been all day.'

'Could get him on the fast ferry I suppose, Shaun?'

'Unfortunately not, sir. I caught the radio announcement at lunchtime. It said that the Phoenix ferry is stuck on the mainland side. No specific reason given.'

'So, what you're saying is that we're effectively marooned for the day?'

'Seems like it, unless you get your surfboard out of the garage, guv.'

Harry laughed.

'So, how did it go with the boys in blue?' continued Shaun as he re-focused upon the Inspector's post-lunch pursuits.

'The Car. Yes …' replied Harry. '… It appears that despite Eva and André remaining divided upon the descriptions of the two people they saw in the vehicle, they have at last reached some sort of consensus on the model.'

Gateaux walked across to the table at which his colleague was sitting and laid the book he had carried into the room on top of a number of open files.

'Seems that we're looking for one of three. Either an Austin Healey 3000, this one here,' he said as he flicked to a middle page, marked with a fluorescent orange tag. 'Attractive little beastie isn't she?'

'Um, just a tad, guv,' agreed Shaun as his eyes filled dreamily with visions of himself sitting in the 1950's classic.

'The second possibility is this, a Jaguar XK,' continued Harry, turning the pages to the next paper marker.

'Oh, wow,' said Shaun as his dreamy state intensified.

'Or finally, this beauty, a MGA roadster. You'll note that they're all fairly similar in appearance so I suppose it's little wonder that Eva and André cannot agree.'

'Yes, suppose they do look alike in many ways, sir, though I wouldn't say no to the chance of owning any one of them.'

The sergeant's eyes remained fixed upon the picture of the MGA as he spent a few seconds drooling hopelessly over it while reading the short piece of accompanying text. His fixation seemingly at an end, he snapped out of his classic car fantasy and looked up towards the waiting Inspector.

'I can read your mind, sergeant, but I think you might struggle to squeeze Bev and the kids into one of those.'

'Yes, guv. Don't think it would go down too well if I brought one of those home. So what's our next move on this car search?'

'Well, I've asked Simon and Gavin if they can compile a list of all the cars and their owners on the Island that fit these descriptions. I've suggested they speak first with the vehicle registration department though that's only the start of it.'

'How do you mean, sir?'

'Well, I'm sure a number of these particular cars will normally be in private, static collections. Because of that, they may not need to be officially registered as they're simply not expected to appear on the public highways.'

'So, where to then, guv?'

'Well, I've suggested their next stop is to speak with someone from the Island's Vintage Car Club. I'm sure those two sources should provide us with most of the vehicles fitting our specification.'

'Presumably the two lads will keep us posted on how their list is progressing?'

The Inspector nodded.

'And what about the final post-mortem results then, guv. Did Jeff come up with any more answers when you spoke with him?'

'Certainly did. He's now prepared to say, beyond all reasonable doubt, that our victim was dead before arriving at Santille.' confirmed Harry.

'All the facial and neck injuries are consistent with a fall from some height, perhaps a few metres or so onto a solid object,' he added.

'The deckchair box or site skip, sir?'

The Inspector paused.

'We still don't know. The tests are still continuing.'

'And the fall would have been fatal?' enquired Shaun further.

'Immediate, was the word Jeff used.'

'So death had nothing to do with that granite stone inside the chamber against which his head rested?'

'Apparently not though to be fair to him, Jeff did actually suspect that that might be the case when the discovery of the body was first made. However, the stone did yield a potentially very interesting find. You may remember from our earlier discussions?'

'Oh yes?' said Shaun inquisitively.

He hesitated for a moment as his grey cells searched every pigeonhole of his brain for recovered information relating to the stone. His mind returned a blank report.

'Not sure I can recall that exactly, guv?'

'Well, sergeant, when I spoke with Jeff on site on Wednesday morning we discussed an apparent inconsistency, assuming that is, that the victim was dead on arrival at the dolmen, between the position of the head relative to the small inner granite stone and small blood stains that were found, one on either side of the stone,' replied the Inspector, his reply semi-laboured as if affording the time for Shaun to re-register its content with some future permanence.

'The interesting point is that though we now know both bloodstains originated from one large bruise around the left eye, only one of the marks is thought to have been made from the initial impact of the victim's head,' he added.

'So what are the conclusions then, sir?'

'That is the puzzle, sergeant. Jeff says everything points to the body having been placed initially with its head resting against one side of the stone. That left the first spot of blood. Then for whatever reason yet to be established, and some while later, the body was rolled over through a hundred and eighty degrees. As the head fell and came to rest against the ground on the other side of the stone so the second bloodstain was left. Scuff marks on the ground around the body reinforce that theory and suggest that at this same point in time the body was also pushed into the tight crunched up position that we found it in, with the victim's knees left almost touching his chin.'

'Why do that though. Surely if you were dumping a body you'd simply do exactly that, just dump it and run, wouldn't you?'

'You would think so, wouldn't you, but for the moment we must add that mystery to the painfully expanding list of unknowns.'

'Do forensics know, guv, how much time elapsed between the initial placing of the body and it subsequently being moved?'

'Not exactly, but Jeff is suggesting that we are talking about one to two hours later.'

'That time frame might coincide with the arrival of the tour bus, sir?'

Harry nodded firmly. 'Indeed. We know the victim was at breakfast and we have reported sightings of him at the hotel up to around 7.45am. The tour left at 9.00am without him and his body was found at Santille at approximately 10.30am.'

'The group didn't report seeing anyone else on site did they during their visit; guv?'

'Well, if they did, they're all keeping quiet about it.'

'So if they didn't see anyone there, it could be that whoever left the body in the chamber might have been in hiding close by during their site visit?'

'Yes, that may be something we need to consider, Shaun.'

'And the crunched up foetal position. Did Jersey Museum's archaeological people conclude that to be significant at all?' enquired the sergeant.

'Well, it did lead us along varying lines of investigation at first, particularly as history suggests that burials in dolmens were performed with the bodies being positioned in the very same foetal position. But that's as far as we've taken the possible link so far.'

'Anything else interesting from the boffins, guv?'

213

'Yes, just one thing. Forensics, if you remember, found what appeared to be the scattered leftovers of a partly consumed chicken sandwich lunch, apples and two empty beer cans in the field adjacent to the monument where we now know the body was brought to site from.'

'Yes,' confirmed Shaun.

'Well, the post-mortem has shown there to be absolutely no trace of chicken or apple in the victim's digestive system nor any traces of alcohol in the body either.'

'And what about the food scraps and the beer smelling patch of grass that Nick discovered inside the site?'

'Yes, interesting, that,' replied Gateaux.

'Nick suspected the patch to have been locally saturated with beer … And tests have shown that to be the case. What is more, the beer found was the same type as that which would have originally filled the cans found empty on the other side of the bushes in the field. As for the bits of food, tests also show that it was part of the same meal found scattered in the neighbouring field.'

'Seagulls perhaps, sir?'

'Well, that might explain the scattering of food over the bush but I don't think our feathered friends are very proficient in the beer can slinging department.'

The sergeant laughed.

'And the partial consumption of the lunch wasn't by birds, guv?'

'Not wholly. Jeff has found very definite human bite marks in the sandwich fragments collected which might be useful later if we can find a matching set of incisors.'

'So if there was no trace of chicken, apple or alcohol in the victim's body, are we concluding that the perpetrator, or perpetrators of the crime ate Andrew Price's lunch?' enquired Shaun, a wisp of surprise and disbelief at the hypothesis edging his response.

'Well, it's possible of course, and I did discuss that with the forensic boys but I tend to favour their conclusion.'

'And that is, sir?'

'That is, that for whatever reason, those involved tried to create the illusion that the victim had died sometime AFTER lunch on Wednesday,' replied Gateaux, emphasising the word *"after"* as he sought to reinforce the importance of the apparent lunch-taking deception. 'The beer was simply discarded, albeit rather crudely, to leave two empty cans adding to the appearance that food had been taken. Then, for some reason, the whole lot was rather messily thrown across into the field, perhaps in haste to conceal it,' he continued.

'But why try and conjure that illusion at all, guv? The body ran the risk of being found well before lunchtime and indeed that's exactly what did happen. And why dump the body at this site in the first place?'

'Yes, those two things are nagging away at me as well, sergeant?'

Gateaux paused and habitually rubbed the palms of his hands together. 'Anyway, post-mortems aside, how did you get on while I was away?'

'Well, I spent a while looking back through the items you asked me to, and I also spoke with Mel.'

'Did she remember where she'd put the note?'

'Unfortunately not. All she told me was a repeat of her interview statement, in which she recalled the note reading something to the effect *"Meet you soon at the Cotte, Thanks Andy"*. I spent a while after my chat with her just thinking about the message and that entry in the diary.'

'And where did your head scratching take you?'

'Well, nowhere really. But I guessed if I sat and thought about them long enough it might trigger something.'

'You've been watching too many movies, sergeant. Did you find any time to review any of the statements at all?' said Gateaux, as he continued his search for some value from his sergeant's endeavours.

'A bit of a blank on that as well, sir, I'm afraid.'

215

'Um,' said the Inspector with a small sigh of resigned frustration.

'Yes, not my most productive piece of work, I'm afraid, guv,' admitted Shaun, a disconsolate air breezing through his voice.

'Well, at least the only way is up, as they say. Come on, let's go and do some real detective work. Did the guys downstairs manage to catch up with Sumo and Walsh?'

'Yes, sir. Appears that the two walked into the station about forty minutes ago.'

'Hope they didn't hurt themselves on the granite,' said Gateaux with a self-congratulatory snigger at his attempted quick jibe.

'Good job Nicki didn't hear that one,' replied Shaun as he offered an obligatory smile in support of his boss's feeble attempt at stand up comedy. 'She'd have you joining Kevin and me on the stage next.'

'So back to our builder friends,' said Harry as the joviality was brought to an abrupt halt.

'Yes, guv. I'm told that they were very keen to visit the station, following a little nudge in the right direction from Charlie and Danny. Sally phoned me a few minutes ago to say though that the two are beginning to kick up a bit of a stink on account of the waiting time to be interviewed.'

'Oh, is that so?' said Gateaux, a dismissive, unsympathetic note wrapped around his short response.

'Yes, sir. They claim that they are busy people and that time is money.'

'Okay, guess we better see them then before they accuse us of making them skint,' added Harry, the same lack of compassion still soaking his vocal chords.

Within seconds the two men had arrived in the foyer area serving the basement terrace of interview rooms.

Sally, the duty officer, looked up from her desk.

'Hello, sir. Hi Shaun.'

'Afternoon, Sally. I'm led to believe that you need some

reinforcements?' enquired Gateaux. 'Giving you a spot of bother, are they?' he added, directing a nod towards the waiting lions' dens of interview rooms beyond containing Sumo and Alec Walsh.

'You could say that. They resemble life-forms but I'm convinced they've a few essential pieces of DNA missing.'

'So where exactly are they now, Sally?'

'Mr Gills is along there in room one, sir and we've put Mr Walsh just here in five,' she continued, pointing to the door just beside her.

'Think we'll do Walsh first,' said Harry as he looked across to his sergeant. 'Let Sumo stew a little longer.'

The Inspector walked a few steps forward and opened the door to interview room five before walking in, closely tracked by Shaun.

The door closed with a resounding thud.

Twenty minutes or so later the two re-emerged.

'Useful, guv?' enquired Sally as Harry sidestepped back to the desk.

'Don't think our man Mr Walsh is ever going to win the orator of the year award,' he replied, a strained expression of frustration tugging across his face.

'Um, that bad, was it? Guess you'll want to see Mr Gills now then?' enquired Sally. 'Let's hope he has more to say?' she added.

'Well even if he only says "Hello" that will be one more word than we got out of his side-kick,' replied Gateaux.

'Come on, let's get this over with, sergeant.'

'Would you like some shin pads?' enquired Shaun as he waved a couple of small cardboard-backed notebooks in front of Harry's eyes.

The other two joined in a short burst of laughter. With the repartee soon extinguished, Sally led the way along to the end of the corridor and stopped outside room one.

'He's all yours, lads. Good luck.'

The two men glanced at each other, then across to Sally, before turning back to face the door.

'Right, it's now or never,' said Shaun with a smile.

The Inspector grabbed the handle, turned it and swung open the door.

'Blow me down if its not Tweedle Dum and Tweedle Dee,' came a loud greeting from the seated figure of Sumo as the duo entered the room.

The new arrivals said nothing.

'You could have got your mate to change out of his ballet gear,' continued Sumo as he looked across at Harry wrapped in his second-skin cycling outfit.

'This happens to be Inspector Gateaux,' said Shaun.

'Black Forest or Strawberry,' said the big man instantly with a broad grin.

'The Inspector's heard them all before so you might as well spare us the comedy. I'm Sergeant Shaun Carak. We met earlier.'

'Yeah, my memory does extend beyond half a day,' said Sumo rather animatedly.

That animation continued as he pushed the fragile looking table in front of him to one side and stood up, leaving his chair to crash backwards with a loud crack on to the tiled floor.

'Right, lads,' he said as he took three paces across the room to where the recent arrivals now stood. Opening his shoulders, he stared at them both in turn from close range.

'Can you say what you want to say and then let me go? I've got better things to do than hang around this dive. To be quite honest, my patience ran out about half an hour ago.'

'That'll make a refreshing change,' said Harry.

'What do you mean by that?'

'You being honest.'

Sumo's face articulated forwards towards the Inspector's to the extent that Harry's image of him became a blur.

'And what exactly are you insinuating, mate?'

218

'Right, Mr Gills, can you return to your seat please.'

There was no response.

'Your seat NOW,' repeated Gateaux, his voice elevated to match the menacing tones of his oppressor who then dropped his shoulders and backed off a few paces, muttering under his breath.

'Something to say?' enquired Harry.

'Yeah. Just how long are you going to keep me here? If I leave some of my guys out on that site for more than half an hour unattended they'll need re-training. I have got a business to run you know. Time's money and money's time.'

'Yes, so you've already told us,' interrupted Shaun.

'Look, Mr Gills. I've got a murder inquiry to run, so sit down and shut up until I ask you to speak,' demanded Harry.

'Bit of a toughie for a ballet dancer your boss, isn't he?'

Shaun quickly raised his hand to his mouth to muffle the imminent germination of a laugh.

With one final stare at the colossus before him, the Inspector marched purposefully past him and pulled the interviewee's chair and table back into their original position.

'Right, Mr Gills, you heard me … SIT.'

'Blimey, what the hell do you think this is, Crufts?' he replied, an anger of defiance underlining every word.

'SIT,' said Gateaux once again as the erupting larva flow of volcanic colour began to flow rapidly into his cheeks.

'Look, I'm not going to say it again, Mr Gills.'

Sumo lumbered backwards a few paces and reluctantly rolled back into the seat, some exaggerated grunts of resistance accompanying his retreat.

'That's what I like to see, co-operation,' said Harry, as he moved away and walked around to the other side of the table to take the vacant seat beside Shaun. 'Perhaps we can now begin.'

'Yeah, okay, okay. Just get on with it, Inspector.'

'Right, you are Mr Adrian Gills of "Moai Lodge, St. Saviour," … Yes?'

Sumo nodded.

'And you are the managing director of Colcroft Construction Ltd?'

'Yes. Yes. Yes. I told all this to your sergeant when he quizzed me earlier,' replied Sumo, an angered cocktail of frustration still bubbling in his voice.

'Well, I'm asking the questions now.'

'Okay, so that's my CV. Can we come to the point of all this.'

'All in good time, Mr Gills. I believe my sergeant here has visited you on two occasions in the last twenty four hours or so.'

'Yeah, always pleased to welcome guests.'

'And I understand from him also that you confirmed during one of the visits a knowledge of an incident back in 1998 between a hotel guest and one of your employees. Do you remember the detail of that incident?'

'Yeah, vaguely,' replied the big man, his arms now folded tightly.

'Okay, let me try and unlock some of those vagaries,' said Harry as he leaned to his side and reached down to the floor to retrieve a buff coloured file.

Placing it on the table, he opened the cardboard flap and took out two sheets of paper. 'Letter number one,' he boomed, slamming a copy of a typed letter down on the desk in front of Gills, before ironing one curling corner firmly flat with his hand. 'Dated seventh August 1998 and addressed to Colcroft Construction and your good self, its sender was the hotel's manageress at the time, a Miss Connie Chiwer.'

He looked up briefly.

The impassive stare that greeted him remained as intense and defiant as ever.

'Okay, Mr Gills, if you don't want to look at it I'll read it to you.'

'What ever you want, mate?'

Gateaux took to his feet, snatched the letter from the table and began a slow paced circuit around the small room as he recited its content.

Mr Adrian Gills
Colcroft Construction
Moai Lodge
St Saviour

Coburg Hotels Group
c/o Coburg Hotel
St Helier
Tel: 01534 949444
Fax: 01534 949445
e-mail: coburg@islelink.co.uk

Our Ref: AA/jt/1844
07.08.98

Dear Mr Gills

Hotel Coburg Façade Cleaning Contract: Incident 6th August 1998.

We write further to the incident that occurred between one of our guests and one of your employees during the afternoon of Thursday 6th August 1998.

As you are aware, this incident involved one of your operatives, a Mr Alec Walsh, allegedly confronting and subjecting one of our guests to a torrent of verbal abuse which proved deeply upsetting to both the guest involved and fellow guests who found themselves in the same area of the hotel at the time.

Yesterday, you informed us by telephone that you had since spoken to your employee regarding the allegations and that he confirmed that the incident did indeed occur as reported by us. I trust you agree that this is totally unacceptable behaviour and must not be repeated by any of your site staff.

We consider the incident to be a serious breach of contract, as described in clause 3.4.1 and must insist, as a result, that your employee Mr Alec Walsh is relieved of his duties on this site with immediate effect.

We look forward to receiving confirmation of your prompt action in satisfying this request.

Yours faithfully

Connie

Miss Connie Chiwer.

cc

Mrs D M Preston. Coburg Hotels Group.
Mr D G Gardner.   Gardner & Westwood Solicitors.

'Very well read,' said Sumo patronizingly as he clapped his hands three times.

'The Inspector can read it to you again if you're that impressed,' said Shaun as he rose to the bait of mockery.

Gills turned and refocused his stare towards the seated sergeant.

As the facial jousting continued in silence, Harry returned to his seat and placed the letter on the table, before stretching his arm to slide it across and under the nose of their megalithic guest. 'You recall receiving this letter? … Yes?' he continued, his brusque tone seeking to put an immediate halt to the ongoing duel of derision between his colleague and Sumo.

Gills exchanged one final penetrating stare with the sergeant before dropping his head and looking down at the document placed in front of him.

'Well?' said Harry as the giant skipped quickly through the text.

'Yes, I remember it,' he said, a wave of dismissive inevitability lacing his response.

'Good. Next point then,' said the Inspector as he reached again inside the same buff file and produced a second letter.

'If I may read this piece of correspondence to you?'

'Do I have a choice then?' enquired Sumo, his belligerence now having switched to overdrive.

'Not really.'

'This letter is dated 10th August 1998 and is a reply to that one in front of you from Miss Connie Chiwer,' he continued as he waved the new piece of archive correspondence in the air.

Gateaux remained seated as he relayed the detail of the response.

Miss Connie Chiwer　　　　　**Colcroft Construction**
Coburg Hotels Group　　　　*Moai Lodge*
c/o Coburg Hotel　　　　　　*St Saviour*
St Helier　　　　　　　　　　*Tel: 01534 912812*

　　　　　　　　　　　　　　10.08.98

Dear Miss Chiwer

Thank you for your letter dated 7th August 1998, reference AA/jt/1844.

We deeply regret the incident that occurred at the hotel recently and offer our sincerest apologises to both the Hotel Coburg and your guest for the trauma and embarrassment caused by one of our employees on Thursday 6th August 1998.

Please be assured that Colcroft Construction Ltd do not, and will not, tolerate such behaviour and have now dismissed Mr Alec Walsh from this company for gross misconduct.

We look forward to maintaining our good working relations with the hotel and hope we can now consider this unfortunate episode to be at a close.

Yours faithfully

Gills

Mr Adrian Gills. Director.

Rendition over Harry, as before, pushed the letter across.
'I presume you recall this communication as well?'

Sumo's reticence returned.

'Yes or no?' demanded Harry. 'Simple question requiring a simple answer,' he added.

The silence advanced to a faint nod.

'I'll take that as a yes, shall I?'

'Yeah, take it how you want.'

'Okay. So have you seen Mr Walsh since the writing of that letter?'

'Perhaps a few times around town.'

'That's a change of tune,' interrupted Shaun. 'Just this morning you were telling me that you'd not seen this guy since the incident in '98.'

'Yeah, well I made a mistake, didn't I?'

As he spoke he raised his arm and mopped a few beads of sweat from his forehead.

'Making you a little warm are we … ?' enquired Gateaux. '… Let's raise the temperature just a little.'

'What d'you mean?'

'Well, we have reason to believe that your ex-employee, if "ex" is the right term, is still working for you and has been seen working on your site this week.'

The Inspector leaned forward and, resting his elbows on the desk-top, propped his chin upon his clenched hands before locking the focus of vision intently into the foreboding-filled eyes ahead of him. 'You never sacked him after that incident, did you? For whatever reason, you told the hotel that Alec Walsh had been sacked but you kept him on, didn't you?'

Sumo said nothing, his stare directed toward infinity.

'Think the Inspector's waiting for an answer,' interrupted Shaun once more.

'Well, I haven't got one, have I,' replied Sumo explosively as he raised his upper body slightly in his chair and thumped both clenched hands on the table.

'Okay, take it easy, sir,' said Harry as he tucked his hand back inside the folder.

'Just wish I'd had a chance to fill that thing with mousetraps,' said Sumo as he looked down at the cardboard document holder.

'It is already,' replied the Inspector sharply. 'And we're going to catch you in one of them in a minute.'

As Harry's hand reappeared from its floor level paper chase it had in its grasp a photo.

'What's this, holiday snaps now?'

'I should save the comedy for later. You might need it to cheer yourself up,' said Shaun.

As with the letters moments earlier, Gateaux slid the photo along the desk.

'That's the kid that got done in, isn't it. Your chum showed it to me yesterday.'

'Yes, but I didn't say anything then about him being done in, as you call it, did I?' said Shaun.

'Don't know, but you wouldn't be sniffing around like you have been if he'd died of boredom, would you?'

'Well, perhaps he would have only died of that if he'd spoken with you, pal?' replied the sergeant.

Sumo raised a brief snigger.

'So now who's the comedian then? Look, as I told you yesterday and I'm telling you today, I've never seen the geezer before in my life.'

'What would you say if I told you that this poor lad was the very same lad involved in the incident with your Mr Alec Walsh back in 1998?' enquired Gateaux.

'I'd still tell you that I've never seen him,' replied Sumo, as he slipped effortlessly back into his now accustomed aggressive response mode.

'If that's the way you want to play it, we've got other places to visit and more accommodating people to speak to right now, so how about if we come back later and you give us some answers,' added the Inspector, a non negotiable emulsion of contained anger now brushing in his response.

Immediately Sumo took to his feet. 'Look, I've done nothing wrong and I want out of here … NOW. I came here voluntarily, in good faith, and I want out. It's a free country and I'm a free man,' he shouted, his anger amplifying with each word.

Instantly the Inspector rose, almost combatively, from his seat.

'You might be free at the moment, but if we don't get some answers soon, that could all change.'

'Look, I've told you all I know.'

'Come on, Shaun, we've got other more productive things to do with our time,' said Gateaux as he began his retreat towards the door.

Shaun stood and followed closely behind.

As they neared the door Sumo, who had himself risen rather sluggishly from his chair, stepped across in front of them blocking their exit. 'You can't do this. You've no right.'

'I want answers and you're not ready, it seems, to give them to me. It's as simple as that,' replied Harry, his uncompromising mood still pasted upon each word from his mouth.

'I think that gives me every right, don't you, sergeant?' he continued, turning to look at Shaun for support.

Shaun nodded.

'We can hold you for a while longer, you know and after that then we can of course arrest you, if you'd prefer?'

'On what charge?' exploded Gills as the blood rush to the head threatened to reach Niagara proportions.

'How about wasting police time for starters and, if you carry

226

on standing there, we'll do you for obstruction as well,' added the sergeant.

With obvious reluctance Sumo moved to one side, allowing the Inspector to reach around and open the door.

As Harry and Shaun made their exit and crossed the threshold into the corridor, a young duty officer approached to take their place in the room.

'Keep an eye on him son,' said Harry. 'He's a bit of a loose cannon just at the moment.'

'What did you go and tell him that for, guv?' said the waiting Sally. 'You'll have him quivering in his boots now, poor kid.'

'Oh, you've got to keep these young-uns on their toes, you know,' replied Gateaux.

Though she considered it cruelly undeserving, Sally reacted with an impulsive though conscience riddled giggle.

'So what do you want us to do with the two guys now, sir?' she enquired as her involuntary facial contortions erased themselves.

Harry paused and looked up at the small wall mounted clock that read four twenty five. 'We'll give them an hour or so to calm down, I think. Then we'll give them one last chance to avoid staying here tonight in your little B and B.'

'Okay, no problem, guv. We'll see you at around five thirty then?'

'Fine,' replied Harry.

'Come on, Shaun. Let's catch up with the others again upstairs. They should all be back by now.'

The two men turned and made their way towards the corridor exit, marked above the door with an illuminated lime green sign.

CHAPTER NINE

Before long the hub of the investigation had returned to the quintet of collective minds occupying room four.

'Right, thanks to you all for your promptness,' said Gateaux as he began addressing his crime team once again. 'As promised, I'll keep this very brief as I've got to be away soon myself. Oh, and Shaun's got some baby-sitting to do, so we mustn't keep him either.'

'Trust you've got plenty of nappies, mate,' said Kevin as he looked across to his colleague.

The others laughed.

'Before we start though, I have a big favour to ask you all,' continued Harry.

The four before him looked up from their seats in silent anticipation.

'I know how valuable the weekends are to each of us, but I'm very mindful that every guest on that fateful archaeological tour last Wednesday returns home tomorrow. Right now, we still have more questions than answers but with a bit of luck and a big effort I'm still optimistic that we can still crack this case before the group leave the Island.'

'What you're trying to say, guv, is that you'd like us to come in tomorrow?' interrupted Nicki.

Harry hesitated before replying.

'Well, yes, that's about the long and short of it. I do apologise about the very short notice, but, to be honest, I'd really hoped we might have wrapped things up before now.'

Kevin lifted his arm.

'Sorry, sir, but I can't make tomorrow. I'm flying over to the mainland first thing with the wife and kids. Not back until Wednesday, I'm afraid.'

'Okay, fair enough, so what about the rest of you then?'

'I'm okay for tomorrow,' confirmed Ami.

'Yes, count me in as well, guv;' said Nicki. 'A bit of overtime might come in quite useful just now' she added.

With two down and one to go Harry looked across at his sergeant.

'Suppose you better include me as well then,' added Shaun, a discernable air of reluctance moderating the tone of his response.

'Thank you very much. It is appreciated,' said Gateaux as he offered a grateful nod to the three volunteers.

'Right, Nicki, Kevin. Back to today's news. How did you get on with the bank manager?' he continued.

'More to the point, did you get me any spare cash?' asked Shaun, leaning forward and turning to look at his two colleagues.

'No cash, mate, but some useful information.'

Shaun rolled back into his chair as Kevin turned to face the Inspector. 'Before I tell you about the meeting at the bank, sir, we've had a response from the French police in St. Malo who have spoken with Woody Tambeau's family in a nearby village.'

'Did they have anything interesting to tell us, Kev?'

'Yes, guv. Seems that the family are certain that the beaded wrist band with the surf motif found in the tractor bucket at their farm doesn't belong to any of their lot.'

'How certain?'

'One hundred per cent according to Inspector Fabienne L'Horizon in St Malo.'

'Good. Well that narrows our field of inquiry down a bit.'

'Didn't you say earlier, sir, that we're fairly confident that the bangle didn't belong to the victim either?' enquired Ami.

'That's correct. I raised the issue with Mr Price when I met him yesterday and he's sure his son wouldn't have been into wearing anything like that.'

'So the very strong conclusion, guv, must be that it belonged to the person or persons who brought the body to the site?'

'It's beginning to look that way, Ami. Is there any chance of tracing where the item originated from, Kev?'

'Already done, sir. Turned out to be a lot simpler than you might have expected,' interrupted Nicki.

'Danny drove around the surf shops this afternoon. He found a small beach hut down at St Ouen owned by a local group of surf bums. One of them, a girl by the name of Kirsty, makes these bangle things by hand as a little side line.'

'I presume that means that they're all very individual in design then?'

'Yes, all totally unique.'

'So, is there any chance of finding out from this Kirsty character, the name of the person who bought our little bangle?' asked Gateaux with an expression that begged the answer to be "yes".

'Unfortunately not, guv. That's where the simplicity ends. Kirsty reckons she's sold about a hundred or so over the years, but has absolutely no record of who bought them or when they were bought. She did say though that a dozen or so of them were given away as gifts at various times to a number of individuals within her immediate circle of friends. Anyway, we've sent the item onward to the laboratory to see if they can come up with something for us to go on.'

'This circle of friends … Did we manage to get a list of them from this Kirsty character at all? There's always a chance that it might throw up an interesting name?'

'Sorry, sir, I don't think that was done,' replied Nicki, turning as she spoke to invite a contribution from her seated neighbour, Kevin.

He shook his head.

'Well, can you put it on the shopping list of things to do in the morning then?' said Harry.

'I'll leave that one with you, Nicki, perhaps, as your side-kick is off on a jolly,' he continued.

'Yes, no problem, guv.'

231

'Any excuse to get down on the beach, eh?' whispered Shaun.

Nicki smiled. 'I'll go over early tomorrow morning, sir,' she continued. 'I think there's a good swell expected so the local surfing crowd should be out in force.'

As she finished, Ami raised her hand tentatively in the air at half-mast. 'I hope this isn't a silly observation, sir, but a number of the remarks you've made recently appear to suggest that you're convinced that we are looking for more than one suspect in the solving of this case?'

'Not silly at all,' replied Gateaux. 'Following the lab and fieldwork, forensics carried out a partial reconstruction this lunchtime of events at the Santille site on Wednesday morning. Their conclusion is that, given the terrain, the dense foliage and the activities that we now know took place, it was impossible for the body to have been transferred from the tractor to its resting place by just one person working alone.'

'So how many are we looking for then, guv?' quizzed Shaun.

'Now that's the sixty four thousand dollar question, isn't it, though Jeff says that he is ninety-nine percent confident that we're looking for two adults. They deduced that after their tests on the footprint impressions found on the dolmen site and on the ploughed field immediately adjacent to it.'

'Both males?' asked Ami.

'Possibly,' replied the Inspector. 'Both footprint trails found were from large shoes, size ten plus.'

'Have to check out Sumo and Walsh's boots later then?' suggested Shaun.

'Yes, I'll leave that unenviable task to you, sergeant.'
Gateaux swivelled his head fractionally and re-focused in upon Kevin.

'Back to your meeting with the AMC Bank. Anything to tell us?'

'Well, sir, Nicki and myself met with Dwight Henderson, the manager of the AMC in Princes Street, as planned this afternoon. Quite an impressive organisation, it turns out, with an extensive international network of branches and nearly eleven thousand staff worldwide,' replied Kevin.

'Company profile aside, Mr Henderson allowed us to look at the employee record on Andrew Price. As we knew already, it confirmed that he had a six-month contract with them in the early part of 1998. During that time, he spent approximately two months under the direction of a Miss Georgina Le Ferne, setting up a new computer system for the personnel, administration and internal finance departments,' he added.

'And did he have access to those departments worldwide as a result, Kev?'

'It would seem so, sir.'

'Has anyone spoken with Miss Le Ferne yet?'

'I spoke with her very briefly, guv, an hour or so ago but she was having breakfast at the time,' said Nicki.

'Breakfast?' cried Gateaux, his voice raised slightly as he endeavoured to grasp the seemingly eccentric notion of one consuming cornflakes and toast in the middle of the afternoon. 'Breakfast … At this time?' he continued, his voice still elevated an octave as the cornflake conundrum continued to confuse his cerebral regions.

'Yes. Miss Le Ferne, you see, is currently in the middle of a one year sabbatical at an AMC branch in Seattle,' she said as the solution to the breakfast riddle was dispatched.

'Okay, I'm with you now.'

'Well, sir, we just managed to catch her as she was starting her day but she didn't have much to add. She remembered Andrew Price, a quiet unassuming lad, she described him as. Definitely knew his stuff as far as computers were concerned but nothing much else to report.'

'And did we find out what he did for the other four months of his contract when he wasn't with Miss Le Ferne?'

'Yes, guv. It seems he then worked for the International equities department, again setting up and developing computer systems,' added Kevin as he took over the conversation from his colleague.

'And again, that would have allowed him access to those departments worldwide?'

'Yes, sir, all four corners.'

'So who exactly was his boss in that particular department?'

'I wish we could give you a clear answer to that one,' replied Nicki as the baton of discussion was returned. 'All it had typed in the file were the initials A.A. and a scribble that the manager thinks reads as L.I.B? He said he'd try and find out a little more about these mysterious characters and establish who they are and where they are now. He's going to call us as soon as he finds out anything useful.'

'The systems our Mr Price developed and adapted for AMC?' said the Inspector enquiringly as his eyes switched back to Kevin.

'Yes, guv?'

'Were they solely for use here on Jersey, Kev?'

'No, far from it. Mr Henderson informed us that the systems that Andrew Price and his team of colleagues developed have over recent years been adopted, more or less, as the *de facto* standard throughout the global AMC networks.'

The Inspector paused and scratched the side of his head vigorously.

'Problem with nits, sir?' enquired Shaun.

The Inspector laughed. 'No, just collecting my thoughts.'

'I'll give you a penny for them,' added Shaun.

'Well, that'll be about three pounds fifty you owe me then, sergeant.'

This time it was the turn of the seated quartet to laugh. As they did, Nicki called out.

'If you offer Shaun a penny for his thoughts, guv, you'll end up with some change.'

The laughter intensified for a moment before being watered down by the loud tap of a pen on the table at the front.

'If we can just get on, I've got to be away soon,' informed

Gateaux as he sought to spoil the "end of week" banter. A civilised hush of anticipation returned to the forum.

'That information you gave us a few moments ago, Kevin …' continued Gateaux. '… There appears to have been a huge amount of trust placed in Andrew Price by the bank particularly as he was only there on a six month contract. He seems to have had almost unlimited access to what many in the AMC organisation probably regarded as classified information.'

'That's right,' said Nicki. 'Dwight Henderson said there was actually good reason for placing such trust in Mr Price.'

'And that reason was?'

'Well, guv, prior to the six month Island contract, we discovered that he'd worked for nearly eleven years at one of their London offices. Henderson has spoken to a senior partner in London who remembers Andrew Price. Seems they had no complaints about his work during his period of employment with them. Perhaps more to the point, they couldn't praise his enormous efforts and input highly enough.'

'And who did he work for there?'

'That, like the situation here in Jersey, seems a little unclear at present. Henderson, through his London contacts, is trying to establish that information for us as we speak. From what we have learned so far though, Andrew Price's work in London was of a similar kind to that which he was doing over here.'

'Um … Very interesting indeed,' said Harry as he paused for a moment's reflection.

'So, just to sum up,' he continued as his mind computed and reviewed the salient details. 'It's probably fair to say that in the eleven and a half years or so that the victim worked for AMC, he came to know intimately the bank's global computer systems and, perhaps, more importantly, had what amounted to unlimited access to the information they contained.'

'That would seem a fair assessment,' said Nicki.

'Yes, I'd agree with your conclusions, sir,' added Kevin.

'Okay, moving on. Did you find anything about his salary?' enquired Gateaux.

'Did indeed," continued Kevin. 'The guy certainly earned a sizeable remuneration for his efforts, both in London and in Jersey. Big enough to put a big smile on my face.'

'But was it big enough to afford some big spending?'

Kevin paused before continuing.

'Well, I've done a few quick calculations, sir, but I'm finding it very hard to reconcile that his resulting disposable income could have funded the Aladdin's cave of books and computer gear we know about, not to mention the extravagances afforded to his father which we're told included paying off the mortgage.'

'I thought as much. Anything else to add?'

'Not for the moment, guv, but I've left a photocopy of the victim's personnel file in your office in-tray.'

'Great, thanks. I'll try and have a read of those later if I get a chance,' replied Harry. 'And you, Nicki. Anything else at all?' he added as he continued to cast his eyes randomly along the line of seats.

'Yes, sir. I did a bit of scratching around as you asked to see if I could find out a bit about our doorman friend over at the Coburg.'

'And what did you find?'

'Well, you will never guess what he was doing before he became a doorman a few years ago, guv.'

'Go on, surprise us, Nicki.'

'Well, it seems he lived in Winchester before moving over here. Ran a small building construction business before selling it on to, wait for it … Mr Adrian Gills.'

She paused and awaited a reaction from those around her.

'Sumo?' replied the Inspector, his short response richly toned in disbelief. 'You mean Joe Masters knows Adrian Gills on a business level?'

'Yes, sir. They seem to have been buddies since army days according to one of Mr Master's past business associates who Inspector Scally managed to hunt down for me.'

236

'Sumo in the army?' cried Shaun. 'What was he, a tank?'

An artillery barrage of laughter ricocheted around the room.

'Well, that certainly adds a new dimension to our inquiry,' said Gateaux. 'Do we know how and why the sale of the Masters business came about, Nicki?' he added.

She nodded confidently. 'It seems that Sumo wanted to expand his construction business beyond the shores of Jersey at the same time as Joe Masters was looking for an easier life. He is nearly twenty years older than Mr Gills, you see.'

'So Masters sold out to Colcroft Construction and then moved to the Island?'

'That's correct, guv, but he didn't relinquish total control of his business interests in Winchester, nor ownership of a luxury house on the outskirts of the city. Interestingly, he's still listed on the register in Companies House as a non-executive director of the Winchester operation which calls itself Colcroft (Southern) Ltd. It's a sister operation to the one run on Jersey. It also has one of its directors named as Alec Walsh.'

Gateaux rocked back in his chair, crossed his arms, and then raised one hand to scratch his forehead yet again as he sought to calm the violent storm of fresh scenarios now washing around ceaselessly in his mind. 'Looks like you might just have opened a veritable can of worms here, Nicki,' he said as the mind-storm of computation abated for a brief moment. 'We have Sumo and Walsh … Do we know where Joe Masters is right now?' he continued as he scanned the seated ranks before him for an answer.

'No. I did quiz reception at the Coburg but Mr Masters has not been seen about the hotel today,' replied Nicki. 'Seems he phoned in sick first thing. We did ask Lucy if she could find an excuse to phone him at his home this afternoon.'

'His Jersey home or his Winchester home?' enquired Gateaux.

Nicki paused.

'Um … The Jersey home, I believe. I don't think Lucy's

aware of the Winchester residence. Anyway, she got no reply apparently.'

'Okay. Think we'll have to track down our elusive doorman and pull him in for a chat as soon as possible. Is there anything more to add?'

'Yes, sir, just one other thing,' she added. 'With the doorman "absent without leave" so to speak, Kevin and myself, out of idle curiosity, managed to sweet-talk the cleaning maid into letting us have a quick peep inside the chap's hotel office this afternoon which she was cleaning at the time.'

'And did you find any little treasures to satisfy your curiosity?'

'More than little treasures, guv. Gold nuggets more like. We found a large bound report in one of his cupboards which it turned out had been produced by external consultants for the Coburg Hotels Group, the consortium which owns and runs the Coburg itself.'

'We also found a number of loose documents and minutes all appearing to relate to a series of meetings by the Coburg Group's main board,' interrupted Kevin. 'Seemed to span the last couple of years or so at least,' he added.

'Did you mention your findings to Lucy?'

'Yes, sir. We showed everything we'd found to her,' continued Kevin.

'The report and other documents turned out to be photocopies of highly confidential information, the original copies of which are stored in the hotel's basement vaults. Apparently the vaults are secured and accessed via a highly complex computerised retrieval system and code known only to a privileged few,' added Nicki.

'Do we have a list of this privileged few?'

'Yes, Lucy did give us the names,' said Kevin.

'And was Joe Masters among them?'

'No, guv.'

'Did you read the report at all?'

'Yes, very briefly. It seemed to revolve around some master plan for the future of the Group's empire and its funding.'

'So what was Lucy's reaction to your discovery?' asked Shaun.

'Well, she was totally gob-smacked that we had stumbled across the information,' replied Nicki as she turned and addressed her colleague.

'And did you tell her where you'd found it all?' enquired Gateaux.

'No, we thought we'd try and keep that from her for the moment, though she wasn't too happy about it,' she replied.

'But I guess we can't keep the secret from her for long in the interests of the hotel's security? We'll have to tell her some time soon for sure,' added Kevin.

'We just thought it might be useful if you had a chance to have your chat with the doorman first before exciting the hotel too much towards his involvement in a possible case of corporate espionage,' said Nicki. 'Whatever his motives.'

'Yes, you might be right.'

With the Inspector's final word a short hiatus in the conversation descended across the room.

'Er ... That's all for now, sir,' continued Nicki as the veil of silence was suddenly lifted.

'Yes, thanks to you both for that. Good team-work,' said Harry, nodding appreciatively to the two.

He raised his arm and snatched a quick glance at his watch. 'Right, ten minutes left before I must be off. Ami, can you briefly fill us in on what you found out during your afternoon walkabout around the corridors of the Coburg?'

Just as she was about to speak there was a knock at the door.

'Come in,' called out Harry.

The door opened allowing the fingers of a hand to wrap themselves around the exposed frame, followed soon after by the head of Sally.

'Sorry to disturb you, guv, but there's been an interesting

discovery at the Coburg which we thought you should know about as soon as possible.'

'Oh, yes?' said Gateaux, his response over-dosed in anticipation.

'We've just been informed that the remains of a lap-top computer, which might have belonged to Andrew Price, have been found in one of the skips of rubbish on the Colcroft building site. Seems the alert followed an anonymous tip-off to the station.'

'Has anyone informed forensics?'

'Yes, sir and I believe that they're looking at it now.'

'Okay, thanks for that, Sally. I'll see if I can squeeze a visit to the site when I return to the hotel in a short while.'

'Just before I go,' continued Sally, her hand still wrapped firmly around the door frame for balance as she sought to prevent her contorted posture from being launched unceremoniously across the floor in front of her. 'You will be back downstairs soon, won't you?' she enquired, a hint of pleading weaved in and around her words.

'Yes, won't be too long now. Shaun and myself should, I hope, catch up with you again at around five thirty, as promised.'

'Good. It's just that Mr Gills and Mr Walsh are beginning to get a bit agitated again.'

'Well I guess this latest development should serve to calm them down a little perhaps,' said Harry, looking across to Shaun.

The sergeant nodded.

Content that the cavalry would be returning to her side in the not too distant future, Sally's head disappeared and the door closed.

Gateaux hesitated before returning attention to his seated colleagues.

'Sorry about that, Ami. You were just about to tell us how you got on with your walkabout?'

Ami coughed gently.

'Yes, sir. I managed to cover most of the rooms on the third and fourth floors, knocking on those that we got no answer from yesterday. A few more people seemed to be around today but those that I spoke to didn't really have anything new to tell us. The handful that did recognise the victim from the photograph described him as a shy person, very much giving the impression of being a loner.'

'Anything else?'

'Yes. There was something, which didn't seem that important until a few moments ago when Nicki and Kevin told us about the documents that they had found in Joe Masters office.'

'Well, share it with us nonetheless.'

For a second time, Ami coughed softly. 'It's just that I stumbled across the discarded remains of a photographic montage dropped in a dimly lit corner alcove of a small meeting room on the fourth floor. It showed the past, present and future construction projects as carried out by the Coburg Hotels Group. I made a note of the company that had given the presentation, Malgra Associates, and made contact with their senior partner, a Mr David Drains.'

'Did he give you a flowing response?' interrupted Shaun with a laugh.

'Get a life,' whispered Nicki.

'Anyway …' continued Ami. ' … Mr Drains told me that the information had formed part of a presentation given by Malgra some weeks ago on behalf of the Coburg Group in front of some fairly influential financiers. The main purpose of their efforts and those of the Coburg board was to drum up some support and, more importantly, some funds for the Group's ambitious expansion plans. He seemed somewhat surprised that we had found the information lying around as we did. Malgra had assumed that the hotel had either put it all in safe keeping or destroyed it after the presentation.'

'And what projects did this montage show exactly?' enquired Harry.

'Well, it started with a few pictures of the Coburg Hotel itself undergoing cleaning of its perimeter walls in 1998. Fairly minor works really. Then followed some artist's impressions of the new annex wing to the hotel which, as we know, is currently underway.'

'And then?'

'Well, sir, then came the exciting bits. Some very detailed sketches, this time showing proposals for a huge new conference centre and luxury hotel on the waterfront, which included a casino. That's scheduled for completion in 2005 it seems. An accompanying piece of text at the end talked of other more ambitious plans aimed well into the future.'

'And what sort of projects were they then?'

'Well, they included a spectacular glass-domed extension to the waterfront leisure and entertainment centre, an art gallery and a huge public aquarium. But the *pièce de résistance* was an elevated monorail transport system which linked all the waterfront facilities to the town centre.'

'Um … Work for a lifetime if you're a builder by the sound of it,' commented Kevin.

'Perhaps Colcroft Construction are aware of that, guv,' suggested Shaun.

'How do you mean?' enquired Harry.

'Well, I've been doing a little research on them just recently and it would seem that they have been going through some sort of rapid expansion programme of late. I spoke with a builder friend of mine this morning and he said that Colcrofts have been packing the newspaper pages with their recruitment ads recently. And Nicki told us earlier, of course, about their acquisition of the building company in Winchester. It might be that Sumo is gearing up in the expectation of taking on this roll-over portfolio of work?'

'I'm no businessman, Shaun, but that sounds a bit of a risky strategy to me. Gills would need to be fairly confident that the work was there and be equally confident that he would get it, wouldn't he?'

'Well, yes, guv, but I get the impression that Sumo is extremely well informed on the Hotel Group's future plans.'

Before Gateaux could investigate his sergeant's hypothesis in more detail Ami raised her hand. 'Excuse me, but I've got something to add on that.'

'Yes, please, carry on, Ami.'

'Well, when I quizzed Lucy indirectly on the subject yesterday, sir, she said that Mr Gills is forever plugging away for information on future work plans and he keeps her and the hotel sweet with freebie little bits of work here and there. Significantly, perhaps, she did say that there has been more than one occasion when she's felt that he has been one step ahead of her in his knowledge of the Coburg's future project ambitions.'

'Um … Interesting. Perhaps we'll quiz Mr Gills on his apparent talent for crystal ball gazing when we see him in a short while,' suggested Harry.

'So, do we know anymore about how Lucy and the hotel find Sumo and his company generally?' he continued, as he scanned his audience for a response.

Shaun looked up. 'Yes, guv. She understands that he does have a reputation for being a bit of a no-nonsense character on site but to her and the rest of the Coburg management he puts himself across as the perfect gentlemen.'

'I must say, sergeant, that I find the notion of our friend Sumo being perceived by anyone as the perfect gentlemen a little disturbing. But presumably, if Gills does know about the future Coburg Group plans and is relying on them to support his own expansion, he can't afford to be any other way with them. If Colcrofts put a foot wrong they could risk jeopardising the likelihood of taking on any of those future projects.'

'Could be a very expensive mistake to loose out on the work, what with all the resources they seem to be collecting together at present … ' interrupted Ami. ' … Interestingly, sir, Lucy did tell me that Colcrofts nearly lost the current annex contract because of the incident back in 1998 during the façade cleaning job. Seems they earned a reprieve on account of their swift and decisive action in responding to the hotel's grievances at the time. Because of that their slate is fairly clean and Lucy added that there's no reason why they shouldn't continue to do any future projects with them.'

Just as she finished her sentence, the Inspector began pacing in front of the display board and scratching the side of his head feverishly.

'Thinking again, guv?' enquired Shaun.

'Um, just a bit,' said Gateaux as he stopped his excited quickstep and looked across to his sergeant. 'What we've been talking about over the last five minutes or so might well explain one reason why Sumo's so reluctant to admit that Mr Walsh is still very much a part of his company. He's just scared that he might lose the next contract. And Walsh is keeping quiet probably because Gills is sitting on him. Perhaps we'll touch on it and raise this with the two downstairs later.'

'Yes, should be an interesting little session,' said the sergeant.

Harry nodded. 'Okay, if there's nothing else then, we'll call it a day. Thanks everyone and see you tomorrow ... Oh, and have a good weekend, Kevin.'

'Will do. Thank you, sir. I'll be thinking of you all.'

'Oh, I'm sure you will ... Get lost, and don't forget the postcard.'

The meeting at an end, the four stood and with the exception of Shaun filed out quickly from the room.

As he waited a few seconds for Gateaux to complete a few jottings in his notepad, the sergeant looked at his watch. It read five twenty. 'Did you say that you were going to the hotel now, guv? It's just that I've got to be away by six o'clock at the latest, otherwise you may have my murder to investigate and Bev will be the prime suspect.'

'Don't worry, Shaun. I'll make sure you're away in good time. We'll see Sumo and Walsh first, and I'll attend to the hotel later.'

Shaun smiled as the early wrinkles of anxiety melted from his face.

'I can't be too long myself anyway,' added Harry. 'As I said earlier, Mel's invited me to the farewell barbecue on St Ouen's beach tonight.'

He hesitated and re-engaged thought mode. 'Tell you what, why don't you come yourself? Bring the kids. I'm sure there will be plenty of room on the bus for them. I'll clear it with the Coburg when I go over there shortly but I know there'll be no problem.'

'Yes, that sounds like good fun. Thanks very much, guv. I was wondering what I could do with the little brats tonight.'

'Right, that's sorted then.'

'Shall we go and find Sally?' continued Gateaux as he made his first steps towards the door.

Minutes later the two found themselves back downstairs.

'That's what I like to see, punctuality,' cried Sally, looking up at the clock on the wall that had just ticked over to five thirty.

'How's Mr Angry?' enquired the Inspector.

'Getting angrier, guv. The sooner you get that obnoxious character out of my hair the better.'

'Proving a little bit of a pain, is he?'

'No, he's proving a large pain.'

'He's not stopped bad mouthing for this, that, and the other, since you left him earlier.'

'Right, let's see our Mr Gills straight away then. See if we can't calm him down a bit,' said Harry. 'We'll catch up with Mr Walsh straight after,' he continued as Sally began to escort the two men back to interview room one.

'Let's keep the Joe Masters connection out of the conversation for the moment, Shaun,' said Harry as he approached the end of the corridor. 'We need to get the full story from Masters himself first,' he added.

'Understood, sir,' replied Shaun as the three arrived at the door to room one.

'Ready?' enquired Sally, her hand poised expectantly on the door's white enamelled handle.

The Inspector nodded.

'Good luck again,' she said as she opened the door.

The two men stepped aside and waited as the ashen looking figure of young Eddie made his exit.

'Thanks a bundle for that. Think I need a long lie down,' he said, forcing every last fibre of energy to extract a smile.

As the two crossed the threshold, the fire-breathing response from Sumo was instantaneous.

'About time too. Say what you want to say and then I want out.'

'In a bit of a hurry, are we, Mr Gills?' enquired Shaun calmly, as he sought to damp down the tinderbox before him.

'Well I am now, no thanks to you and your ballerina friend,' he replied, his rage-saturated voice lifting an octave with each syllable. 'Look, not only have I missed an afternoon on site but Friday is wages day. The lads want their money by four o'clock. Now I won't be able to sort them out 'til the morning. They'll be charging me interest if I'm not careful. That's if they don't chuck me in the concrete wagon first.'

'Well they'll just have to wait then, won't they?' said Shaun.

'And another thing,' shouted Sumo, his body still agitated by the earthquake rumbles of hostility within. 'If it gets back to the hotel that I'm in here being quizzed by you lot I'll be done for.'

'And if it gets back to Lucy and the hotel's management that you've been telling them porky-pies you'll be done for as well,' added Harry.

'And what's that supposed to mean, mate?' enquired Sumo as his voice level normalised for a few seconds.

Harry leaned across the desk and once again stared at Gills from close range.

'Look, I'm a very busy man, my sergeant is a very busy man and you keep telling me that you're a very busy man as well. So can you cut it with the clever talk and stop messing about because I've got better things to do with my Friday evenings than share them with the likes of you.'

For a moment Sumo flinched as the first atom of apparently weakened defences exposed itself. Before he'd had a chance to reply, the Inspector continued his barrage.

'As I suggested during our first little chat, you never sacked Mr Walsh in 1998, did you? You told the hotel you had because you wanted to keep them under your wing. You dared not appeal against their request to dismiss Walsh because you knew if you crossed swords with them it might kill off any chances of future work. And you also knew they had enough work to keep you going from now until retirement if you played your cards right. Tell me I'm not right Mr Gills?'

The Inspector sat back and arched the upper part of his back gently across behind the seat as he awaited Sumo's response.

Silence descended upon the room.

Gills dipped his head and began combing randomly through his thick mop of hair with his fingers. Suddenly, a large drop from a river of perspiration fell from his forehead and splashed on the table as he flicked his head back up and looked forward.

'Okay, Okay, so I didn't sack Walsh after that bust up in 1998. Can I go now?'

'That's more like it, Mr Gills. Co-operation at last. If you'd said this earlier we could have all had a pleasant afternoon.'

'I was hoping I'd never have to tell you 'cos I didn't want it getting back to the hotel.'

'But you ran the risk of them finding out that you were here,' snapped Shaun.

'Well, that was a lesser risk I was prepared to take.'

'Of course there were other reasons why you didn't sack Walsh, weren't there?' said Harry. 'At the time, you had him ear-marked to look after the Winchester operations which you were then planning to take over?'

'How did you know about that?' demanded Sumo as he pushed his arms down against the table and slammed himself back in his chair.

'Doesn't matter just now.'

'All right, all right,' said Gills as he relaxed his arms. 'Alec Walsh happened to be one of the best carpenter-foremans around back in 1998, still is. If I'd got rid of him then, someone else would have picked him up straight away. Tradesmen like him are worth their weight in gold on this Island and if the client wants quality, and I am to make any money, then I need skilled craftsmen around me. He was something of a Jack-of-all-trades and knew a lot of useful people as well. I saw him at some point in the future as the right person to create the links between the Winchester based business and here.'

'So how did you manage to keep Mr Walsh out of view of the hotel's management for so long?' asked Shaun.

'Didn't have to, did I? They never knew what he looked like in the first place.'

'So they just took you at your word that he'd been sacked?'

'Well, yeah. They had no reason to disbelieve me, did they? You're not going to tell them, are you?'

'No reason to, unless they ask.'

'Will they ever ask that question then?'

'Depends where our investigations take us,' replied Harry. 'But they might be curious, as indeed we are, as to how the victim's broken computer ended up on one of the rubbish skips on your site. Any bright ideas?'

'Well, that's the first I've heard of it.'

'Well, now you have, what're your thoughts?'

'None whatsoever, except that it didn't get there until after three o'clock today and I was here then, remember?'

'And how can you be so sure when it might have got there?'

'Because the skips were booked for changing around mid-afternoon today, that's why. Check with the lads on site if you don't believe me.'

'Might just do that, Mr Gills,' said Harry.

With that, he pressed down on the table and stood from his seat.

'And just one other thing, Mr Gills. How much do you know of future work plans by the Hotels Group?'

'Why do you ask?'

'Well, you seem on quite a radical expansion plan at present. It must be in preparation for something big?'

'Yes, it's called ambition, pal. There's loads of work out there and I want more of it. No crime in that, is there? Now can I go?' responded Sumo as he shuffled uncomfortably in his seat and prepared for an exit.

'For the moment yes but I might want another word tomorrow.'

'Well you know where to find me. I'm not going to do a runner anywhere if that's what you are worried about.'

'I'm glad to hear it.'

With that Gills rolled forward, flicked the chair from behind him and stood, followed closely by Shaun.

Bathed in an eerie silence, the three men left the room and walked to the small desk at the end of the short corridor behind which sat the lone figure of Sally.

'All finished, guv?'

'Nearly. Can you arrange for some dabs from our friend. Then he will be free to go.'

'What the hell do you need those for? I've done nothing wrong,' shouted Sumo as the colour of anguish that had been in retreat returned instantly to his face.

'Calm down, Mr Gills. You were doing so nicely. It's only a routine request in this case.'

'Routine? So you do this to every one who walks in through the station doors, do you?'

'Well, not always, but it's in your own interests. Who knows what prints we might find on that trashed computer, for example?'

'Well I'm telling you now, whatever prints you find on that computer thing, they won't be mine.'

'In that case, you've nothing to worry about then have you?'

said Harry. 'You all right here then Sally while Shaun and myself go and have a chat with Mr Walsh?' he continued.

'Yes, no problem, sir. Charlie's on his way down very soon to take over from me for a while. In fact here he comes now.'

'It's all right, you know … ' interrupted Gills. ' … You don't need reinforcements. I'll be a good boy.'

'Pleased to hear it,' said Gateaux. 'Right, we'll be off now,' he added as Charlie made his way around to join Sally behind the counter.

'Yes, thanks, guv.'

'And thank you, Mr Gills, for your time,' said Harry as he looked back at the big man whose body now slouched across the counter, fingers tapping a frustrated dance on its cup-stained mahogany top.

'Pleasure was all mine, I'm sure, Inspector … Oh, and Sergeant, of course.'

'Come on Shaun, let's go and see Mr Walsh. Still in there, is he?' enquired Gateaux as he looked across at Sally and nodded to the room adjacent to the desk.

'I hope so, unless he's dug a tunnel.' she replied.

Harry laughed before taking a few steps sideways and entering room five, followed closely by his sergeant.

Ten or so minutes later Alec Walsh, flanked by the two men, found himself back at the charge counter.

'Sally gone?' enquired Shaun.

'Yes, about five minutes ago,' replied Charlie.

'Mr Gills as well?' asked Harry.

'Yes, sir. We managed to get some prints from him.'

'Good. Can you do the same with our man here and ensure you get a contact number. Then we'll let him leave.'

Gateaux turned to face Walsh. 'You are on the Island this weekend if we need to catch up with you again?'

Walsh nodded.

'Right, see you later, Chaz,' said the Inspector as he returned his attention briefly to the counter and then across to his sergeant. 'Come on, let's get going.'

250

'So do you think Sumo and Walsh are involved in Andrew Price's murder?' enquired Shaun as the two made their way up the double flight tile-covered staircase.

'Don't know yet. A few theories are beginning to gel in my mind though.'

'What do you think about the computer in the skip, guv? Mr Walsh didn't seem to have much to say about it, did he?'

'Mr Walsh hasn't had much to say all afternoon, Shaun. But then I think Sumo put the kibosh on the guy's ability to offer any meaningful information long before we got to him, simply to protect his own business interests.'

'Yes, I guess you're right, sir.'

Harry stopped and looked at his watch.

'Right, it's five fifty. We better be off. Just need to quickly phone our lads about the car,' he said.

He pushed open the double doors that accessed the first floor corridor.

Suddenly he was stopped in his tracks.

'Sir, Sir,' thank goodness I've caught you, shouted Gavin.

'Your ears must be burning, Gav,' said Harry as the constable came to a standstill in front of them.

'How's that, sir?'

'Well, I was just about to give you and Simon a ring. Just to see how you got on this afternoon.'

'I'll tell you what, guv, there're some seriously nice cars on this Island.'

'I don't doubt it. So how many did you find that fitted our description?'

'Well, we've spoken to the vehicle department and Don Roseisle, secretary of the car club. Between them we have a list of around twenty red Austins, Jags and MGAs on the Island. We've seen about twelve of them so far but none appear to have been on the road on Wednesday morning. Simon and myself are both on duty tomorrow so we'll finish the others off in the morning.'

251

'Fine, I'll catch up with you then.'

Gavin nodded before continuing on his way back through the double doors to the staircase beyond.

'Right, it's definitely time to get moving now, sergeant.'

'Yes, guv.'

'And don't forget, Shaun, if you do want to bring the kids to the barbecue tonight, you'll need to be at the hotel in around an hour's time. The bus is leaving at seven o'clock prompt.'

CHAPTER TEN

'Hi, Gats,' said Mel cheerily as the bright green 'T' shirted figure of Harry jumped on board the vintage red bus, his rapid approach from the hotel's door and down its sweeping granite steps having been witnessed just seconds earlier by the eagle eyes of some of the other passengers waiting patiently in the vehicle.

'Good evening, sir,' cried Cyril.

'Or should I say foggy evening?' he continued, exaggerating a forward stare into the grey gloom beyond.

'Let's hope it clears up soon, eh?' replied Gateaux before turning to face Mel. 'Bet you were beginning to think I'd miss the departure, weren't you?'

'Yes, the thought had entered my head … So what were you doing in there?' she replied, gesturing quickly with her finger towards the entrance of the Coburg.

'Being a bit cheeky actually. I was a little short of time this evening so I raced home on my bike, grabbed a few bits, pedalled back and then talked reception into letting me use the staff wash-room to change.'

'Lucy didn't mind, did she?'

'She wasn't about, so I asked her colleague instead. Think her name was Liane.'

Mel nodded.

Suddenly the nod froze in the down position. 'Hey, great shorts. Been shopping in Hawaii, have we? … Can see why you wanted to change in the hotel,' she added as the Inspector chose the moment of friendly ridicule to sidestep past her.

'You should thank your lucky stars I didn't cycle to St Ouen. You might never have seen them in all their glory.'

'I think the whole Island should consider itself lucky you chose not to do that, Harry. Would have scared most of the wildlife away for evermore. To be honest though, I was half expecting a call from you to say you'd decided to go ahead by bike. What's up, you're not going soft in your old age are you?'

Gateaux laughed. 'No, I did think about taking the trusty old machine. I was even going to offer you a seat on the handlebars but this weather shattered those dreams.'

Mel smiled, her face pinking slightly.

As the two paused for a moment in conversation, Solly suddenly cried out.

'Hi there, Inspector. Mighty good to see you again.'

Harry looked up.

'Gee, think I'll put my sun-glasses back on if you're wearing those breeches tonight,' continued the American as he and his fellow passengers focused hypnotically upon the Inspector's psychedelic fashion statement.

Mel joined in the chorus of amusement while Lauren swivelled her body and slapped her husband pathetically on his tree-trunk forearm which was covered partially in a body-bursting blue flower patterned shirt.

'Don't be so unkind, cherry-pie,' she said before offering a token wave of apology for her husband's comments along the aisle in the direction of Gateaux. 'Your breeches aren't exactly what you'd call plain Jane?' she added, turning her mind to the two new continents that called themselves Solly's legs and which were concealed, in part, by a wigwam-sized pair of red, white and blue striped shorts.

Instantly he stretched out an arm and pointed forward. 'Gee sugar-plum, they're a mighty lesser risk to the optic nerve than those things.'

Harry said nothing, continuing his side-step shuffle into the second row to take a vacant seat behind Mel.

'Bet you wish you'd gone by bike after all, don't you, Gats?' she enquired, crunching the ageing green leather upholstery as she swivelled in her seat to face him.

'Yes, you might be right.'

He paused before continuing.

'Anyway on to other matters. How many are you expecting tonight?'

'Um, should be twelve from the hotel and us three …' she replied, nodding across to include the flat-capped figure of Cyril. ' … Plus of course your sergeant and his two kids, though he's leaving it a little late if he wants to join us,' she added, squatting as she spoke to cast a wide scrutinizing arc through the array of windows as far as the ever worsening visibility would permit.

'Perhaps he's lost in the mist,' came a shout from the driver's cab.

'Talking of which … ' interrupted Harry. ' … Are you confident we'll find the beach later in this?'

'No problem, Gats,' replied Mel instantly. 'Our guys over at St Ouen have just phoned me to say they've found a fantastic sun spot,' she added, with reference to the advance party of Coburg staff who had made their way to the site earlier in the day.

She looked at her watch.

'Time to go, is it?' asked Harry.

'I'm afraid so. We'll give Shaun another minute or so and then we'll have to be off … You are sure he was coming, aren't you?'

'Well, he certainly seemed more than keen when I asked him an hour or so ago.'

'Okay. Let me just do the register and we'll see if he appears,' she added before taking a few advancing strides and standing in the aisle by row three.

'Right, starting with you at the back.'

'Hi, Miss Mel,' cried young Munro, waving frantically.

'Hi, lads.'

Having ticked the Milner family from the list her vision moved progressively nearer as she signed off, in turn, the fellow attendees.

Registration complete, she retreated to retake her seat under the watchful gaze of the Inspector.

'All present and correct?' he enquired, leaning forward in his chair.

'Yes, all here, Gats, except for your mob.'

'Um … I guess we can't hold on any longer, can we?'

'No. I think we'll have to forget them unfortunately. It's just gone seven and the barbecues will be firing up about now.'

A momentary flutter of despondency wisped across Gateaux's face. 'Really sorry to mess your plans about, Mel. I'll have words with my sergeant next time I see him.'

'Don't be silly, Harry. It's not your fault.'

Consolatory remarks delivered, she looked over to Cyril, his concentration locked into the horse racing pages of the newspaper that was spread wide across the steering wheel.

'Cyril,' called Mel.

There was no reaction.

'Cyril,' she repeated, this time louder.

The newsprint twitched as the driver flicked his head up.

'Sorry, girl, miles away … Time to make a move, is it?'

'Certainly is. Next stop St Ouen if you would kindly oblige.'

'Coming right up,' replied Cyril as he hurriedly folded the paper and then adjusted his body slightly to stuff the crudely origami-ed heap unceremoniously behind his seat.

Returning to face the front, he quickly extended his arms and then arched his spine with equal speed across the backrest of his chair. Pre-trek exercise finished and with a painful groan that suggested he should do more, he reached down to the small switch on the dashboard that operated the door mechanism. The two concertina panels closed to seal the vehicle shut with a dull thud.

As Cyril continued with his "pre-flight" checks and switched on the ignition, Mel reached for the microphone. She stood and spun to face her audience.

'Okay folks, welcome to the world famous Coburg evening barbecue.'

'Hooray,' came a muffled cheer from Munro and his brother at the back.

'Thank you,' said Mel as she looked up and waved.

The two lads shared instantly in a fit of giggles.

'Shush,' said Alison.

Quiet returned, inviting Mel to continue.

'Now, it's probably not escaped everyone's notice that there's been quite a bit of fog around today, but I'm told that we've found you a great sunny location and we're going to have a fun time, aren't we?'

The bus rocked to a loud cheer of passenger accord, a friendly contagion initiated yet again by the Milner juniors' ear-shattering shrieks.

'Yep, a barbecue to remember,' added Mel warmly. 'So if you all sit back and relax, our journey should take us around half an hour or so, depending upon any delays caused by the traffic or the fog.'

'Or this old crock of a bus,' whispered its driver as he hooked his head across his shoulder and winked to the now seated host.

'Okay, Cyril, let's get going.'

The instruction taken, the red jalopy shuddered nervously across the cobbled driveway as it headed towards the stone pillars that flanked the exit to the main Esplanade road.

Just a few metres on and still within the granite clutches of the hotel's walls, the vehicle lurched violently forward and came to a sudden halt, necessitating those on board to grab instantly for the closest fixture for fear of otherwise being slung mercilessly into orbit.

'It's Shaun … He's made it,' shouted Gateaux as he looked through the windscreen to see the faintest outline of his colleague jumping like a madman on the tarmac ahead, his wildly gyrating arms stirring the fog-soaked air above.

Oblivious to the Inspector's instant identification, Cyril pulled back his side window, allowing him to cantilever his upper body into the open air and contort his head awkwardly around to the front. 'You on a death wish or something, mate?'

As Mel and the other passengers focused their thoughts

257

toward the "jack in the box" sergeant outside, so Harry suddenly switched his to the developing plight of the driver.

Leaping to his feet, he reached across to grab the back of Cyril's tweed jacket in an effort to prevent the already twisted body contained within from loosing its seesaw battle with physics and falling on to the cobbles below.

With Cyril's fate still hanging, quite literally, in the balance, dependent wholly upon the breaking strain of either the jacket's fibres or Gateaux's arms, Mel leaned calmly across to the Inspector's side and dabbed the switch to open the doors.

'Sorry about that,' shouted the sergeant jovially as he arrived at the foot of the steps.

'You know how to cut it a bit fine don't you, Shaun?'

'Yeah, I'm really sorry.'

'Thought you were bringing the kids?'

'I did. They can't be far behind. I had to run on ahead when I heard the bus firing up and do something to attract your attention.'

'Well, you certainly succeeded in doing that,' said Mel.

As she finished her sentence, two young joy-filled faces appeared and tucked up tightly to each side of their father.

'Hi, Zoe. Hi, Josh,' said Harry warmly as he rotated his upper body just enough to greet the new arrivals eye to eye.

'Hello, Mister Gateaux,' replied the youngsters as they strained their necks to maximum elevation from their lowly position on the driveway below.

'What's that man doing?' cried Zoe as she stared with increasing amusement at the panic crazed figure beyond who was scrambling to rescue himself from the salivating jaws of the cab side window.

'Is he drunk?' enquired Josh.

'Yeah, is he dad … Is he?' asked Zoe.

'Hope not ... He's our chauffeur for the night' said Shaun as he glanced at the semi-inverted view of the driver and then adjusted his view a few degrees to the left to look at the Inspector.

'Do you need any help there, guv?'

'Keep him out of it,' shouted Cyril from the cab.

'Guess not,' whispered Harry.

'Right, come on, you lot, on you get, otherwise we'll be late and our dinner will burn,' urged Mel, as she ushered the two children and their father on board.

'You'll definitely find some seats up there. We've a bit more space than usual. Everyone's baggage has been taken on ahead in the hotel's van,' she whispered as the family passed by.

Immediately, the two youngsters ran off excitedly to the back to test out their host's pledge.

'Now, be good and behave yourself,' called out Shaun.

Parking themselves in a vacant row just in front of the Milners the two dropped their two small rucksacks to the floor. Instantly, they turned and, kneeling on their seats, peeped their heads nervously across to begin a quick visual assessment of their young compatriots for the evening, Andrew and Munro.

While the tentative and silent appraisal carried on at one end of the vehicle, so Cyril, at the other, his life now out of danger, continued to restore his hair and clothing to something resembling an un-twisted state of normality.

Semi-presentable once more, he looked up to the standing figure of Shaun. 'You should get your kids to teach you how to cross the road properly,' he said, his response enthusing the sarcastic overtones of a person not overly impressed by the sergeant's circus-like entrance minutes before.

'Whoops,' whispered Shaun as he sidestepped past Mel and then exchanged a few quiet words with Harry before raising his head to search out his children. 'You okay back there?' he enquired.

'Yes, dad,' came the instant reply through the crowd of seated passengers.

Acknowledgement received, Shaun took his seat in the second row just across the aisle from Gateaux. Suddenly his eyes caught sight of the Inspector's colour-blitzed shorts.

'Gee Whiz, 'you on a dare, guv? Tell you what. It's lucky you're in the police force … You'd be arrested for wearing those things otherwise.'

At once, Mel dipped her head and buried her mouth in her hand as she endeavoured to asphyxiate the onset of laughter. As her efforts continued, Cyril, fresh from his escapology routine, suddenly called out.

'Right, I'm ready. Let's try again.'

He turned his head to give Shaun a quick cautionary stare.

The sergeant jabbed his head sideways as if oblivious of the driver's intimidating glance and looked out of the window.

As he did, the bus door snapped shut.

Within minutes of guiding the vehicle back onto the open road, Cyril eased down gently on the throttle and sat back as he steered the machine on its passage around the concave inner arc of the Esplanade towards its west coast destination.

Mel stood, microphone in hand. 'Just going to make sure everyone's okay, Gats.'

Harry nodded.

As she disappeared Shaun leaned his body partly across the aisle.

'So, did you have time to do all your unfinished tasks back at the Coburg before coming tonight, sir?'

'Just about, but it was a bit of a race.'

'Did you see Lucy, guv?'

'No, she wasn't there. I'll catch her in the morning.'

'And what about the computer that was found in the skip. Did you have a chance to see it?'

'Very briefly. Jeff's over at the site right now … Said he's going to spend a whole week in a pub when this case is over to celebrate the end of us chasing him around.'

Shaun laughed. 'So, when will his conclusions be ready for us?'

'Well, sergeant, he knows we're pushing him hard for answers. He's going to get his guys on the Island to do some analysis this evening on the computer "find" and has persuaded the Southampton lab to work through tonight. He's very confident that he'll have more to report by morning.'

As he finished talking, Mel returned to retake her seat. She'd barely had time to take her first breath of relaxation when there was a light tap on her shoulder.

It was Gateaux.

Mel slid around in her seat as the Inspector spoke.

'Looks like we have quite a few of the same faces here tonight who travelled on this very same bus on Wednesday morning?'

Mel paused and flicked to the guest list attached to her clipboard on the seat beside her. 'Yes, you're right. A good number of the twelve here came on Wednesday. The only absentees are Bob, Doris and young Luke. Why do you ask?'

'Just a thought.'

'Steady on, Gats,' interrupted Mel with a broad smile.

The Inspector reciprocated before continuing.

'Well, I was just thinking that, perhaps, with the similarities to Wednesday's journey, fog and route excepted, we could maybe treat this as an impromptu reconstruction?'

'If you think it might be useful?' she replied.

'Well, yes, I'm really in need of some fresh leads right now. If you could run over the events of Wednesday morning again it's just possible that the familiar surroundings might just throw up something new?'

Mel shuffled further around and then leaned sideways to prop herself against the brass plated rail that separated her seat from the one behind. Shaun closed in, as she relayed her recollections of that fateful day one more time, from the breakfast presentation through to the discovery of the body.

'And that's where you came in,' she said, concluding her résumé.

Report delivered, Mel quickly recoiled her body back to the front and gently massaged her neck with both hands.

'You all right?' enquired Harry.

'Yes, fine thank you. Just felt a little twinge that's all,' she replied, twisting her semi-recovered neck muscles to turn and face the Inspector once again.

'Just going back to the moment at the hotel when you realised Mr Price was missing … '

'Yes, Gats?'

'Well, I know we've asked this question many times before but can you try again and remember where you put the note given to you by Lucy?'

Mel hesitated.

'I'm really sorry … I've racked my brains these last two days, you know. I recall dashing back into the Coburg as soon as I realised that we were one passenger short. That's when Lucy gave me the piece of paper.'

'And then what happened exactly?' enquired Gateaux in a soft almost hypnotic tone, as if attempting to extricate, via some trance-induced state, the second by second movements of the elusive message.

Mel returned a silent, hypnosis-free stare of bemusement in reaction to the Inspector's exaggerated delivery of the question before continuing. 'Well, that's where my memory does a bit of a runner. As I said earlier, I had Joe search the bus and I've had my bags, pockets, everything inside out. I can only assume that I dropped it in a bin somewhere but exactly where is anybody's guess.'

Words delivered, she turned her body back to face the front for a further session of self-administered neck therapy.

As she did, the bus was illuminated by an intense shaft of sunlight.

'Blimey, who turned the light on?' shouted Cyril as the vehicle escaped momentarily from the sea of fog that had enveloped its journey since leaving St Helier.

A riotous cheer echoed round the vehicle.

With the solar celebrations still ongoing and Mel's neck

cramps for the moment seemingly forgotten, she swivelled excitedly in her chair to face the two men again.

'Mind that shoulder of yours,' said Harry.

'I've got it, I've got it,' she cried before pirouetting back in her seat and springing herself forward to a standing position. In the same elastic movement, she reached forward and pulled down the black leather sun shield from the top of the windscreen.

A silence of anticipation suddenly descended as the buzz of passenger conversation which had, until now, succeeded in drowning out the noise of the vehicle's ageing mechanics, ceased.

The silence continued as each passenger strained to discover the object of Mel's sudden exuberance.

'Would you believe it?' she said as she flopped back into her chair and twisted again to look at Gateaux and then across at Shaun. 'It was up there all the time,' she continued as she quickly thrust out her hand and passed a folded piece of white paper to the Inspector.

'The note?' enquired Shaun, his enthusiastic voice filled with the same impassioned feeling of anticipation.

'Yes. I remember now, of course. There was a particularly bright sun on Wednesday morning as we tracked our way through town. It was flashing directly through the windscreen and into my eyes so I pulled the visor down, as I've just done. When I'd read the note, I then tucked it away up there in the fold of the hinge.'

'For safe-keeping?' enquired Shaun.

'Exactly. And of course as soon as the sun wasn't a problem any longer I must have pushed the visor closed, complete with Andrew Price's note, and that's where it stayed until now.'

'What have you found, miss?' shouted Munro from the back row.

'Nothing really,' said Mel, standing quickly and turning to respond to the young Milner. 'Just a little game we're playing.'

263

'Can we play, miss?' shouted Andrew.

'Now you've started it,' whispered Harry.

'Well, we're finished for now Andrew,' she continued. 'But there's plenty of games for you to play when we get to the beach.'

'We need to get this over to forensics as soon as we can,' interrupted Harry as he looked over and carefully offered the open piece of paper across to his sergeant.

'I'll see what I can do, guv. Have you got your phone on you by any chance? I've left mine in town unfortunately.'

Without a further word, Gateaux shuffled forward in his seat, pulled a mobile phone from the pocket of his beach shorts and handed it across the aisle like a relay baton into the firm clutch of Shaun's outstretched hand.

'I'll phone the station straight away and see if someone can meet us over at St Ouen to take this note back to town. Do you think there'll be anyone from Jeff's bunch around tonight to look at it?'

'Well, he was at the hotel just half an hour ago. It's possible he might be able to arrange someone to look at it, that's if he's still there. If you do manage to speak with him, find out if they have any handwriting experts who we can pester?'

'For what, guv?'

'Well, we can't take for granted that this message was written by our victim, can we?'

'No, I guess not, sir?'

'Speak with the Coburg as well if you can. See if they have documentation around with the victim's own handwriting on it. Oh, and one other thing, Shaun.'

'Yes, guv?'

'Whoever you do chat to, try not to be too long. The battery is running a bit low. I've not had a chance to recharge it today.'

'Understood,' said Shaun as he slid back in his seat and tucked his shoulders around tightly in an effort to create an acoustic barrier between him and the juggled combination of engine noise and conversation that had now recovered to its fever pitch level of before.

While the sergeant's dialogue with the station HQ disappeared into his fat-wrapped biceps, Harry turned and moved forward across his seat.

'Mel, you mentioned a little earlier that the only absentees tonight, from the archaeological tour earlier in the week, are Doris, Bob and Luke Bass.'

'Yes, that's right, Gat's.'

'Did any of them give their reasons for not attending?'

'Well, the evening's not compulsory of course. I did invite Doris and her husband but she said it wasn't really their scene. They simply wanted to spend the last night of their holiday enjoying a quiet evening at the hotel.'

'Yes, I can appreciate that a beach party might not be their cup of tea. Bob didn't strike me as the surfing type.'

Mel laughed. 'To be honest Harry, I'd more or less counted them out before I'd even asked them but I think I really put the mockers on it when Doris asked me if there would be any Glenn Miller music and I said probably not.'

'Oh, you party pooper.'

Mel's laugh returned for an encore.

'And so what happened to Luke?'

'Well, he did say he was coming when I spoke with him yesterday afternoon but he didn't show tonight. I guess he just found something better to do. We did ask around the hotel, and even sent someone up to his room, but it appears he's not been seen around at all today, though his car's still in the basement car-park, we're told, so he can't be far away.'

As Mel completed her sentence, Shaun moved across and hovered a small blue and white cased mobile phone in front of the Inspector's eyes.

Instantly, Gateaux grabbed the object with a swatting motion.

'So, did you find anyone who wasn't down the pub then?'

'Yes, guv. I spoke with Kevin at the station. He's going to

send young Steven over to meet us down at the beach when we arrive.'

'What on earth is Kevin still doing at the station?'

'Funny, that's exactly what I asked him. Seems he had a bit of a conscience about abandoning ship this weekend so he's putting in a few extra hours this evening.'

'That's what I like to see, devotion to duty … He's not after a pay rise as well, is he?'

'Wouldn't put it past him, guv.'

'And did you find Jeff across the airwaves?' continued Harry.

'Incredibly, I did, sir. He said he should be able to find someone to look at the note fairly quickly, just as long as we get it back to town tonight. That's hopefully where young Steven comes in.'

'Okay, that's good.'

'Couple of interesting messages for you waiting at the station as well, sir.'

'Oh yes, sergeant?'

'Firstly, the computer in the skip. It's definitely the one from Andrew Price's room. A quick check on the serial number found that they match records found at his Winchester address.'

'Good. That was nice and easy. Suppose it's too early for any fingerprint results, is it?'

'No, guv, they've come up trumps with those as well. There were quite a few on the thing, many as you might expect belonging to Mr Price, and a few mystery ones, yet to be identified.'

'Have they had time to compare these against those of our builder friends?'

'They certainly did but there's absolutely no match.'

'Okay, and what was the second message?'

'Winchester phoned back. Seems this morning's fire at the father's house was, as they suspected, no accident. It definitely started in the computer study and Inspector Scally has told us that investigators have concluded that petrol was used as the accelerant.'

'A fire? Is Andy's father, okay?' interrupted Mel.

'Yes, don't worry. He wasn't there at the time, mercifully,' replied Shaun. 'He was already here on the Island to identify his son's body'

'Um,' whispered Mel, her face shadowed for a moment with a glaze of melancholy.

'And he's not returning to the mainland until tomorrow morning at the earliest," continued the sergeant. 'He had wanted to get back today after hearing about the fire but the fog has cost him a flight and the fast ferry isn't running.'

'Do Winchester know approximately what time the fire started?' enquired Harry.

'Seems to have been in the early hours, sir. Apparently the fire brigade were called out sometime around 4am this morning. We're told that the house was well ablaze by then. The brigade estimate is that it probably started at approximately 3.30am.'

'Fire, what fire?' snapped Jamie, stretching his body to lean forward from his fourth row seat.

'Oh, nothing important, sir,' said Shaun, turning briefly to address the curiosity filled passenger.

Jamie snorted as if to pronounce his displeasure at being omitted from the hot-press gossip and rolled reluctantly back into his chair.

The Inspector inched forward once more between the semi-stooped bodies of Mel and the sergeant. 'This bus is not the place to continue our inquiry, you know?' he whispered. 'I'm beginning to think I should have stayed at the station, after all.'

'Don't be silly, Gat's. You've had a tough week,' said Mel. 'You deserve a bit of a break. And it's Friday night so what better time to start one.'

'Yes, maybe you're right?' replied Gateaux as his tensed body eased back in the seat, his mind fizzing in an effort to make some coherent sense of the rapidly evolving pool of information.

As the computations continued, Cyril shouted from the front of the bus.

'Not far away now, girl. Fog seems to be getting thicker again though.'

Mel looked forward.

'Yeah, amazing how it rolls in over here, isn't it,' said Shaun.

He turned and looked intently out of the window in search of any visible landmark that might offer a clue to their current location. 'Where on earth are we?'

'Airport,' replied the driver, his stern response suggesting that he was still far from returning to full diplomatic relations with the young sergeant since the latter's stuntman arrival at the start of the evening.

'Still nothing flying then?' enquired Mel.

'Only seagulls I should imagine. I understand the place has been shut all day. The planes that were on the ground first thing this morning got away but that's it. Nothing has arrived at all, so I'm told.'

'That's left a few unfortunate people floundering around then?' suggested Mel.

'Yes lass, just a few. They've always said the airport should have been built on the east of the Island.'

Suddenly there was a tap on Shaun's shoulder from the bat-eared Jamie. 'Did I hear the driver say there are no aircraft flying?'

'Tell you what, mate, for a little guy you don't miss much do you?' said the sergeant.

Jamie said nothing.

'Yeah, nothing's flying because of the fog. Happens a few times a year actually.'

'Hope it's clear for tomorrow. Think most of us are flying back in the morning,' interrupted Kathy from her seat across the aisle from Jamie.

As the news of the airport's closure filtered through the bus the pattern of conversation underwent a metamorphosis from beach party enthusiasm to an indecipherable series of anxious, mini-conversation exchanges.

'Dad?' called Munro.

'If there isn't a plane to take us home tomorrow will you build us a raft?'

The anxiety levels lifted slightly as a wave of laughter rippled through the rows.

'I don't want to go anyway,' said Andrew.

'I want to stay here and build sand castles forever.'

'Hope it is clear tomorrow,' said Mel quietly. 'I could well do without that hassle in the morning.'

As she finished speaking the vehicle, for a second time, popped out into daylight through the shroud of pea-souper mist.

'Hooray,' came another chorus of euphoria from behind, this time louder than before and accompanied by a parallel chorus of applause.

'Picked a lucky spot here,' said Shaun as they turned off the main coast road and descended slowly down a sun glistening granite slipway towards the beach and the waiting entourage of hotel staff.

'Still pretty grey down that end though,' he continued, pointing in a southerly direction to a mist-swirling blanket, punctured just occasionally by the piercing light of La Corbière lighthouse in the distance.

'Yes, a bit murky,' agreed Mel as she looked along the coastline.

Suddenly Zoe and Josh appeared.

'Dad. Dad. Can we get off the bus?' asked Zoe.

'Come and sit here for a minute,' said Shaun as he motioned the two towards him with his hand and coaxed them somewhat reluctantly onto the vacant seat beside him.

'We've not stopped yet.'

'We have now, dad,' cried Josh seconds later as the vehicle lurched forward and juddered to a heart stopping halt on the edge of the sand dusted cobblestone slipway.

'Please. Please. Can we go, please, dad?' repeated Zoe.

Mel turned to face the sergeant's daughter whose young arms wriggled busily in her attempts to disengage herself from her father's protective clutches.

'If you just stay there for a little while longer, young lady, we'll be leaving very soon,' she said with a wink of her eye.

Zoe sniggered and instantly relaxed her arm-stretching attempts at parental liberation.

Order temporarily restored, Mel reached back for her microphone and then stood to face her attentive group of beach-goers.

'Right, we're here,' she cried, an animated exuberance filling her enthusiastic announcement.

Instantly, that same bag of joyous excitement from the guests re-opened and exploded into a resounding cheer.

'Just a little bit of an intro before we do depart.'

'Sorry, can't hear you, miss,' came a muffled cry.

Mel paused to allow the last decibels of vocal celebration to evaporate and then pointed towards a side window. 'Thank you. As I was saying, just a few words about tonight … If you look over to your right.'

All heads turned to look outside towards a group of six adults, their frenzied energy in preparing the barbecue feast and the vibrant summer coloured beach wear combining into one blurred rainbow of activity.

'Is that where all that fog comes from?' enquired Zoe as her little arm stretched out across her father's nose to highlight two of the Coburg's staff who were fighting comically to control thick clouds of smoke wafting from the recently fired barrels of charcoal.

'I hope not,' said Shaun. 'Or we'll not see the beach soon and we don't want that, do we?'

Zoe dropped her arm back to her side and shook her head.

Mel crouched so that she was at eye-level with the young girl. 'Actually, that's a very important point. I'll tell the others,' she said.

Her private words spoken, she stood and put the microphone to her mouth.

'Can we all take care and look out for each other tonight. We don't want to lose anybody if this weather should unexpectedly start rolling this way.'

'What is the good old British weather doing tonight then?' shouted Solly.

'Well, I'm informed on good authority that we're past the worst of it. With any luck it should begin to slowly clear very soon.'

'Yeah, and I guess by then it will be dark,' replied Solly, as he popped a golf ball size piece of chewing gum in to his cavernous mouth. 'Thank you, Ma'am,' he added, his words straining to escape as he turned to divert his early chewing actions out of the side window.

'One final word of advice,' continued Mel. 'If there are any brave souls among you who are planning to have a paddle or surf, the tide is just about on the turn again now and there may be some deceptive currents around. We have actually employed the services of two of the beach's resident lifeguards tonight so if you do venture into the sea, please stay in groups between their flags.'

A murmur of approval at the request bounced around the four walls of the bus.

'Right, let's go,' she added, turning to Cyril and signalling with a firm nod that the doors could be opened.

As they slid back, a warm, almost Mediterranean sea breeze flooded invitingly in.

'Me first,' shrieked Zoe as she skipped excitedly down the steps and rolled playfully onto the soft golden sand below which had begun to vibrate gently to the sound of pop music emanating from the cooking area beyond.

'Me next,' added Josh with equal zeal, brushing swiftly past Mel to follow closely in his sisters wake.

'Can we go now, mum?' pleaded Munro.

'No, you sit there and wait patiently for the other passengers to leave,' insisted Alison as she placed her arm, seat-belt fashion, tightly across his chest.

'But, mum, we'll miss the games,' he continued.

'Yeah and I bet everyone's scoffed all the food before we get there,' added his brother to compound the weight of kindred protest.

'Quiet now. You both chose to sit here, so you'll have to wait politely for the others to get off.'

'And as for the food, the lady said it wouldn't be ready until half past eight. Look, it's only half past seven now,' continued their mother, as she extended her arm and wrist-watch under the concerning eyes of her two sons.

Back at the front, Shaun left his seat and squatted down in the aisle beside the Inspector.

'You okay, guv? You've be staring into nothingness out of that window for the past ten minutes.'

Gateaux looked around. 'I'm still thinking that I should be somewhere different right now, like back in town at my desk. We still have too many questions and not enough answers and this crowd all disappear tomorrow.'

As the conversation continued, the two stood and joined the exodus for the beach.

'Come on, sir. Tonight's a chance for a good unwind,' said the sergeant as he stepped from the bus onto the soft powder sand.

The Inspector followed behind and dropped his less than enthusiastic foot heavily onto the beach. 'Any sign of the lad from the station to collect Mel's note?' he enquired.

'Seems not at the moment, guv. I'll give him a few more minutes and then I'll phone the station. Come on, let's go and grab a beer and chill out with the others.'

As the men wandered towards the refreshment area, the disembarkation continued behind them.

'What a gorgeous evening,' cried Rachel as she jumped from the vehicle. She turned and looked back up the steps towards the figure of Mel who, in the role of "ship's captain", had remained "on board" to guide the final bodies from their seats.

'Just hope this sun lasts,' she added, raising her crossed fingers and pointing to the cloud-free air.

'Let's hope so, Rach. I'll be with you in a minute as soon as I've got the last few safely off.'

Within minutes the bus was an empty shell once again.

As the children engaged in an absorbing digging game of treasure hunt, supervised by a couple of the hotel's staff, so the cluster of beer and wine consuming adults looked out to the horizon and the slowly receding sun.

'Anyone for a paddle?' shouted Tony as he placed his empty beer bottle on one of the small plastic camping style tables beside him, stripped off to his black swimming trunks and began jogging down the beach.

Within minutes of his invitation, the beach echoed to the racing feet of Craig, Alison and Lauren, as they stampeded their way towards the "pied piper" and the crystal shimmering temptations of the gin clear warm waters beyond which slowly lapped the golden shoreline.

'Not coming with us, Rach?' shouted her husband as he turned and continued with a backwards run towards the sea, allowing the chasing pack to pass him by.

'No, I'm happy here with my drink and the music, thanks,' she replied with equal volume. 'Doesn't look like he'll be showing off on his board tonight. Just a tad calm, I think?' she added as she turned to Mel.

Collecting a bottle each from the nearby ice cover box, the two then joined their fellow alcohol absorbing compatriots to watch the now distant figure of Tony as he ripped his way through a sand storm "wake" in pursuit of the aquatic enthusiasts ahead of him.

'Bit of an ace on the old board is he your husband?' enquired Harry who had caught the gist of the girl's whispered words of conversation.

Rachel paused for a moment as she considered the Inspector's hidden talent for lip-reading.

'Er … Yes, he likes to think he is. Can't get him away from this place when the surf's up.'

This time it was Harry's turn to pause for a moment's thought as he looked out across the mirror flat waters in the distance.

'Um, can see why you said that's he's not going to be too happy tonight.'

'A bit of an understatement that, Inspector, but at least there's more beer for us while he's gone.'

Suddenly the Grand Canyon sized figure of Solly stepped forward. 'Think I might join them as well,' said the American as he looked seawards and then began to drag his skin-tight 'T' shirt from his body.

Harry edged across towards Mel. 'Reckon he'll need a crowbar to get that thing off?'

Mel turned instantly, her hand smothering her mouth. 'Don't make me laugh, Gats,' she muffled, her face reddening as she strained to damp down the tickling of funny muscles within her. 'It's embarrassing,' she continued, her voice breaking slightly as an escaping pulse of laughter punctuated her response.

'And who said whales couldn't run?' called out Shaun as he joined the remaining beach crowd in viewing the amusing spectacle of "Uncle Sam" thunder his sand-shattering frame seawards.

'What time did you say high tide was, Mel?' questioned Jamie.

'Think it might be in the next few minutes if that great lump of lard dives in,' added Shaun.

As the laughter and exchange of blubber related one-liners continued to ebb and flow, Harry took a few steps sideways and reached for another beer.

'You all right, Inspector?' enquired Cyril, from his paper reading perch at the end of one of the tables. 'You look as though you're on Mars, heading for Mercury.'

'Just a busy week I guess, that's all. Hopefully, I'll wind down with a few more of these inside me,' he said as he raised his can of beer towards his drinking compatriot.

Cyril reached across and lifted his half drunk glass of orange juice. 'Cheers,' he said as the glass and tin can moved in for a gentle collision.

'Yes, cheers, and thanks for getting us here safely. Lovely old bus you've got there by the way.'

'Yeah, she's a good old girl is old "Bertha",' replied Cyril as he turned his head slightly and offered an affectionate smile in the direction of the vintage red machine. 'Not put a foot wrong, she hasn't, in the twenty or so years I've owned her. Can't say that about many vehicles on the road today of course, unless you ride a bike.'

'Don't you believe it, Cyril. Even my cycle's had a few things drop off it this year already, and I only bought it in February. Must say though, your old workhorse stops pretty smartly.'

'Just as well with people like your sergeant around,' replied Cyril as he looked a few metres in front of him and nodded discreetly in the direction of Shaun.

Shaun, in ringed conversation with Rachel, Mel and Jamie, quickly looked over his shoulder.

'You'll have to speak a bit softer next time,' said Harry.

'Well, you saw him. Nearly ended up as a road marking, just like the other joker on Wednesday morning.'

'What other joker?'

Cyril paused before looking a few metres across to Mel.

She looked across. 'Yes, Cyril?'

'Who was that guy who tried to pick a fight with the bus the other morning?'

'A fight?' she enquired, her head drawing back slightly in bemusement.

'Yeah, you remember, that young lad in his flashy sports car who nearly drove in to old "Bertha" just before Wednesday's archaeological tour.'

'Wasn't that Luke?' interrupted Rachel.

'Oh yes, that's right,' replied Mel. 'He turned up late for the tour on Wednesday. I believe he'd only got off the boat that morning, and then had to take his brother somewhere which left him running a little late.'

'Yes, nearly made a right mess of that red car of his,' added Jamie.

'Red car?' said Harry, his statement racing with the infusion of excited curiosity. 'Can you remember at all what make it was?'

'Haven't you switched off from playing detective yet, Gats?' cried Mel as she stepped across and wrapped her arm around his shoulders.

'Come on, chill out, it's party time.'

'No, this is really important, Mel,' said the Inspector as he turned and placed his partly consumed can of beer on the table. 'Is there anyone in this group who might know what car Luke was driving?'

'I think Solly might have been chatting to him about it,' said Mel.

'You might have a bit of a wait to ask him in that case, guv,' added Shaun. 'He's still out there doing an impersonation of an oil tanker.'

As the others laughed, Harry put his hand across the top of his eyes to screen them from the setting sun and squinted out to sea.

'They'll be in for food soon, Gats,' said Mel. 'I'm just going down there now to give them the shout.'

'Okay, fine,' he replied.

Mel turned to her side. 'Rachel, is there any chance you could go and find Rozella for me? Tell her to round up the kids. Food's ready.'

'Yes, no problem, Mel.'

'Cheers.'

Within minutes of the junior's call to order, the beach was lit up by wisps of sand dust trails as the children, led by Munro and Andrew, raced to initiate the queue for food.

'Is there any chocolate cake?' enquired Munro as he looked hopefully up towards one of the hotel staff.

The woman nodded.

'And there's lots of chicken and steaks and salad,' she added.

'Can I just have Chocolate cake?' asked Munro.

'Yeah and me to,' asked Andrew.

'Can I have some chips with mine?' enquired Munro.

As the nouveau cuisine conversation continued, attention from the beer tent group of adults was drawn back to the water's edge and the food seeking clan of returning sea-life, led by Tony.

'The water's lovely and warm,' he shouted as he neared base camp. 'Just what you need to build up a decent appetite.'

As the adult group dried off and began joining the meandering queue of "little people" towards the food-laden tables, Harry, flanked by Mel and Shaun, stood to one side and awaited the arrival of the monster from the deep.

'You guys worried I might drown or something,' said Solly as he approached the barbecue zone and looked across at the three.

As he spoke, Lauren walked over.

'Here's your beach bag, sweetheart.'

'Gee, thanks sugar-pie,' he replied, before bending slowly down and pulling out a duvet sized towel which he then flicked over his head and wrapped across his shoulders.

'Solly,' said Harry as he watched him begin his slow return to the vertical. 'I believe you were talking with Luke on the morning of the dolmen tour about his red car?'

Solly paused for a few seconds and looked skywards.

'That red car that nearly hit the bus,' added Mel, as if seeking to kick-start his apparently stalled memory.

'Oh, yes,' said Solly as the grey cells shed their crust of sea-salt and re-engaged gear. 'Mighty fine MGA, it was … What a beauty! … 1961 model … Sixteen hundred engine.'

'Can you recall anything else of that particular conversation at all?' enquired Gateaux, a rush of adrenalin-fuelled urgency in his voice.

'Well no, not really, only that the guy had arrived on the Island that morning with his brother, that's all, Inspector.'

'Okay, that's great. Oh, and just one other thing, Solly, before you go. Can I ask you to keep the detail of our little conversation from the others,' he continued as he looked across the beach to the massed ranks of adults and children in the food queue.

'Sure can, sir. Not a word.'

'And that applies to the rest of you, if that's okay,' added Gateaux as he glanced in turn at Lauren, Rachel, Mel and Shaun.

The four nodded in consenting solidarity.

'Thanks for your co-operation.'

'Just mighty pleased to be of assistance,' said the American before turning and leading his wife away to join the back of the line, followed closely by Rachel.

'Before you go, Mel … And you as well, Shaun,' said Harry.

The two turned.

'I just can't believe this car link to Luke Bass hasn't come out sooner.'

'Well, perhaps the lad was keeping it under wraps when we spoke with him, guv, and no one else thought it was relevant.'

'Yes, maybe,' said Harry, a wisp of frustration glazing his response. 'Anyway, I need to get back to the office, guys … Like now. I'm beginning to think that this case is about to enter the fast lane. If I leave it a moment longer I fear it might just explode out of control,' he continued, that same adrenalin rush now performing cartwheels in his body. 'Mel, any chance do you think that Cyril could whiz me back to town?'

'If you really must,' she replied, her voice drowned in a clear pool of disappointment.

'Do you want us to put a blue light on the bus for you, sir?' mused Shaun.

The Inspector remained impassive.

'Apologise to the others for me, can you, Mel?' he said.

She nodded and then took a few strides sideways to speak with Cyril.

Gateaux looked across to his sergeant. 'What did you do with that note, the one Mel found in the bus?'

'I've put it in an envelope, guv, which you'll find in a small locker just above the drivers seat.'

'Great, I'll get it back to town at the same time. Who knows where young Steven's got to. I presume he's still not showed?'

'Haven't seen him yet, sir, but I'll be phoning the station in a short while anyway. I'll see what's happened to him?'

The men's conversation was suddenly ended as the bus fired back into action, blasting a small cloud of dense exhaust fumes across the sand.

'Nothing like the fresh sea air to exercise your lungs, is there?' said Shaun, as the diesel-scented breeze wafted past them and ominously onward towards the gaggle of eager partygoers and feast of smoking food.

'Mel, have you got your phone with you just in case I need to buzz you or Shaun?' shouted Harry as he began a fast walk towards the bus that had just completed a spin turn and was waiting at the edge of the slipway.

'Yes, Gats,' she replied as she waved a green leather pouch in the air.

'Great. You can catch me at the station if you need me. Don't bother phoning me on my mobile. It's out of juice. Incidentally, what time do you expect to finish here?'

'I guess we'll be away around midnight, weather permitting,' replied Mel, her voice raised to fight the rippling flutter of the light sea breeze.

'See you later then,' said Harry with a quick wave, as he jumped back on board the vehicle.

Within seconds, the vehicle had begun its laboured crawl back onto the main road.

'Trust when he says "see you later" he means the morning?' enquired the sergeant.

'I guess so,' replied Mel as she skipped forward and waved to the departing "Bertha".

'Come on,' said Shaun. 'Let's join the others and get some food, before it all goes.'

CHAPTER ELEVEN

Twenty-five minutes after its exit from the party night exuberances at St Ouen, the bus, now commandeered by Gateaux for his return to town, came finally to a bone shaking stop at the entrance to the town's Rouge Bouillon police station.

'How's that then, sir? Door to door service,' said Cyril as he slapped the palms of his hands down firmly on the steering wheel and habitually arched his upper body back across the top of his seat.

Harry stooped slightly and looked through the side window at the main door to the building, its traffic-exhaust soiled glazing faintly illuminated by a single street lamp, whose orange glow fought to penetrate the dense foliage of a partially enveloping tree.

'Um, not quite as inviting as a beer on St Ouen's beach, is it?' he said with a resigned acceptance that he had forsaken the barbecue extravaganza for a night at the office.

'If you have any regrets, Inspector, I'm going straight back now.'

'Yes, thanks for the offer and, tempting though it is, there's far too much to get my head around here right now unfortunately.'

'Fair enough, can't say I didn't ask,' replied Cyril, before rocking forward in his seat and flicking the dashboard-mounted switch to open the door.

Harry extended his arm forward and shook the driver by the hand. 'Thanks for the taxi ride. Just sorry I had to drag you away from all the fun.'

'Oh, don't worry about that. The music was beginning to give me grief anyway. To be truthful I was glad to get away and give my head a rest.'

Harry's appearance back in the station's lobby was greeted

instantly by a duet chorus of cat whistles and laughter from the late shift of Julia and Charlie as their eyes zoomed in magnetically upon the luminescence of the Inspector's evening wear.

'Jeepers Creepers, guv, you sure those things are legal?' said Charlie.

The Inspector looked down at his colour radiating attire and then across at the duo.

'Perhaps he's come to give himself up,' said Julia laughing. 'So what happened to the party then, sir?' she continued.

'More to the point, what happened to your messenger lad?' enquired Harry.

'You mean young Steven?' asked Charlie.

Gateaux nodded.

'Oh, he came back here. Claimed he couldn't find you in the fog.'

'Pathetic excuse. Think we'll have to enrol the kid in the scouts so that he can do his orienteering badge, in that case.'

'That's a bit advanced for him at the moment, guv. He still thinks the only use for a compass is to draw circles with,' added Charlie.

'Yes, and the only "North Pole" he knows is that dive of a pub down the road,' said Julia as she made her small contribution to the good natured verbal tirade. 'We were going to send him out again but Shaun rang in literally a few seconds ago and told us that you were on your way. I must say his call was a bit of a surprise to us. We weren't expecting you back at all this evening,' she added.

'To be honest, I wasn't expecting to be back this evening either. Thing is though, I needed to find some quiet space to get a few ideas straight in my mind which were just beginning to click into place when I was down on the beach.'

'Must be all that sea air, sir.'

'Well, guv, sea air or not, we're glad you are here now. A lot's been happening,' interrupted Charlie. 'Kevin's been trying desperately to reach you on your phone.'

'Oh, it's on the blink at the moment unfortunately ... Is Kev upstairs?'

Charlie nodded. 'Yes, he's in your room.'

'While the cat's away, eh,' said Harry.

'Delusions of grandeur, more like,' added Julia.

'Nothing grandiose about my room.'

Julia smiled.

Small talk at an end, Gateaux bade his farewells to the two and headed upstairs. 'Hi, Kev,' he called as he pushed the half open door to his office back on its hinges. 'Burning the midnight oil, are we?'

Kevin looked at his watch that read ten past nine. 'Don't think I'll get much past the ten o'clock oil, sir. I'm up fairly early in the morning for a flight at eight.'

'Yes of course ... So how have you been getting on in my absence?'

'Well, it's been quite an eventful evening since you left, guv. I have been trying to track you down this past hour but then they told me you were on your way.'

'Yes, apologies for the phone. As I've just told Chaz, the damn battery is on its last legs. In fact, I must sort that out now before I forget,' said Harry as he pulled the cellphone from his top pocket and then moved around to the side of his desk to plug it into a small black box mounted on a file-stacked shelf.

'Nice shorts!' said Kevin loudly, as the infamous beachwear came in to full view.

'Don't you start.'

'Last ones in the shop, were they, I presume?'

The Inspector remained un-phased by the evening's next helping of taunts. 'I've heard every one liner in the book tonight, including that one.'

'I bet you have,' continued Kevin laughing.

Gateaux waited for the amusement to subside. 'Right, Kev. Do you know if anyone at all phoned from the Coburg tonight? I did ask Liane to call the station to let us know if they'd established Luke Bass's whereabouts.'

'Er, yes, she did phone. About eight thirty. Apparently, there's still no sign of the chap. Seems he's done a bit of a Houdini on us and disappeared into thin air.'

'Or fog,' added the Inspector. 'Okay, so what else has been going on then?' he continued keenly as he returned to the front of his desk and took to his seat.

Kevin reached across for a scrap of paper containing some scribbled notes. 'Firstly, I had calls from both the Southampton laboratory and the local lab.'

'And ...?'

'Fascinating development actually, sir.'

'In what way?'

'Well, Southampton has said that despite the two samples from the builder's skip, namely the paint flecks and the clothing fibres, having only just reached them, they are now ninety-nine per cent certain that the deck-chair box is the object which proved fatal for our victim when he fell onto it. I've put their faxed preliminary report in your tray.'

'So why the laboratory's one per cent doubt, Kevin?'

'That's the really intriguing bit, guv. The doubt is because the local labs have reported that the sand samples found on the victim are matched by both the beach sand around the deck-chair box, and what we understood to be builder's sand in the skip.'

'Intriguing is the word,' replied Gateaux, an air of puzzlement dusting his face. 'What you're saying then is that until we get the Southampton results on the paint and fibres from the building site, there remains an outside chance that Andrew Price fell on the skip also, or at least came into contact with the sand in it?'

'Indeed, sir, it's going to be a bit of a nail biter this one, until we can speak to them again in the morning, and even then it might be too early for a definitive result?'

The Inspector stood and paced the room in silence for one complete circuit before returning to his resting place. 'Did you say, Kev, that the stuff in the skip is builders sand?'

'Well, that's what we've been led to believe. We spoke with some lads who were still working on site this evening. They weren't Colcroft's direct labour, just sub-contractors, but they said they'd definitely seen Colcroft's men using the material for everything from batching concrete for foundations, to pipe laying.'

'And can you use raw beach sand for that sort of thing. It sounds a bit iffy to me?'

'I asked Doctor Preben at the St Saviour labs that question, guv?'

'And what was the expert's opinion?'

'Well, the Doc just laughed. He said that while they might have used sand in its unrefined form to build the dolmens five thousand years ago, it's a definite no-no for modern day construction. It needs to be put through controlled washing and cleaning processes first.'

'And had Colcroft's stock pile been cleaned?'

'You're joking, guv. Preben went on to say that he had found a variety of sea life in the bucket load he was given to analyse. Claimed he's saving it all for his tea tonight!'

'What for … SANDwiches?' replied Gateaux, as he emphasised the vital noun in his word-play.

'Very good, sir. I've always said you were cabaret material.'

Harry laughed before continuing.

'So, did Colcroft have any comment at all to make on the contaminated materials?'

'Well, I did manage to get through to Sumo tonight by telephone but he got all defensive as soon as I raised the issue and then said I was spoiling his Friday night out with the lads.'

'Well, he should have left his phone at home then, shouldn't he? Did he tell you anything else?'

'Not a lot, guv. He insisted that the sand we found is only used to mop up oil spills, nothing else. Then he hung up on me.'

'If that's the case, then all I can say is that Colcrofts must be very careless with their oil.'

Kevin nodded.

'Think we'll call our friend Sumo back in again tomorrow. Shaun will be pleased when I tell him. So have you anything else to tell me?'

'Yes, sir. Winchester phoned again. They've finally received the results on the Telecoms trace from Andy Price's phone line … And, wait for it … '

'Yes, yes,' said the Inspector excitedly.

'Well, nearly all of the calls turn out to be e-mail links to either the AMC banks in Jersey or London. They traced them back a couple of years and the pattern's the same.'

'So where does that leave us?'

'Nowhere exactly, guv, at this particular moment, but the work is ongoing.'

'And what about the fire, Kevin? Did Winchester give any up-date on that by any chance?'

'Yes, they did. It appears that they managed to salvage a computer hard disk from the charred remains at the house and have somehow succeeded in building a computer around it from which they've accessed much of the data it contained.'

'Don't you just hate these clever computer types, Kev. Too smart for their own good if you ask me?'

'Yes, I know what you mean.'

'Top marks to them for accessing the information nonetheless.'

'Yes, guv, but it seems that it took them a little while to get around the password problems before they eventually triumphed.'

Gateaux hesitated before responding.

'Don't suppose the password had anything to do with our "3456BC" teaser?'

'No, sir. Sadly it wasn't that simple, though I understand it was tried initially as a possible way into the system. All it means is that our cryptic combination remains a mystery, I'm afraid.'

'What did they find once they'd analysed the disk?' enquired Harry, an increased sense of urgency now creeping into his voice.

'Well, guv, the incredible reality seems to be that it was absolutely saturated with confidential client files from AMC banks around the world. Inspector Scally said that he had spoken with a number of very senior personnel at AMC who confirmed the content of the files as having originated from both local network and wider mainframe databases. AMC, understandably, were somewhat shocked at the revelations, to say the least.'

'How shocked exactly?'

'Potentially apocalyptic is how the bank put it according to the Inspector. They're dreading any leak to the press until they have a fuller understanding of this apparent breach of their security.'

'I bet they are. So, did forensics manage to pull anything else useful from the ashes?' said Gateaux.

'Not a great deal. The fire seems to have been fairly catastrophic. They did recover a few other computer pieces that they're trying to rebuild in a similar fashion, I assume. On the back of their findings and the other identifiable remains they've had their experts make an assessment of the storage capacity and content of our Mr Price's little home-based computer empire.'

'And what was the answer, Kev?'

'The conclusion seems to be that it probably held a sizeable proportion of the bank's computer information, from internal administration through to the execution of deals and even personal client details, age, shoe size, the lot. As you can imagine, that further revelation only served to magnify the shock wave already reverberating through the corridors of AMC … And that's not all.'

'Think I might need a stiff drink if it gets any more incredible,' said Harry, as he sat up attentively in his chair.

'Well you better start pouring now then, sir.'

A momentary hush fell on the room.

Harry's body twitched slightly in eager anticipation as he leaned forward and began tapping the top of the table quickly. 'Come on, Kev, I can't bear this amount of suspense on a Friday evening.'

'We had Mr Henderson from the bank on the phone to us late this evening. He's finally put a name to those initials A.A, which appeared in the victim's personnel file and related to a senior work colleague. Transpires they belong to Anthony Astey ... or ... dare I suggest, one Tony Astey, perhaps?'

The silence returned as Gateaux sat back, lifted his head and stared trance-like at the ceiling. Meditation over, he looked back at Kevin.

'You mean the same Tony Astey who is staying at the Coburg. Rachel's husband?'

'We've not had the chance to quiz him yet, guv, but it seems a bit too much of a coincidence, doesn't it? I mean it's not a particularly common surname around these parts.'

'Well, if it is the same guy then he was clearly being a little economic with the information he gave us during our interview with him. I distinctly remember him telling Shaun and myself that he didn't know our victim except for the occasional sighting around the hotel.'

'Do we know where our Mr Astey is right now, sir? Is he over at the beach party?'

Gateaux nodded. 'He was when I left about half an hour ago.'

Suddenly the Inspector pointed across the desk to where his mobile was still buzzing away in recharge mode. 'Kev, can you pass me the phone there and the clip of papers beside it. It has a copy of Mel's guest list and their departure times tomorrow.'

Kevin reached out to his side for the items and then swung his arms through ninety degrees to offer them across the table.

'Cheers,' said Gateaux as he began running his finger instantly down the register of names.

'Here we are … Mr and Mrs Astey. One thirty flight to London Gatwick, Saturday 16th.'

'Do you think we should pick up Tony Astey now then, sir?'

'Well, he's not leaving the Island until tomorrow lunchtime. Perhaps we'll leave him down at St Ouen just now. I don't want to send the troops storming in there and cause a scene. That would spoil it for the others.'

'Yes, understood, guv.'

'But, sergeant, we'll drag him in here first thing in the morning before he's had time for his eggs and bacon.'

'Right, sir. I'll get that arranged on my way out. Is it okay if I call it a day? I promised Bev I'd be back around ten?'

'Yes sure. Thanks for your efforts and have a great weekend.'

Kevin stood instantly and began his retreat towards the exit.

'Oh, one last thing, Kev, before you disappear … Do you know if there's anyone at the AMC Bank tonight if I need to speak with them?'

'No, not now, guv. Mr Henderson phoned me just before he and his colleagues left for the night, around eight forty-five. When we spoke he told me that the bank has called an emergency board meeting in the morning. Seems their top brass are flying in from all corners. He said he's sent you an e-mail to that effect, together with some extracts from Anthony Astey's personnel file apparently.'

Immediately, Harry leaned forward and fired his computer into action.

'Yes, here it is. Astey's employee file and notification of the board meeting, as promised,' he cried excitedly. 'Seems the bank's hoping for my attendance tomorrow … Henderson's even attached an agenda.'

'Mind you change out of those shorts before you go, sir.'

'Sorry, didn't catch that,' said Gateaux, as his mind remained fixed in cyberspace.

289

'Nothing. Er, is that all for now?' continued Kevin as he hovered anxiously across the office threshold, his body now split by a room portion in "chat" mode and the remainder in "ready to sprint" mode in the corridor

'Yes, that's all. Thanks for your help.'

Before the short-lived echo of Harry's appreciative few words had evaporated, the door had closed and the Doppler effect of disappearing footsteps filled the passageway beyond.

Back in solitary confinement, the Inspector picked up his desk phone.

'Hi, Julia, any chance of sending someone out for a bag of chips or something? Oh, and a nice cup of tea wouldn't go amiss.'

'No problem, I'll get young Steven to pop out for you.'

'Just make sure he doesn't get lost this time.'

'Yes, guv. I'll tie a piece of string to him.'

'Great, thanks,' said Gateaux.

His meal ordered, he replaced the phone and then reached forward to pull the stack of files and papers from his in-tray. With the characteristic efficiency of the organisational maestro that he was, the administration tasks began.

The Inspector had just opened the personnel file relating to Andrew Price when the phone rang.

'Sir, it's Shaun.'

'Hi, how's the party going? Sounds lively enough,' said Harry, raising his voice to a semi-shout as he endeavoured to compete with the Richter scale thump of dance music firing down the communication line from St Ouen.

'Great, thanks. Just wondered how you're getting on,' replied the sergeant, with an equal elevation of his voice.

As the larynx-rasping conversation between the two continued, the Inspector began to relay the evening's developments while at the same time flicking his attentions sub-consciously between the personnel file belonging to Andrew Price on his desk and the screen version relating to Anthony Astey.

The lively exchange suddenly stopped.

'Sir, sir you still there?'

There was no answer.

'Sir, you okay?' repeated Shaun, this time louder.

'Err … Yes …still here,' came the slightly laboured response. 'I've just noticed something in these personnel files, sergeant.'

'Sorry, didn't quite catch that,' replied Shaun as the background beach music began to nudge ever nearer to sand-atomising levels. 'Hang on, I'm just going to find somewhere a bit quieter.'

'Think you might be gone a little while then, judging by the noise,' shouted Harry.

Having sought refuge behind a nearby beach hut, Shaun picked up the conversation once more. 'Okay, sir, try again.'

'Yes, that's better,' said Gateaux as the volume of dialogue returned to the comfort zone once more. 'Right, I think I may have just hit on something,' he added.

'What's that then, guv?'

'Well I have two AMC personnel records in front of me right now. One for our victim that Nicki left earlier and the other for Anthony Astey, which was e-mailed across this evening. I've just noted their staff numbers, which are similar. 9214AP and 8467AA respectively.'

'So what's the connection exactly, sir?'

'There's no connection, Shaun. It's just the pattern that's important, numbers and then the initials.'

'Sorry, I'm still a bit confused, guv?'

'Our mysterious entry in the victim's diary, remember … "3456BC",' cried Harry, as the copious excesses of adrenalin building in his body raced to his vocal chords.

'The code has nothing to do with the age of the dolmen, or a password for any of Price's computers. It's an AMC staff number,' he added, the euphoria of his conclusion enthusing his response.

'Brilliant, sir. Think you've cracked it?'

'Not quite yet. The problem now is that we won't know who the code belongs to until morning when the bank re-opens. How I'd love to be able to turn the clock forward.'

'Pity it's not Solly's bank,' said Shaun instantly.

'Sorry, sergeant, now it's my turn to be confused.'

'I said "pity it's not Solly's bank". If it was an American bank you were phoning it would still be open, wouldn't it?'

There was a short pause before Gateaux replied. 'Tell you what. For that last comment I'm going to buy you the biggest pint of beer you've ever seen in your life next time we're down at the Peelers Arms.'

'And what's merited that generosity, guv?'

'The AMC branch in Seattle. They must be ten hours or so behind us, I guess. If you remember, Andy Price worked for someone during his contract work here who later moved to the United States?'

'Yes, that's right, sir. Georgina something or other, wasn't it?'

'Yes it was.'

As the conversation ceased for a short moment, Gateaux flicked frantically through the pages of the victim's employee file. 'Yes, here we are, Miss Georgina Le Ferne and there's a contact number for the office she was transferred to. I'll phone her straight away. See if she can find anyone to help us out on this one. I'll speak with you later, Shaun … And thanks.'

'Okay, guv. I suppose we'll be here for another couple of hours or so if you need me. If not, I'll catch you in the morning.'

'Yes, sure. Enjoy the rest of the party. Oh, and sergeant, try and be in by eight if you can. There's a lot to sort out before all our holidaying friends begin their returns back home.'

'I'll do my best, guv, headaches permitting.'

The Inspector replaced the handset and continued his study in silence.

Half an hour later that peace was suddenly broken by a knock at the door.

'Come in.'

'Room service,' called Julia as she entered. 'One bag of chips and a hot cuppa, as requested,' she continued before placing the package of food in a small clearing on Gateaux's desk.

'Thanks very much,' said Harry as he unwrapped the takeaway feast, surveyed its aroma-filled contents and then stabbed his wooden fork into the first unsuspecting chip. 'And what happened to Steven this time?' he added.

'Who knows? We sent him out ages ago. I guessed you couldn't wait much longer so I went out myself.'

'Oh well, I'll have his bag for breakfast when it arrives … If it arrives?'

Julia laughed before stepping back towards the exit. 'I'll be downstairs if you need anything else, guv.'

The door closed.

EARLY NEXT MORNING AT THE INSPECTOR'S OFFICE …………..

'Morning, sir,' said Shaun as he walked in through the now open door.

'Yes, Hi, Shaun,' replied Gateaux, raising his head slowly from his desk-study pose.

'Enjoy the chips, guv?'

'Oh … Still smells, does it?'

'Yes, you could say so. It's either that or you're wearing a particularly dodgy aftershave. I'll leave the door ajar for a moment, shall I, sir?'

Harry nodded. 'Tell you what, Shaun, you look a bit rough. Good party, I take it?' he enquired as his interest was suddenly drawn to his sergeant's paled expression, one which bordered dangerously, it seemed, on the very edge of life itself.

'Yes, we had a fantastic time, thanks, and to cap it off I won the sand castle competition.'

Shaun hesitated.

'If you don't mind me saying, guv, you don't exactly look the picture of freshness yourself. Long night as well, was it?'

'Yes, very long. Hardly seemed worth going home in the end. I couldn't sleep for this case buzzing away incessantly in my head. The only sensible thing was to turn around and come straight back here. Think I'd just started my fourth black coffee by the time the sun came up.'

Shaun stepped forward and picked up the empty mug from Harry's desk.

'Fancy another? I'm off down the kitchen now.'

'Yes, that would be great. Think I might need to be wired up intravenously to that drink machine soon,' replied Gateaux as he mustered a token smile of appreciation that was suddenly distorted wildly by a lion-wide yawn.

'Anything new that I should know about since we last spoke?' enquired the sergeant as he made his initial strides backwards towards the door.

'Where do you want me to start? I called in at the hotel early this morning in the hope of speaking to Lucy about our missing persons, Luke Bass and Mr Masters?'

'Did you talk with her, sir?'

'No, I was too early but I did manage to solve one outstanding riddle while I was there.'

'And which one would that be?' enquired Shaun.

'Well, sergeant, guess who was on duty at the door when I arrived?'

'Er … Our elusive Mr. Masters perhaps?'

'The very same,' replied Gateaux.

'As soon as I walked into the Coburg he pulled me to one side. Said he wanted a private word.'

'And what exactly did he have to tell you?'

'Quite a lot actually. He, like you, had also read the local newspaper on Thursday night and the lead story about the failed appearance of the Spitfire on the Islands. Masters knew we'd catch sight of the article as well and immediately realise that his alibi for first thing Wednesday morning was somewhat flawed. Seems he was going to speak to us, in confidence, a little earlier but he's been at the hospital on and off over the past few days, having some tests.'

'Hospital, sir?'

'Yes, turns out that he was at the doctors on Wednesday morning on account of a few problems recently with an irregular heartbeat. He was afraid of the consequences if the truth got out about his time off during that day, and Friday, when he phoned in sick.'

'What consequences?' enquired Shaun, his eyes awash with curious bemusement.

'He was concerned that if any suspicions about this blip in his health, temporary or otherwise, got back to the hotel's management, then it might have put his job in jeopardy. Said he couldn't risk that and then proceeded to give me a fairly unconvincing sob story about how the job means everything to him.'

'Did you have a chance to check out the doctor story, guv?'

'Yes, we found from his employee file that his GP is called Linda Trott. As luck would have it, she has an early morning surgery on Saturdays and it's only just around the corner from here. I've just got back from seeing her. She confirmed his Wednesday morning appointment, the heart condition, and the subsequent period in the General Hospital for tests on Friday. She couldn't divulge much of his medical history but seems he's had the condition for some time. Interestingly, it appears that his previous doctor in Winchester had recommended Mr Masters to seek a less stressful work life on health grounds.'

'Maybe that advice was the catalyst for him to release his overall control of his Winchester building company, guv, then sell out to Colcrofts and move over here for the hotel job?'

'Yes, that might seem a plausible chain of events, sergeant.'

'Did you quiz him about his connections with Colcroft Construction?'

'No. The hallway wasn't the place for an interview. It was beginning to get a bit busy, so I've arranged to meet him again at twelve o'clock today, back at the Coburg in his office,' replied Harry.

'Can you make a note of that, sergeant? And when you've done that, can you make that cup of coffee you promised me a few minutes ago. I'm parched?'

'Yes, sorry, sir.'

As Shaun added two more strides to his snail-paced advance towards the door, the Inspector's phone suddenly rang.

The snail stopped once again.

'Gateaux?'

'Morning, guv. It's Kevin at the airport.'

'Thought you were on holiday,' said the Inspector.

'Well, I am, but I thought I'd just give you a quick buzz while we're waiting for the plane … It's been delayed for a short while. I was wondering how it all went last night after I left?'

'Well, I had a very interesting chat with the AMC Bank in Seattle.'

'With the victim's old boss, I assume?' quizzed Kevin.

'Yes, exactly. We asked her to investigate the reference "3456BC" for us, the reference we found in the victim's diary on Wednesday.'

'Er, right, sir,' said Kevin, as a semi state of confusion began to germinate.

'You see, we eventually concluded from AMC employee files that the reference might be a personnel number for one of the bank's staff.'

'Oh, I see … And was it, guv?'

'Certainly was. It turned out to belong to one Brett Cramer.'

'And which branch is he working at now?'

'Well, that's just it, Kev. Brett Cramer retired from AMC's

London office around fifteen years ago. Seems he then spent his time helping with his son's holiday park business down in Cornwall somewhere.'

'So why did our victim seem so interested in a retired staff member?'

'You might well ask? What is more intriguing though is that we discovered, through the Seattle office that our Mr Cramer still appears on the payroll. Has done ever since retiring, much to the consternation of AMC. When they investigated it further they found the salary going through to him to be quite astronomic. Well into the hundreds of thousands of pounds each year.'

'Wow, not bad for someone in retirement, guv?'

'Wow is the word if the figures are correct and there's no reason to suspect that they are not?'

'The bank has its board meeting later this morning, doesn't it, sir. I guess this latest addition to the agenda will probably transform the current crisis into all out panic?'

'Yes. Dwight Henderson, the manager, said much the same thing when I spoke to him a few minutes ago,' replied Harry. 'I've been invited to the meeting, as you know. Won't be able to stay for too long though as I've promised Mel that I would pop back to the hotel around eleven to bid the guests farewell, minus Tony of course. He's got just a few more questions to answer before we let him near a plane.'

'I thought earlier that the guests had already started leaving.'

'Sorry, how do you mean?' puzzled Gateaux.

'Well, I bumped into Luke Bass here a little while ago, sir.'

'Luke Bass … So he's turned up at last has he … I thought he was going back on the ferry with his car?'

'I think he still is, guv. I didn't have long to talk to him at the time but I gathered that he was simply dropping his brother and brother's girlfriend at the airport. The lucky couple were off to Paris for a break.'

'How the other half live! So do you know where young Mr

Bass is right now, Kev? It's just that I'd really like to ask him a few more questions before he departs.'

'Unfortunately not, sir. I said goodbye to him about ten minutes ago and I've not seen him since. I presume he's on his way back to town?'

Suddenly the clarity of Kevin's voice disappeared into the mire of the airport's loudspeaker system which exploded into life.

'WOULD ALL PASSENGERS ON FLIGHT JJ044 TO LONDON GATWICK PLEASE MAKE THEIR WAY TO GATE 10'

'Sorry, guv. That's us. I'll have to go, but hope the day goes well for you all.'

'Yes, cheers, Kev. And have a good time yourself. Say hello to Bev and the kids again for me.'

'Will do, thanks.'

The Inspector placed the receiver back down and swung around to face the front of his desk.

'Thought you were never going to finish,' said the waiting Shaun, an empty mug still in each hand.

'Did you get most of that, sergeant?'

'Yes I did, guv. You really did have an action packed Friday evening, didn't you?'

'Yes, and I was supplied with some drinks as well,' replied Harry, a thick slice of sarcasm rolling from his rapidly drying lips.

'Okay, message received and understood.'

Within seconds the sergeant had completed his return journey to the kitchen. 'Hot dishwater again I'm afraid,' he said as he placed the two overflowing cups on the table.

Gateaux stretched his neck forward and looked inquisitively into the nearest mug.

'I see what you mean. Not exactly cappuccino, is it?'

The sergeant laughed.

298

'So what's the order of play then, sir?'

The Inspector paused for a few seconds.

'Well, Nicki and Ami have gone over to the Coburg Hotel to pick up Tony Astey. He should be here soon. First though, I've got that meeting to attend to over at AMC.'

'I'd love to be a fly on the wall at that one, guv.'

'Yes, indeed, and I'm going to be one such fly. Should be quite lively.'

'So do you want me to start interviewing Mr Astey while you're away?'

'No, I think we'll let him stew for a little while. But you can try and find out something about a brother that Luke Bass was apparently over here with. As you probably gathered from my conversation with Kevin a few moments ago, he saw Luke at the airport this morning, dropping his brother and girlfriend off for some flight to Paris?'

'Do you think Luke is wrapped up in all of this then, sir?'

'Could well be, particularly as we now know that he owns a classic car that just happens to fit the description of one we're looking for.'

Gateaux looked at his watch. 'Right, it's nearly nine. I'd better be off. Can't keep the bank manager waiting.'

'Anything else for me to do while you're away, guv?'

'Yes, there is one other small task. Could you wait for Nicki and Ami to get back from the hotel? I need them to go to the airport and quiz the airline that took Luke's party to Paris. I don't know which one that is mind. They'll have to find out for themselves. And if they see Mr Bass on their travels, tell them to hold on to him and call me straight away. I don't want him going anywhere.'

'No problem. I'll catch you later,' said Shaun as he held the door open and nodded to the departing tracksuit clad Inspector, his red cycle crash hat tucked tightly under his arm.

Just a quarter of an hour or so had passed when the door suddenly crashed back open and the Inspector reappeared.

'Everything okay, sir? Thought you weren't leaving the meeting until around eleven,' enquired Shaun, clearly surprised at Gateaux's premature return.

'I wasn't, but Dwight Henderson has found a name to those initials L.I.B which appeared beside Tony Astey's initials in the victim's AMC employee file. They just happen to belong to Luke Bass. Seems that both Luke Bass and Tony Astey worked for the same trust fund team at AMC for some years and, more to the point perhaps, still do.'

'So Mr Bass must, like Astey, have known our victim fairly well then, guv?'

'Yes, but again you wouldn't believe it from his interview statement either, would you?'

Harry stretched across to the side of his desk and began rustling frantically through what had, until that moment, been a neat stack of ordered papers.

'What are you after, sir?'

'That list of Mel's, highlighting departure times,' replied Harry, a heightened state of urgency vaulting through his agitated body.

'There it is,' replied the sergeant, pointing to the other side of the desk.

The Inspector instantly snatched forward before sitting back and scrolling his eyes down the record of passenger travel details.

'Are Nicki and Ami at the airport, Shaun?'

The sergeant nodded. 'Yes, they phoned while you were out to say they've arrived. No sign of Bass but they're speaking with an airline at the moment about the Paris flight.'

A shot of hyper-activity suddenly fired through the Inspector's veins. 'Shaun, can you quickly dive next door. Phone the docks and see if they have any record of a Luke Bass travelling back to the mainland today in an MGA.'

A couple of minutes later, the sergeant returned.

'Luke Bass isn't going on the boat is he?' said Harry confidently.

'No he's not but how did you know that, guv?'

'I've just spoken to Nicki. She's been told that there are no flights to Paris today … Well at least not direct anyway. What's more, the girl's found that there's a booking today for a Mr L. Bass, travelling on the two fifteen flight back to London City and another record showing that he had in fact just got off a flight,' said Gateaux. 'The reason why Kevin saw him earlier had nothing to do with Luke Bass's family or friends. He'd just got off a plane,' he added, as a Vesuvian lava of adrenalin began to bubble violently within him.

'He'd just flown in! … Where from, guv?'

'From Southampton, sergeant. He travelled out Thursday evening apparently. It should only have been an overnight stay and he was due to return yesterday morning but the closure of the airport on Friday because of the fog put paid to that. My guess is that he was returning in the hope of giving everybody the illusion that he'd never left the Island.'

'Must have been something important to warrant interrupting a weeks holiday to take an overnight flight back to the mainland, sir. Do you think he might have any link to the fire at the Price's residence in Winchester? It can't be more than twenty miles maximum from the airport and it's quite a coincidence that his little excursion occurred at the same time?'

'Well, my money is very definitely on him having some part to play in it, sergeant … So what did the ferry company have to say?'

'Yes, Phoenix ferries have in their records that Bass came over with the car alone on Tuesday and not Wednesday as he led us to believe. They also said that the vehicle was collected from the hotel's car park by one of their people this morning for its return, as freight only, on the lunchtime sailing today.'

'So it's waiting at the docks as we speak?'

'Yes, guv.'

'Right, Shaun. Get on to Phoenix ferries straight away and tell them the car's not to be moved. Can you send someone

301

down there straight away to keep an eye on it? I'll get in touch with Jeff and see how he wants to play it. And when you talk to the ferry company, ask them to inform us immediately if Luke Bass checks in at any time as a passenger.'

'I thought you said he was booked on a flight later today, sir?'

'Yes he is, sergeant, but if he rumbles us he might try and get away by sea. I'll quickly phone Lucy now at the hotel and see if Mr Bass has made an appearance yet. He's sure to at some point - to collect his things and complete the illusion that he'd been on Jersey the whole time,' replied Gateaux.

'And while you're speaking with the ferry company I'll phone Nicki again and ask her and Ami to maintain a vigil at the air terminal and to keep an eye out for Bass. I'll also get her to speak with the airlines and put a block on him leaving the Island by air. Come on, let's get going. There's not a moment to lose.'

Shaun stood and began a quick retreat once more towards the door.

'Before you go, sergeant?'

Shaun looked up.

'When you're done, meet me back here and we'll head off to the Coburg. If my hunch is correct Luke Bass should be back there very soon and he'll be keen for plenty of people to see him if my theory is correct.'

'He perhaps will be less keen when he sees us, eh, guv?

Gateaux smiled and nodded.

FOUR MONTHS LATER ....

Surrounded by a vocal ensemble of fellow lunchtime devotees of "The Peelers Arms", Harry placed his empty beer glass down on the bench of the sun-drenched pub terrace and reached for his mobile phone.

'Quiet, you lot, just for a minute.'

A semi-hush descended momentarily upon the group, the

residue of conversation now choked out by the rumble of passing traffic as the Inspector began punching the numbers on his keypad.

'Hi, Mel, it's Harry.'

'Hi there, Gats, how are you? Gee, it sounds a bit noisy there. You sitting in the middle of the Esplanade or something?'

'Yeah, nearly. We're all down the "Peelers" right now, celebrating.'

'And what's the occasion?'

'We've wrapped the hotel case up.'

'Oh, very good, congratulations.'

Suddenly another voice shouted down the line.

'Helloooooooo, Mel.'

Harry nudged the interloper gently away from his side. 'Sorry about that. It's just Shaun messing about. Think he's had too many lemonades.'

Mel laughed.

'Anyway, wondered what you were up to tonight?'

'Well, I suppose that depends upon what the offer is, Harry?'

This time it was the Inspector's turn to return the jovial accord. 'I was wondering if you fancy meeting up at "Popeyes" later, usual time?'

There was a brief pause.

'Yeah, sounds good to me. I was at a bit of a loose end tonight as it happens. Any chance you can tell me the full story of the case over dinner. I've only had a few fairly disjointed snippets from you over the past few weeks?'

'Yes. Sorry about that but I had to keep a lot under wraps until the court case was over.'

'So will you give me the full unedited details this time then, Gats?'

'I guess so, if you're really that keen to talk shop all evening. The whole saga is going to be public knowledge fairly soon anyway so you might as well be the first to hear it.'

'Great, look forward to it.'

'And I've a little idea to put to you when I see you,' said Harry.

'Oh yes … Sounds interesting. What is it, Gats?'

'No, not just now. It's a surprise. It will have to wait.'

'Oh, that's not fair. You'll have me in suspense all day now.'

'Afraid so.'

'All right. So I'll catch you at eight then. Anyway, must dash. I've another tour to host soon.'

'Yes, see you later,' said Gateaux before putting the cellphone back down on the table.

'Glad you're off that thing,' called out Shaun.

'And why's that, sergeant?'

'Well, it's your round, guv. Can't escape it by ignoring us to chat up the girls, you know,' continued Shaun as he pointed to the offending item on the table.

The group laughed, signalling the return to the traffic-drowning banter.

THAT SAME EVENING AT POPEYE'S RESTAURANT ....

'So your initial suspicions towards Colcroft Construction, this Sumo character and Alec Walsh being involved in the death of Andrew Price were completely unfounded, Gats?'

'Indeed Mel, as too were our suspicions suggesting the hotel's doorman, Joe Masters, to be implicated in the crime in some way.'

'Those particular trails were completely wild goose chases then?'

'Well, not entirely. It did throw us off the scent initially I'd admit but the Coburg learned a lot of useful things out of it. I'll tell you a bit more about those in a while.'

Mel reached over to her glass of white wine and took a quick, though delicate sip.

'I still can't believe that Rachel's husband was involved,' she said as she placed the glass back on the table. 'Poor girl, is she okay, Harry?'

'As okay as anyone can be whose husband has just been locked away for twenty years,' said Gateaux, a wisp of sympathy creeping into his reply.

'I really must get in touch with her. Is she back on the mainland now?'

'As far as I know.'

Suddenly the shadow of a waiter rolled across the table.

The two looked up.

'Are you ready to order, madam, sir?' he enquired, nodding with subtlety to each in turn.

'Er, yes, please. Can you tell me what is the soup of the day?'

'It's clam chowder, madam.'

'Um, lovely,' replied Mel as her appetite kicked into a higher gear.

'Think I'll have the chowder then for entrée please and the grilled red mullet for main course.'

'And your side dishes, madam?' continued the waiter as he pointed delicately to the list at the base of the menu.

'Oh, think I'll go for some sautéed potatoes and the vegetable selection, if I may.'

'You may indeed. Thank you. And you, sir?'

'Yes, I'll have the wild salmon for entrée and the red mullet also for main course, please.'

'And your side dishes, sir?'

'Sautéed potatoes and the vegetable selection as well, thank you.'

'Very good, sir.'

'Copy cat,' whispered Mel.

Gateaux looked across and winked.

'And can I get you any more wine at all?'

Mel offered Harry a discreet shake of her head.

'Perhaps not just at the moment,' he said.

'Very good, sir,' replied the waiter as he leaned across and lifting the two menus, folded them neatly closed, tucked them under his arm and then disappeared.

'Right, let me continue before our meal arrives,' said Gateaux. 'It turned out that the whole conspiracy was dreamt up by Tony Astey when he worked for AMC back in the early nineties. He teamed up with Luke Bass soon afterwards and the final piece of the jigsaw came when a computer maestro by the name of Andy Price turned up on the scene to work alongside them. Seems that the trio developed a bit of a reputation as the dream team as far as their employers were concerned. Top drawer whiz kids was how they described them.'

'Well, they obviously weren't that smart or they wouldn't have got caught I guess.'

Harry laughed.

'So what exactly was this conspiracy?' continued Mel as she reached forward for her glass of wine.

'Well, it was simple really. Tony and Luke as fund managers, through their varied and very wealthy clientele, basically had a controlling interest over literally millions of pounds. Their clients relied on them to invest the monies on their behalf and expected a favourable financial return from the professional services they had chosen to employ.'

'So did that not happen then?'

'Well, to a point. The clients got a financial return but not quite as much as they should have got. Not that they would ever realise it,' replied Harry.

'How's that?'

'Well, each time the bank, through this "dream team", conducted any form of investment for these clients, they would charge a fee. Nothing unusual in that, of course. Normally that fee would be based upon a percentage of the transaction involved. Tony, together with Luke, creamed off each time a fraction for themselves from any financial gain before adding the bank's percentage fee as agreed. A veritable pot of gold it proved to be as well.

The conversation suddenly halted as a serving trolley appeared at the side of the table.

'Excuse me madam, sir,' said the waiter.

A hush descended.

Mel and Harry sat upright in their seats and watched as their entrée dishes were presented in front of them.

'Bon appétit,' continued the man as he nodded invitingly to each in turn and then spun the trolley around and rolled it away.

'Looks good,' said Mel.

'Smells good as well,' replied Gateaux.

As their cutlery made its first advances towards the gourmet introductions before them, the conversation picked up once more.

'So if their money was disappearing, did the clients not suspect any wrongdoings?' enquired Mel.

'Seems not, for two reasons primarily. Firstly the amounts being drawn fraudulently from each account were relatively minor when compared to the huge sums of money typically invested. And secondly, in many cases the clients had no detailed knowledge of the mechanics of the particular investments anyway. Their bottom line was simply how much their return was. If their investment returned, say, 7.25% instead of the deserving figure of, say, 7.255% they would be none the wiser.'

'And in time, I suppose, the pennies that the team accumulated from each deal grew to pounds,' suggested Mel.

'Yes, many hundreds of thousands of pounds actually.'

'But surely these banking organisations have foolproof security systems to counter such fraudulent activities, don't they?' enquired Mel as she leaned gently forward and carefully lifted the first mouthful of soup.

'Well, yes, but you see the three had total command over the very computer systems that monitored and policed such breaches. Very simply, they bypassed the security protocols because they controlled them, replied Gateaux.

'And this technological side of things is where Andy Price came in, I assume?'

307

'Exactly, Mel. Through his intimate knowledge of the computer networks and procedures that carried out each transaction, he was able to dive into the client accounts at any time he or his co-conspirators, Tony and Luke, desired.'

'But I still don't see exactly how they extracted their monies?' said Mel as her initial offering of soup continued to hover precariously at the edge of her lips.

'Well, as far as the external investment organisations were concerned, the transactions went through honestly and the returns by them back to AMC were made legitimately also. It was only when those funds returned to the bank that Andy, together with the other two, massaged the figures via the software systems, so taking their small cut, before passing the often not insignificant remainder on to their respective client.'

Mel, though limited in computer techno-literacy, continued to stare forward as the Inspector unwrapped his lay-person's account of the case. The same cooling spoon of clam chowder waved nervously about her mouth.

'Tell you what, Mel,' said Harry as he looked at his dining partner's gastronomic balancing act.

'This food's too good to interrupt with involved shop talk.'

'Yes, think you're right, Gats,' she agreed as her eyes dipped quickly to view a rapidly developing skin of soup creep purposefully across her spoon.

The conversation, prompted by Harry, instantly took on a transition from crime solving police talk to the ever more jovial appeal of cosy evening small talk as the two tucked with enthusiasm into their immaculately presented dishes.

As they did so, a light ripple of chamber music from a stage mounted string quartet began to breeze across the table as the live ensemble struck up the first chords of their evening programme.

'Think they must have been waiting for us to finish playing detective,' said Harry.

Mel smiled.

Soon immersed in the fine mist of classical music and wine, the meal moved on from entrée to main course as the conversation continued on into the slow burning embers of the night.

'Are we finished, madam, sir?' enquired the waiter who, totally oblivious to the conversation-entrenched couple, had moved in at close quarters.

The duo looked up.

'Did you enjoy your meal?'

Mel glanced down at the mirror clean white bone china that now remained on her place setting.

'Think the plates say it all.'

The waiter smiled appreciatively.

'Yes, excellent, thank you,' said Harry as he offered a paralleled commendation.

'Would you care to see the sweet trolley at all?'

Mel sat back in her chair and lightly patted her stomach. 'What do think, Gats?' she said, a deft shake of her head suggesting a very definite response of "no".

'I don't think I could eat another thing just now. Perhaps later?' she whispered.

'Think I'm with you on that one, Mel.'

Gateaux looked up.

'Could you ask again in say half an hour. Perhaps we could have that other bottle of wine in the meantime.'

'Certainly, sir. Same again?' enquired the waiter.

Harry nodded firmly.

'Right, Gats, let's just finish that intriguing little story of earlier. You'd just finished telling me about Andy Price's involvement. Tell me a little more about how precisely the three fitted into the scam?'

'Well, in its early days, I suppose you might call it a trial period, Tony Astey and Luke Bass worked from the Jersey office of AMC with Andy providing the computer expertise from the bank's main headquarters in London.'

'I didn't realise that Andy worked for them before he came to the Island?'

'Well, we didn't for some time but it seems that he was almost part of the furniture. Held in very high regard by all of his superiors and many of his colleagues whom we spoke to.'

'The powers of secrecy, eh,' said Mel as she took another sip from her glass.

'Quite.'

'Excuse me, sir,' announced the waiter. 'Your wine,' he continued as he carefully pulled the empty bottle from the small ice bucket at the side of the table and replaced it with the freshly uncorked new one.

'Thank you,' said Harry before turning to face Mel once more. 'Well, the plot really took off though when Price came to Jersey. When the three realised how successful their new venture was proving it took on a whole new dimension.'

'In what way, Gats?'

'Well, they decided to go big time with a view to expanding the fraud on a truly global scale. Tony relocated to the head office in London, while Luke stayed in Jersey. With the funds they had already accumulated they set up Andy with a mini version of the AMC at his father's home in Winchester, of all places.'

Mel listened intently as the ingenuity of the trio's endeavours continued to unfold.

'Between them they now had total access, in theory, to a significant number of transactions passing through the bank. And that's when it began to go pear shaped.'

'So what was the reason for that?'

'Well, Andy, as I said, was one of the leading lights behind the setting up of much of the computer software. He'd added quite a few personalised tweaks to safeguard the protection of the three against any risk of detection. Suppose you'd call it an insurance policy. The ultimate scenario, it turned out, should their involvement have ever risked exposure by their employers, would have wiped out theirs and the bank's systems completely.'

'Guess that would have made a few headlines, Harry.'

'Certainly would but it would have left the group in the clear. That was the important point. And any subsequent collapse of the bank in those circumstances would probably have provided them with a tasty payoff. It was a win-win situation really as far as they were concerned.'

'So how did all this lead to Andy's death?'

'Greed is the simple answer. The root of many an evil deed, I'm sure.'

Mel nodded in silent agreement.

'It seems the agreement from day one was that the proceeds from their little jolly would be split four ways,' continued the Inspector.

'Four ways?' quizzed Mel.

'Yes, the split provided a quarter share to each of the big three and the other quarter was divided among a number of co-conspirators who worked primarily in the bank's I.T. department,' replied Gateaux. 'Recently though, Andy had announced that he'd included what I suppose amounted to a time bomb in the customised software that he'd developed. If his cut of the proceeds didn't increase to a specified amount by the last seconds of year 2001, then the whole scam was off and the offending software anomalies would basically melt away forever,' he continued.

'And how much exactly did he want, Gats?'

'Well, he was looking for an additional twenty five per cent cut of Tony and Luke's earnings, if you can call them that? That would have given him over a third of the total monies accrued.'

'Um, I see … I guess he was fairly confident that the others would agree, albeit reluctantly.'

'Yes, Mel. The other two had become accustomed to their affluent lifestyle. There was no way that they were going to risk losing it. Andy had even given a title to his trump card in some

311

computer data we deciphered, calling it "2001, a cyberspace odyssey". The fact that the three men all happened to be at the Coburg that same week back in September was no co-incidence.'

'So they'd arranged a meeting to try and resolve Andy's claim for what amounted to a pay rise then?' enquired Mel.

'Very good. That's one way of putting it. I'll make a detective out of you yet.'

'I'll stick with holiday rep-ing, if that's okay. I wouldn't be very good when it comes to arresting people. I could never give detention to people when I was a school prefect.'

Gateaux smiled. 'On more than one occasion with this case I was beginning to think I'd lost the knack to arrest people myself,' he replied as he leaned to his side and then arched across to hover the recovered new bottle of wine above Mel's empty glass.

Mel nodded.

'Anyway, the real tragedy of their reunion turns out to have been a bit of an accident. Seems that on the Wednesday morning of your tour the trio had pre-arranged an early meeting first thing, down on the beach front. We found an entry in the victim's diary, mentioning 8am on that day which we now assume referred to the meeting time. During that liaison, the three got involved in some argument over this division of their funds, an argument prompted by Andy's "space odyssey" sting. Seems the argument became increasingly heated and next thing, a spontaneous burst of anger from Luke, directed at Andy and intended apparently as a fairly innocuous scuffle, ended up with the lad loosing his balance and falling to his death from the seawall onto a steel box at beach level.'

'Poor kid,' said Mel, her face paling slightly. 'So what about the note I was given from Lucy that morning written by Andy. The one I eventually found on the bus. Where does that fit in to all of this?'

'Transpires that was written by Tony Astey after he and Luke had disposed of the body. He'd returned from Santille that morning and had a quick shower to get rid of any sweat, dirt and, no doubt, blood before scribbling that partially smudged note. The two didn't realise at the time that the hotel had some handwriting of the victim on file which we could use later to compare with that on the note you collected.'

'Very clever,' said Mel. 'Of course, the message *"meet you soon at the Cotte de l'Arbre"*, which I thought Andy wrote and which seemed a little odd at the time, would now make perfect sense in a way if Tony wrote it. He wasn't at breakfast on the Wednesday morning. Because of that, he wasn't to know that the tour route had been reversed.'

'Exactly, Mel. Tony had quizzed Rachel as to the last stop on the tour. She told him Santille, as she had assumed the route would be like the endless other tour routes she herself had hosted before it.'

'And of course Rachel didn't know any different because she'd missed breakfast also.'

'Precisely. By leaving the body at what they understood to be the final stop on the excursion and by making the scene appear as though Andy had at least started his lunch, they hoped that by the time the body was discovered, it would appear that the person had died sometime later in the day, by which time Tony and Luke's alibi was firmly established because they had been with your group from the start.'

'Ingenious, Harry.'

Suddenly the waiter reappeared at the table.

'Are you ready for dessert yet, madam, sir?'

'I'm nearly there,' said Mel.

'Perhaps fifteen more minutes or so if you'd be so kind?' suggested Harry.

'Very good, sir,' said the man before turning and moving across to the party of four seated at the adjacent table.

'So how did the body arrive at Santille, Gats?'

'Well, after the initial panic at the realisation of their deed,

313

the two had to work fast to cover their tracks before the beach warmed to its daily arrival of sun worshippers. They managed to get Luke's car down the slipway, bundled the body into the boot and then drove to the site,' replied Gateaux. 'Their initial plan was to simply carry the body up to the stone chamber and dump it there via the main entrance track but when they arrived they were greeted with the attentive eyes of both Eva, who lived just across the road from the dolmen, and André the local fruit and veg man who was doing his daily rounds. That completely washed away "plan A",' he continued.

'So what was "plan B" then?'

'That was a little more bizarre. They drove around the lanes to the back of the monument where they found a farm. By chance, the owners were away on holiday.'

'And then?'

Before replying, Harry paused for a moment and lifted his glass.

'Just a bit of oil needed to soften the old larynx. All this talk has left my throat like sandpaper.'

'Good excuse to join you,' said Mel as she lifted her glass and took two lingering gulps.

The two placed their glasses simultaneously back on the table.

'Well, they dumped the body in the bucket of a farm tractor. After that, they drove across the ploughed field at the back of the site and hopefully out of view of any nosey neighbours. Of course, it now turns out that Luke was driving the thing with his gloves on. Hence no prints to help us.'

'So what clues did guide you on your way?'

'Well, for one, we found a hand crafted surfer's bangle in the tractor bucket in which the body had been placed. It took a while but we finally tracked its ownership back to Tony. There's another little twist in that particular story. I'll tell you about it in a minute,' replied Harry. 'As well as the bangle, though, we also discovered that the body had been dragged on to the site through the perimeter hedge. Forensics made a perfect match between fibres found on the damaged foliage and fibres found both in the boot of Luke's MGA and from samples of his and Tony's clothing. Took forensics some time to come up with their conclusions though. Seems that after the trip to Santille by Bass and Astey, Luke went and got his car valeted thoroughly, inside and out.'

'Of course, that would explain why his car was dripping wet when he pulled onto the hotel's forecourt on Wednesday morning,' said Mel.

'But he didn't clean it enough to fool forensics,' added the Inspector.

'To the power of modern science,' said Mel as she raised her glass and took two further slow motion sips to toast her proposal.

'To modern science,' said Harry as he lifted his own glass and took a quick gulp before continuing. 'The other intriguing little tale regarding the bangle I promised you about came out of the position in which the body was found.'

'Explain,' demanded Mel as she slowly lowered her glass to a slightly shaky landing on the table.

'Well, after the body had been left and both Luke and Tony were back on the bus, Tony suddenly realised that he'd mislaid his treasured item. Having failed to locate it elsewhere he guessed it might be with the body in the dolmen although it was too late by then to go independently in search of it as the tour departure was imminent. And they couldn't risk missing the trip or their alibi would have been destroyed. Then, to add to their woes, the two soon realised that the tour was operating on a reverse route. Tony knew that if the bangle was with the body and was found by the police then any trace would probably end up on his doorstep and that's when the anxiety levels began to hit overload.'

'But the thing was in the tractor bucket all the time, wasn't it, Harry?'

'Yes, that's correct, Mel, but Tony wasn't to know that. As soon as your tour bus stopped, he raced ahead to see if he could find it. That's when the body got turned over from its original resting place. It was also the point at which Tony pushed the body further back into the chamber in the pathetic attempt at trying to conceal it. In his panic, he also tried to hide the pack lunch that he himself had partly eaten, by throwing it and the emptied beer cans over into the adjacent field. As I said earlier, the two had wanted to create the illusion that the victim had died after lunch, but the reversed route now made a mockery of their plans.'

'Yes, their sprint to the site … Of course,' interrupted Mel. 'After our arrival at the parking slot at Santille for the dolmen, Tony, Luke and Jamie raced off towards it. That must have been why the other two tripped Jamie up along the way. They simply didn't want him finding the body before the main group arrived.'

'Yes, I guess so,' said Harry.

'So, Gats, what about the events back at the hotel - all that business with the break-in to Andrew Price's room and the dumped computer in the builder's skip?'

'Well, that was another deviously executed plan which went wrong. You see, Tony managed to get the master key to all the rooms from Rachel.'

'From Rachel?'

'Yes. He made out he'd locked her and himself out of their own room and duped his wife into asking one of the maids who she knew from her previous years working there, to lend them the key. Little did Rachel know that Tony only wanted it to gain access to the victim's room.'

'But what for?'

'Well, after Andy's death, Tony and Luke panicked as they couldn't be totally confident in the circumstances that their own "foolproof" security software would work as intended. As a result they seemed hell-bent on destroying anything that might implicate them in the plot and that basically meant destroying as much of Andrew Price's computer-ware as they could. So intent were they, that Luke even travelled back to the mainland on Thursday evening and torched the Price's family home in Winchester. Did a good job of it as well. Took our computer boffins many sleepless hours to salvage anything meaningful from the ashes.'

'And the computer in the builder's skip was put there by Tony?'

'Yes. Tony had learned that we had Mr Gills and Mr Walsh from Colcrofts at the station for questioning. He thought that by throwing the gear in the skip it might increase suspicion towards the builders. Unfortunately for him, he obviously wasn't thinking straight and left the thing with traces of his own fingerprints.'

'So were Colcroft Construction totally vindicated?'

'In the case with Andrew Price, yes, but not in their relationship with the hotel,'

'How's that, Harry?'

'Well, their link with Joe Masters, the doorman, was not as innocent as it seemed. Sure, Mr Masters had been told to slow down on health grounds by his doctor and as a result had sold his business to Colcrofts who were keen to expand. And the reason they were keen to expand was that they knew everything about the Coburg Hotel Group's expansion plans down to the smallest detail. They had access to so much inside information, on tender prices, for example, from other interested companies bidding for projects, that they could intervene at any crucial moment and guarantee winning that work over for themselves.'

'So how did they get access to all the privileged information?' enquired Mel.

'Quite simple really. They had Joe Masters working for them on the inside, spying. Regular little James Bond he turned out to be.'

Mel sat back and took a deep breath. 'I'm stunned. He seemed such a nice, genuine sort of chap.'

'Well he's gone now, as have Colcrofts. Dismissed by the Hotel Group from all future work,' said Harry.

'Not only were they corrupt in the sense that they were involved in a world of industrial espionage, but their working practices were exposed as a bit of a fraud, as well. We discovered that they were even using unrefined beach sand straight from the bay to supplement bona fide construction materials. Who knows what's in many of their buildings? Probably find seaweed and the odd crab if you look hard enough.'

'That's incredible, Harry. And all happening under our very noses?'

'Indeed … I guess it's when it's right in front of you that you often miss it though, isn't it?'

Mel nodded.

'So back to the banking conspiracy. What about the funds that the group had accumulated over all those years? Where did that all end up, Gats?'

'Well, ultimately, the monies became neatly camouflaged as a salary to a previous employee, our mysterious Mr "3456BC", or one Brett Cramer. Though that employee had long since retired and was a totally innocent bystander, our fraudsters kept his internal account open. It provided a useful smokescreen through which to dispose of the money which was drip fed into a Swiss bank account and then distributed as agreed.'

'And poor Rachel suspected nothing?'

'Nothing at all. She just took it that her husband earned a good wage. Don't think there's much more to say really, Mel.'

'Um … Very interesting, Harry, and congratulations I guess … Cheers,' she said as she lifted her rapidly emptying glass one more time.

Gateaux followed in mirrored precision. As the two glasses touched lightly, the waiter appeared.

'Dessert?'

Mel offered a single nod to Harry.

318

'Yes, we're ready now,' he said as he glanced upwards to the notebook ready attendee.

'Madam?'

'Think I'll have death by chocolate.'

'Yes, I'll have the same,' said the Inspector.

Mel looked across the table and smiled.

'Thank you,' said the waiter before turning and for the third time rolling the sweet laden trolley away from the table.

The couple stared briefly at each other and exchanged a second synchronised wink.

'Hope the sweet doesn't live up to its name, Mel, otherwise I might have just conjured up my next case.'

'But for someone else to solve presumably?' she replied, a broader smile now illuminating her wine-tanned face.

'Right, Gats, when you extended this dinner invitation you said that you had an idea to put to me,' she continued, a taste of excited expectation teasing her palette.

'Yes, that's correct. Just a quick sip of wine and I'll tell you what it is.'

While Gateaux lifted his glass the table descended into silence for a moment as in the distance the light airs of chamber music played on.

THE END.